Never The Dawn

By
Grey Wolf

SCIMITAR

EDGE

Published by Scimitar Edge
An imprint of Purple Unicorn Media

ISBN 978-1-910718-43-8

Front Cover and all illustrations by Derek Roberts

Map on the back cover thanks to Analytical Engine

Never The Dawn

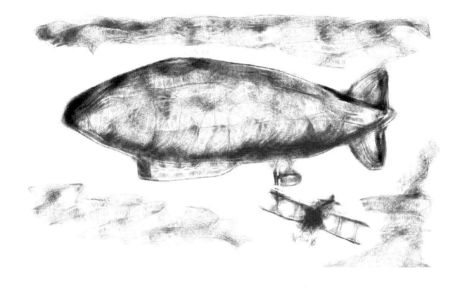

Chapter One - The Herald
West Africa

The sun glittered off the open gunports as the behemoth of the skies began its descent over the fabled city of Timbuktu. Home to the Empire's Forward Command, the son of the Emperor had come in person to inspect the troops, and to impart his own glory and honour upon the men and women desperately fighting for the name of Albion in these Godforsaken parts.

"Begin counting us in", Grand Captain Elijah Ramirez spoke into the web-like microphone before his throne-like position upon the bridge.
"One hundred" echoed a voice from out of the tinny speakers, "Ninety-nine, ninety-eight"
"Prepare to deploy" Ramirez bellowed and a half dozen underlings rushed out of the room, trained and ready to do his bidding.
"Passing over the palace now" reported a junior officer, her black hair streaming down her back over her gold and black uniform.
"Steady as she goes" Ramirez demanded
"Steady, aye!" the barrel-chested black man gripping the spokes of the huge wheel rolled the words off his tongue

Imperial Prince Alexander Roberto Heinrich looked out through the reinforced viewing port and saw the traditional buildings of mud and brick give way to the splendour of the marble palace, built in the heart of the city where once the mosque had stood. It was an amazing sight, made the more so since the marble had been imported from Italia, the water was channelled through a network of canals from the Niger River, and not less than two thousand slaves had died in the two decades it had taken to build. As a grand gesture of the power of Albion, it was without equal, given the circumstances of its construction.

"Eleven, ten, nine, eight", the tinny voice continued to count down over the speakers but was drowned out by the sudden hullabaloo upon the bridge.
"Deploy!" snapped Ramirez, and from a score of openings the ropes snapped down to the waiting crew below.

"Power back!" a tall man, his head crowned in a golden topknot snapped
"Powering to zero", the raven-haired female said calmly
"Steering locked", the black giant eased his words into the ether
"Take-up!", a second female officer reported from the forward viewing deck.

Below them, as they settled scarcely yards above the ground, a crew of hundreds of black slaves, ridden by their masters, had snagged the ropes, and were easing the gigantic craft into its berth.
"Lock down underway" the second female reported
She was stocky, not more than five foot tall, with the white blonde locks of an Icelander.
"Locked!" she replied, as the ship steadied and settled slowly to a standstill.

Ramirez rose from his throne-like seat, and nodded slowly around to the bridge crew,
"A good landing, ladies and gentlemen. We depart in thirty-six hours"
It was tradition that they would have half that time to themselves, and even as the words were spoken, junior officers were approaching senior ones all over the vessel to have their cards marked. They would have exactly fifty-percent of downtime to themselves, but if they reported in more than ten minutes late they would find themselves in the brig.

Alexander Roberto Heinrich turned away from the viewport, and walked slowly towards the Captain,
"A smooth flight, sir, and a very smooth landing."
Ramirez took the praise as befitted his station, and made no direct reply. Instead he asked,
"Will Your Highness be dining in the palace tonight?"
"I think not", Alexander laughed, "Cousin Gunther is not an inspiring speaker, I wish to avail myself of the pleasure of his company as little as possible"
What he meant was that the formal ball set for the following night would be enough of a drain, and he could do with some time to himself.

"You are welcome to dine with myself and the senior officers", the Grand Captain offered, and he seemed sincere.

Alexander was impressed; Ramirez had the reputation of a surly, haughty individual and to be invited to his table was praise indeed.

"If you mean that, sir, I would be most pleased."

The Grand Captain was taken aback by the acceptance, but his offer had been made in truth, so he nodded quickly,

"Yes, Your Highness. Midnight should find us ordering at The Lion and Lamb, if that is not too late for you?"

Meals round here rarely began before nightfall, and at this latitude ten o'clock was the earliest one usually saw anything like a nightlife in Timbuktu.

"I will be there, sir. Make sure there is a seat for me"

"I will scribe your name on it personally" Ramirez assured him.

With a nod, Alexander took his leave and made his way along the companionway to the ramp, joining a small throng of officers and passengers as they headed down off the *Xerxes* towards the ground, incongruously green in this desert location.

~

"I do not like it"

There were a great many things that Imperial Duke Gunther Luis Leander may have speaking of, not least the arrival of his cousin within his viceregal city, but there was only one which was occupying his attention at the moment.

"We do not know how it was done, sire"

General Alberto Smith was a career soldier, a self-made man, owning the ribbon of a Companion of the Golden Cavalry, and what he did not know about war was not worth knowing...except that somebody appeared to know it.

"A dozen patrols have perished in that area alone", Luisa Maria Valdez was all Galician, a strong woman of thirty, renowned for her wrestling, her cardplay, and not insignificantly her ability to read the enemy, who were numerous.

"I can read the dossier", Gunther was surly, upset with the news, not just because of the arrival of his more illustrious cousin, but because it caused great unease within him, "What I need to know is whether there were any common denominators?"

"It is hard to tell" Smith pointed out, "Each patrol was annihilated, their bodies not found until days, even weeks afterwards"

"Tell it from the beginning", the Imperial Duke leant back upon his tiger-skin couch, about as expensive an import here in the heart of West Africa as one could get, Italian marble always excepted of course.

"Patrol G-P-095", Luisa began, "They are assigned random numbers by Cyclops."

"I am aware of that" Gunther grunted.

"Of course. This patrol was on a routine mission to exterminate a Fulani rebel cell in an area we had recently pacified."

"How well pacified?" the Viceroy interjected.

"Ten thousand slaves, and ten times that number dead"

"Go on"

"The patrol initially reported strange lights in the night sky - one of their reports even mentioned...'willo the whisps'"

"Fancy?", it was a question.

"Description, I think" the woman officer replied without hesitation.

Gunther picked at an ingrown hair upon his chin,
"Very well, how experienced was the commander?"

"Group Leader Sasha Johns had ten years in the field"

"Here?"

"No, sire, eight in China, one in Georgia"

"Georgia?", Gunther raised his eyebrows; it was a particular Hell-hole

"Yes sir. She transferred to here at her own request, upon attaining the Golden Lion"

"I see"

That honour allowed the recipient to request a stationing that would further their own martial prowess. It was not a cop-out, even less a way out, and Sasha Johns had swapped one never-ending war for another. She had wanted to be in West Africa, and she had taken the chance with both hands.

"What about her second?" Gunther asked

"Patrick Luis O'Donahue..."

"I have heard of him..." the Viceroy interrupted, "I had not known he

10

was dead"

"We have not released the news to the broadcast stations", General Smith sounded somewhat apologetic, "It would be too severe a blow to morale if not handled in the correct manner"

"A more glorious death is being arranged for him?" Gunther asked

"The first occasion such a thing comes along"

The Viceroy nodded, gave up on his chin and nibbled at an olive, "How many of these incidents has there been?"

"Twelve" Luisa wondered why he was asking

"All patrols completely destroyed?"

"Yes sire"

"And none of these would qualify for inserting the Hero of Gondar into as a casualty?"

"With respect, sire, every patrol was wiped out in an almost identical fashion. If we could not release news of O'Donahue's death for the first one, we could not for any other."

"The incidents are that alike?" Gunther furrowed his brow, and when he did so his brow was most deeply furrowed indeed

"Almost identical" Luisa responded, "An initial report of strange lights, then mention in various idioms of beings of light..."

"How so?" Gunther rubbed at his head, "Various idioms?"

"Willo-the-whisp, faeries, angels, daemons, giant glow-worms..." the Galician explained.

"I see..."

There was silence for a moment, then the Viceroy collected himself, "And now this?" he said.

"Yes sire, it is all part of the same pattern" Smith was confident

"A dozen patrols, and now this?" Gunther pressed.

"Yes sir", Luisa was keen, certain.

"Thirteen", Gunther sat back and stared into the overhead lights, "It was number thirteen..."

"Er, we don't think that was significant...not numerically, sir" Luisa managed after a moment..

"You are a soldier, I am a governor", he stirred himself, "It does not matter whether it was significant, but if news gets out then the rebels and the disenchanted will find their own significance. I do not care about the number for its intrinsic value, but only for the galvanising effect it will have on destabilising elements here."

"I see", General Smith finally managed a genuine smile, then frowned, "Do you think They know that?"

"Who is 'They'?" the Viceroy asked, petulantly.

Smith and Luisa exchanged glances, then the general replied, seemingly addressing his reply to the Viceroy's maroon-slippered feet, "The Fulani are not doing this themselves, and there is no way that the Egyptian Caliphate have weapons so exotic and this powerful."

"That is for certain" the Viceroy frowned

"The rebels must be receiving help from an outside power." Smith finished.

"Hmm...", Gunther lay back upon the pillow and massaged his temples, "Someone with the technology and the power, and the will to defy us..."

"At a minimum", Luisa looked quickly at the general, who nodded his approval.

"Europa? Halych? Kazan?" Gunther reviewed the other global empires with a technological level equal to Albion's, "I suppose that Brasil or Zanzibar could have afforded the technology, if not developed it."

"We have done some investigation, sir" Luisa was almost apologetic.

"I suspect there are no traces to anywhere, and nothing to indicate that the Fulani did not manage this for themselves?", Gunther may have been an Imperial Duke but he had not attained his viceregal status by being stupid about international politics.

"Nothing until tonight" Smith said

"Ah.." a slight smile played upon the Viceroy's lips, "Somebody slipped up?"

"Not quite, sir" Luisa managed.

Gunther looked back at the photographs set out before him, the scenes of devastation and destruction captured in silver by the overflight of Colonel Stavanger's Wildcats. Whatever had destroyed Fort Bastion was far from an ordinary rebel activity, far indeed from anything that any power ought to be able to project into the heart of occupied West Africa without leaving an obvious trail to follow. Many may hate the globe-spanning empire of Albion, but few could do this to it, and of those who could - how could it be done and not be obvious?

He stared particularly at a shot showing the armoury; it had been blasted apart, apparently from the inside, the radius of the blast levelling buildings, trees and railstock as it went. But there was nothing in that armoury that could have done that - even a perusal of the confidential Section 11 report, here before him, stated that. None of the Special Units had anything there, none of the Scientific Faculties had rented premises in the fort, none of the Shadow Organs had come near to it. So, only the enemy could have made the armoury blow up like that, and to do so they would have had to penetrate it...and if they could do that, then nowhere was safe.

"I do not think I will like your answers" Gunther commented soberly, "Please make sure they are accurate before speaking them. My mood is turning decidedly sour"

~

"A hundred whores!" Sub-Commander James Bach bellowed, and the whole assemblage collapsed into laughter.

Imperial Prince Alexander Roberto Heinrich thought to himself that it was a long time since he had felt as relaxed as this, a long time indeed since he had felt as free to laugh as this. He raised his tankard to his lips and took a deep draught, as the female Sub-Commander, Katerina Delilah Spinks, she of the raven hair from the command bridge of the *Xerxes*, took up the slack with her own story.

Without listening to her words, Alexander watched her lips, imagining them on his member, and feeling it respond to his imagine, getting painful before he began to think of pigs and cows, and hens to cool off his ardour.

"Excuse me, sir"
For a moment, the Imperial Prince feared he had been rumbled, then he saw that the red of the uniform of the man before him was not the garb of the waiters at The Lion and Lamb, but was the more

resplendent uniform of the Imperial Messengers, part of the Red Guard.

He sobered up immediately.

"What is it?" he turned away from where another officer from the airship was now beginning his funniest tale, "Is my father...!"

"The Emperor is fine", this Messenger had the cool of a thousand cats, and the hauteur of a fair proportion to speak like that, "You are requested and required to present yourself at the Imperial Gate with immediate effect"

"Immediate effect?!" Alexander could not believe he was being spoke to this in this manner

"If you questioned the order, I was instructed to quote a biblical passage to you - 'Every man of the children of Israel shall pitch by his own standard, with the ensign of their father's house'"

Alexander's blood ran cold, *Numbers 2:2*, there could be no doubting that the message came from his father, himself. He nodded, and the Messenger disappeared. The Imperial Prince reached across and picked up a silver salt cellar, banging it down. Most of those around him stuttered to a halt and looked at him in surprise,

"I must leave", he said, and motioned for the Grand Captain to join him as he rose.

"What is it?" Elijah was coolness itself despite the half dozen beers he had imbibed.

"A summons from my father. I would suggest that when you leave here, you instruct the *Xerxes'* constables to issue a five-hour warning."

Ramirez was silent a moment, then nodded,

"It will be done. I will have the bridge crew on a three-hour whip."

"That is wise"

Alexander squeezed his hand, and then was gone, leaving behind a perplexed but extremely worried Airship Captain.

- - - - - - -

The Imperial Gate had once been a gate, but was now a slab-sided edifice of a building, constructed from imported granite, and with few adornments to show that it symbolised anything in particular from the

14

Empire.

The long low automobile drew up with a sharp exhalation of steam, the boiler spraying hot water onto the flagstones below, its egress spurting occasional puffs of superheated water into the atmosphere. One of the newest vehicles from the Imperial Pool, it had come at once upon the prince's urgent command.
He stepped out now, dipping his hat to the chauffeur who nodded and withdrew a discreet distance into the shadow of some old mudbrick conglomeration.

Alexander approached the steps and looked the pair of guards in the eye,
"If you have not been ordered to expect me, I will leave now" he said.
"We are expecting you, Your Highness", the more burly individual on the right stepped forward and yanked open the door, "Please go straight through"
"Thank you"; courtesy was at all times the mark of one born of Imperial rank.

It was as well that he had that instruction for the entrance foyer was dark and uninhabited. Passing beyond into a corridor, he found warming light, and soon heard the agitated hub-bub of voices coming from behind a sturdy oak door. He raised his fist to knock and it was opened.
"Cousin"
Ramona Elise Carding was a bastard, but an Imperial bastard and whilst she enjoyed none of the privileges of rank, she had enjoyed almost all those of birth, and had risen within the shadow service to head up this viceroyalty. She motioned her better-born cousin into the spare seat around the mahogany table, and indicated to the technician before the televisual apparatus to do whatever it was that he did.

Alexander sat transfixed as the one-foot diameter circle within the oak surround began to display pictures, live from a camera somewhere else. It was magic, as far as most people were concerned, but a whole Imperial organ was dedicated to it, of which the branch his cousin belonged to was simply the most...scary. As an Imperial Prince he felt that he could use that word, if even only within his own mind.

"What is...?" he began.

But the pictures displayed their own message.

"Holy Battle Rabbit..." said an old man opposite, the oath a favourite of a service that did not consider itself bound by any rules, even those of the Imperial Church.

"Elven Battle boots!" another responded, rubbing at the bridge of his nose.

Alexander took this for the noise that it was, and waited until somebody said something that had quality to it, as well as quantity. He was not surprised that it was Ramona,

"We have seen the answer to questions we had only just begun to ask" she said.

"This is directly upon our borders?" Alexander could not keep the shock from out of his voice.

"It is what is causing our borders to fall inwards", the old man had apparently now recovered his composure.

"I do not understand" the Imperial Prince looked to his cousin in confusion.

"The Viceroy has yet to inform you" she said.

~

Fort Hardcastle was seven hundred miles South of Timbuktu, upon the Black Volta river, and as advanced a forward base as Albion had across the whole benighted theatre. Home to a thousand men and women, it presented a bluff black-stone front upon the riverbank, cannons protruding like the snouts of fearsome beasts, mortars hidden within the main courtyards, ready to launch deadly hidden fire upon anyone so foolish as to attack.

But attack they did, from out of the trees, a dozen moving globes of light, with hundreds of half-naked natives running silent in their lea. It was eerie, that was the first thought of the sentries upon the walls, then to wonder what was causing the phenomenon, then to rush to ring out the alarms.

But it would not have mattered had they done so at once, for no gunfire could shatter the hovering lights, and no matter how many

16

scores of natives behind them fell, the globes advanced inexorably.

- - -

"There is no point!" Salvadore Hans Kant was the Imperial Chaplain of the fort, and despite his calling a committed pragmatist, "Your machine can do nothing to them, Commander. Fly yourself North and give the warning"
Swift Commander Tomas Thorn looked at his boots, and then nodded, "Your wisdom is worth twice my valour. Die with honour"
"We shall try", Jessica Parker was the Governor of the Fort, a woman in her forties, strong and weatherbeaten. She looked the Commander in the eye, and then they hugged like colleagues usually did not.
"I see" said the priest.
"God-speed" she whispered.
But Thorn was already striding towards his aerial craft

The globes of light moved through the walls as if they were butter, and themselves a hot knife. In their wake, the natives crawled and clambered, slipped and fell, but were always ready to move up and take their comrades' places.

- - -

"It does not work!" Lieutenant Severian Pole slammed a fist down upon the bastard apparatus, "I tell you Captain, it is a pile of junk"
Herbert Kinsale moved past him and ran a hand along the transmitter.
"It was never that much more than a pile of junk in the first place", he said, "Are you sure that we cannot repair it?"
"I cannot repair it!" Pole stressed the first person singular, "If you can, sir, please be my guest"
"No, I cannot" Kinsale rose up from inspecting it, "What is wrong with it?"
"It doesn't work!" Pole was not unaware that the fort was under attack, and felt trapped up here in the tower.
"Leave me", Kinsale settled himself into the only chair within the cramped room, "I will ponder on it"
Halfway to the door, Pole turned and stuttered,
"Sir...but sir that is insane!"

"Thank you, lieutenant, I wish you well"
Then he was alone, but not for long.

- - -

"The Wildcat is away", Jessica moved into the tower room slowly, "What of this?"
She indicated the machinery all around that was singularly doing nothing.
"Whatever they are doing, it is killing this" Herbert Kinsale gestured the fort's governor to a perch upon a unit of redundant equipment.
"They are not....right" Jessica held her head in her hands, "The Empire cannot even conceive of this technology, I cannot see Kazan or Europa managing it"
"Or Halych or Brasil or Zanzibar or the Caliphate..." Kinsale slammed a piece of equipment back together, "Let us see what that does"
"Indeed?", Jessica was on her feet to watch as the commander replaced it into a series of relays that were deader than an emir's dinner.

For a moment nothing happened, then suddenly a cacophony of voices erupted over it.
"You repaired it?!" Jessica eyed him with newfound wonder.
"No", Kinsale shook his head, "I changed its function. We can receive again but never send."
"Oh..." she was crestfallen, "What good is this?"
"Listen to them" he advised.

Together they listened, and learnt. They were not alone in being destroyed. . .

~

"Ten forts", General Alberto Smith spoke in a voice that the night had deadened, "All destroyed, all over-run with no survivors"
"But this time we have something to go on", Ramona Elise Carding rarely came within spitting distance of the Viceroy, but the shadow service had certain powers reserved to it in emergencies, and however much he may despise her birth, the Viceroy had no choice but to have her at this meeting.

"Cowards..." Archbishop Paolo Jansen was unrepentant in his condemnations, seeing it as his duty to hand down scorn upon the weakness of others.

"Do not be a fool", Gunther found his voice, "The pilots will have been ordered to leave, and will have seen enough firsthand to know that resistance was useless"

"What more could one pilot and one aerial machine do that was not being done already?" it was Luisa Maria Valdez who spoke, as ever at her general's right hand.

"These lights..." Samuel Guy was an octogenarian, and though he might look his age he did not act nor feel it, heading up the Merchant Community within Timbuktu, and an ever-present in the council of the Viceroy who respected his tremendous knowledge and great experience.

"A trick..." the Archbishop was scathing, "A clever trick"

"So clever that guns could not fell them?", Commander Tomas Thorn had been admitted to this council as an observer but few were going to deny him his right to speak, "So clever that a direct hit from a mortar killed only those natives standing behind?"

"Then it was not where it seemed to be" the Archbishop snapped.

There was a moment of silence, before the Viceroy spoke again

"Cousin, is that feasible?"

Startled to be addressed in such a friendly fashion, it took Ramona a moment to realise that the enquiry had been directed at her,

"At the limit of theory, some speak of light-patterns, cast from behind but created some distance ahead"

"Explain that?" Samuel Guy was never reticent in coming forwards

"Light can be weak as well as strong... Imagine a thousand weak and pale beams, on their own they are nothing, but project them towards a common area and the beams will merge and strengthen. This could give the appearance of there being an object, made up of light, at the conjunction of the beams..."

"Science..." the Archbishop protested weakly.

"Were there a thousand natives standing behind them with light-beams?" asked Samuel Guy.

"That would appear to be the problem, sir" Ramona deferred to his age.

"And the lights never dimmed no matter how many natives we killed.", Thorn had been there, so his words carried weight, "We could kill natives, we could cut great swathes through their number, but the lights moved ever onward."

He was clearly shaken by the experience.

"We are left with answers that we do not like", Gunther summarised, "Let us hope that our cousin's mission is successful."

"Let us pray" said the Archbishop.

And this time nobody challenged him.

Chapter Two

"Approaching the drop zone", Sub-Commander Katerina Spinks studied the gyroscope carefully, "This is where the Wildcats said we should be."

"Draw back on the engines" Grand Captain Elijah Ramirez intoned.

The behemoth that was the *Xerxes* began to stall in midair, no great problem at this height, but one which would keep it temporarily at the position it now held relative to the ground.

"Your Highness, it is time.", he spoke through the speaking tube directly to the gondolier hung crazily beneath the airship, a place where pleasure-seekers would dare to go, or where observers would feel right at home as if aloft upon a crow's nest. None of them, though, would have the external door open.

Imperial Prince Alexander Roberto Heinrich looked around the men and women crowding the small space with him. His mission of inspection and invigoration had rapidly turned to one of daredevil proportions, suicidal proportions if he had paid any attention to the priest who had given him his blessing prior to take-off.

"Mark" he said, not addressing an individual but as a signal to synchronise their timepieces.

"Quickly, your highness", the strain in the Grand Captain's voice was evident; whilst this manouevre would hold the airship in position in long enough, it was not one that could be easily repeated if they did not rapidly take advantage of it.

"You all have your orders"

Prince Alexander threw himself out of the open doorway, followed a moment later by first one, then another, of the chosen. Before long a dozen figures could be briefly seen in the Moonlight, before they fell and every man and woman was left to their own devices. For his part, the prince simply followed the procedure. He had done this twice before on much less hazardous occasions, once back in Albion itself across the Atlantic, and once over the Highlands of Scotland. He put every iota of his being into the operation, and some time later was drifting to a dignified, if jolting halt, upon the plateau below.

As he cut the strings and gathered up the parachute, he looked around.

On all sides the land dropped back into the jungle, deadly trees and open swathes of swampy water. That was why it had been so important to land here, on the high ground, where survival was better assured.

This was near to one of the lost forts, perhaps one of the lesser ones, Fort Antioch, a bluff outgrowth of rock upon a cliff edge overlooking the Bagoe River. It was one of the many lost the previous night, and a target that had been picked almost at random - almost in that the larger edifices had been ruled out beforehand.

"Here, sire", a bald-headed woman stomped across to him, daggers whirling in her hands, an intense frown upon her face, "Where is the fort?"
"Was", he said, and pointed to the West, off the plateau and at a junction of a couple of waterways.
"That is a fort?" she sounded dubious.
"It was a fort", he corrected her, "It is now just a pile of rubble"

"That is what my eyes tell me", the speaker was tall, rangy and sported a single stripe of hair down his scalp, "It is just a pile of rubble"
"It was not yesterday morning." Alexander told him.
"As you say, sire", the voice did not sound at all convinced.

"Where in Tarnation are we?", the speaker this time, still dragging his parachute behind him, was a wiry Irish man, "If this is not Hell's own waiting room itself..."
"It is that Liam", the tall man said, with a rare spark in his eye, "But men still live here."
"Men are stupid", he finally cut himself free from the knotted strings he had been trailing, "Men live in the most benighted places..."
"Then you are in the right place", the woman bared her teeth in a semi-grin.

"Enough of this", Alexander had let it go on long enough for them to let off steam, but there was a mission to complete, and discipline needed to be reimposed, "Let us get on..."

They began to move out, picking up the others as they went, moving slowly down the slope towards the jungle.

~

The main railyards were some distance to the North of Timbuktu, so as not to spoil the aspect of the vice-regal city. Usually moderately busy with importation of foodstuffs, goods and luxuries from the coast, today it was a heaving mass of belching, burping machinery. Not only was every siding full of locomotives, box-cars and wagons, but a whole stream of flat-bed cars had come in, upon them iron monsters who were now contributing their own smoke, steam and noise as they were worked up, and slowly driven out. Albion had taken losses on a scale all but unprecedented in modern times, and this was their response.

Ramona Elise Carding stood upon the observation platform of the Imperial Gate and watched them come. It was inevitable, of course, but she was far from certain that it was a useful, or even a sensible response. The battle-wagons came in two sizes, first the cottage-sized trapezoids leading the way, guns bristling from their sides, an observer in a conning tower of sorts, their segmented tracks clanking around the outside of the whole side-section of the vehicle. Then there were the true leviathans, comparable in size to the chapels that the Imperial Church had built in every town the Empire had ever conquered. Slower than the trapezoids, these were forming a separate column to the rear, their tracks gigantic but only one-fourth the height of the vehicle, their body-shape more than of a wedge, sloping up from the front to twin gun ports at the top where large-calibre muzzles protruded. As they came nearer, it became obvious that their sides were bristling with smaller guns as well, and the true enormity of their main weapon became obvious. The conning tower on these vehicles was squatter, wider and boasted twin machine-gun mounts, offset to either side on traversable platforms. A crew of five could be seen at the head of each leviathan, but in battle the number would be smaller, depending on the type of enemy encountered. Inside the smaller battle-wagons, a crew of a dozen laboured intensely, within the larger ones were upwards of a score of men and women.

She conceded that it made an impressive sight, awe-inspiring in the literal sense of the word, but the enemy was not here in Timbuktu, but hundreds of miles away to the South...though she conceded that that might not be the truth for all that much longer. Her pondering having left her in, if not quite two minds, now at least one-and-a-half, she blanked her mind and concentrated on taking in the visual display that was rapidly proceeding towards her. Smoke, steam and dust was being blow to the East by a friendly wind, and the proud pennants and banners flying in their multitude from each battle-wagon were snapping and flapping in a most encouraging manner. The trapezoids were a dull green, shading into yellow and brown patches, an attempt at camouflage by a Quartermaster who was clearly not sure exactly where they would be seeing action. The wedge-shaped battle wagons were gigantic blocks of moving darkness, a matt black effect contrasting with the black field of the Imperial Ensign, if a dull black can contrast with a shiny black.

They were not, of course, coming to the city. The vibrations alone would probably have brought half of the older buildings down. Rather, they were approaching the outer ring road, and even now turning to parade around the Eastward side from where they would head South towards Fort Striven, thirty miles away. From there it would be up to the Elite Marshal whose pennant flew from one of the rearmost leviathans to decide how to deploy them, always taking into account the advice of the Viceroy that was. The Viceroy, for his part, was seeming to be pleasantly open to taking advice from his council, so as things currently stood Ramona was happy with the arrangement. War, though, had a habit of changing things at a moment's notice, and she had her own agents within the Elite Armoured brigades, especially for this reason. They would report in time, if necessary.

"Mistress"
The old man had emerged from a doorway, hidden behind the stack of a giant chimney, and approached her slowly.
"Wolfgang?", she turned, a little surprised, "Is there a problem?"
"Not enough that they would call you", he admitted, explaining why the telephone embedded in another recess of the chimney stack had not been the means to call to her, "but young Francis called from Downer Field."
Ramona walked across to her elderly lieutenant, all thoughts of the

battle-wagons sliding from her mind,

"Whilst he calls here, his superiors call the palace, and the Viceroy deliberates with General Smith over whether there is anything they need to tell us."

"Yes", Wolfgang was already heading towards the doorway, continuing to talk in his certainty that she was accompanying him, "He reports that of the twin Wildcats that went out early this morning, only three have returned."

"Have the others landed at forward airfields?", she asked, disappearing now into the doorway herself.

The stairway inside was spiral, lit by occasional electric lights, not a few of which were flickering, and boasting a single hand-rail nailed into the wall.

"He does not think so. One of the Wildcats that did return was badly damaged...seared he called it, as if it had been too close to a fire."

"Or a bright and burning light?" she raised her eyebrows.

"Yes.", he saw no reason to point out that this was her words, not those of her agent in the Imperial Airforce; she would no doubt keep the two things separate in that great mind of hers, "Francis is not of course admitted to the command tower or the officer's mess, so all of his observations are made from the hangars."

That was a valid point - Francis was eighteen, a trainee engineer in the Airforce, and the second cousin of a shadow service operative; recruiting him had been easy, given the usual complications that attended such missions, but his youth and relative low-birth had its downside.

Every pilot in the Imperial Airforce was an officer, usually of some noble rank, though it was possible to transfer from the Airship Service or even from Commercial Airflight if one had shown the necessary prowess. The command tower would be where the Station Commander and the Grand Captain in charge of the aerial wings would be discussing things. The officers mess would be where all the pilots were.

But even so, Francis had done them a valuable service in telephoning in his observations. If it turned out to be nothing of import, it was still valuable in that it told them that the young man remained both willing to operate under these conditions, and able to do so.

They stepped off the stairway into a small office, where Wolfgang eased himself into a battered armchair beside a coalfire, and Ramona closed the door, then put the kettle on the stove.

"What do you think has happened?" she asked him.

Wolfgang leant back and drew a pipe and pouch of tobacco from out of the folds of his jacket, carefully beginning to stuff the brown flakes into the bowl of the former,

"My instinct says that the Wildcats ran into something."

"Mine does also", she banged around, spooning tea leaves from the tin into two earthenware mugs, and sniffing at the milk in the bottle, "and I do not think we should wait and see whether my dear cousin decides to take us into his confidence once again."

"How do you mean?", the old man said, tapping down the tobacco.

"Was I being obtuse?", she turned and smiled at him, "I meant that we should not take an absence of information from the palace as a sign that nothing is wrong. If my cousin does not contact us over this, I think we should still look into it ourselves."

"It would not be the first time he has left us out of the loop" he agreed.

"Or simply been plain wrong in his assessment", she said, turning back towards the stove.

~

He had waited until nightfall, moving slowly through the grassland away from his shattered machine as the sun had slipped beneath the sky. He knew he was lucky, more than lucky, but whatever had done the damage to his Wildcat had not been like anything he had heard of before. Something had come from nowhere, burnt up his engine, but left him unhurt. With a great deal of luck, and he dared to say a great deal of skill, he had managed to bring the thing down on a relatively flat service at as low a trajectory as he could manage. He had seen from the air that others had not been so lucky, spinning down in an uncontrollable descent to smash upon the rocks below. But he had always prided himself on his dead flying skills, having learnt on gliders at his uncle's estate in his youth.

Born thirty years ago in Cornwall, Lucas Tremayne was the grandson of a count, a noble enough birth to gain him admittance to the flying arm of the Imperial Airforce, his application boosted by his uncle's letter of support. His first few years had been spent in desultory campaigns in the Caribbean, flying against rebels, against smugglers and against the occasional slaver daring to operate without an Imperial license. Since then he had served in Georgia, in Abyssinia, and now for two years had flown his Wildcat out of bases in West Africa, fighting the never-ending war on the only front where the Empire of Albion never seemed to make gains.

Now, he crept silently towards the treeline. The grass had been good for landing the shattered aerial vehicle in, but was no good at all for hiding him in anything like the long-term. The only reason that nobody had come looking for him yet was that there were easier pickings on the rocks below, and he had every intention of not being up here when they did come.

His uniform was a dull green, though on parade it was a shiny leather black like many of the services who claimed descent from the defunct Imperial Guard. Out here, black would have doomed him, and those in charge of day-to-day things were well aware of this and had issued a green combat suit, a colour it was hoped would blend in equally well in forests or woodlands as in grasslands or fields. He did not know if it had helped - maybe there were Fulani watching the wreck, and he had evaded them. Maybe there were not and his precautions were more than was necessary, but since he did not know which was the case, it was obviously better to be safe than sorry.

Reaching the tree line, he pulled himself over a fallen log, and finally had the cover to defecate, an urge which had been growing more uncomfortable with each passing hour. Finished, he knelt against a tree trunk and observed the gathering darkness. If the lights came, he would see them from far away, but before the lights, the Fulani had always been hunters, warriors to be feared and he had certainty that they could move stealthily in the darkness.

His service pistol had been lost in the crash and it would have been far too risky to try to prise it out of the shattered footwell, risky and obvious if anybody had been watching. Now he crawled around and gathered sticks, stripping the bark and sharpening their points with the knife on his belt. A pointed stick was exceedingly primitive, but sometimes the Fulani themselves were armed with little more, for all the vaunted support of the Egyptian Caliphate. He waited until the Moon was obscured by clouds, and began to feel his way through the trees, deeper into the forest, biting down on a primitive urge to turn and run back into the open. Survival was never easy, and required strength in all things. He could just about remember his father saying that to him, before he had gone off to get blown to bits in Georgia when he was seven; but now he chanted it to himself like a mantra, inside his mind of course, for only a loon would talk aloud in these circumstances.

~

They had made camp in the ruins, sleeping during the day, taking it in turns to watch, although there seemed nothing around to pay attention to them anymore. Even the corpses seemed to have gone - that was the most eerie thing of all. The fortress was a shattered ruin, its inhabitants almost certainly dead...but they were not here.

When dusk fell, Prince Alexander Roberto Heinrich gathered the rest of his group together, excepting only Liam who remained on watch. They crouched in the lea of what had once been a gunport, the massive artillery piece now strangely twisted and thrown upon its side, the roof collapsed in a shower of rubble all around it.

"Where to now?", the bald woman had her knives sheaved on either hip, "I take it, we're not staying here?"
"There's nothing here", the speaker was black, his muscles seeming to have been carved beneath his flesh
"We report on what *is* here", Alexander snapped, "- the devastation, the lack of bodies..."
"That's just freaky", she was young, lithe and sat with her back to the blasted gunport.
"It is what the Emperor needs to be informed about."

That more or less killed their arguing; nobody was about to argue Imperial will with the son of the Emperor himself.
"We've been all over this place", the young woman tried a different

tack, "Everything is the same - blasted rock, twisted metal...and no bodies!"

"Yes" Alexander's voice was soothing; he recognised a dangerous level of tension when he heard it in a voice, "To be brutal, its impossible that the Fulani moved them all..."

"Or ate them all", the black man smiled a glistening white arc.

"That too", Alexander conceded.

"Are they not dead after all?", Liam strode over, handing over the watch to his rangy comrade with a stripe of hair.

"It is one possibility", Alexander had been thinking about it all day, when not sleeping, "Maybe they surrendered..."

"To the Fulani?!" Liam was incredulous; long practice had shown that such an action replaced a probable quick death in battle, with an almost certain lingering death by torture.

"There is obviously a lot more going on than we understand", Alexander was not one to be intimidated, "These lights..."

"Beings of light are they?" Liam had been pondering this in his solitude.

"Daemons?" whispered the young woman.

"If they're angels, we're fucked!" the black man laughed..

The young woman scowled at him.

"There are many theories", Alexander's voice was stern, "We are here to ascertain the facts."

"Then we do move out", the bald woman smiled in her own private victory.

"Ten minutes", the Imperial Prince acknowledged, "We are going to try to backtrack the enemy."

Nobody said anything; in any ordinary circumstance the idea of tracking a Fulani warband back to their camp would have been madness. These were not ordinary circumstances, but whether that made it better or worse, none could say.

~

"We do not know", Imperial Duke Gunther Luis Leander had got tired of saying this in the last few hours, first to General Smith and his advisors and now to the full council.

Ramona Elise Carding glared at her cousin across the table, "You had a duty to inform us."

"I am sure you had your own methods of finding out", Samuel Guy looked at her with a measure of annoyance.

"The point is taken, sir" Ramona chomped down on her anger, "*Do you know more than we do?*" she asked the Viceroy.

"Let us stop this", General Alberto Smith was tired, not only of all this bickering, but in his body, having been awake since the early hours when he had been overseeing the detail of Prince Alexander's mission.

"Yes", Luisa Maria Valdez as ever backed up her commander, "The details are uncertain, but the simple fact is that the patrol was ambushed and the three who escaped were lucky."

"God's will", Archbishop Paolo Jansen did not like remaining quiet for long.

"As you say", Gunther nodded a politic nod at the churchman, "Luck is God's gift to the brave."

"And the unlucky ones?" Ramona frowned deeply.

"God's will is multi-faceted", the Archbishop smiled across the table.

"What do the survivors say about the ambush?" Samuel Guy sipped at a tall carafe of iced water before him.

"Nothing useful", the Viceroy said reluctantly, "One moment they were flying in formation, the next there was a blinding flash, most of the Wildcats fell away, and the few survivors staggered off home."

"Source of the blast?" Wolfgang Kessler rarely attended these meetings, but had been brought along by Ramona.

"No source" General Alberto Smith had read all of the reports numerous times, "There was no visible point of origin."

"What about the damaged machine?" Wolfgang pressed.

"What of it?" Gunther stared at the old man across the table, seated at his bastard cousin's right hand.

"It was seared - hit but not destroyed", Ramona picked up the thread, "A full report would be appreciated"

"I have it here", Smith tossed it across to her.

"Sire", an Imperial Messenger hovered on the edge suddenly, his red uniform shining in the reflected light of the dimmed gaslights, "I need to deliver this."

"Approach", Gunther rose from his seat and took the sealed envelope. He read it slowly and dropped it on the floor

"What?!" Ramona rose from her seat.

"They are attacking" he said, his voice but a whisper.

"From the South?" General Alberto Smith rose also to his feet, concern etching his tired features.

"No..." Gunther leant heavily upon the table

"No?" Ramona cast an urgent glance at Wolfgang who rose and moved towards the shadows.

"No..." the Viceroy repeated, "They are attacking New Lisbon..."

~

New Lisbon was one of the coastal enclaves held by the Empire on the Southern Coast. Massively fortified, it was deemed impregnable by experts who should have known better, but who had nothing to go on but their own experience, and the long history of the Empire behind that. Huge ramparts crowned with guns of all calibres towered up on the landward side, a series of enfiladed rampways leading through giant gates into the city within. On the seaward side, massive moles curved out towards the sea, artillery positions encased within them, large railguns able to run along their length to give added firepower.

At the centre of the city stood the citadel, a fortress within a fortress, its walls as impressive as those on the outer lines, a garrison of a thousand Elite Guard encamped within. Not that they stayed there much of the time, of course. Abidjan, despite its formidable appearance, was a trading post, and the land to a hundred miles around was seen as its natural hinterland. Small forts, more akin to the keeps of medieval times, guarded the roadways, whilst heavily armed parties roamed the area, negotiating with natives on the one hand, seizing what they wanted on the other. The former trade consisted in a large part of ivory, cocoa and diamonds, the latter almost entirely of slaves who were herded into New Lisbon, and sold at the great slave market on the docks. A healthy specimen could fetch as much as a thousand crowns, to be resold no doubt at ten times that once he or she arrived safely across the ocean in Albion itself. A few enterprising traders bought for the European market, but that had collapsed almost entirely since the rise of Europa a century ago, Albion's rival now controlling the trade through the interior desert and having revitalised the markets of Tripoli with their conquests.

At night, gigantic searchlights swept both the landward side, and out to sea, occasionally picking up figures moving furtively in the darkness, or a ship trying to run past the outer moles without being detected. The former would be seen off with the sharp bark of artillery pieces, the latter with the boom of naval cannon from one of the cruisers moored at the harbor edge. There was rarely a quiet night in New Lisbon.

This was not least because a twenty-four hour vigilance meant that it was always somebody's rest period, and off-duty soldiers and sailors mingled at every hour of the day and night with merchants, shipmen, and the type of adventurers that an outpost like this always attracted. The taverns, brothels, opium dens and theatres did a roaring trade twenty-four hours a day, whilst the cinemata showed the newest films imported from Albion proper, those with sound having supplanted the once-ubiquitous silent film over the last decade. The markets of the city were always open, the boast of the trader that anything could be bought for a price a true one, although for the more exotic orders a customer might have to wait twenty-four hours whilst the item was bought, or stolen, by the stall-holder.

Justice was administered under the Uniform Code of the Empire, *"One Law for all His Majesty's subjects"* as the words carved into the local courts proclaimed. Constables in the black-and-gold uniforms favoured by the local administration patrolled the city streets, breaking up brawls, hauling the collapsed drunks away to the tank, and shooting people as a last resort. The Uniform Code was a clear guideline; those involved in brawls would be held overnight, and then released on their own sufferance - if they came back again within a month for the same offence, it would be a week behind bars and three months parole, if again within this period a month behind bars and six months parole. Fighters, soldiers, sailors, adventurers even should not be unduly punished for doing what came naturally, but if they persisted in breaking the peace they would either learn or end up at the highest end of the penalty scale. By the same token, a collapsed drunk would be sobered up, fed and returned to society the next day. Persistent offenders would come before the courts to have their ability to manage their own lives judged, and if found wanting would be sentenced to a period of hard labour, a certain cure for drunkenness as the mines, quarries and timberyards that served as the destination for such a sentence were a long way away from any city, and prisoners did not get paid enough to use the officer's taverns, even if their entry into such an establishment would not have resulted in them being beaten to death.

- - - - - - -

When the attack came, nobody noticed at first. Even when the alarm was raised and the guns on the outer ramparts began firing nobody took a great deal of notice. It was an almost nightly occurrence, and the sounds and life of the city all but drowned them out anyway. People began to wonder when the number of guns engaged increased until it seemed that the entire outer defences must be engaged, but the small crowds that began to drift towards the viewing platforms were enervated with a sense of excitement, the prospect of seeing a really big Fulani force be blown to bits before their eyes.

It was only when the first explosions began to occur behind the ramparts that the city as a whole took notice. It had been decades since an enemy had managed to land a shell inside the city itself, and at first there was a kind of nervous excitement, with people laughing that this would be something to tell their children about, that they were there when for the first time in ages the city came under bombardment.

Then the outer gate blew apart. Everybody noticed that, and suddenly excitement gave way to fear.

- - - - - - -

Inside the citadel, City Governor Maximilian Christopher Schenk, of the famous London Schenks, was beginning to know the same feeling himself. Combined with a not unnatural worry for the defences of the city, and indeed the safety of his own person, was the fear of being the first in a glorious line to fail in such a dishonourable fashion. True his great-grandfather, the last of the great Dukes of Middlesex, had been beaten by Europa at the Battle of Trier, but that was not only a century ago, but was against a major power, and had been, at that dark period in Albion's history, just one in a number of defeats that had come the one upon the other. But to be in charge when a major Imperial bastion such as New Lisbon fell...to natives! That was unthinkable. He had already ordered his personal slave to bring him the cyanide.

In the meantime, he was going to do all in his power to prevent the eventuality from occurring, and to save the good name of the Schenks, even if he himself were tarnished in the process. In this endeavour he was, however, hampered by a distinct lack of knowledge. The reports coming in from the front were often garbled, frequently panicked, and usually terminated in screams or a horrifying gargling that did nothing for the telephone operators nerves. Those reports which were coherent seemed to have been sent in by children, or the insane, unable to properly describe what they were seeing. He was beginning to think that there was nothing for it but to go and see for himself.

The destruction of the outer gate sealed his mind on that one, and he hurried down from the Operations Room to the vast courtyard below. A score of armoured wagons were in the process of working up, great gouts of steam and smoke rising into the air. Most rested upon six thick rubber tyres, though a few had a tracked section behind. All were encased in armour, bristling with guns, and crowded round with Elite Guards busy readying themselves for the task ahead.

"Sire", the Grand Captain in charge of the squadron stepped up to him, "We have got news that the enemy have broken into the city."
"Yes", there was not much need for any other answer, "May God help you smite these craven heathen"
"Thank you, sire"

Grand Captain Domingo Green was not one personally inclined towards mixing faith with war, but he understood the Governor's sentiments, and it would not have been politic to have said anything else. He turned as one of his lieutenants ran up, a woman with scarlet hair flapping behind her in the exhaust of one of the massive vehicles
"Sir, we stand ready to open the gate"

Domingo looked briefly at the Governor who nodded, and turned back to the woman officer.

"Make it so" he said, trying for a grand-sounding phrase in case this battle ever got written up as an Imperial Epic. They would, of course, have to win it first.

The gates were the height of four men and the width of six laid end-to-end, and were operated by a mixture of hydraulics and old-fashioned counter-weights. They creaked slowly back against the strong towers of the gatehouse, and one by one the armoured wagons rolled, bounced and clanked out of the citadel and onto the Imperial Avenue, usually the scene of grand parades on Empire Holidays, but today crowded with people running in every direction. A quick burst of machine-gun fire over their heads got rid of most of these from the roadway, and the sudden choice of being run down or fleeing to the side dealt with most of the others. A few unfortunates fell under the massive wheels and were crushed to death, but one could not say they had not been given fair warning. This was war, and one did not stand in the way of the Elite Guard.

Up ahead numerous fires now lit the night, all seeming to be coming from the area of the walls, whilst a great pall of smoke was beginning to drift over the city, blocking out the stars and adding to the unease felt by those now faced with something never before experienced in these parts. But the Elite Guard were veterans of a dozen wars and campaigns, Grand Captain Domingo Green himself having spent six years in Georgia where the Last Bastion of Christendom in Asia was being slowly torn apart by the allied forces of the Khanate to the North and the Caliphate to the South. It was every Imperial soldier's duty to spend at least one tour helping to prop up the accursed kingdom, and Green had seen more action there than he had on all of his subsequent postings put together. He was coolness itself as he looked out through his vehicle's viewing slit, though he could not quite scratch the itch of concern that something very unusual was happening here, and that that in itself made it the more dangerous.

Gunfire now began to echo around them as they pushed towards the ruined gate, the houses in this area beginning to blaze as the conflagration spread, the guards from the walls retreating street by street as they fought for every yard of ground.

The first armoured wagon, one of those with a tracked section behind the wheels, edged forward into a billowing cloud of smoke, and then blew up, the gun mounted on its rear section tumbling end-over-end to smash down alongside the Grand Captain's own vehicle, the shells for it cooking off and sending fiery streamers into the night.

As a trained unit, the squadron spread out, seeking firing positions and beginning to pour fire into the smoke. Domingo's own vehicle edged to the left and nosed through a kitchen garden to rest in the lea of a potting shed. The rear hatch popped and a half dozen Elite Guards leapt out, rocket-launchers at the ready, spreading themselves out in the lea of the garden wall, seeking targets in the oiling black.
"Anything?" the Grand Captain popped the roof hatch, and looked out.
"I can see some sort of lights amongst the smoke, sir" one of the men by the wall reported hesitantly, "They seem to be bobbing about as if they are alive."
"Fire at the lights", Domingo was having no truck with any superstition. If the lights were moving, then the enemy were carrying them, and as they could not see the enemy directly, this was target enough for him.

Five rockets streamed out of their tubes, flying into the darkness and impacting with a shattering blast. The armoured wagon itself joined in, firing the twin cannon in its nasal port, whilst Domingo snatched the binoculars from around his neck and tried to fathom out what was happening amidst the flame and smoke and burning debris.
"Something's coming out", the speaker was a woman soldier, the only one who had not fired her launcher already. She sighted on the emerging ball of light and fired.
The rocket seemed to go straight through it, and impacted behind against a collapsed pile of masonry. The light came on.
"What the Hell is happening?" one of the men was up on his feet, panic beginning to well in his voice.

The light was rapidly nearing them, and now they could see that it came on alone. Somewhere behind, they could make out the creeping crawling shapes of a Fulani warband, but nobody was holding the light, there was nothing tethered to it, no sign at all that it had any substance, but as it moved it cut a swathe through masonry and timber, making a path for those who followed behind.

The cannons in the armoured wagon's nose were chattering away, slamming shell after shell at the light, with absolutely no effect. The panicking guard turned as if to run, and Domingo shot him down. The last thing the city needed was a rumour that the Elite Guard was panicked.

"Withdraw in good order!" he commanded, "Assume new firing positions and engage at will."

With that he slammed the hatch closed and disappeared below,

"Head to the left and try to get behind the bastards" he bellowed to the driver.

"Aye, sir"

The armoured wagon began to move out.

Chapter Three

He powered back on his joystick and let out a sigh of relief. It had been rough coming over the jungle, and only now that he had finally arrived had the winds eased. Floating gently on the thermals, he guided the light-weight aerial machine towards the target destination.

Admiral Hans Orlando Colbert had not been a happy man when his radio operators had informed him that New Lisbon had gone off the air, and all of his attempts to get a sensible answer from any of the patrol ships in that area had failed. Oh, true, some of them had replied, saying that daemons were in the process of taking the city and that it was every one for themselves. The Admiral suspected that somebody had had rather too much to drink, or perhaps smoke, and had mentally filed a report about such unprofessional behaviour, but the patrol ships were a long way from where his fleet was based, and he could do nothing immediately about it.

Instead he had ordered one of the experimental Hell Cats aloft, co-opted a pilot from the Imperial Airforce, and told him to seek an answer, and not to return until he had one. Thus, Captain Francisco Endymion Johns was now approaching what looked most certainly to be the *ruins* of New Lisbon. The Hell Cat was a machine built to attain high altitude on its experimental rocket engines, then to cut them off and glide silently, until it needed to use the engines to repeat the process again. Johns had trained on gliders in his youth, a common past-time for those of Britannic birth who would later enter the Imperial Airforce. He knew how to get the maximum time aloft in one, and he was using all his skills now to drift towards the city, without, he hoped, alerting the enemy to his presence.

If there were any enemy... So far, all he had seen were smoking piles of rubble, gaping holes in the outer walls that must be truly devastating up close, and blackened patches that must be the remains of wooden dwellings. He turned his attention to the citadel, still standing tall in the centre of the city, but looking somehow odd, strange in its alignment. Beyond, the moles of the harbour seemed to have been blasted apart, great gaps letting the sea surge through, and some score of ships lay sunken or on their beam ends in the oily water. It was clear that something truly devastating had happened here, but quite what it was he could scarce imagine. Where were the enemy? *Who* were they?

"Ah nuts..." he sighed to himself and put pressure on the joystick, forcing the Hell Cat lower, and closer. The Admiral would not be happy with a partial report.

Now he could begin to make out the remains of armoured vehicles, strewn around and blasted apart in the vicinity of the main landward gate. Nothing was moving, not even surreptitiously, and even the carrion birds seemed to be absent. That was wrong - unless it was some sort of gas weapon. Maybe that would account for the garbled reports the Admiral had received - a hallucogenic gas preceding the attack? If it was also toxic, the carrion birds would not touch the corpses...but...

He was closer now, looking down on the area directly before where the gate must have been. There was nothing left of that, and the whole area had been burnt, blasted and otherwise demolished. His eyes caught more detail now, an overturned armoured vehicle in the middle of a sideroad, another that appeared to have driven headlong into a house which had collapsed in upon it. But there were no bodies - not a one! His spine tingled, and he shivered. There were stories about cannibal bands among the Fulani, and the many tribes they had subsumed within them, but he had not seen any credible evidence of such acts. But what if the absence of the dead was because the enemy had eaten them? Or was his mind beginning to run too far ahead?

He shook his head to clear it.
"Focus on the facts" he told himself, "The Admiral will make any suppositions necessary."
From what little he had seen of the Admiral Colbert, Francisco rather thought that he was a man prone to making his mind up regardless. It would not do to seem to interfere in that process.

Something moved! He scanned the horizon, and then the ground to either side - nothing. Below, something was slinking from shadow to shadow. He angled the craft in lower, knowing that soon he would lose altitude altogether and have to fire the rockets - that for certain would wake up whatever enemy force was hiding out here!

It was a lion, no doubt freed from some private menagerie by the destruction of the city, and now roaming...looking hungry. That seemed wrong. Surely, there were bodies somewhere, or wounded, or the weak - something that a healthy lion could feast on? But he was seeing none, even as he passed along the pockmarked strip of the Imperial Highway and came upon the citadel itself. Now, he could see what was wrong with it - its entire upper third was missing, blasted somehow from aloft and shattered in the courtyard below. He could make out broken vehicles and upturned guns amongst the rubble...but no bodies. What the Hell was going on?!

Passing the citadel he was over the commercial district. Here fire had also done its work, smoking ruins testament to its destructive power. The market was a mass of overturned stalls and burnt-out sheds, produce trampled, seared or smashed all about. The surrounding buildings, once fine townhouses more recently used as large emporiums, were all in ruins. But there were no bodies.

Now he was at the docks, and flying so low that if he did not engage the rockets soon he was going to ditch in the sea. Given that it was full of the twisted steel of wrecked ships and a noxious mixture of leaking fuel stuffs, he certainly did not fancy trying that. The gigantic warehouses along the wharves were in ruins, the cranes collapsed and twisted in upon themselves, railcars and locomotives thrown about as if in the temper tantrum of an immature god. Something moved amongst these...another lion....another hungry-looking lion. He certainly did not wish to land here!

With a final sigh and a short prayer, Francisco fired the rockets, and was thrown back against his seat. At least that meant it had worked - the test pilots had had a thirty percent casualty rate, and there were rumours that the production model was not much better. He had been quite happy flying Wildcats until the Admiral had assigned him this mission, so thus far it was two out of two for success in engaging the rockets. The problem with thirty percent was that it was around a one-in-three chance. Could he make it back to the fleet base without having to fire them up again?

~

The room appeared empty at first, and Ramona paused, puzzled, upon the threshold, then she saw him, standing in the shadows by the fireplace, as if frozen in time.
"Cousin?" she said tetchily; he had asked for her, and now was acting like this?
"Oh...?" Gunther Luis Leander blinked and then nodded, "Have you heard from Admiral Colbert's fleet?"
"The fleet?", it was unusual for the shadow service to have operatives in the Imperial Navy, but it did have some. Regardless, she had not heard from any of them.
"No, apparently" he smiled at her, and handed over what he had been holding in his hand

Ramona took it and skimmed it quickly in the firelight,
"Utterly destroyed?!" she whispered
"I was beginning to suspect that" the Viceroy said, at last moving from his frozen pose, and settling into a seat, "Did you notice the part about no bodies?"
"It was an aerial surveillance..." she shrugged.
"Read it again" he advised, and reached for the carafe of brandy.

She settled herself into a chair across the rug from him, and read it more carefully,
"Ah", she said at length, "A Hell Cat... I have not seen one close up."
"Nor I", he admitted, "But I keep abreast of reports"
"Perhaps you do", she conceded.
"With their rocket engines they can drift very close to the ground before firing them again to attain altitude."
"As this Captain Johns reports", Ramona had now understood what she passed over on first reading, "There were no bodies at all?"
"Nothing living, nothing dead - well, nothing living apart from two lions"
"Lions..." she sighed and leant back.

"I doubt that they ate them all" Gunther sipped at his brandy.

He did not bother to offer her one - if she wanted one, she could help herself. That was the privilege of rank.

"So...we have three mysteries" Ramona closed her eyes, "What are these balls of light, who is behind them..."

"And where are all the bodies?" Gunther slammed his glass down, "Of those three I think the last one worries me more!"

"What do you mean?" she opened her eyes, frowning at him.

"Whatever the balls of light are, they are a weapon. Whoever controls them, they are an enemy. But removing all the bodies? How is it even possible, and why?"

"I understand. The thing done for no reason is worse than that which is fearsome, but essentially understood."

"Sire", General Alberto Smith stood in the doorway, "The Europan Consul requests an immediate meeting."

"What...now?" the Viceroy raised himself to his feet, "Its the middle of the blasted night!"

"You *are* awake, sire. I did not think I could unreasonably refuse to pass on his request."

"Very well. It is a rare occasion when Europa acts like this."

"I will come too", Ramona had also risen, "Too many strange things are happening"

Her cousin looked at her and laughed,

"What you mean is that you are worried that you did not receive warning of this either."

"That is true"

Together they exited the room in the wake of the general.

"I don't understand", Sarah Maria Gonzalez was the bald woman with the knives. She was a veteran of ten years incessant warfare since she had graduated from the cadets in her teens, and for her to admit to not understanding something, was quite...something.

"Nor me", Liam looked around them in some wonder, an emotion he was thoroughly unused to feeling.

"What is this?", the black warrior was the son of a freedman and a whore, but he had adopted a surname for himself, and his prowess on the sportsfield had led to a commission in the army. After five years fighting for the Empire in the Caribbean he had been promoted and sent to West Africa. Sporting the somewhat grandiose name of Valerius Gallant, the first in breach of the custom not to glorify Rome since the Europans took it a century ago, he was nevertheless proud of what he had achieved, and at the same time in no way ashamed of his origins.

Now, he crouched down over a concave cavity in the rock, seared clear of all vegetation as it was for hundreds of yards around them. The cavity looked like someone with a giant spoon had scooped up some iced cream, but this was solid rock, and what sort of spoon could do that, even metaphorically speaking?

Prince Alexander Roberto Heinrich came across and knelt beside him, running a hand over the smooth contours of the indentation. It was about three foot in diameter, and as smooth as a whore's backside.
"There's another one over yonder", Andreas Demetrius Xian was half-Greek, half Moor, a product of the Empire's refugee communities in New London close to the Imperial Capital. Now, he stood and pointed to a space in the shadow of the cliff-face, where running water cascaded down to make a fine spray that was hiding the indentation to normal eyes. But Andreas had perfect vision, some even said too perfect as he claimed that he could see static electricity upon cats in a storm. Maybe he could; why would it not be possible for a defect to make you see more, not less?

Alexander, Liam and the rangy warrior with the single stripe of hair down his head walked across. The latter was called Badger by his friends (and very short-lived enemies) but went formally by the ancient name of Richard John Fitzherbert. As such, he was one of few in this part of the world who could claim an entirely Britannic origin, as if that was, in these days, something to be proud of. Maybe that was why he preferred the monicker 'Badger', preventing himself from having to protest his lack of false pride. Noble genealogy was a complex subject at the best of times.

"It is identical" Andreas declared.
"In size as well?" the Imperial Prince bent down to it.

"Exactly"; when Andreas was around one did not need the measuring tape.

"What is the distance between them?", Sarah Maria meant to tease him, but should have known better.

"Ninety-five yards" he said, and shrugged.

"I think there's one over there..." Badger was shielding his eyes against the spray around them with one hand, pointing off to the right, and some way ahead with the other.

"Not a square then" Alexander mused aloud.

"You need four fixed points to determine a shape", Andreas pointed out helpfully.

"Find the fourth then"

Half an hour later they had six of them, and calculations, backed up by Andreas' uncanny instinct, had confirmed that the indentations were forming the apexes of an octagon. But, perplexingly the two missing points failed to turn up.

"It could be that there was something else at those points", Alexander had stripped off and was bathing in the cool water of the cliff-side fall, Sarah Maria and Valerius with him, as the others kept watch.

"Yes", rumbled the black warrior, grinning as he sized up the woman next to them both, "As we don't know what these things are, we don't know what it means when they aren't there."

"Its crazy", Sarah Maria stepped out of the spray to urinate away from the pool, "Nothing we know of can make such a mark on rock like this, but we speak as if that was no mystery at all"

"It is all mystery!" the Imperial Prince called from out of the waterfall, "But we have to concentrate on one part at a time."

"Oh shit" said Liam, then louder, "Shit! Shit! Shit!"

That got everybody running, the three naked warriors snatching up weapons and flinging themselves flat, whilst the rest of those on guard took notice of the direction of Liam's call and began to circle round.

It did not take a genius to know what the problem was. A giant orb was descending out of the sky, glowing with unnatural light, and about to land less than a hundred yards from where they were.

~~*~*~*~*~*~*~*~*~*~*~*~*~*~*~*~*~*~*

Dawn had found them still at work, not an altogether unknown event, but one which was generally the exception not the rule. Even now as the flames of mid-morning burnt heavily down upon the Viceregal capital, the senior officers of the shadow service were bent to their work.

"The Consul was not exaggerating", Wolfgang leant back, looking deathly tired, and showing all of his seventy-plus years.
"You should sleep", Ramona rubbed at her eyes.
"Let us finish this first", the old man said, "Ten desert forts have been wiped out in the last..." he looked up at the clock upon the wall, "thirty-six hours."
"In his wisdom, the misbegotten Emperor in Salzburg has declared war on the Caliphate."
"Which would be amusing if it were not...dangerous", the third officer in the small office was A W F Bannister, known to his friends as Awfy and to his enemies as Alehouse Whorebitch Fuckwit. He had come to the service in an extremely roundabout way, one which made leaving behind his prior life not only impossible, but undesirable. As long as they were not too often reminded of it to their faces, the other senior officers went along with things.

"You believe that the Caliphate is not responsible?" Ramona looked up from the pile of papers before her.
"I believe they are not capable, Mistress" Awfy said, "If they were, then our Western border would not have stood for two decades"
"Unless the Caliphate is behind what is happening with the Fulani", Ramona shook her head, "But I am become convinced they are not"
"Then, Mistress..." Awfy stood and stretched the muscles of his back, "Why do we have five teams working on the Caliphate?"
"Precisely *because* Salzburg has gone and declared war upon Egypt" Ramona pushed the stack away from her and leant back, "But you are correct - that is not the real problem"

There came a knock at the door, locked and sealed as they had settled down to work. With a sigh Ramona pushed herself to her feet and slotted the key into the lock, also spinning the combination on the second lock until it read the correct four digits. Outside, one of the younger operatives stood together with an Imperial Messenger..

Ramona raised her eyebrows; for the latter to penetrate the interior of the Imperial Gate he must have had a very good explanation for the guards on the door.

"Mistress", the young man sounded unsure of himself, "I was instructed by the guard commander to bring this gentlemen straight to you"

"Very well", Ramona waved him away, "What is it?", she addressed the red-uniformed man.

Impassively he handed her an envelope, sealed in crimson wax and with the imprint of a signet ring upon it.

"Oh..." she looked round at Wolfgang and Awfy, shrugging apologetically, "I am unable to open this in your presence"

"Of course Mistress", Awfy was gone in a moment.

Wolfgang took longer, rubbing his back, and looking a little perplexed as he rounded the corner.

Alone, Ramona broke the seal and read the two crisp sheets of white paper within.

"You are come straight from Albion City?" she asked the Messenger at length.

"Yes", he made no use of her rank, "Aboard the airship *Pandora* which arrived half an hour ago."

She had forgotten that it was closing in on Midday; in her mind it was still night-time, her lack of sleep having confused her. Now she cleared her mind of other things, and looked again at the letter,

"This must have been written right after the destruction of Fort Bastion" she said.

The Imperial Messenger did not reply, but that was of no matter as Ramona was by now talking aloud solely for her own benefit,

"That means that that attack was sufficient proof...but of course it came upon the loss of a dozen patrols...but even so"

She looked up at the Messenger who was still standing there,

"You may leave" she said.

"No", he shook his head, "I am instructed to guard you with my life"

Ramona was somewhat taken aback by that, her hand going to the sword and pistol at her side,

"I can guard my own life" she snapped.

"Nevertheless, I am so instructed."

"Very well", she knew a lost cause when she met one, "Lead on"

As they reached the entrance hall, Awfy came out of the shadows and bowed respectfully at her,

"We understand you are required elsewhere" he said.

She bit down on her shock, and nodded. How they knew was perhaps a testament to their skills in the service, but to have knowledge aforehand of what was in a sealed letter conveyed on the person of an Imperial Messenger? She would have words with someone..when she had time.

"His Imperial Majesty has summoned me to Albion. I must leave immediately."

"The writ of the Emperor is mighty indeed" he said, quoting if not scripture, then somebody's interpretation of scripture. The Imperial Church was very fond of such sayings.

"Look after Wolfgang", she said to him quietly, "His mind is as fine as ever, but the body begins to fail."

"As you wish, Mistress"

He would rather she had left him in charge, but deep down knew that such would have been an unforgivable breach of protocol and a vicious slap in the face for the old man. This way perhaps he could dominate proceedings, whilst still appearing to be a loyal servant. Come to think of it, that had long been his forte.

Outside, a small automobile was sitting in the sun, its driver fanning herself with an elaborate swan's feather fan, her colleague standing outside of the vehicle, a gun in each hand.

"This is not very inconspicuous" Ramona pointed out to the Messenger.

"I am only the Messenger" he pointed out in turn, "They have orders of their own."

They approached the vehicle and climbed into the back, the guard climbing in beside the driver, and the woman sealing the whole thing with sliding armoured plates as she powered up the engine. A few clanks and hisses later, and they were underway, rising rapidly to a speed of sixty miles an hour as they hit the major thoroughfare and tore down it towards the airfield.

Despite herself, Ramona found the motion of the vehicle lulling her to sleep. Realising that to fight it was stupid, she gave herself up to it, and was surprised to be woken what seemed like but seconds later.

"We have arrived" the Messenger was opening the door on his side, "The airship *Elysium* is ready to depart"

Ramona knew that she was tired then; her mind had heard that he had come in on the *Pandora* and unthinkingly thought that he meant to go out on it, but no airship turned itself around in a couple of hours, certainly not one that had just crossed the Atlantic. The *Elysium* was a sister vessel, ploughing the commercial routes and making a small fortune for her owners as it did so in significantly less time than even the fastest of merchant ships.

She followed the Messenger across the grass to the boarding ramp, vaguely aware that the vehicle and its inhabitants had sped away behind her, presumably to their next assignment...whoever they had been. It was nagging in her mind that she could not identify them, but she was overly tired, and maybe a proper sleep would help.

"Let me show you to your cabin", the Messenger seemed to be trying to be everything to her, from bodyguard to ship's guide.

"There is no need", she snapped back, harsher than she had intended, her temper shortening the longer she remained without proper sleep.

"I will accompany you anyway", he pointed out, "I cannot guard you from afar."

"Oh very well", she sighed and let herself be escorted. Whoever had given the man his orders had been very clear about where and when they could be breached, if ever. She was not going to be rid of him so easily.

~

Richildis was not dead, that was about the only thing she was sure about as she crawled through the jungle and tried to block the memories of that awful night from her mind. Oh, was it God's punishment for her sins? But did not far more men and women all have much greater sins than her? But they were dead, and she was not, but had she been the cause of their death? Oh woe...! She blocked it

48

out again, and thought of the fluffy lambs of her childhood.

Some time later she regained her sense of place and time and looked around her, realising that she had come to a clearing in which a crystal pool shone in the sun that filtered down from the trees above. Her strength sagged as she focused on her tired limbs and blistered feet, and some deep instinct made her take cover beneath a fallen log.

Several hours later she awoke, to find the pool now at dusk-time the drinking ground for an astonishing variety of wild animal, not many of them looking particularly friendly. She froze in fright, feeling her urine puddle warmly about her body, later cooling uncomfortably until the last of the animals was gone with the new dawn's light.

She crawled out and cleansed herself in the pool, also drinking as deeply of it as had the fiercest of the animals. Afterwards, she resumed her walking, now at a slower pace, keeping her mind more focused and beginning to ask herself where it was exactly that she was going. That seemed to be a question for another day, so she forced herself to think back upon the recent past, and shuddered.

She had told her husband that she was going to see a sick cousin aboard one of the merchant ships in the harbour, but as soon as he was out of sight, she had hooked up with Jamie and been led by one of the secret ways out of the city and into the jungle where her lover awaited. Rann was a runaway, a murderer sentenced to five years hard labour in one of the quarries of the interior, but having successfully made good his escape and now roaming around the outskirts of the city. She had met him when accompanying her husband on one of his slaving raids, Rann emerging from the shadows to watch as she had defecated, and then to seduce her and take her anally before she truly knew what was happening. It was a new experience for her, and the power of the fire in her loins and the excitement in her mind had led her to take chances that she would never have taken otherwise.

Jamie was the son of a good family, but seventh or eighth by birth, and had fallen in with a bad lot. He knew how to get out of New Lisbon better than even the Governor or his staff would know, and for a price he had taken her a half dozen times to secret meetings with her lover.

Her husband was too caught up in his work to truly notice, and she had been free to live one life of respectability on the surface, and another of depravity beneath it.

Then had come the Night. She had been sucking hard when the gatehouse had exploded, and had bit down in shock, causing Rann to rear violently and throw her to the ground. She suspected that she was only spared his wrath by the evident emergency above them in the city. All fire and ardour gone, he had dashed off to meet up with others of his kind and see what they could do to help. And that was the last she had seen of any of them. Abandoned and alone, she had hidden whilst They destroyed the citadel, and watched in awe as the fiery orbs had descended from the Heavens. Then she had got up and wandered alone

She was still wandering, still alone, and getting very hungry now. She knew people were supposed to kill animals and eat them, supposed to be able to light fires with sticks and roast them, but she had no idea how any of that was achieved. Berries were good sustenance, and Rann had in the past shown her which ones were poisonous and which ones not. But they scarcely filled the void, and she knew she would soon weaken if she did not eat properly.

Something moved in the half-light before her, and she froze. Perhaps instead of eating an animal, one was destined to eat her. But it was no animal, it was a globe of light. She watched with a mixture of terror and awe as it approached her, then with a flash both she, and it, were gone.

A snake slithered across the ground.

Chapter Four

With engines roaring, and their wings and tail-rudders straining at the air, the dozen aeroplanes launched themselves fully into the sky, and were quickly roaring away to the South. Behind them, Francis Elias Bannerman watched the flight of Wildcats go, and knew worry.

Something bad was happening; even if he had not felt the slowly rising panic amongst the officers, and heard the shriller voices in the commanders, the evidence of his own eyes would have told him that. Downer Field was home to four wings of Wildcats, the foremost aeroplane in the Empire's armoury. It was part an interceptor, part a scout, and part a terrier, a truly multi-function machine, and by far the best blend of all these qualities that the Empire had ever known.

But this was the last wing, the last dozen machines taking to the sky under a Grand Captain who had looked both young and scared as he had briefed his pilots. Something was devastating the patrols - the first had come back with three (better, two and a half) machines, the next with four, the third wing with only two machines. What had happened to the others it seemed nobody knew for certain. Even from the hangars he could hear the conversations, the whispered confidences, the hysterical laughter that accompanied them.

Lights had done this, lights rising or falling, or zooming or hovering...or perhaps doing anything at all. Lights which could somehow sear an aeroplane as if it had parked too close to a bonfire on Saint Richard's Night. Light which seemed to be alive in its ability to move. But lights which those who survived had seen either only at a distance, or but fleetingly, for too close a call would doom the machine.

Now, the final flight was launched, the Station Commander having gathered what seemed like the entire priesthood of the airfield to pray for their mission before launching upon his soliloquy. Francis had been too far away to hear, but the effect on the men and women had been noticeable, though not consistent. Some had looked shocked, even downcast. Others stoic and determined. A few had positively glowed with religious ardour - those, he thought, would be the first to die.

Now, he bent to fuel a Scavenger, an older aeroplane, ten years outdated, its twin wings making it look like the thing of romantic legend, rather than of true and ugly menace. But a decade ago it had been the terror of the skies, and its kind had remained in action in the Empire's backwaters - where the enemy did not have aeroplanes, the second-rate bested their complete lack of such machines. Modernity had come upon Downer Field over the last couple of years, the four flights of Wildcats pushing the Scavengers aside, but now, in these straightened circumstances, the Station Commander had ordered all of the remaining older machines readied for action.

There were a score of them in storage, but a rapid evaluation had shown that only eleven were flight-worthy, with perhaps two to three of the others capable of being made so in a day or two. The others were rotten, collapsed in upon themselves, and only good for spareparts - a good motto, if any machine ever made it back to base needing some.

"Is my old steed ready?"
Francis snapped to attention, feeling a strange stirring in his loins,
"Captain Meredith, sir!" he ejaculated.
"At ease, man", Guy Simonis Meredith was fifty now, a veteran and a legend, and had never expected the summons to fly again. He had long been enjoying his desk, and the desks under his command, but the Station Commander had cited the Viceregal command to him, and truth be told Meredith had been keen to test his mettle once again.
"The...the machine is ready sir", Francis found his voice stuffed deeply down his trousers.
"Good, good", Meredith patted first one, then the other of the wings nearest to him, "In battle I need one hundred-fifty percent, you do understand?"
"Oh yes, sir!" Francis splashed his words upon the man before him, "This will be the best aeroplane in the whole Viceroyalty!"
"Good", Meredith laughed, showing teeth that, crazily, still shone white, "You may scribe your name into its log."
"Oh God sir!", Francis leant back, panting, "Thank you sir!"

"As you will", Meredith gave the Scavenger one last look, then headed across to the officer's mess.

~

She no longer knew the passage of days. At the back of her mind, she knew that something had happened, but that she retained no memory of it. She wandered the jungle, feeling as if the answer had been in her grasp but had slipped from it. But other terrors lapped at the edges of her mind, and she shut them all out, regardless.

The cottage was a ruin, half-overgrown with vegetation, but with some roofed portions remaining, and the shadow of a kitchen garden still poking up from amongst the ubiquitous weeds. Richildis looked at it in wonder, then slowly crept into its lea, edging towards the doorway with fright and hope mingling within her breast. She knew a bit of history, her husband had seen to that, feeling that ignorance of the Ivory Coast was unpardonable as he did his business there. Fifty years ago, settlers from New Lisbon had spread out into the hinterland, setting up farms and looking set to establish themselves for life. But the Fulani had driven them out - not in one go, but in repeated attacks, a campaign of attrition over ten years that had eventually seen even the most determined and committed leave. Only the quarries had remained, armed punishment camps for New Lisbon's worst offenders, and with their perimeters and machine gun nests, they had survived the attacks and become the isolated outposts of today, linked by highways that only armoured battle-wagons kept in operation.

But this cottage must date back to that time of hope, when the men and women of Albion thought that they could properly make a new colony in this part of Africa, perhaps to join up with the Viceroyalty being established to the North in the fullness of time. The latter had become a permanent fixture upon the map of the world, but the inland colonies of New Lisbon had not, and even most of those who lived there now knew nothing of them, would indeed have been surprised to have heard that the city had once had networks of new settlements spreading out into the hinterland...except of course that nobody lived in New Lisbon now, Richildis had seen that with her own eyes. It was as benighted a place as this smallholding...except that perhaps this ruined cottage might offer her salvation.

She crept through the doorway, a few rotten timbers to one side all that remained of the door, and entered the dank interior. As her eyes adjusted she could see the outline of a fireplace, a few collapsed heaps that must once have been the furniture, and a network of threads upon a wall that was probably once a tapestry, though it now looked to be held together by cobwebs, such as was left, that was.

She wandered from room to room, if the subdivisions still deserved that name, coming to a place where the roof still stood strong upon walls that seemed thicker than the others. A small alcove was set in the farthest wall, and a piece of rotten wood was still nailed to the wall at the back of it.
"Lord Jesus", she fell to her knees, addressing not what was there in fact, but what it might still symbolise...

Something glowed from without, and for a moment she thought that the Lord had come. Then the ball of light came into sight, and she remembered...and she screamed...

~

Five, four, three, two, one...
He moved quickly across the path, counting the patrol of the sole guard on duty to the second, to merge back into the darkness on the other side.
Lucas Tremayne did not pause to count himself lucky. It was not luck, it was skill, but hardly a rare one, and he had managed it only because his senses had been heightened enough to note the existence of the Fulani outguard down here in the darkness. If he had blundered in unawares, he would be dead now - or worse.

With no other plan in mind, he circled the camp's outer defences, noting that the only sounds he could from within were the orderly movings of warriors. On the one hand that was good, for no prisoners were being tortured, or worse. On the other hand, it was bad, for it meant that they were not going to be at all distracted. He paused against a tree, watching a young warrior use the woods for his

54

toileting, and pondering his chances. If he continued to blunder through the jungle in the hope of reaching somewhere friendly, the odds were that he would end up captured, or better yet killed. But if he could make the Empire aware that he was out here, they might launch a rescue mission for him. He wasn't sure what the odds of that were, but it seemed a better hope to wish for than to blunder into salvation.

Every Fulani band had some sort of radio, though often it was an antiquated heavy thing that a specially-trained runner would carry on his back. It was always a mistake to under-estimate the Fulani, to think of them as savages or primitives. They might not often dress fully, and as often as this they would be unshod, but they were suited to the environment, knew the ways and paths of the jungles, and they were fearsome warriors. The Empire's technology might impose a superiority in a specific area, or for a specific operation, but it could never be overlooked that much of West Africa remained in Fulani hands, and that Imperial attempts to settle and pacify the interior had met with very little success over the past half century.

On the other hand, they saw the men and women of the Empire as some sort of Hellspawn, not worthy of the treatment they might give to other tribal groupings, and to be tortured, killed - or worse. Lucas could not remember reading about or hearing about a single occasion when the Fulani had agreed a prisoner exchange, not even one for a huge ransom as noble families sometimes offered for the return of their scions. This was their code, and it was one the Caliphate was not altogether happy about in its allies, as it deprived them of desperately-needed funds, but the war was not about money, and Imperial prisoners were simply animals to be used and killed as their captors desired it. Lucas had no illusions about what would happen to him if he was captured, and like many other officers he carried a cyanide pill in his jacket pocket - the problem was, as many had found to their terrible pain, that getting it out and using it was not normally a luxury the enemy afforded you, as like as not he would take you by surprise.

Lucas knew of some officers who had pre-empted this and placed the ampoule already in their mouths before going into an engagement, and of a fair few who had accidentally bitten down on it and dropped dead as they ran, or leapt, or rolled in the heat of the combat. It was a preferable death than that which the enemy had in mind for you if you survived, but it was not an honourable one, and it was something that the Marshals of the Army often railed against in their speeches. It was better to enter combat believing you would survive and emerge victorious, than to take every precaution in case you did not. The former gave you spirit, honour and valour, the latter made you sluggish, overly fearful and prone to accidents of the kind above. Lucas knew that he would need all of his valour for what he was about to do, and the cyanide capsule stayed safely stowed in its metal tube.

The warrior had finished his toilet and was turning back towards the camp when Lucas leapt on him and garroted him with a twine he had formed from the metal lacings at the bottom of his jacket. Like the sharpened sticks he still carried slung across his back on vine-strappings, it had been a way to make the best of a poor situation. His jacket now flapped outwards, but it was a small price to pay for a useful weapon. The warrior had made no cry and now lay dead in a depression where the pilot had rolled him.

He now began to creep towards the camp proper, ears and eyes open and spread wide as Advanced Training had taught him to do. It was the same sort of skill one needed in an aerial dogfight, the ability to see or sense an enemy coming at you from the edges of your vision, or to hear when something was out of place, and move before it came upon you.

He rolled, and the warrior who had leapt on him from out of a tree hit the crowd with a thud. Before he could rise or issue a cry, Lucas had impaled him with a sharpened stick, ramming it through the eye socket into the brain. They never made any noise after that.

Withdrawing it, he held it in one hand as he now knelt in the shadows eyeing the open ground of the campfire. A couple of figures were moving on the other side, preparing some sort of animal for the evening meal, whilst a couple of makeshift huts beyond them served as shelter from the not infrequent rain. His keen eyes crept slowly over the rooves, until he saw a vine unnaturally looping down and back upon itself - that would be the camouflage for the radio aerial, a vine wrapped around it to prevent it from shining in the Moonlight.

Nodding to himself, he circled round, garroting another guard who was looking with concern into the trees where his comrade had still not returned from his toilet.

Lucas sprinted across a patch of open ground, crawling through the undergrowth to the back of the shelter that housed the radio. He could hear a single voice within, repeating what sounded like a coded phrase into the microphone. He hoped it was a case of bad reception, not of faulty equipment - that would be a terrible irony, to risk all this to steal a radio that did not work. Now up close, the pilot could see the burly operator sitting back, sweat glistening on his bare arms and torso as he took a swig from a glass bottle, probably some sort of fiery mix of herbs and spices and as like as not alcoholic for all of Islam's theoretical ban on such things. Peering through the slats, Lucas was able to see that nobody else was within the shelter - if he could enter with surprise, there was a chance he could deal with the operator, and get away the way he had come before the alarm was raised.

A bright light shone down upon him, and Lucas paused stunned. He knew of no occasion when the Fulani ever used floodlights, both lights and generators being too heavy, too cumbersome for use this far into the jungle. Perhaps it was of Imperial origin, maybe an airship drifting low and scanning the ground? He turned to wave to it, and froze.

Before him was a ball of light, gaining swiftly upon his position. Before he could form a more coherent thought than that, both Lucas and the light were gone...

Chapter 5
Albion City (Imperial Capital)
Empire of Albion

"My wishes are not to be respected then?!", Dionysus Rothgar Excelsior stood in a pool of almost blinding light and appealed to someone unseen, far above.

"They are not" boomed a voice, artificially magnified until it seemed as if it came from every corner of the great room.

"I should not have to work with my father's bastard...!" Dionysus protested.

"Your work, as all work, is the Emperor's" the voice above was having none of it.

"Then pass my protest to His Majesty!" Dionysus commanded.

"Denied!" boomed the voice.

"How can *you* deny me?!" he demanded.

"By the power invested in me by His Imperial Majesty William VI"

"You are just a mouthpiece..." Dionysus began, but he knew he had gone too far.

A pair of naked slaves approached, lightning rods in their arms.

"Alright", he spread his arms wide before them, "I get the message."

"You will meet your sister at the airfield" the voice added, calmer now

"Half-sister", Dionysus protested, then as the slaves twirled the rods towards him, added hurriedly, "I will meet her"

"Then go, there is but little time"

He went.

- - -

Golden Field bristled with guns. Perimeter ramparts were topped with turrets, the muzzles of others poked up from pits dug alongside the fairways, and yet more were to be seen in the form of truly enormous armoured battle wagons lumbering slowly from point to point on a leviathan's guard duty.

One of a number of airfields on a spoked radius surrounding the

Imperial Capital, it could handle a half dozen airships at a time, with more room for tethered vessels on the ground. A network of roadways ran between the landing areas, the battle wagons and supply vehicles moving at a constant speed between them.

A single tower spiked up into the air, over twenty storeys high, a mixture of precious metals and high quality reflective glass cladding its sides, and clusters of banners and smaller flags sprouting like copses of trees upon its flanks. The first sight any visitor to Albion City would get would be this phallic symbol of Imperial majesty, an awesome reminder that the Empire could afford to use its wealth in such ostentatious decoration.

On the uppermost floor, a handful of technicians attended to the radio mast that spiked up as a natural extension of the structure, whilst the duty officer of the moment looked out at the scene before him, counting down mentally the imminent arrival of one certain special vessel. Whilst flights from all over the continent of Albion were the most common here, those from across the Atlantic were not so uncommon that they marked a special occasion, and a regular service even ran to the Viceroyalty of West Africa. This particular vessel would not have attracted undue comment were it not for the passenger aboard whom, he knew, had been summoned home on the personal order of the Emperor.

- - -

The *Elysium* descended rapidly, teams of slaves rushing up from underground pits to secure the guiding ropes, and tie the airship down. Even as the Grand Captain was announcing their arrival over the speaking tubes, an armoured wagon, gigantic tyres taller than a man was high, bounced across the hard-packed grass towards them.

Ramona Elise Carding was moving slowly down the gangway when half a dozen white-and-gold uniformed individuals leapt from the rear of the wagon and raced towards her,
"The Emperor commands that you are to come with us at once" a woman said, long blond hair snapping in the breeze, sub-machine gun held nonchalantly in her arms.

"Then I shall obey" Ramona allowed herself to be led around behind the enormous vehicle and up a ramp to its interior.

It was moving even before the ramp was closed on its hydraulic lifts. She scrambled for purchase after the guards and emerged into what could only be described as a room, six foot square, lined with benches, with small narrow tables in the centre. Another half dozen guards were sat motionless, but standing at the head of the room was a man she could recognise, even after all this time.
"Brother..." she whispered
"Half-brother" he snapped, "And the better half"
She seated herself beside a trim raven-haired woman, whose bulging midriff was most definitely a mark of pregnancy,
"As happy to see you as ever" she smiled.
"Likewise!" he growled, and threw down a folder onto the table nearest to her, "Read that"

Then he was gone, climbing through a companionway up towards the command deck of what was truly a miniature landship. Ramona reached for the document, and pulled it towards her. None of the guards did anything, there was no conversation, no sly looks, and no impatient shuffling. Presumably only the best had been chosen to pick her up. She smiled at that; no doubt that was another thing putting brother Dionysus's back out.

Despite its elaborate folder, the document inside was brief and did not take her more than a couple of minutes to read. Ten minutes later she put it down, having read it five times, including twice from the bottom up. She thought she had the measure of it, but was confused as to what it had to do with her...

- - -

Battle Commander Ignatio Hunt was the duty officer of the moment in the imperious tower. Having watched the airship arrive, he now watched the armoured wagon thunder out of the airfield, between the gigantic gates. He waited a moment until it was on the Imperial Highway, and crossed to the telephone set in the farther wall of the control tower.

None of the technicians was about; their checks done and their measures taken they would be back below in the radio room, listening to and conversing with transmitters from all across the Empire, all across the planet. Ignatio knew he had the time to do what was necessary, the time and the privacy for, other than the technicians, nobody could access this level without his personal authorisation. He picked up the head of the telephone and blew down the tube. In a sleepy village it might have woken the operator up from a slyly-taken doze, but here at the heart of the Empire it would go straight to a duty handler in the vast Exchange visible over the horizon from the tower.

"Order of the Dragon" he demanded, when the operator answered, "Connect me to the Office of the High Dragomaster."
Two minutes later a voice came on the line,
"I am Acolyte Bryn Magnuson, how may I help you?"
"A message for your master"
"Please dictate it; I am proficient in ten languages and have a typing speed of sixty words per minute"

Ignatio nodded to himself; it was always an intriguing contest of wills this part
"Arapahoe"
"Of course", it was the native language of choice for all high-level coders.
Ignatio began...

"The snake", Sulvia Theresa Bartholema put out her hands, and the hissing serpent was placed into them.
She caressed its skin, feeling her excitement rise with the motion.
"It is ready to do good service" she said.
"Yes Mistress", the naked youth took it back and placed it into the deep cylinder from which he had drawn it
"Two minutes before Midnight" Sulvia said.
"Yes Mistress"
"Let all know of The Rising!" she intoned breathlessly.
"It shall be so, Mistress

- - -

The building was nothing out of the ordinary from the outside, a dull stone blockhouse on the outer edge of the Imperial Capital, close to the massive railyards and almost underneath the more recent addition of an elevated railway that led deep within the heart of the administrative zone.

Nor did the doors provide any clue; the loading bay looked long unused, the doors covered in blistered paint, and rotting wood, but solidly barred with heavy timber planks nailed over them. The side door was a bare nothing, openable only from the inside, an emergency exit perhaps, or perhaps even just a wall feature within, the only sign of its previous life as a door being what remained on the exterior. The front door was reached by climbing a half dozen steps set parallel to the wall of the house, steps which had once had a railing on the exposed edge, but this had long ago gone, leaving only small holes in the outer edge, and a somewhat precipitate drop for the unwary.

The door itself was a faded black, the spotted remains of gold lettering flaking upon its surface. An "A" and a "u" could be seen - 'Auction' perhaps, perhaps not. There was no door knocker, no bell-pull, no way to gain the attention of anyone within but to knock heavily and hope that they could hear. What windows there were were shuttered, both outside and in and offered no glimpse into the heart or soul of the building, presuming it had one.

With no warning, the door now opened and a young woman exited, her cheeks flushed a rosy red, the curls of her auburn hair tied back in a single braided band. A shawl was wrapped tightly around her torso, whilst the trails of a white cotton dress blew in the breeze below. A man's eye would be drawn to these features before noting what she carried; a woman might have noted the steel cylinder clutched tightly in her arms and remarked upon its likeness to a milk churn.

Nobody would have stopped her, though, but perhaps a bold man would have spoken and tried to proposition her, for all that what she carried all but precluded her from being a whore. But there were no men here, no women here. The street was deserted, litter blowing in the wind that whipped low and stirred up whirlwinds in its lea. Further away there was a rumble of vehicles, then a train sliced through the scene, barrelling upon the elevated railroad, absent one moment, here the next with its sudden cacophony, and then gone again leaving what now felt like an eerie silence.

The woman headed up the street, purposeful, lugging the cylinder as she went, the unseen muscles in her arms bulging tight and strong. At the junction she looked both ways, but the crossway was as deserted as the road she had walked up. She smiled a secret smile to herself, and passed across the roadway to a door set in the side of an ancient chapel. A key slid from a hiding place upon her person, and balancing the cylinder upon her hip, she unlocked the door and passed swiftly within.

- - -

James stopped what he was doing with a guilty start and looked up,
"Er, hello!" he called out, hurriedly buttoning himself and grabbing a faded altar cloth to swing about his person as he turned to greet her.
"I bring the future" Sulvia placed the cylinder reverentially upon the long-abandoned altar.
"The future?" James felt that it was safe to move now, and crossed the dusty concourse to her side, "The Rising?" he asked.
"As prophesied!", Sulvia swayed and he longed to reach out and catch her, but she never ever quite fell, and he had given up hoping. Only his dreams alone saw him play the gallant hero to her needs.

Another dull rumble signalled the passing of another elevated train, then all was silence again. James cast the young woman a glance, excited and yet disturbed by the look of rapture upon her face, and the swaying of her hips as she caressed the shining steel of the cylinder,
"A new...way is...coming!" she breathed.
"It is", he could agree with her wholeheartedly, even if he had to move closer to the altar table to hide just how it was manifesting upon him.
"It is two minutes before Midnight!"
"Yes" he let go, and held the sides of the table with strong hands as another part of him gave up the unequal struggle in such close

proximity to the living goddess.

"Let all know of The Rising!" she intoned, swaying.

James could only nod; the rising of his own kind had now spent its force, and he was wondering just how we was going to clean his trousers before going home. If his mother did not notice, his sisters would and they would give him such a ragging...again!

~

They wore yellow, a colour uncommon and unpopular with most formations within the Empire and, it was rumoured, adopted by the first Guardians for that reason. Yellow was now a colour of esteem; people would stop and nod, or bow if the wearer also wore the other badges of rank. Yellow could get you a free drink, or the use of a love-slave; it could feed your family for a week at someone else's cost, or it could get you tickets to the theatre, the cinema, sports games, or even the erotic shows. It could, of course, also get you killed.

Heart Intrinisia Lennard wore her yellow robe with pride, her hair in shapely ringlets, her arms and thighs bare, uncovered by the robe. Underneath she was naked, as the Law demanded, and about her brow she wore a thin brass circlet. This had been her life since signing on as a cadet in her fourteenth year. Ten years later she could not imagine life outside of the Guardians, or life without such intimate contact with Cyclops.

In the popular imagination, Cyclops was a single entity, one giant machine that did things, nobody knew quite how, but that was just how the Guardians portrayed it, and was how all those who mattered wanted it to seem. In truth, Cyclops was a thousand machines, most here in the Imperial City, but with extensions of its being in London, in Timbuktu, or in a dozen other locations around the Empire. Simple telegraphy kept them all in contact, mathematical codes encrypting the entries from dedicated stations, messages passed along dedicated lines that a whole sub-section of the Imperial Navy had sworn to protect from any enemy who would cut the cables, or dredge them.

But, whilst Cyclops was many, and whilst it had its arms in far-flung places, its heart was still in Albion City, and all of its appendages still fed into the central well. Heart was tending this, a vast array set in vacuum-packed tubes, covering perhaps a football field's worth of space, but several banks deep, and requiring constant monitoring less a single burn-out lead to a section failure and that to a computational error that could be the difference between life and death for hundreds.

For whilst Cyclops had a huge mind, it had only one eye, and that would be focused on the task given to it, not on what might go wrong within it. Like any machine it would not know if it was broken - ask an aeroplane not to start its engine if the propeller is fractured, or a locomotive not to pull its carriages if the bogey of one has split. Its single eye was upon the matter at hand - it took a hundred pairs of eyes to watch it, a thousand to care for it, a score of thousand to ensure its safety.

Heart watched as a series of flashes at the edge of her vision indicated an input from one of the Rods at the consoles on the periphery. When she had first come here as an impressionable teenager she had dreamed of one day seducing a Rod, loving him, having him as her own. But time was a teacher, and she now knew what the word eunuch meant, knew from deeper examinations that the Rods existed to serve, Master Slaves to the system, incorruptible and sworn into service of the machine.

They were the lynchpin between the machines in other locations, the messages received via the secure telegraph, and the information that was input into the heart of Cyclops. A Rod could read a coded message in seconds without recourse to texts. The best could look at a sequence of flashing lights and know not only what it asked, but where the question had come from. There was pride, and there was love, but there was never superiority for above everything else the Rods remained slaves, not of any person or corporation, but of Cyclops itself, and the Empire as a whole.

Above all of them, of course, were the Lord Guardians, the shadowy rarely seen figures who thought in sharp equations and could do twenty things at once. Only they alone wore underwear, wool from the farther reaches of the British Isles, and they alone shaved their heads.

Some said there was a symmetry in the two things, the fibres round their genitals replacing those shorn from their pates. But a lot of what some people said was rubbish, so one never knew. The women amongst them were also Lords, also dressed the same, shaved the same, and thought the same. It was the ideal of equality to which the rest of the Empire strived, made the starker by service to the Machine, a thing without sex, a thing which seemed to exist on another realm altogether.

~

The armoured wagon had slotted into an underground bay like a ship to a wharf. The bays were open at all sides, only the stone platforms around the midriffs of the vehicle, and the stairwells by the rear served as entry and exit points. Ahead, the stone platforms merged with a flooring that swept away into the distance, but beneath it was a maintenance deck from where appliances and small vehicles were rolled out to see to the leviathan's needs.

Dionysus had left as soon as the vehicle had docked; in truth, he had been already out, standing proud upon the carapace as they had come in, and docking completed, he had stepped up to the stone platform, and strode hurriedly away. It had been a full two minutes before Ramona had come up the stairwell, striding behind a half dozen white-and-gold guards, taking her lead from them, and not noticing that her brother was receding into the dimly-lit distance.

She had continued to follow them, as they had walked from the platform, across the concourse to a cylindrical tower set within an open area, and waited for an elevator that had taken them to the surface. Emerging in an ornate garden, she had allowed herself to be led through a door manned by heavily armed and armoured Red Guard, into a large and airy hall where an ugly man in a dirty robe had bid her wait.

Half an hour later, somebody finally came through the curtained doorway that she had had her eyes upon. For a moment she did not believe it, then she was up on her feet, running into the wizened one's embrace,

"Augie!" she all but screamed, "I do not believe it!"
"Please believe it, my child, for belief is all that holds these old bones together."

Augustus Simeon McLeon was a hundred years old, born in a time when Roman names were still the vogue, and twenty years before had been an old man charged with tutoring the bastard child of an Imperial dynast. That awkward teen was now a mature woman, and the old man was now an ancient one, but he lived on, and as long as he lived he held Senatorial rank; nothing could take that away, but death itself.

"Things must be bad, my child" he said, and Ramona was transported back to a time over half her lifetime away, "for them to recall you from where I know you do good service."
She smiled at that, happy to know he had looked out for her in the letters and communiqués, still bubbling in the delight of finding him alive, and hale.
"Its bad" she shuddered, "I had not known how bad until..." and she frowned.
"Until, my child?"
"Until my brother handed me a folder upon my arrival"
"He spoke to you?", Augustus' voice was full of sudden hope
"Only because he was commanded. He still hates the fact of my existence."
"Oh..." he was downcast, "I am sorry."

She shrugged,
"I never hated the fact of his. He was always too sensitive."
"But he has done well for himself in the years between" Augustus pointed out.
"Free of my presence, you mean?" Ramona pulled the old man to a seat beside her on the bench, "Maybe that is why he hates me - he thinks that I will be a block upon his talents"
"His mind is the problem, in that case" Augustus shook his head sadly, "Family should always pull together"
"That is precisely his problem, he does not want me to be family"
"You speak true, child"

"Rise and...!" an authoritative voice began, entering the hall from the shadows, but seeing the ancient one stuttered to a halt, "I apologise Your Eminence, I had not know that you were here."

"I rise" Augustus looked the newcomer up and down, seeing a woman of slowly maturing years, proud in her bearing, and vain in her power, "You will speak with due reverence to the daughter of a dynast"

The woman reddened, but did not dare contradict one of such rank, "Of course, Your Eminence"

She stood and waited whilst the two of them hugged, and the ancient man retired behind the curtain, then aware that he was probably still watching her, she coughed,

"Highness, you will please attend upon the Great Chamberlain"

"Of course", Ramona inclined her head.

The Great Chamberlain was the Voice of the Emperor, the most powerful officeholder in the whole of Albion. A shadowy figure, he lived beyond the light, unseen by most of those who spoke to him, but always doing the Emperor's will.

She followed the woman through a door hidden in a recess, and down a dark passageway into one better lit and carpeted. A minute later this gave way to a corridor more ornate and furnished, and after a short expanse of this, into a marbled entrance hall. Occasionally they had passed a pair of patrolling guards, white-and-gold and sub-machine-guns at the ready. Arriving, they passed between a pair of ironbound oaken doors and into a room where the natural order of things seemed inverted.

Pools of light lit the dark, a cliff seemed to rise at the far end and where there should be a roof, there was . . . something else, a place populated by voices that boomed down towards a man still standing in the largest of the circles of light.

"You will not leave our presence!" the voice was magnified as if to come from all around.

"You overstep..." the figure began, but the approach of the naked slaves cut him off.

"My brother!" Ramona breathed, turning to the woman beside her...but she was gone, her duty done and taking advantage of the first opportunity to be rid of her unwelcome charge.

68

"Approach, Daughter of Albion!" the unseen voice boomed out, there being little doubt whom was being addressed.

Ramona walked forward, a little unsteadily, especially when a spotlight fixed its beam upon her. It halted beside her brother, and she halted inside it with a shuddering motion.

"You have read the briefing?" the voice demanded to know.

"Yes" she said, simply.

"Something is very wrong", the unseen Great Chamberlain fairly growled his words, "You two will work together to find out what."

Ramona cast a glance across at Dionysus, his face a mask of impotent fury, his feet glued to the floor, his hands to his sides, his teeth clenched, and his eyes blazing.

"I look forward to it" she told the voice.

"You will speak also", the voice was subtly altered, different banks of speakers directing it at the prince who stood frozen in time.

"Yes" Dionysus growled, unable to manage his fury any better or his words any greater.

"The Grand Master of The Order of The Unicorn will see you now."

"At last..." Ramona breathed, the document having preyed hard upon her mind, the chivalric order seeming an irrelevance, at best an anachronism, but here in the Imperial Capital they did things differently, and she was about to find out just what the hints and teases in that document had alluded to.

"This way", this slave was not naked, wearing a coat of mink, and a hat of felt. He held a six-foot lightning rod in his arms, its base between his bare thighs, its shaft where his genitals would have been had they not been removed.

Neither Dionysus nor Ramona had anything to say as they followed him into an invisible opening, and beyond to their appointment.

~

The Northern outskirts of Albion City were the salubrious suburbs, not so much through an accident of local geography, but through the pattern of development of the whole Albion continent. Road and rail-lines from the North-East came into the Eastern hub, whilst the vast majority of such communication links were from the West and South, and came into the gigantic Western hub. The South of the city had sprawled into a massive industrial zone, whilst the North had been where the Emperor's family had their palaces, where the nobles of the Empire had conglomerated in the early years, and whilst most of the parkland was now overgrown, and some of the older palaces demolished and replaced with salubrious squares of elaborate townhouses, there were still open areas, where the roads ran between the trees, and where the houses were set back from the road in their own grounds.

The steam limousine swept along the road at a fair sixty miles an hour, sleek and black, with silver leopards rearing out of the hood, and a banner fluttering from the rear. This did not mark it out as in anyway unusual, here in the Imperial Capital - everyone who was anyone had their personal symbols adorning anything that they were allowed to, not least their methods of getting around. In times past that had been carriages and stage-coaches, and in the parties of horsemen that every noble travelled in. Now, they were seen on every type of vehicle, and the modern steam limousines were fast become the vehicle of choice for the elite.

Ignatio Hunt sat in the rear, legs crossed as he gazed thoughtfully out of the window. In front his driver and bodyguard drove, and watched; one could never be too careful, especially if one was allied to an Order. Off-duty, he was no longer a Battle Commander in the Elite Guard, but a member of the nobility, albeit a minor one, and therefore doubly a target if anyone was bold enough. They had tried twice before, once killing his driver of the time, the second time nicking his own arm slightly with a bullet. He wore the scar as a mark of honour in bed; it had a definite aphrodisiac affect upon the young married women he was becoming famed in certain circles for being able to service. Of course, that was another danger in itself, but a cuckolded husband would challenge one to a duel not shoot from out of the trees.

They swept round a lazy bend, then straightened out before slowing as they approached a pair of high silver gates on the left. Two men in leopard livery stepped out from concealed positions and, checking up and down the road, unlocked the gate. The limousine swang in and accellerated up the roadway towards the house set in the distance at the edge of a private woods.

Ignatio's family had always had money, but titles had been few and now only his older cousin's line still bore one, Count of Mar, for all that none of them had set foot in Scotland for generations. He had inherited a fair share from his grandfather, and made more by business dealings in association with the Dragon, but whilst the latter had raised the funds for the purchase of the land, and the construction of the house he was now stretching his limbs before, it was always the more dangerous of his wealth, as what was given could be taken back, not directly for it had been payments, not gifts, but if he did not keep in with the Dragomasters, they would find a way of punishing him - several ways, actually, all of them painful.

A naked slave girl came down the steps and brushed against his side. He tousled her hair, then indicated the driver
"Service Karl, he's more in need of it"
The driver nodded his thanks, and led the girl away towards the barn. The bodyguard completed the lockdown of the limousine, then rose to await his master's command.
"Check on the household, then choose one of the girls for the night. I have some important calls to make"
"Yes sir", the guard beamed and trotted into the house.
A little munificence could go a long way, Ignatio thought to himself.

He passed swiftly through the entrance hall, filled with ancestral paintings of people he could barely remember even when he looked at them, which was not often. Mounting the marble and oak stairway, he crossed into a master bedroom, and locked it behind him. He had several sleeping quarters around the house, just in case someone sent somebody after him here, which so far they had not. This room was one of the less luxurious but had a few advantages. He quickly disrobed and took a shower from the cubicle set dead centre of the room, then walked naked around whilst he towelled himself, running over in his head the conversation he was going to have to have soon.

From a walk-in closet, he pulled on comfortable leggings and a wrap-around cloak. The household slaves in the basement kept the building at a comfortable temperature, and if it had not been below his level of dignity he could have walked around naked without feeling any chill. In the heights of Summer, the position was reversed, but his overseers made sure everything was just as comfortable.. Taking a long cool drink from an icebox, he opened what appeared to be a cupboard door, set a foot off the ground, stepped lithely up to the lip, and climbed the tightly-wound staircase within, up several floors to the eyrie at the top. Bolting the door behind him, he settled down before the radio equipment and turned it on. Whilst it warmed up, he finished the drink, placed the glass carefully on the edge of his desk, and drew out the code book from the hidden drawer beneath it. Without the weight of the glass, the counter-weight would not have shifted to allow the lock to open. It was ingenious, if simple.

Direct communication was always more complicated than passing on a message, but there were things that could not be said to an Acolyte, and this was one of them. Focusing his mind on the pages before him, Ignatio began to tap out the introductory sequence, identifying himself and requesting personal conversation. It could take anything up to an hour for the High Dragomaster to reply, depending on where he was, and what he was doing, when the call came in. Ignatio placed a plump cushion beneath his rump, and settled in for the long haul, replaying once more what he was going to have to say. It could go either way, he knew, and there was no point worrying about it...yet.

Chapter Six
Albion City (Imperial Capital)
Empire of Albion

The machine juddered, and a spew of ticker-tape began to emanate from a slit in its side. Brand Endeavour Rourke scooped it up in his hands, letting it feed through his fingers as he read the cryptic symbols upon it. He pursed his lips and looked across to where a Rod was rattling his fingers across an input board. Whatever the Master Slave was doing was resulting in this. He watched a bit longer to make sure of a direct correlation, and then rose.

Moving between chuddering banks of machinery, smelling of hot oil and rarified air, Brand made his way to where a Lord Guardian stood frowning at a flashing board of electric lights. It was a male - sometimes it was hard to tell in the absence of hair - and the light shone fiercely off his bald pate, indicating a fresh shave that morning.

Brand sighed inwardly, and clicked his heel, bowing his head to face the floor,
"Lord Guardian" he said.
The man took a full minute to reply, but one did not hurry them. Their minds were giant calculating machines, and they needed to complete the calculation underway, and park it before being able to pay attention to a mere flesh-and-blood interruption.

"Speak" the man's eyes slowly cleared, and he regarded Brand with a detached interest.
"Sir", Brand raised his eyes as protocol now allowed, "Cyclops is spouting gibberish."
The Lord Guardian narrowed his eyes, and from a voluminous pocket raised a short staff,
"You will justify that statement or face the consequences."
Brand had anticipated this and prepared a speech in case his conscious mind failed him. As it was, he had kept his wits about him,
"N--G-H A-S-W" he said, "The feed is giving out three-letter bursts with no words in them."

Whatever he had been expecting it was not for the Lord Guardian to turn and run away. But that is what he did. Brand stared after him open-mouthed, and then looked back to where the Rod was sitting. The eunuch was still busy inputting readings he was receiving from another location into the data well, and Brand had no doubt that Cyclops was equally as busy spouting gibberish from the ticker-tape.

A Red Guard appeared on the balcony above, an unprecedented sight but one that at least made sense. The Reds were the Guards of Last Resort; an Elite Guard in white-and-gold would have been far more unsettling. Now another pair stood next to him, looking down over the well, weapons to hand but held loose and pointing towards the floor. Somehow, Brand did not find this at all reassuring.

An elderly Lord Guardian now pushed his way amongst them, raising a bullhorn to his lips and blasted the whole vast room into silence.
"Oops" he said, but nobody dared to laugh. A moment later, with the help of a Red Guard, he had the feedback suppressed, and his voice boomed out like the thunder of the Gods, or the Great Chamberlain on a bad day,
"All work is to cease!", he swallowed, "All work is to cease!"
People stared up at him in disbelief.
"Rods are to gather in the Watching Room, Guardians in their zonal groupings. Now!"

People moved, slowly at first, and then faster as the Lord Guardians began to move about them, beating the slower ones with their staffs set to slice through the nerves. Yelps, squawks and a few effeminate screams, mainly from men, echoed through the air until all the dawdlers were in their proper space.

All around red lights were now flashing, Cyclops feeds from all around the Empire that were now going unanswered. A few shrill whistles came, signalling that Cyclops was shutting down processes that were already beginning to spiral out of control without their human overseers.

All eyes looked up at the elderly Lord Guardian as he once more raised the bullhorn to his lips,

"Station 55 has been infected by an outside source. All Rods are to clear down their data relays and pass test transmissions to the well. All Guardians will operate under their zonal Lord Guardian and tend to the output. All operations are now under the security edict of the Red Guard"

For a moment everybody just stared at him in thunderstruck silence, and then pandemonium broke out

~

The rain lashed down, drenching the windows of the elevated train as it thundered through the darkness of early evening. Inside, the air was full of the smells of mustiness, clothes slowly steaming from the heaters placed beneath the footrests on the seats. A child ran up and down the aisle, sometimes lending a swipe to someone unfortunate enough to overhang even slightly into what the child saw as a play-space. Somewhere someone was snoring loudly, somewhere a drunk was singing, guzzling on a bottle in between verses.

Solomon Hankey was reading an essay on the History of Kazan, or more particularly the khanate's conquest of Astrakhan at the end of the nineteenth century. It was not a very good essay, being stilted and full of quotes from obscure authors, or even more obscure commentators of the period. But it was correct, and factual and he could not fault the research that had gone into it. If the student intended to go into publishing after completing her doctorate, though, she would need a slave to work alongside her, perhaps an aged ex-secretary from one of the estates out in the West who had come to the end of his useful life and been sold on cheap to whatever institution would have him.

He would grade it high, he knew, and it was not simply that the author was a beautiful woman, or even that she was a dynast. Perhaps they came into it a little, but he could feel the power of her mind, even through her parlous use of words. It would be good to have someone like that on the faculty again.

Hell, but he was getting old! Almost fifty he had been at Saint

Michael's for over thirty years, first as an undergraduate now as senior Professor of History, and where had all those years gone? To be sure he could recount significant events a-plenty, both the happy and the sad, but so often when he looked back it seemed like only yesterday when he had been drinking wine at Orlando's and urinating on the slaves sleeping in the basement. He had no children of his own, and though he had hoped at first to be an uncle to those of his sister, or his brother, nothing had come of that. His brother had been killed in action at Gondar...twenty years ago now, it was. His sister had declared herself a lesbian and married an old crone from Wales; God alone knew where they were now. He suspected he would have heard if they were dead.

Was it too late for him personally? Fifty was not so old. As if to prove it to himself, he set the essay back inside his black leather case and looked around the carriage. There, that young woman with the curly brown hair, holding some kind of bundle in her arms - she was beautiful, and if he focused on her he could feel a stirring in his loins. So, what was stopping him from getting up and walking over to her? More fools tried and failed every day than ever anyone suspected; at worse he would just be another of them. In his mind he resolved to do just that, but in his body he did nothing.

The train began to slow and the brakes screeched out a warning as they bit. He looked through the runnels of water on the windows, peering into a darkness lit by stuttering gaslamps, not recognising this part of the city at all. Then he saw that she had moved, stood up and risen, passing through a door that a young man in a black coat was holding open for her. On a whim, Solomon rose, hefted his case and followed her, only just avoiding having the door slammed in his face by the unsuspecting youth. This latter gave him an odd look as he made his own way down, but did not look back.

Solomon buttoned his coat, and straightened the hat upon his head. The woman was bending over a bench, fiddling with whatever it was she held in the bundle. Wondering if he had gone truly mad - or truly sane - he walked across to her,
"Can I help you with that?" he asked gallantly.

Sulvia turned, serpent wrapped around her wrist
"Yes" she said.
And plunged the reptile's fangs into the academic's open neck.

~

Bryn Magnuson moved away from the telegraph and rubbed down the ache in his back. At thirty he had gone about as far as any Acolyte could without embarking upon the next step - and that was not something to be taken lightly, if at all. Some never took it, and grew old still doing the chores of a man a third of their age. He did not want that for himself, hence his dedication beyond the ordinary call of duty.

The room was small, packed with machinery and occupied by three of them. One was close in age to Bryn, a woman with all the signs of advanced pregnancy upon her, and the lethargy to go with it. The other was also female, straight from the schools, and with all the annoying mix of ignorance and hauteur that Bryn found disgusting in such creatures.

"Switch to Arapahoe!" Bryn commanded.
The pregnant woman reached out slowly and reset the links, the younger looked up at him in confusion.
"A what?" she said quietly.
He frowned,
"Where do you hail from?" he demanded.
"London" she snapped back.
"London, England?" he checked.
"Do you know another one?" she was defensive.
"Three actually" he said.
She just looked back at him with incomprehension.

He sighed,
"What would you have done if I had said switch to Brasilian?"
"Er?" she looked at the links before her, "Sommat with these...I remember you said"
"Or Norse?" he tried; maybe Iceland was a less obscure place in her mind.
"Um..." she pulled a couple of links out and then let them dangle from

her hand, "Dunno..." she said.

"Maybe you should just take a break", he wasn't being kind.

"Alright" she shrugged, rose and left.

Bryn completed the realigning of the links for her.

"You are being hard on her" the pregnant woman said from behind him.

"Hard?" he was astonished, "I did not even shout at her."

"Maybe, but you treat her like an idiot."

"She *is* an idiot!" he protested.

"She is young and ignorant", the woman heaved herself up to her feet, "but if she was stupid she would not have been chosen by the Order."

He nodded, having to concede that point to her.

"She will learn" the woman said, and moved towards the door, "We need food"

"It is unseemly to speak in that way" Bryn said, but she just laughed

Alone, he bolted the door shut behind them. Sometimes it was better to simply do things yourself.

- - -

Ten minutes later he was happily receiving and transmitting in Arapahoe, so practised at it that he was able to man both his own and the young woman's terminals at the same time. It was all routine stuff at this time in the evening, but it was routine that kept the Order going, and much of it was nevertheless of some import - it was after all always useful to know that nothing had changed. A change was more significant by far, but sometimes could be missed at the beginning if one was not also watching what stayed the same.

The telephone rang.

Bryn looked at it and let it ring again, then picked up the receiver, "Yes" he said.

"Operator speaking"

"Yes" he said, again; it was like this every time.

"I have a call from Serenity Field for the High Dragomaster"

"I will take the call" he said, as he did usually.

"I will connect you."

Some thirty seconds later the line clicked and he said,
"I am Acolyte Bryn Magnuson, how may I help you?"
"Do you own the registration of the airship *Prometheus*?" an unfamiliar voice asked.
He frowned,
"I will have to check for you. Who is it calling?"
"High Engineer Balthazar Smith", the voice was cultured, educated, "I am duty engineer at Serenity Field for this evening."
"Please wait whilst I retrieve the information"

Bryn rose and unlocked the door, stepping out into a sober corridor, concrete floor, yellow-painted walls and spartan lighting. It was home to him, and he hardly noticed it, walking swiftly to the right, as the passage headed slightly downwards, and emerging in a large room where a single old man sat at a desk whose ramparts were of bulky documents.
"Dragomaster Spinks" he said and waited.
The old man put down a pen and regarded him over the wall of documents,
"Bryn..." he said at length, recovering the other's name from some private store.
"Sir, do we own the airship *Prometheus*?"
"*Prometheus*?", Spinks raised himself to his full height, about five foot, and came slowly down the wooden stairway, "Well, that would be yes and no."

"I see", Bryn was not unused to such ambiguities, "I have the duty engineer of Serenity Field asking this of me?" he clarified.
"Hmmm..." the old man seemed to stare into the middle distance, then sighed, "Oh very well" he said petulantly.
"Sir?" Bryn blinked
"Tell your engineer that I will attend him within half an hour."
"Oh...yes sir, of course."

Bryn hurried away and returned to where he had come from, catching the young woman kneeling in front of the telephone, rocking back and forth lasciviously as she whispered to the person on the other end. He snatched it from her, and sent her sprawling to the floor.

"High Engineer?" he demanded.

"What, nah its Bob" a young man said in confusion.

"Where is the duty engineer?" Bryn demanded.

"Who?", Bob was clearly out of his depth.

"I was speaking to High Engineer Balthazar Smith!" Bryn yelled at him, "Fetch him for me immediately"

"You fucking mad or what?" Bob, whoever he was said, and slammed down the telephone.

Bryn looked at the dead instrument in his hand with bemusement, then as he saw the young woman crawling towards the door, her dress rucked up above her naked behind, he realised what had happened.

"You stupid bitch" he spat and crossed to tower over her, "What do you have to say?"

She tried desperately to say nothing, attempting to slither out beneath him, but Bryn grabbed hold of her hair and yanked hard on it,

"Answer me!"

"Get off you bastard" she squirmed and hit him hard across the nose, creating a gushing fountain of blood which splashed fiercely onto her face, "Fucking let me go!"

Bryn collapsed to the floor, grabbing at his injured genitals, still feeling her vicious kick, blood pooling beside his head, and his vision swimming in and out. The young woman clambered to her feet and stood swaying above him. Then something warm and pungent splashed down upon him, before she was gone.

"Ungh..." the Acolyte said, "Ungh a-ugh-ugh"

But there was nobody to hear him.

~

"Cheese and wine?" the slave was female, naked and very old.

Ignatio Hunt grimaced at the sight of her,

"Yes please" he said and took them off the proffered silver platter.

The ugly crone moved on, and the Battle Commander bit down upon a salted cracker covered in a creamy goats cheese.

"Awful do" a heavy man in a gown one size too small for him sat down beside him, making Ignatio bounce as he did so, "Hideous just hideous"

Ignatio had to agree, but was unsure about doing so openly

"The cheese is nice" he said.

The man gaped then laughed, then clapped him hard on the back, causing the cracker to fly out of his hand and land on the expensive rug in front of them.

"I am famed for my cheeses" he said.

Ignatio had not survived in the Order without having a sharp ear and an even sharper mind. He staggered to his feet and bowed,

"My lord"

The heavy man beamed,

"As you say" he said, "Here, let us go upstairs"

"Um..." Ignatio had learnt to be wary of such open-ended invitations

"My niece and her husband await"

"Oh..."

Still none the wiser, Ignatio nevertheless followed after the heaving straining man as they mounted the two dozen marble steps and emerged on a wide landing.

"You may be surprised" his host said, which did not altogether bode well.

Ignatio followed him down towards a wooden door with ivory handles, and inside as an unseen hand gripped the interior handle and swung the door open before them.

"The Lord High Dragomaster!" a naked black slave announced, "And guest"

Ignatio frowned a killer frown at the slave, then shrugged. What else would he have been announced as? It was the way of the Order to make members those of other organisations, but not to grant them rank. Guest was probably much more befitting than 'associate' or a number of other things he could have said.

Two people were seating chastely on a sofa covered in the hides of white tigers.

"Uncle", one of them, a black woman rose up and kissed the big man on the cheek.

"Sir", the man remained sitting, speaking in a toneless voice.

Ignatio could see why - he had no eyes, only pits, no ears, only holes, and no nose, just a stub. His mouth, though, remained apparently untouched.

"Sit down" so far his host's tone remained pleasant towards him, and Ignatio sat on the sofa opposite the couple, thankful when the big man pulled over a rocking chair of immense proportions and lowered himself into that.

"I am Lucille Drusilla Marguerite" the woman said, and Ignatio could only admire her dark coffee skin, and the exquisite high cheeks of her face, comparing her mentally to several of the slave girls he had bought at the market on his only visit to the Southern Islands.

"My niece was born free" the High Dragomaster could probably read his thoughts, "My brother had...interesting ideas."

"I am Jesus", the man coughed, "Maria", he coughed again, "Jones"

"Honestly" the High Dragomaster bit back a laugh he had clearly bitten back many times before.

"I was used" he coughed, "and abused" and again, "by...by", he breathed deeply, bringing up a vile globule of black spit that he dribbled onto a silk handkerchief more by luck than judgment, "the Serpent"

"I....see..." said Ignatio, wondering if the poor man's mind had gone the same way as most of his body.

"No you do not", the High Dragomaster motioned for a slave to approach from out of the shadows behind his rocking throne, and took a dossier from the man's hands, "Read that", he held it out to Ignatio

With mounting horror, the Battle Commander read, and swallowed hard.

"This..." he shook his head, "A chivalric Order stoops to this?"

"The Serpent is the most debased" Lucille spoke sonorously from beside her mutilated husband, "They have lost all honour and dignity and worship now the animal inside them."

"To be true", her uncle interrupted her, "they worship the Serpent - quite literally"

"And use it as a weapon", Ignatio closed the file with a shudder.
"It gets worse" the High Dragomaster said.

Ignatio could not begin to imagine how.

Balthazar Smith was not a happy man. Not only had that bastard Dragon hung up the telephone on him, but nobody was answering when he finally managed to telephone back. Now he had a dozen Elite Guard swarming all over the hangar, demanding entry into the *Prometheus* but without word from the Order he was reluctant to give them permission, knowing full well the weight of wrath that could land upon his head if he made the wrong decision there. If he could only hold things up for another two hours then the night duty engineer would be here, and he could hand it all over to that poor bastard - Eli or Hieronymus, probably, poor sods.

"This is not acceptable"
Balthazar was getting fed up with this woman. True, she was possessed of an astonishingly good body, lustrous blond hair and an intriguing face, but her eyes were dead as coal and her tone was the annoying buzzing of a wasp. The submachine gun slung over her shoulder, and the knife that stood prominent at her belt however prevented him from voicing these observations to her.
"An answer will be forthcoming from the Order shortly" he said, for about the twentieth time.
"It is no doubt a false registration", she was now convinced of this, her earlier uncertainty dispelled by the High Engineer's failure to get an answer from the Dragons.

"And if it is not?" he asked, again, but again she did not address that point. She knew it would be on his head but what did she care?
"My men will begin removing the offending...items" she said.
"No they will not" Balthazar knew that the game was getting ever more dangerous.
"I have the power to clap you in irons" she warned.
"Not if I am doing my job" he snapped.

She turned and strode away to discuss something with two of her lieutenants. Balthazar did not like the look of this, and was getting sorely tempted to just let them in - it was a fifty-fifty chance, after all, but he would prefer to bet his life on odds that were somewhat better than that.

An old man walked into the hangar, immediately stopped by two of the Elite Guard who rushed forward to block his passage.
"I came forth from the Father and am come into the world" the old man said to them, and they saluted and fell back in shock.
"What is this?" the woman had now stepped up to the old man, her gun all but poking him in his chest, "How do you know the pass-phrase?"
He smiled at her,
"And as they spake unto the people, the priests, and the captain of the temple, and the Sadducees came upon them"
"What?" she all but dropped her weapon, "I do not believe you!"

Balthazar stepped forward and bowed,
"Dragomaster" he said.
The old man nodded but frowned,
"You speak my rank but not my name" he admonished.
"I apologise, sir, but I do not know your name."
The Dragomaster frowned, did some quick calculations in his head then nodded,
"The Acolyte did not inform you that I was coming."
"He hung up on me" the High Engineer protested.

"Can we please get to the matter at hand?", the woman was looking from one to the other, "If you truly are a Dragomaster, I am Battle Captain Juliana Frederica Hoare of the Elite Guard."
"Juliana?" the old man cocked his head to one side, "Unusual under the Embargo...", he pondered, "You must be related to the Duke of Wichita."
"He...is my uncle" the woman admitted.
"Yes", the Dragomaster turned to where the airship lay like a sleeping leviathan, "What is the problem?" he asked.
"It is perhaps best if I show you", Balthazar did not feel like his words would be worthy of what he had to describe.
"Very well"

The three of them approached the ladder leading up into the hold of the airship, where two Elite Guard stood on duty, weapons at the ready, watching their approach with some concern.

"Stand down" Juliana commanded, and with relief they did so.

"The generator is connected to the lighting rig", Balthazar pointed out, "We can all see"

Without word or comment, Dragomaster Spinks climbed up the ladder into Hell.

~

The station was twenty foot above the road, rainswept, cold and dimly lit by a few spluttering gaslamps. Ordinarily all but abandoned after the afternoon rush, it was unusually crowded this evening. Constables, doctors and bureaucrats crowded the tiny waiting room, and out along the platform. In the distance the thunderous beat of a Red Guard armoured wagon could be heard as it responded in its own time.

"What the Hell?" Thomas Helios Kahn was a good-looking man in his mid-forties, his receding hair swept up into a rakish peak, and the muscles in his body rippling as he moved. He was not moving now though, standing stock still, staring down at the hideous sight before him.

"Doctor", the Chief Constable for the District rose from beside the body, "May I have a word?"

Kahn allowed himself to be led to the far end of the platform, where the Chief Constable stood with hands on hips and chose his words carefully,

"This is not the first such death" he said.

"In what way?" Kahn chose his own words carefully, as well.

"A month ago a drunk living in the streets was found dead like this, two weeks ago a runaway slave in one of the back alleys. Just last week a young girl"

"I have not heard this" Kahn's tone was accusatory.

"With respect, Doctor, Mercy Hospital does not receive reports of the deaths of slaves and outcasts."

"And the girl?"

86

"Yes", the Chief Constable looked down at the shiny black leather of his boots, "We were not sure"

"Of the diagnosis?" Kahn was scornful.

"Of course not", the Chief looked into his eyes, "We did not know her status."

"You had better explain that" Kahn was beginning to get a nasty feeling about all this.

"There were some of us who argued that as her hands were fresh she had to be an abductee, something like that"

"But?"

"Nobody ever reported her missing, and as she had been well...violated in the weeks before...it was decided to call her a whore"

"Despite the law?"

"Illegals operate them despite the law" the Chief Constable pointed out, "All we did was to classify her..."

"Falsely" Kahn completed the sentence for him, "A coin cannot be head and tails together; despite seeing the head, you called it tails...it was after all, there anyway beneath it"

"I would ask you not to judge us" the other said.

"Ask" Kahn spat on the man's shoe, "Now what about this one?"

They walked back towards the body, the tension between them dampened by the rain, and by the immediacy of the task at hand. To tell the truth, Kahn did not know what he would do about their 'oversight' - that was a question for another time. This one was more immediate.

"He was found by a teenage girl" the Chief Constable shrugged, "As far as we can tell she came up here to catch the next train"

"Where is she now?"

"In the Station House"

"There is no telephone up here", the doctor looked about.

"She ran to the corner beneath the bridge to place the call"

"Dedicated of her", Kahn had passed beneath the bridge upon his arrival, and would not have liked to linger there alone in the darkness, even with his skills.

"She was waiting by the steps as we arrived, talking to a young male"

"And?"

"Young males do not hang around when the Constables arrive" he pointed out.

Below them, the groaning, grinding sound was getting louder, indicating the nearer approach of the armoured wagon of the Red Guard. Depending on their orders, they could close this investigation down right there and then.

Kahn knelt beside the body and did his own quick investigation of the wound

"Definitely a snake bite" he said, "Lethal in seconds.... Administered to the open neck... Looks like our victim was not suspecting.... Do we know who he was?"

"Not yet", the Chief Constable hated admitting that fact in any case, least of all in this, "We suspect that the murderer took his wallet, anything he was carrying."

"Where would he be going around here on a night like this?" Kahn asked

"To the train?" suggested the Chief Constable.

Kahn shook his head

"An open neck, an almost dry coat - he had just come off the train. Where is there for him to go around here?"

"At this time of night?" the other scratched at an itch upon his forehead, "Unless he had business with any of the companies here...and not many of them work at night...there are only a dozen or so inns, mostly dives, some second-class music..."

"So he came here to meet someone..." Kahn finished.

"I am the Constable" the other reminded him.

Before the discussion could proceed any further, the crowds upon the platform parted to admit a phalanx of Red Guard, only six in number, but bulky with their weapons, and led by a broad-shouldered woman who removed her helmet as she came upon them.

"Sirs", she looked from one to the other, "Under the direct orders of the Great Chamberlain, I am placing three units of the Red Guard at your disposal. Please instruct us as to your immediate requirements"

~

The telephone rang. Lucille Drusilla Marguerite froze in mid-sentence and stared at it. Her husband dropped the glass he was holding. The High Dragomaster stopped with an olive halfway between the bowl and his lips.

It rang again.

"Intriguing...", the High Dragomaster heaved himself to his feet and crossed to the shadowy table where the onyx instrument was placed. Casting a look of confusion in Ignatio's direction, the head of the Order picked the offending instrument up.

"Code?" he snapped, curtailing whatever anyone was about to say unless they spoke the required lines

"And he did that which was evil in the sight of the Lord and followed the sins of Jeroboam" ; it had clearly been on the other's lips, ready to be spouted.

"Arthur Spinks?!", the High Dragomaster rocked back on the balls of his feet.

"My lord, there is...a problem"

"That I surmised", the High Dragomaster dragged the telephone across to the nearest chair and threw his bulk down in it, "But what is it?"

"I am at Serenity Field with the duty engineer and a squad of the Elite Guard...and the mutilated bodies of a dozen children"

"What?!" he dragged the cable of the device clear of obstructions and placed the receiver more closely to his ear, "Did you say dead children?"

"Thankfully...for them"

"That is terrible", the High Dragomaster felt that he was missing something, "What am I missing?" he asked.

"The airship *Prometheus* apparently"

The High Dragomaster frowned,

"If I recall, that vessel is subordinated to the Lakota Corporation"

"Which the Order owns" Spinks pointed out.

There was a pause, then he replied

"I am not sure that that fact was ever supposed to be spoken on a telephone."

"That is no matter", Spinks brushed it aside, "The registration documents carry our stamp of authorisation for Central Airspace."

"Very well... The dead children were aboard the *Prometheus*?"

"Yes my lord, a dozen of them all most terribly mutilated.!"

"That does not seem possible" the High Dragomaster shook his head, "But ignore that - it happened, it is possible. How has it happened? What do the crew say?"

"Apparently the *Prometheus* came in with a training crew, declared themselves without load, and they left. It was only when the duty engineer was moving her into the hangar he... came upon the bodies."

"Registered commander?"

"Bigfoot..."

There was silence whilst the High Dragomaster regarded the receiver as if it were some kind of fabulous beast itself

"Shall I guess that nobody said anything?"

"It was thought to be a Lakota name" Spinks said, sighing heavily.

"Bigfoot...!" he shuddered, "Ship's Medical Officer?"

That was always recorded even on a training flight; in emergencies it might prove necessary to get hold of them at once

"Maria Magdalena" Spinks tone was halfway between gloating and despair.

"I am...unhappy" the High Dragomaster said.

"Yes my lord...I thought that you would be"

"Could you make me less unhappy?"

"I am endeavouring to do so, my lord"

"Try harder!"

The High Dragomaster slammed down the telephone and rose slowly to his feet, leaning heavily upon its arm

"Battle Commander, I feel I am in need of your expertise. If you could accompany me to my study"

"Of course, sir" Ignatio put down his long-empty glass and rose quickly.

"Lucille dear", the High Dragomaster addressed his niece, "If that telephone should ring again, tell the man on the other end that I do not want to hear from him until morning."

"Of course, uncle"

He kissed her once on the cheek, and then they were gone, hurrying out of the room and back along the corridor to a much smaller door at the farther end.

"Close the door"
Ignatio closed the door
"Sit down"
Ignatio sat down.
The High Dragomaster gave up on the idea of rounding his great desk, and instead lowered himself into a seat in front of a gasfire, lighting it himself,
"No slave is ever allowed in here" he explained.
"A wise precaution, sir"
"Yes, it is"

With the gasfire now a roaring delight, the High Dragomaster leant back in his chair and regarded the newest addition to the familiarities of his inner circle,
"Why do I appear to own an airship full of dead and mutilated children?" he asked.
"Because someone is trying to discredit you?" Ignatio thought it a good and reasonable answer, but made it a question in case there was a hidden reason he ought to have been aware of.
"Yes, but assuming that neither Bigfoot nor Mary Magdalene is actually the culprit, what is going on?"

Ignatio paused for a moment, then decided that if one had three strands, one probably had a ball of string whatever it might look like to the naked eye,
"If all these events are connected...then we need to understand just what or who is driving things."
"If we knew where the Grand Temple of the Serpent is, I would happily order it to be destroyed", the High Dragomaster pointed out, "It would have been done months ago."
"And the events in the palace, sir?"
"Even the Emperor does not call back a bastard cousin from West Africa on a whim; it is as you say - something more..."

The telephone rang. The High Dragomaster stared at it in fear and loathing
"Sir?" Ignatio prompted him as it continued to ring

"I...", he picked up the receiver, "Dragon" he said
"Unicorn", the voice on the other end crackled, "We need to meet."

Chapter Seven

The trees had long given way to a desolate grassland, a landscape frozen at any time except for the height of Summer, and in the distance the rivers could be seen floating with ice, navigable if one took care but cold and icy even when the sun was shining in the sky.

The airship came up from the South, weighted ropes slamming into the ground, followed swiftly by Elite Guards swarming down the ropes to grab them and begin to tether the mighty beast as it bobbed around in winds that even at a quiet time like this threatened to send unsecured items tumbling across the ground.

"Where in the name of the Holy Trinity are we?!", Dionysus Rothgar Excelsior looked out from a viewing port on the command bridge, and did not like what he saw.
Grand Captain Shauna Nixon looked from one of their exalted guests to the other, and smiled thinly to herself,
"They call this place the Yukon."
"A Native name?", Ramona Elise Carding spoke from a viewing port almost diametrically opposed to that where her half-brother stood.
"I would imagine so", Shauna looked at the clock upon the wall, "We are on time. A Ranger patrol should be here in ten minutes to take you to your destination."

"This is a load of mutilated sperm", Dionysus sagged heavily, "We are sent to the Ends of the Earth!"
"At least it is still Albion", Ramona snapped, "In Africa we send people to far worse places that the Empire does not own."
"Africa!", Dionysus spat, "What do I care about Africa?"
"Everyone should care..." she began.
"Oh shut up", he leant heavily on the wall, "Where the Hell is that patrol?!"

As if on cue the radio crackled
"*Ardent*", the female officer who answered was lithe and leggy, thin of face and haughty of demeanour, the usual mark of a noble-born in the inbred Azteca lands.

"Ranger Patrol 6, Commander Vincento Lanfranc"
"Halt at one hundred yards and secure" the radio operator commanded.
"We are complying."

"One hundred yards..." complained Dionysus looking out at the landscape.
"If you are not too weak, I will see you on this Ranger vehicle", Ramona turned her back on him and descended to the hold and the ladder leading down to the frozen earth.
"If you leave us here I will personally kill you", Dionysus looked at the airship's commander.
"You will not need to", Shauna looked up from the report she was filling in, "If I leave you here, the Emperor will have me executed."
"At least *that* is right", Dionysus reluctantly followed his bastard sister towards the ground.

Ranger Patrol 6 proved to consist of a low-profile tracked vehicle, thin on armour, short on guns, but with whole compartments given over to surveying operations and to survival equipment.
"Ranger Commander Lanfranc", Vincento presented himself as Ramona climbed up the steps in the vehicle's outer shell.
"Ramona Elise Carding" she nodded back, "shadow service"
There was a moment of silence, then an awkward cough. A woman emerged from behind the Commander, coming into the light of the outside from the shadows of a doorway
"Karina Mimosa" she said, "We share a calling"
"Then we are sisters"

"Not to me you're fucking not", Dionysus hauled himself up the side and stared daggers at his half-sister, "You will not talk about me in my absence."
Ramona made to retort, but the other shadow operative had a hand on her elbow, so she relented.
"You may talk about yourself now," she said as if in riposte.

Dionysus drew himself up to full height,
"I demand the rights accorded to an Imperial Prince"
Vincento Lanfranc looked from one to the other, and shrugged,
"I am sure that you will find no disrespect here, Your Highness"

94

"Good", Dionysus headed inside, out of the cold, and took a chair for himself.

The others piled in after, Karina eyeing the chair with a frown, and positioning herself against the outer wall as the vehicle began to get underway again.

"So what is all this nonsense about lights?" Dionysus had not been happy about being sent on this mission in the first place; now, he was positively furious.

"The base has copies of all records" Vincento explained, adding "Your Highness" for good measure.

"When did they first manifest?" Ramona wanted to know.

"Six weeks ago, or thereabouts" Vicento replied.

"I wonder..." Ramona said aloud.

"We have wondered" Katrina assured her.

"Speak sense woman!" Dionysus scowled at her, but did not press for anything more.

The vehicle continued to press its way over the tundra, edging towards the base, right on the edge of the Northern Sea...

~

She was naked, strung upside down and bleeding from a dozen orifices. The basement smelt of blood and piss, and rebounded to her whimpering. The screams that had started the session were now dulled by torment, and the inhumanity of her position.

Bryn Magnuson laid the rod gently in the crevice between her legs and smiled,
"You know what will happen if I apply the charge here" he said.
"No...." she whimpered, because she did know.
"Tell me where is Bob? That is all I want to know"
He made his voice sound soft and caring, though in truth he wanted to slice this girl's belly open and rip out her innards. The Dragomaster supervising the session would not have allowed that, though, and to defy him would have led to his disgrace.

"Clerkenwell" she whispered, "He's in Clerkenwell"

"And what is his full name?" Bob moved the rod symbolically in its slot.

"Robert Herodius Lane!" she screamed, "That's my Bob!"

"Let her down" the Dragomaster came forward into the light, a rotund little man with a shiny bald spot on the crown of his head, "She will go to the mines"

Bryn grinned, and cut the ropes, allowing the girl to fall in a heap amongst her own mess. A woman in the mines would have a hard time of it, especially so a young and beautiful one. If it became known that she was of an Order, things would go even worse for her. He could hope.

Two slaves dragged the sobbing girl from the basement, whilst another pair came in with mops and buckets. Bryn accompanied the Dragomaster up the stairs into the light, such as it was. A blood-stained bandage still wrapped around his nose, and he walked with a definite limp.

"The local branch of the Order will see to this Bob" the Dragomaster assured him.

"I want him sliced into a thousand pieces!" Bryn growled, angrily

"No", the Dragomaster stopped and stared at the Acolyte,, "You have had your Revenge. Now focus back upon your work. There are dangerous times ahead."

"Dangerous?", Bryn was interested despite himself.

"You will see", said the Dragomaster, "You will see..."

~

Something screeched in the trees, perhaps an owl but probably not. With the Moon hidden by the clouds that did not so much scud as drift slowly across its face, an eerie darkness had enveloped the place of the dead. Family mausoleums, ornate stones set up to honour individuals, even tombs set into the rockface, all were here, and in the dim light shadows seemed to flit between them.

In the distance, spires and towers could be seen thrusting high in the lights of the streets below, but there were no lights here for who visits a necropolis at night?

Ignatio Hunt moved slowly from stone to stone, pausing behind an angel with outstretched wings as there came another screech from the woods. He smiled to himself; the first time he had not been so sure, this time he knew it for what it was. Everything depended on what their attitude to this was; they had asked for, so presumably they were going to go ahead with it - but why? If it was a trap, then he would spring his own on his master's behalf.

"Truce", the voice was silken and came out of nowhere, some distance ahead.
The High Dragomaster paused in his advance and Ignatio could just about make out that he nodded
"Truce", he said.
"There is no one in here, but I", the voice appeared to be coming from a large mausoleum, probably built of white marble, but in this light the domed structure could have been the ugliest of grey cements, for all that Ignatio could tell.
"The family Bonville", the High Dragomaster appeared to be reading an inscription above the door.
"Something of a family hideout" said the Grand Master of the Order of the Unicorn.

And with that they were gone from sight. Ignatio lay low, watching, careful not to give his own position away. In the half hour that the two men were in there, he had managed to pinpoint the position of two of the Unicorn's guards by careless or restless actions upon their part.

Both men emerged together, silently and walked apart without a word. Ignatio let his Master pass him by, whilst noting where two other of the Unicorn's guards had been as they closed in on their master. The owl that was not an owl screeched again, and the group moved away, out of his field of vision towards the darkness of the trees

Ignatio turned slowly to follow the High Dragomaster with his eyes, noting his gait, his silence and his direction. That was wrong! He was about to dash after his master but another got there first, Kimlara stepping forth from her hiding place,
"Sir, it is this way" she said, confused.

There was a loud bark, and the woman collapsed to the floor. The High Dragomaster continued moving in a straight line, away from her.

Now Ignatio could hear movement to his right, a lot of movement, people passing close by his position as they fanned out amongst the memorials to the dead.
"Oi, what do you want?" a thin male voice came from a tapering column ahead, Bartolomeo, Ignatio recognised from the twang.
One of those he had addressed shot him down.

In the receding distance the High Dragomaster had reached the limousine parked by the gates. A sudden staccato burst of gunfire blew away the men inside of it. Ignatio remained where he was, puzzling over things, determined to remain unobserved so that there would be some witness to events to speak of them on a future occasion.

It was half an hour later before two trucks rolled up at the gateway, one hitching the battered limousine up onto its flatbed, the other a canvas cover over benches which could sit the score of men and women who now emerged out of the darkness to take their places.

As the trucks spluttered back into life and roared away, Ignatio practiced stretching exercises on his muscles whilst remaining stationary. An hour later he was rewarded when he saw a man move slowly out of cover from the trees. This individual unscrewed the sight on a rifle, and slung the weapon over his back, before making his own quick way to the gates and out.

Even so, it was another hour before Ignatio moved. He ran swiftly, bent low towards the Bonville mausoleum, and shot the padlock off the door, something that the Grand Master must have replaced on his way out. He checked his pace now, and walked with soft, easy steps into the darkness, his nose telling him that something was wrong. It smelt of death - not old death or decay, but new death, fresh and messy and very very smelly. Pushing the door to behind him, he drew a box of long-life matches from his pocket and lit one.

The High Dragomaster's features stared up at him, from a body missing the majority of its chest. The burnt and blackened hole could

98

mean only one thing - a high powered lightning rod. On an unsuspecting victim the effect could be instant death, without the chance even to begin to utter a cry. Ignatio had heard nothing, and it looked as if his master had suspected nothing, or at least not enough.

He bent, and keeping the match held aloft with one hand, used the other to draw the knife from his belt, and to slice quickly through the flesh and bone of the High Dragomaster's right hand. Pocketing the fingers, Ignatio extinguished the match and waited for his eyes to accustom themselves to the tiny amount of light coming in through the crack of the door.

Only then did he open it, and slip out, rolling to one side just in case, but nothing happened. The dim light was much clearer than inside the sealed room, and he scanned the rest of the necropolis - nothing. Swiftly he ran down the hill, towards where the outer boundary was a six foot high metal fence, set against a brook. He fancied his odds that way far better than the others.

~

Tears ran down her face, pooling a moment at the base of her cheeks, then dripping onto the newspaper spread open before her on the desk. Page 6! How cruel and unjust was that? Such a mind, such a mentor, and his death relegated to page 6... Blinking, and running a hand through her now thoroughly-tousled hair, she read again the details, finding in them no sense or logic at all. What had been doing there, and why had he been killed? Nothing made sense anymore.

The telephone rang. Oh blasted, instrument! She stared at it a moment, resolved not to answer. It stopped ringing, and she rose to walk towards the kitchen in her small student apartment. Small, it may be, but ornate it was, as befitted the daughter of an Imperial Duke.

The telephone rang again. Clearly whoever it was had made a resolution of their own. Annoyed, she slammed down the mug she had just picked up, and snatched up the receiver,
"Helena Larennia Alexandra" she said formally.

"Aha, miss...er, Highness", the man on the other end was clearly unused to initiating such conversations, at least over the medium of the telephone, "My name is Chief Constable Charles Ronaldo Harkness. I...that is we believe that we need to speak to you...at your convenience, of course"

"Speak to me...?" Helena's tone was dead, "About Professor Hankey?"

"Exactly", the man sounded relieved, "I am in charge of the investigation into his...ah, his death..."

"Murder" she said, having been well able to read between the lines in the newspaper.

"Ah yes...his murder, quite so...", the Chief Constable seemed to be talking to somebody behind him, probably with his hand over the mouthpiece for the sounds came across only as a muffled murmuration.

"I understand the history of the Khanate is of interest to you?" he asked after a moment.

"It is on the syllabus", Helena sounded as confused as she felt, "If I was not interested, that would force me to be"

"Oh...quite", Harkness realised that his beating around the bush was having the effect of simply confusing himself, "Miss...Um, Highness, an essay with your name on it and Professor Hankey's signature was found in an inn not far from...from the murder scene."

"My essay?" she frowned.

"It was about the....er....[here, hand it over Cain...right...]...the conquest of Astrakhan...?"

"Yes, I handed that in a couple of days ago for marking"

"It, er, has a big A in a circle on top"

What would ordinarily have been excellent news was nothing, now

"Oh..." she shrugged, "Professor Hankey left it in an inn?"

"No", Harkness sounded strangely certain on this point, "If the professor had it on him when he was killed, we believe that someone else left it at the Dog and...er, I mean at the inn."

"Someone else?" Helena said, "You mean the murderer?!"

"Probably...or an accomplice"

"Why would they do that?" Helena was getting beyond puzzled.

"We have a theory...", he sounded unhappy.

Helena had by now dragged the telephone over to a seat before the fire, and sat perched demurely on the edge, the instrument balanced upon her lap,

"I am an Imperial Dynast", she knew he knew that, "Do you think...?"

"Yes, Highness", Harkness sounded relieved at her perspicacity, "We can only believe that it was left as some kind of warning."

"I see", she looked into the spluttering embers of the fire, ignored since she had opened the newspaper onto that inner page, "Somebody is coming after me...?"

"Possibly, Highness...but I have ordered a unit of the Red Guard to deploy at St Michaels University, specifically with orders to protect Oak House."

"I see"; as at home, so here - she would again be hemmed in by guards. The freedom she had sought and loved would be stripped from her, and she would be the slave to guard commanders insistent that she take this precaution or that, that she take no risks, not go where she wanted. "When will they arrive?"

"In about twenty minutes, Highness"

"Thank you"

"Thank you, Highness"

He hung up.

~

They came in the night, two armoured battle-wagons thundering through the defences, machine guns chattering away, cutting down slaves, guards and anyone else who got in their way. At the house, they blasted the turrets, shot up the windows, fired artillery rounds into the coal-holes, the cellar doors. As the frightened inhabitants of the building came running out, troopers leapt down from the wagons, dragging them down, shooting any who tried to escape.

From his fox hole in the woods above the late High Dragomaster's country house, Ignatio watched and fumed, angry at himself for not being able to do anything, but knowing that he could not have got here sooner, except by risking not getting here at all. As it was, he had seen and he knew - what good this knowledge was, he had no idea.

He watched in fury as Lucille Drusilla was stripped naked in the courtyard, and then raped, seemingly to order, before her long-suffering husband was beheaded in front of her eyes. Slaves and servants alike were snapped into manacles, whilst another team, arriving in a simple truck stormed into the house, coming back with treasures and documents, even as the smoke of the first fires began to rise into the night sky behind them.

Once again Ignatio waited until long after the last of the attackers had appeared to leave, and once again he was rewarded with the sight of a trio of troops, their uniforms shining white and gold in the morning sun, departing in one of the late High Dragomaster's limousines which had been stored in a garage, untouched otherwise by their depredations.

An hour after this, Ignatio walked down from the woods and regarded the devastation. What had been a fine country house, with all the appendages of rank, was now a smoking ruin, bodies lying unburied where they had been cut down, any stench from them overpowered by the drifting cloud of residue from the fierce fires of a few hours before.

He knelt before the body of Lucille Drusilla's husband, hoping now that Jesus Maria Jones knew at last some respite from his sufferings. Then, stepping over the body of an adolescent slave girl, he crossed to the stables. Dead horses, blasted grooms, and slain stablehands lay all about; senseless destruction for its own sake, and carried out by the highest in the land...of whom he himself was a part.

His discoveries were repeated a dozen-fold as he circled the smouldering ruin, people killed because they had been there, because they could be. No quarter given, no mercy shown. He doubted even that the ones who had been taken would be any better off - if there was enough power behind this, then slavery was the best option any of the captives would have...even Drusilla.

Returning round the other side to the front of the building, he found that he now had company. A tractor had driven across the fields and was parked upon an ornamental garden, a young man and a teenage girl standing by it, staring at the devastation in absolute shock. Ignatio approached unseen, then coughed. The pair started, an iron bar suddenly in the hands of the man.

"Did you do this?!" yelled the girl.

Ignatio looked at her,

"No, I knew these people" he said, playing it down the middle.

"We saw the smoke as the sun rose" she said.

"Are they all dead?" the young man asked.

"All who are here", Ignatio again hedged his bets.

"What happened?" the girl held tightly onto the young man's hand, "Tell me?"

"It is best that you do not ask" Ignatio advised, "To ask the wrong person could be a death sentence"

"But they can't leave them like this!" the man protested.

"There will be no need", Ignatio was sure of that.

The pair approached the ruin, and Ignatio came alongside, getting a few wary looks, but as their minds returned to full working order, allaying their fears that he was the one who had done this. No one man could have been responsible, no single person this murderous upon their own.

"It is the same everywhere", Ignatio indicated the bodies before the garage.

"But why?" the girl asked.

"Another question that it is better not to know the answer to" he told her.

"What should we do?" the young man asked.

Ignatio nodded - that was better.

He began to give instructions.

~

"Coming into position now", the *S-8* was small as airships went, and usually a scout vessel for the Coast Guard service within the Imperial Navy.

This time, however, it had been borrowed, and whilst it was still hugging a coastline it was far farther North than it usually went, not to say significantly to the West.

The bridge was small, cramped except that the designers had clearly had an eye to functionality and the four-man crew each occupied distinct areas out of each others' way - as long as they remained there. However, this design did not cater for carrying two extra passengers, and First Captain Sophia Hall had not been happy about carrying either of them - but who was she to resist a direct order.

The man was bald and dressed in yellow, and that was enough information for her to wish he was a thousand miles away - or had needed a lift to somewhere that the S-8 was not equipped to go; Kamchatka for instance. But no, his papers had been very clear; he needed immediate transport to the Yukon.

The woman likewise, but she was an oddity. She was clearly frightened, but haughty, at once demanding to know why the vessel flew too low, at another to demand why it flew so slow. Sophia had tried to shut her out, but inside her mind had calculated the odds on the bitch being a non-entity and come up wanting. She was clearly someone, and presumably someone quite exalted. Damn her.

"Landing zone in sight", the duty officer at the navigation console was another woman, tall and Greek, with copper hair and liquid almond eyes.
"Signal the *Ardent*" Sophia knew the command was superfluous but both her guests' had their eyes firmly upon her.
"This is *S-8* calling *Ardent*", the man at the radio station sounded discomfited having to play along so formally for the sake of their guests, "Do you require us to land in any particular place?"

There was a pause, then
"This is Grand Captain Shauna Nixon - land where-ever you want, why don't you?"
It was a fair question; with hundreds of miles of tundra all around them, the only places not to land were in a water course, or in the sea to the North.
"Beginning final descent", Sophia gritted her teeth as she said that. Her guests seemed content, but the Grand Captain would think her an idiot for even saying it. Who was there to get out of the way?

104

"Team go", Rannulph Lindsay was the executive officer on the bridge, and in command of those ship functions not immediate to that location. Upon his command a half dozen men and women leapt to the ground and grabbed the guidelines, pulling the small vessel in, and anchoring it all to the ground.

Sophia straightened her uniform and stood up,

"Lord, lady, we have landed"

"So I see" the woman was not to be impressed with mere success, "It was perhaps a little bumpy"

"Perhaps" Sophia ground out; what did the bitch expect?

"We will head to the base at once", the Lord Guardian was already beginning to walk towards the exit ramp.

"It is several miles away", the woman at the navigation console offered, having the map spread in front of her.

"Nevertheless", the man said, leading his unwilling companion away, "We go now"

Sophia shrugged and held her hands open. What did she care?

Rannulph was listening to someone through his headphones. He turned towards his captain, a look of concern upon his face,

"Something from the rear lookout" he reported.

"Bearing?", Sophia was immediately professional once more

"About 100 degrees....up"

"Up?", Sophia did not like that. There were no Imperial aeroplane bases around here, and none from elsewhere could have the range to reach here, let alone anything from any other nation.

"Er...." Rannulph listened with some consternation, "It is a ....globe of light..."

Time froze, then disintegrated into action.

"Cut the guidelines!" Sophia yelled, "Man the guns, and ready for some damned cute flying!"

"*S-8* to *Ardent*", man at the radio station was almost yelling, "Believed hostile on imminent trajectory"

"Holy fuck!", Shauna Nixon had clearly just realised that for herself, "Commander!" she was yelling to her own bridge crew.

"Lines cut, we have control", the Greek woman reported calmly.

"Reverse full power!" Sophia yelled.

"Full reverse! Full reverse!", Rannulph was yelling into the speaking tube to the engine room.

The *S-8* appeared to drift upwards for a moment, then hovered, then shot backwards parallel to the ground. The globe of light swept in to where it had been, then turned its attention to the much greater target provided by the *Ardent*.

"Open fire!" Shauna Nixon's voice could be heard coming through the radio link that she had left open, "Get this thing off the ground!"

A dozen guns opened up on the globe of light which was now swinging round for a second run at the giant vessel. Any bullets that were on target simply swept right through the thing.

"Now! Now! Now!"

A half dozen ropes were still tethering the airship, but the majority had been cut, and rising at full speed the *Ardent*'s momentum pulled the last few out of the ground, sending them swinging about its flanks as it tried to rise at the fastest speed possible.

"Oh my God..." Rannulph had been looking through the viewing port at exactly the moment that the globe of light had passed through the other airship. For a moment nothing seemed to happen; it was simply as if a torch beam had bracketed the *Ardent*. Then it staggered and then it fell apart. The forward section nosed towards the ground, the rear span out of control to impact heavily in an explosive finish some several hundred yards away.

"Course due South", the Greek woman had calculated, "Our speed is edging beyond critical for this kind of manouevre."

"Enemy bearing?" Sophia demanded.

"Its...uh, closing in on the *Ardent* for the kill" Rannulph managed.

"Lateral 180" Sophia demanded, "Then full power, we are getting the Hell away from here!"

"What about the passengers?" Rannulph had to ask.

"Fuck them", Sophia threw her hands up in the air, "Find a diplomatic way of recording *that* in your log."

"Yes, Captain."

Chapter Eight

"No", Helena said, "No"

The man shrugged and walked away; nothing ventured, nothing gained.

She let out a deep breath and walked slowly round the corner. In this part of the city even the simplest of actions could be misconstrued. Popping out to buy some bread and cheese she had been propositioned three times, and now in the evening a simple journey to a tavern had gone horribly wrong.

Used to the bars and taverns of the St Michael's campus, she had found those in this part of the city a completely different world, and was now heading back to the mean apartment that was all she had been able to afford to rent. For some reason they would not take credit here, and her signed Imperial Chits were laughed at. Having to rely on plain cash was an embarrassment, and one that had led her here.

Dodging the ancient cat, and a pile of worm-eaten clothes that must have been somebody's laundry delivery, once, Helena made it to her door and inserted the key. She had already learnt to lean on the door when she turned it, and then knee it when she depressed the handle. It swung open to reveal a spartan bedroom with two small entrances off it. Around here that counted as salubrious - a separate bathroom, a separate kitchen, even if the first had only a toilet and a sink, and the latter had only a sink and stove and some cupboards. Compared to some places she had seen that morning this was luxury. She was content to be happy enough with it, for now.

But it was freedom. She could not bear the thought of being watched day and night, and told what she could or could not do. She had run before the Red Guard had got there, and gone to ground. It was more instinct than judgment that had brought her here; an anonymous hole where the denizens were anonymous also.

Moving to the kitchen, she turned on the gas and lit a match at the second attempt, applying it to the jet. Filling a kettle with water, she placed it on a hob. Returning to the bedroom, she rummaged in the single kitbag that she had been able to bring with her from St Michael's. Drawing out a small leatherbound book, she perched on the edge of the bed. 'History of The War' it was called, written originally by a nobleman of Kazan some eighty years ago, it chronicled the beginnings of the seemingly never-ending war against Georgia. The start of something that massive fascinated her, the repercussions from the decisions taken on both sides, the echoes that still rang down the years til today.

Professor Hankey would have understood, but he was dead, and she was determined to find out why. Such a mind, such an incisive wit. Cut down on an elevated station in the middle of nowhere - it was not right! She would avenge him if she could. But to do that she needed to remain independent, able to take her own decisions unhindered by authority.

The kettle began to whistle and she returned to tend to it, a slight smile on her face. Yes, this place might be a million miles away from the luxuries of her birth, but it had more freedom than ever those palaces and castles had had. She could take this....she really thought that she could.

~

Work was not the same. The tower still spiked high into the air, its sides still shone in the sun, and the airships still came in from all over the Empire, but Golden Field felt like an orphan now that he no longer dared to put a message through to the Order. It had been five years since his induction, and in that time he had grown used to the familiar feeling that contact would bring. So, he had remained an associate, relatively lowly except that as his outside rank had grown so had his ability to source information, and in turn so had his standing within the Order - until at last, and fatefully, had come the invitation to a party that the High Dragomaster was going to attend.

Nothing had really been right since then, but he had set it all in motion himself, his message to the Order about Ramona Elise Carding, and the deductions they had all made based upon that. Nobody had asked what if he had been wrong; they had come to trust him enough to disbelieve the very idea. Nobody had asked what would happen if, for nobody had foreseen the circumstances that had in fact occurred.

Ignatio Hunt had had no choice but to turn up for work when he was next expected and to hope that his cover still held. Nobody had seen him, either in the necropolis nor at the house, and whilst his affiliation to the Dragons was known on a theoretical level, that made him just one of several thousand mid-level officers making a little bit on the side. His house, his slaves, and even his wine collection owed as much to the Order as they did to his inheritance, but in that again he was hardly unusual. The Order paid as it was given, and many a public official was on the pay roll of one of the dozen chivalric orders.

So far there seemed to be no sign that anyone saw him as anything but another Dragon lackey and he had been driven to work unmolested, recent events revolving around his mind, but not escaping from it.
"*Sargon* coming in on due East zero-zero" a voice spoke over the radio.
He recognised the name; once a King of Assyria in ancient times, 'Sargon' was now an airship run out of Tunis across the Atlantic. A mite puzzled he checked the chart upon the wall; yes, his mind was not playing tricks. He followed the row across, found the code and punched it in,
"Golden Field to *Sargon*, priority"
"Priority aye, this is *Sargon*", the reply was immediate, strained.

He paused and chose his words carefully,
"You are half a rotation out of line, Sargon"
"Confirmed", that threw him, "We have taken casualties and require immediate landing and servicing."
Ignatio stood a moment, hand on his hips, then demanded
"Confirm that - you have taken casualties in an attack?"
"Confirmed", the duty officer on the *Sargon* sounded angry, "We need to land at once"
"Understood"

A deep frown wrinkling his brow, Ignatio stepped towards the internal relays.
"Clear berth 6 immediately" he ordered, "Swing the...", he checked the

manifest, "the *Lusitania* around the perimeter. We need to land the *Sargon* immediately - ready emergency crews to attend to wounded."
"Signal a full alert" his correspondent said.
"Full alert, aye" another voice, down the line echoed back to Ignatio.
"Berth Six emergency clearance"
"Prepare for reception"
"Emergency crews standing by"
"Go go go"

He listened to the chatter with a mixture of satisfaction and trepidation. He knew that his men and women would do their duty and perform well, and assumed that those on board the incoming vessel would do so also. But you could never be sure - this was the meaning of his job.

"Contact..." he paused, remembering the massacre he had been witness to, "ah, contact the Red Guard and request their liaison here immediately"
"The *Red* Guard?" the officer on the other end did not understand.
"Things are worse than they would seem" he said.
"Oh my God..." the man collapsed into muttering, then pulled himself together, "Transmission now, sir"
"Let me know immediately that they respond."
"Yes sir"

- - - - - -

The wounded airship came in low from the direction of the coast, its trim lines blurred by heavy searings, its gondola split almost in two by some external force, and a hole in the upper skin of the gasbag, through which helium was slowly leaking.

For a moment everyone stared at the staggering behemoth, then as it cleared the outer perimeter and approached its allocated berth people ran to their stations. The teams of slaves from the pits were whipped towards the ropes, many taking a fatal lashing from them as the *Sargon* proved unable to hold a position. At last, enough hands were on the ropes to tie her down, the shattered gondola disintegrating as it brushed the earth, the hull itself buckling in upon itself as gravity proved too much for its wounded structure.

A few decades ago this would all have ended badly; an airship with a hydrogen bag would have exploded under all this pressure and few, if anyone, would have got out alive. But the emergency teams swarmed aboard the *Sargon* undaunted; helium was much safer, though the engines could still blow, and the structure still burn. But fire engines were seeing to that risk, pumping foam onto the overheated engines, spraying water onto the skin in case a spark leapt out.

Diego Amadeo Lansbury was a tall man with a swarthy beard, and a bloody gash upon his cheek. As Grand Captain of the stricken vessel he waited until last to leave the burnt-out remains of the bridge. Met upon his descent by a Battle Commander of the Red Guard, he was momentarily taken aback, then regained his composure.
"Commander" he drawled, "I see that things are worse than even I had assumed."
"Yes Captain", the Battle Commander was of a similar age and bearing to him, "We will need to debrief you immediately"

In fact, the Red Guard Battle Commander had no idea what he was doing there, why he was performing a role usually carried out by the white-and-gold uniforms of the Elite Guard, but the duty officer in the Tower had insisted that this was a matter for his men, and even if it proved not to be he was not about to lose face in front of a Grand Captain by giving voice to his doubts.

Diego watched a few moments whilst emergency crews led away his wounded, then nodded
"I will accompany you now"
"This way please", the Battle Commander led him to where a pair of giant armoured battle-wagons had been hurriedly parked, carving giant swathes through the grass, "We will begin enroute"
"Of course" Diego would expect nothing else.

~

The Wildcat was a two-seater trainer version, a type that never saw action on the frontline, but was quite numerous at airbases well behind the lines, such as here at the edge of Albion City itself. It was flying low, skimming hedges and barns, frightening horses and sheep as it shot across the land. The pilot was an expert, a veteran of both Georgia and Abyssinia, and a man who now made a comfortable living teaching other young bucks how to survive those Hell-holes.

Fifty years of age, Leander Cotswold Farnham had been flying since he was seven, and was more at home in the pilot's seat than he was at home in front of a fire. That probably explained why he had gone through five marriages, four divorces and the current incumbent not looking as if she planned to stay around very long; true, she was over thirty years younger than he was, but why marry an old hag when all the young women swooned after a fly-boy? Still, perhaps next time he might pick one just slightly older, a bit more mature about things...though it probably wouldn't make much difference, so why bother?

"Errrrghhh..." his passenger was feeling not at all well. Arthur Spinks had never flown this way before, but given recent events had felt that he had no choice. He had evacuated the Grand Temple of the Dragon as soon as reports began to come in from the High Dragomaster's house, and had scattered the Acolytes amongst the lesser temples in the city. For his part, though, he had a greater role to play, one that required him to head far away from the Imperial Capital.

What reports had come through from the massacre had made it clear that their attackers wore the white-and-gold of the Elite Guard, and since all of the airfields surrounding the city came under the security protection of the same Elite Guard, he had not fancied his chances trying to get out that way. Instead, he had sought out a bastion of the Imperial Airforce, where the Airforce provided its own security with its own ground forces. From such an airbase he had hired an expert flyer by the simplest method possible – gold.

It was a long flight, and they would have to refuel several times, something that the Dragomaster was at least looking forward to, in so far as he could once more place his feet upon the ground. The pilot had assured him that once they were into the mountains, he would be safe enough to fly at a proper altitude, and that this would alleviate much of the discomfort that he was feeling, but Arthur was not at all sure about that.

Flying this way was for crazy people, he was fast becoming fixed of a certainty in that belief. Airships were the luxurious way, and he wished that he could have taken the risk...but he could not have. To get to Navaho City, he had to be undetected, for he was certain in his loins that detection meant death – and therefore, non-arrival.

"Skybird" Leander's voice appeared in his ear by virtue of the helmet that he had been issued with.
Above them, significantly far above them to be little more than a small blob against the whiteness of the sky, a larger aeroplane was floating over the farms and fields. Leander had told him of them, something that Arthur had not been aware of before; extra eyes for the Emperor, or more like the Great Chamberlain, and the only way to evade their notice was to pretend to be a farmer's aeroplane. The spraying of chemicals from the air was a relatively new thing, but here, close to the Imperial Capital, where wealth was congregated, the new quickly became the norm, and as he had expected, the Skybird did not bother them, simply overflying and continuing on its way.

Of course, it did not know that there was anything special to be on the lookout for, so was not being that extra degree of vigilant that might have tracked the tree-skimming aeroplane, and wondered just how vast an estate it was covering.

~

"They are going to try and get another vessel out to us tomorrow"
Ranger Commander Vincento Lanfranc sighed and turned away from the set,
"I am sorry your highnesses, but that is the best that can be arranged."

The three people opposite him viewed the announcement with a mix of different emotions. Ramona Elise Carding was well aware of operational realities, and how the sands could shift from one moment to the next. The destruction of the *Ardent* and the precipitate flight of the *S-8* had been unlooked-for eventualities, and had left the base on the edge of the Northern Sea in an exposed position. The evidence that the globes of light were most definitely still around had been welcome, in its way, but worrying as it appeared that they possessed the ability to effectively cut them off.

Dionysus Rothgar Excelsior was in something of an inner turmoil, the reason for it standing ten foot to his rear, watching on. Naiomi Louise Lindt was demure, slight of build and almost white in her blondness. A Lieutenant in the Rangers, she was absolutely no push-over, and the combination of her terrier-like qualities and her disrespect for his rank, had intrigued the Imperial Prince enough that he had finally given in to her charms. He excused himself on the grounds that it was only an hour after the globe of light had destroyed the *Ardent* and in the throes of relief at surviving a battle, men do funny things. That didn't really explain the half dozen other times they had shared a bed, though, but he was not going to let that shade his thinking.

And yet it did. He had hated this place from the moment he had walked in; small-scale parochial little outpost in the middle of nowhere, their only neighbours Natives who moved around a lot, and who seemed less than totally friendly, if their Medicine Men had really instructed them not to talk to the Imperials about the lights. Perhaps that had only been a rumour, or an excuse by that pathetic excuse of a shadow service operative that they had here. He had loathed her on sight, and her moping over a dead boyfriend, the photographer who had given his life to take the film of the lights, that was just pathetic. A man should be mourned, a glass raised in his honour, but this silly weeping; ugh, it had turned his stomach.

But Naiomi was different, and the prince did not really relish departing on board an airship with these lights around to fly straight through it and slice it in two. He would see what would happen on the morrow; that was good enough for him.

Not so for the third Highness, the woman who had come on board the *S-8* and had moaned ever since she had arrived here. True, she had had some reason to moan at first, the walk across the frozen landscape with only a Lord Guardian for company had been an agony of body and mind, but she had not stopped moaning several days into her stay. She was not about to be silent now, either.

"This really is unacceptable", she droned, "It is as if they do not know who I am"

"Perhaps they prefer you here", snapped Dionysus, who had felt his heart sink when the bitch had walked in from the cold.

Of all the thrice-damned people to be sent here, it had been her - Tabitha Clarissa Theresa, a cousin and a Dynast, and an acquaintance of long, long standing. What was worse was that when they had been younger he had fancied her, Hell he had done rather more than fancy her, but now she was an ice maiden bathing in her own shadows. Her eyes met his, a haughty disdain there for all to see,

"Do not seek to brush me with the same tar as yourself" she snapped.

"Why were you sent here anyway?", Dionysus had never quite figured that out, "What skills could *you* possibly have?"

Other than in bed, he thought, but he doubted she had been sent here to seduce the lights, though perhaps it was worth a try.

Tabitha paused a moment, then decided that the time had come. She reached into an inner pocket of her jacket and drew out a gold card - in truth a thin wedge of gold, imprinted with words and icons, and stamped on the rear with a very particular stamp indeed. She handed it to him,

"Eyes of the Great Chamberlain" she said.

Dionysus was astonished. He took the card and studied it, but what was the point? The fact of its existence meant that it was genuine; nobody forged these. He tossed it back, watching with a tight smile as she made a grab for it out of the air. Perhaps indeed her skill in bed was of some potential use in this role, though not here.

"That is very interesting", Ramona had been paying close attention to the exchange and now nodded as a series of observations came together in her head. The heart of the Empire was so different from West Africa that she was often in danger of missing clues that an operative who had spent all their time closer to the centre of power would have easily picked up.

"Presumably the Lord Guardian accompanies you", she said, "and not the other way round"

"Of course" Tabitha's mouth twisted into a sneer, "Now, what are you going to do to ensure that we *do* get out of here on the morrow?"

116

This was aimed back in the direction of Vincento Lanfranc who inwardly grimaced, but he had hardly failed to notice the developments in the conversation either. To date he had shown her the minimum deference necessitated to an Imperial Dynast, but if the bitch was one of the Eyes of the Great Chamberlain he better make swift to do what he could for her.

"We can bring all three of our armoured vehicles to battle-readiness, and have them secure a perimeter for the arrival of the airship" he said, thinking aloud.

"What good will that do?" Ramona interrupted, not being rude, but because she could not see the logic, "Nothing touches these things, cannon fire from the *S-8* passed straight through it - you saw that with your own eyes."

"What else can be done?" he was confused, looking from one woman to the other, "Either we do nothing and hope, or we do something and hope"

"Do something and hope", Tabitha told him, then turned and walked out of the communications room.

Ramona looked at her half-brother
"Does she think that waving that piece of gold around has placed her in charge?" she asked.
Dionysus considered this a moment,
"Yes", he said, "I would say that she does"

~

"We shouldn't be meeting like this"
"We have a problem"
"But if anyone finds out, they will think we are conspiring"
"Who is going to find out?"
"I do not know", Thomas Helios Kahn ran a hand through his hair and then nodded, "Very well, let us go in"

They entered the inn, a better class of dive than most of those round here, but still a dirty smoke-filled den of noise and iniquity - just right for a clandestine meeting, presuming that nobody had been watching. Of course, it was not a crime for the Doctor in charge to meet with the lead investigator - it was all part of the routine, and happened frequently. But it happened within parameters, and it happened where other people were...not in The Strangled Chicken in Lower Slaughter.

"Two of your finest ales", Chief Constable Charles Ronaldo Harkness banged upon the bartop, then inspected the grime suddenly embedded in the side of his hand.
"My finest...?" Otto Dick was a barrel of a man, with a flattened nose and a scar beneath one eye. In the trade he was known as kind and generous - he always let those who owed him money speak first...though usually to no avail. He had had a few dealings with the Constables, and Harkness was not unknown to come in on occasion in search of something. He nodded at the man, looked the other up and down and decided it was professional, not some personal liaison. He sighed and rolled a barrel out from under a stool,
"My finest" he said, and tapped it.

Some minutes later, the two men sipped at their beer at a corner table beside the fire.
"Well?" Doctor Kahn asked, sitting back, "What is this problem?"
"Helena Larennia Alexandra"
"I am not familiar with the name", Kahn admitted, "but the form suggests a Dynast"
"Hankey had in all likelihood just finished marking her essay when he stepped off the train"
"There were no personal effects on him", Kahn remembered that vividly, as well as he remembered the rest.
"Yes...her essay was found in The Dog and Duck."
"Somebody took it there?" the doctor was confused.
Harkness nodded and drained fully a half of his beer in one go.

"We have been working on the theory that the murderer left it there as some kind of warning"
"By murderer, we mean ..."
"Probably an Acolyte of the Order of the Serpent", the words had been thought for a while now, but were only just spoken aloud.
"I thought so", the doctor stared into the flames, "And by warning you mean that they intended to target this woman?"
"We had to act on that probability."

118

"Yes", he nodded, "I can see that you did...but I cannot yet see why we are meeting in this place, at this hour, alone...?"
"Ah, that..."

Harkness rose and made his way through a shallow crowd of floaters and drifters, banging his empty tankard down to get some attention.
A young barmaid came across and sniffed the empty glass, the surest way to tell. She smiled widely,
"You must be rich" she said, "or powerful"
"I like to think so", Harkness didn't think that telling her he was a Chief Constable would make her happy.
She was bending over, refilling the tankard from the barrel, placed once more beneath the stool, and Harkness drank in the sight of her naked buttocks as her too-short dress rose up.
"Five crowns, sir" she said, and grinned, "And twenty if you want some of the other"
"Not right now", he smiled pleasantly.
"Its fresh now" she said, "Later not so fresh"
"I will bear that in mind"

He carried his foaming tankard back to where the doctor seemed lost in thought, staring into the flames. he had drunk only half his beer, and Harkness did not feel at all guilty about not buying him another. The man had only come here to listen, not to unburden himself as had he.
"We lost her", he said, sitting down, "She ran"
"Helena Larennia Alexandra?" Kahn dragged his eyes away from the fire.
"I spoke to her on the telephone, assured her that a unit of the Red Guard were enroute to protect her"
"But yet she ran?", Kahn was interested despite himself, "She must be involved..."
"That has to be so" Harkness nodded, "But how can I tell an Imperial Duke that his daughter is in league with the Serpent?!"
"I see the problem", Kahn took another sip from his tankard, "What we need is a body."

"Whose?" Harkness was confused.
"It doesn't matter, someone similar to her in size, age and looks. We inform the Duke that his daughter is dead, then we have free rein

against the creature."

"Can you get one?"

"No doubt in a day or two", Kahn shivered, "All it requires is that there be no identification at the point of delivery. We just won't follow it up."

"Then we assuage the Duke, and get down to the real business of hunting down these fiends"

"And exterminating them" the Doctor was adamant about that.

He drained his beer and rose,

"I will be in touch as soon as I have something for you"

"Good"

"One of us should leave before the other" Kahn pointed out.

"You", Harkness looked back at the bar, "I have some business with the barmaid."

~

"Stand by", the elderly Lord Guardian looked at his best men and women, bald heads shining proudly beneath the arc lights, "On my mark"

Fingers tensed as they waited

"Mark!" he snapped, going by the wristwatch upon his left arm.

"Re-initialising external feed", a woman reported.

"Translation in place", that was a man.

"Fortress Wall is holding", another woman.

"Beginning relay to stations now"

The elderly Lord Guardian nodded and left them to it, walking across to a viewing window to look out and watch as the Rods received the incoming transmissions and began to pass them through to the well. For almost a week, the relays had been off whilst work had been done to correct and rebalance the well. Tests had been extensive, including live data from Imperial organs unable to wait any longer. The results had been promising - the repairs were holding, and the well was operating at optimum capability.

A score of new ticker-tape machines had been meshed in, and teams of

Guardians had sat and read every iota of data that was spewed forth, checking it for sense, and for gibberish. It had all passed, and Cyclops was now ready for re-integrating with the outside world. An outside world that was now two steps further away than ever before.

The translation was the first, checking that the incoming coded signals made sense, a dozen young Guardians, barely into their first year, now sitting in rows in an office scrutinising the incoming messages from around the Empire, swapping random passages into and out of code. They could not do all of it, even a thousand of them could not, but a random sampling of everything ought to ensure that no message that was not genuine got through.

But that was not all; the second level was the Fortress Wall, additional relays that mass-translated portions of the code passed by the Rods, and enacted upon them a series of tests. If any test indicated that the code could have a negative effect upon the well, the whole console was isolated by the simple mechanism of blowing the relays, and the whole code dumped to the young Guardians to decrypt in its entirety.

If that did not work, the best minds had a few other suggestions but ones which would require Cyclops to be inoperative completely for a couple of weeks. None of the Lord Guardians could even imagine what the world would be like if that had to happen.

"All systems at optimal", a female Lord Guardian crossed to where he was standing, "Cyclops is firm"
"Open all relays", the elderly Lord Guardian said.
"All relays open", she relayed his order.

Once more, the well was full. Cyclops was back, and the Red Guard banished. The old man nodded well satisfied with the job he had done. The problem was solved, and should not occur again. What had caused it, and why - that remained a different matter, altogether...

~

"Hmmm..." he walked around it once more, then sighed, and sat down, "Hmmm..." he said.

"What does 'hmmm' mean?" Leonie Alessandra was a trainee Engineer, only in her mid-teens, but with a sharp mind and a mathematical brain that had allowed her to bypass whole sections of basic training.

"Oh..." Balthazar Smith looked up, and could not but smile; not only her mind was beautiful, "This was no engine blow-out"

"But the engine has blown out", she pointed out.

"As a consequence, not an act"

She frowned up at the huge airship, the *Cahokia*, new in last night from the deep South and making an emergency landing at Serenity Field due, her Captain reported, to an engine blowout.

"What do you think happened?" she asked, walking to stand under the black and twisted section, and forcing the High Engineer to rise to his feet and follow her, if he wanted to explain, and who would not?

"If the vessel had parked itself in a field full of fire, then the heat would have caused the engine to blow out", he said.

"But it didn't" she pointed out.

"No", he was now standing directly underneath the offending section, "It could have descended too low over a volcano, or even dropped within the heat radius of a major fire - perhaps a forest, or a warehouse even"

"But it didn't", she pointed out, again.

"If the section below had caught fire and burned fiercely, the heat could have caused a blowout"

"The section below is undamaged"

"And perhaps if lightning had hit the vessel and chained from point to point, it could have done this"

"I heard no such report"

"No", he shook his head, "Nor did I"

He moved back to where he had been sitting, and she followed him,

"Is it a mystery?" she asked, intrigued.

"The cause is a mystery" he pointed out, "The actual sequence of events is obvious."

"The why is missing but not the how?"

"Yes", he nibbled on a biscuit, "What do you think?"

It was a fair question; her age was irrelevant, her position all that mattered.

"I think it was attacked" she said, and waited.
He did not explode or turn away as others would have done. Instead he raised his eyebrows, and nodded
"How?" he asked.
"In a way that we do not know how"
He pondered this for a moment, then laughed
"You do not know"
"If it is by a method unknown, then I cannot know"
"Hmmm..." he thought on this, "What do you suggest?"
"See if any other airships have suffered damage alike to this" she said, "Contact all the fields"

Balthazar rose and stared into the middle distance. Ten days ago he would have decided not to, would have thought it too much a risk, even if there was the possibility she was right. But the dead children changed all that, the *Prometheus* even now remained in quarantine. Strange things were happening, and some of them were way beyond his ken. He turned back to her,
"I will do that" he said.
And she beamed.

~

This was not Hell on Earth, but it was close. Sealed wagons transported the chosen through the night, the stink of piss and shit, of fear and vomit pervading all of them as they neared their destination. On top soldiers sang a hearty song, whilst up front the double-headed locomotives could be heard from time to time whistling, as if in merriment. There was no merriment here within, only a grim determination to survive. It was cheaper for the Empire for the weak and the ill to die enroute than to be equipped and issued with rations, and then die a week or two later from exhaustion. Better dead on arrival, than a dead loss in the mine.

Lucille Drusilla Marguerite sat back against the slats of the wagon, chilled to the bone by the cold wind that seeped in, but able to look into the centre of the space, and use her trained night vision to watch for the whereabouts of the murdering bastards that every wagon had a few of. Most of the forty or so people inside were innocents, caught up in somebody else's war, but a handful were always the guiltiest of the guilty, and not a few of those were actually in the pay of Imperial organs who overlooked their actions in return for information. She had already spotted one little shit, too well-fed to be a genuine captive, too cocky to be heading towards his doom; no, he was a professional rider, and she would deal with him when she had the chance.

Others she vowed to look out for; that old black man, struggling to retain his dignity as a pair of white thugs tore into it; the young white male, cowering in a corner as burly men made lascivious advances upon him; the handful of children every wagon held, either torn from their parents, or thrown together by random acts of murder. She watched two now, clinging to each other, a boy and a girl, perhaps cousins, not siblings as one was black, the other white. Though how many would have thought her the niece of the Lord High Dragomaster? She would have smiled at the memory of a hundred shocked faces, if this had been any place to smile in.

The train juddered, and a couple of men standing free in the centre of the wagon fell sprawling, one landing with his face in a pile of faeces to general applause. Then there was another shockwave, and the wagon slid to the side.
"Oh fuck", the speaker was a middle-aged black man, his face a mask of concentration, "We've derailed"

Indeed, that seemed to be the case as the wagon careered down an embankment to end up tilted over at an angle, shit and other things splattered about most of those in its interior. Lucille Drusilla Marguerite wiped it out of her eyes, and looked about. The structural integrity of the wagon still held, worse luck, and a bright light was shining without.
"Fire?" whispered an old woman, thrown against her and seemingly unaware of anything other than the light that now closed in upon the wagon
"Hail Mary, Full of Grace..." began a teenage lad.
But then the light hit.

124

The wagon burst apart, and the light could be seen hovering above, a globe of self-contained luminescence, that seemed to pause then passed on to the next wagon.

As the survivors hurriedly picked their way out through the debris, the globe of light could be seen smashing down the walls of the wagon next along.

Prisoners scattered in all directions, some running down the embankment towards the fields below, others crossing the line to seek shelter in the hills beyond.

"Come" Lucilla Drusille Marguerite took the hand of the little girl, gaining a fierce glower from the young boy

"I protect my cousin" he said.

She smiled at him

"Come, both of you, we must get away from here."

The boy hugged the girl close to him, then nodded at her

"You will take us to safety?" he demanded.

"Yes"

It was enough for him.

Chapter Nine

"Now!"

The half dozen troopers, men and women naked to the chest and glistening in the evening sun, strained and heaved as they pulled the bi-plane out of its underground shelter and up the ramp to the runway above.

Guy Simonis Meredith was standing in the shadow of a tree, eyed glued to the horizon, watching for lights. He straightened as Francis came towards him, and they embraced, kissing on the lips.

"Cyclops has issued a sector map for this area", the eighteen year-old told him, "No enemy activity recorded."

"We all know that means nothing" the fifty year-old veteran slapped him on his behind, "Now wish me well"

"I wish you in my bed", Francis Elias Bannerman had lost all embarrassment and restraint over the last couple of weeks.

"Your bed?" Guy laughed, "I thought mine was the finer."

"Bed!" Francis panted.

Guy laughed again,

"After the mission"

"Yes..." Francis managed to get a hold on feelings that he had never known he had until two weeks ago.

The Scavenger aircraft was battered and blackened, but had held together in a dozen fights. Where the Wildcats had fallen to the lights, the Scavengers had lived to fight another day. They had not of course done any harm to the lights, but had concentrated on shooting up the Fulani warbands who followed in their wake.

"Ready, Grand Captain?", recent weeks had been hard on command ranks, and Meredith had jumped to exalted status with merely the batting of a superbly placed eyelid. The Station Commander was young, had been a desk officer a couple of weeks back, but had survived by his ability to spot an attack and order an evacuation, something his superiors had been sadly lacking in. A native of Normandy, Laurent Clermont Judd was not yet thirty, but wore his new rank with a certain aplomb.

"Just let me know where the bastards are" Meredith let loose his winning smile, causing Francis by his side to shudder and almost collapse to the ground.

"I don't think we will have to", Laurent was blunt and somber, "The way-stations report that they are coming to us."

"Fork and spoon!" , Meredith used an old oath designed to be spat in good company, "Cyclops is wrong!"

"At least it's working again", Laurent was hardly a believer, "Now they just have to make it tell the truth"

"That has something to do with the information we send it…sir",. Francis had read that in one of the learned journals Meredith subscribed to, even though he did not seem to actually read them, merely to use them for show in his quarters.

"Then God help them!" Laurent laughed harshly, "We haven't a clue what's going on so we ask them, they don't know so they tell us nonsense, we make our report and they base their updates upon that!"

"That sounds wrong", Meredith allowed, getting down onto his knees, but disappointing Francis when he headed beneath the aeroplane's wing.

"Is there a problem?" Laurent was all concern; he could not afford to have his best fighter out of the coming combat.

"No problem", Meredith fiddled with the mount of a wing-cannon, "There, I think that fixes its alignment. Too rough a handling of the machine knocks it out of true, and what point is there firing the thing if it doesn't go where you aim it?"

"Hmmm", Laurent was unhappy, "And the Duty Engineer missed it?!" he demanded.

"Because he's an engineer, not a pilot, and not an armourer"

"I see", the young Station Commander sighed, "Write me a report and I'll circulate it to them anyway"

"When I get back", Meredith said.

"Of course"

The Station Commander left the two men kissing passionately.

~~*~*~*~*~*~*~*~*~*~*~*~*~*~*~*~*~*~*

They came on the train, pulling their hideous contraptions with them, unloading them in an area of the railyards cordoned off by their fierce-looking guards, and their enormous dogs.

Awfy was not at all happy to have been selected to come and greet them. He knew full well that when Wolfgang used the term "on the behalf of the shadow service", he really meant on behalf of the Viceroy who was using them to do his dirty work, and without Ramona around to gainsay her cousin, they had to do as instructed.

It didn't mean he had to like it. In fact, liking it was about the furthest thing from his mind, as he took back his pass and walked between the two half-naked men with their unsettling swirling tattoos. He recognised their type only from books - Maoris, or from somewhere near there, fierce warriors all, and perfect for Albion in the role to which they had been assigned. It was now traditional within their cultures after a hundred years of warfare on this scale, but it still made the skin creep just thinking about it.

"Selector Baines", a woman announced.
That was another thing, or two or three thought Awfy. They had damned funny ranks, and whilst the ordinary ranks only came from the South Pacific, they had a smattering of officers, often women, imported from veteran combat units, especially those which had seen action in Georgia and worked alongside the Special Units before.

"Bannister" he said, simply, eyeing the woman up and down, not as a woman but as a strange creature from Hell. She was over six foot tall, slim of waist but burly of arm. Her uniform seemed to consist of a short dress over some coarse undergarments, and her arms and legs were entirely bare. She had spikes embedded into her ears, and her hair had been shaved at the front, but hung down in long blond locks behind. Awfy was not one to judge by appearance, but it was doing her no favours, especially given the Special Units reputation - but that was probably the point.

"I will give you a tour"
Oh yes, that was another thing. They were inordinately proud of their Hellish contraptions. Awfy winced, but nodded his head. Even if he

had been willing to incur the Viceroy's wrath by being rude, he wouldn't have dared with all these scary-looking people around.

"These gases are not the kind you will have read about in history books", she indicated startlingly yellow tanks with dreadful skill-and-crossbones emblazoned upon them in black.
"Oh?" he said, dully.
"We call these Nerve Gases for they seep through the skin and infect the nervous system. Respirators and masks won't help you with these"
"Lovely..." he swallowed.
"And these aren't gases at all", she indicated tanks painted bright red.
"Liquid?" he asked.
"You fail to understand", she shook her head, as if with a stupid child, "These are germs, bacteria, viruses"
"Plague?" he wondered.
"Far worse than that!" she laughed.
He shuddered.

"Selector!", a Maori - or Samoan, or Tongan...if he could ever tell them apart – approached.
"Up-Master Vingatani?"
"Professor Kyle is ready to unload the Device"
"Very well", she made to stride off then looked back to Awfy, "Come - this will interest you"
"Oh good..." he managed, "Professor?"
"From the Hidden University"
"Ah", he coughed to recover the power of speech, "I..."
"He accompanies his creation" she explained.
"Er..."
"Come!"

They rounded one of the hideous red tanks being wheeled down a ramp from its flatcar towards where a heaving, panting steam truck was waiting to receive it. Behind it, a cylindrical wagon still linked to the train was disgorging what looked like a madman's sculpture of an octopus. A bald man with telescope-like spectacles was standing behind it, berating the dozen or so tattooed troopers who were happily ignoring him.

"A paranoid" Baines told him, "But that is the Hidden University, for you"
"Yes", Awfy could certainly agree on that.

The Hidden University was not so much a place, as a co-opting of academics from existing institutions and hiring them onto an Imperial programme they could never escape from. There *were* laboratories, hidden away in the vastness of Albion, but the academics remained attached to their mother institutions, and usually spent most of their year there. A few, though, happily gave their oddballs leave, and Awfy suspected that Professor Kyle was one that his home university had been happy to sign off, and see disappear to a complex somewhere in Alaska, or Kamchatka, or somewhere!

"Can you guess what it is?" the Selector asked.
Awfy bit down an urge to say 'octopus' and shrugged,
"Something very different from what you have shown me" he said.
"True", she seemed happy with that answer, obvious though it was, "It is a light weapon!"

There was a moment of silence, and he realised that she was waiting for him to say something. He managed to shake his thoughts into some kind of order,
"To fight light with light?" he essayed.
"Exactly", she turned to look at him, "You are not so stupid, after all" she said.

Then the Professor was striding towards them, arms waving as if he was an insane bird trying to remember how to fly.
"They do not listen!" he wailed.
"They do not need to, Professor" she seemed to have his measure, "You supervised their training back in Gloryhole"
"But I tell them more!" he exclaimed.
"They already know how to keep the Device safe. I have your signature on the document."
"But..." he shook his head, then looked at Awfy, "What are you?" he barked.
"Shadow Service", Awfy guessed that this was what the man meant.
"Huh", he was unimpressed, "I am genius!"

"We certainly hope so, Professor" the Selector told him.

He stepped back and slapped his arms against his thighs, again like a bird unable to take off.
"The world will echo to my name!" he declared.
Awfy stared at him
"There will be nowhere I am not a God..."
He strode off.

"Er", Awfy was shocked, despite himself, "Delusions of grandeur?"
"If he had been sane he could not have achieved that which he has done" she told him.
"That which you hope he has" he pointed out.
She nodded,
"A test is one thing, I agree - the reality will be in the field"
"How do you intend to get that thing...the, er, Device, *into* the field?"
"Some things are operational security" she pointed out.
"I will accept that", he nodded.
"Good", she turned and pointed towards a shack, "Recorder Vane will complete your visit"
With that she turned and followed the Device towards its destination.

Awfy sighed and strode towards the shack. Maybe this Vane, whoever he was, would simply sign him out and he could go back to the Imperial Gate, make his report, and get some work done.
"Ah, there you are"
She was young, naked and had all of her hair, in the right places.
"Um" he said, confused.
"Come in", she beckoned at the door of the shack, "Mine is an ancient office"
"Recorder?" he asked, confused.
"The rank is a name, a word. You do not think that our troopers run on fire alone?"
"Er..."
"I give the spirit they lack"
She closed the door behind them.

~

The airship was unusual, black of aspect and bearing the lion and the unicorn emblazoned upon its side, the arms of London, the primary city of the province (or as it liked to call itself, the Dominion) of Britannia. It was clearly a vessel belonging to the city government, and there were few who could commandeer such to their own use, or even order it sent far out of its normal flightpaths to West Africa.

Viceroy, Imperial Duke Gunther Luis Leander had been informed of its imminent arrival, as soon as the radio operators were aware, and had himself, and a selection of senior officials transported to the airfield to meet their powerful, if mysterious, guest upon their arrival.

The slaves did their job well, the overseers beating them more regularly in a show of respect for the Viceroy, and the lines were tied down secure. The incoming vessel had been named as the *Londinium*, no surprise there, and records showed that its Grand Captain was one Christopher Nicomedeus Holand, aged sixty and of noble descent, if no significant landowner himself. What neither the radio nor the records showed was just who had decided to come to Timbuktu...

A ramp descended from the lower portion of the vessel and a half dozen Elite Guard descended, their uniforms black and gold, with red flashing in the pattern of units serving in the 'Olde Country'. A moment later a fanfare exploded, trumpeters hidden in the gondola blasting out a melody, followed shortly by two figures at the head of the ramp. One was smaller, the other stocky and dressed in fine clothes, garnered in jewellery. He descended and, reaching the bottom of the ramp, made his way across to the Viceroy where he bowed,

"Count Roger Alejandro Schenk" he announced, "and my daughter, Leonora Bunny"
"Delighted", Gunther bowed back to the Count, shorter and quicker than he had been bowed to, and took the hand of the girl, a sombre-looking individual of about eight, who might have been pretty if she had smiled.
"Good", Roger looked around, and noted the aged Samuel Guy in the delegation behind the Viceroy, "My grandfather was acquainted with you" he said.
Samuel frowned in thought, then nodded,

"Charles Victor, I remember him well"

"Good", Roger returned his gaze to the Viceroy, "There is much to discuss. My servants will remove our traveling chests to your palace"

"Ah yes, of course, please do"

"Yes"

After an uneasy pause, Wolfgang stepped forward, irritated that Gunther had forgotten to introduce his entourage individually,

"Lord Count, I am the ranking officer of the Shadow Service"

"Oh yes", Roger looked the old man up and down, "You don't look like an Imperial bastard to me"

Gunther coughed,

"That was my cousin, Ramona Elise - she has been summoned to Albion to engage in important work"

"Oh", Roger sounded annoyed, "Leaving this...this Wolf?"

"Wolfgang" Wolfgang said.

"Yes" Gunther affirmed.

"Huh" Roger did not bother to hide his disdain.

By now his multicoloured army of servants were beginning to disgorge from the airship, carrying chests, bags and cases. In many cases freedmen, the servants remained tied to their master. Black, Indian and Chinese, they were his prized possessions, even though technically they were as free as he was.

"Order some trucks up from the park", Gunther turned to an aide.

Used to finding General Alberto Smith to his rear, he was surprised again that it was his deputy, Luisa Maria Valdez, who now stood there. Smith had gone South to try to co-ordinate the defence, to try to rally some kind of effective resistance, and it was the Galician who now stood in his stead.

"Yes sire", she sounded disapproving, but understanding that the Imperial Duke was caught in a bind by the need to show hospitality, even to so unwelcome a guest as the Count.

"Now, I will need a top-level briefing on the military situation" Roger said.

Gunther shifted uneasily,

"With respect, sire, unless you have authorisation, your noble rank does not entitle you to that."

"Authorisation..." Roger rumbled the word as if it was an alien curse, "There *is* a High Temple of the Order of the Unicorn within this....city?"
"Yes..."
"Then perhaps we should pay a visit there"

"Your tone is out of order", Archbishop Paolo Jensen moved forward from amongst those arranged behind the Viceroy. Ever a one to feel the position of the Imperial Church keenly, he had a fierce loathing for the chivalric orders and that which they represented within the Empire. The count looked from Archbishop to Viceroy, and then around at the other dignitaries, and nodded,
"Apologies, Highness", he could find respectful words when he wanted, "I only meant it as a reply to your...question"
"Very well", Gunther had better things to do than stand here and argue all day, "We will visit the High Temple on the way back to the palace"
"But I protest!" the Archbishop attempted.
Gunther waved him away,
"Come", he said, "The vehicles are this way"

~

They lay upon the ridge, ducking low as they looked into their binoculars, an artillery bombardment pounding in over their heads and impacting on the river valley stretched out below.
"See any lights?" General Alberto Smith yelled in a moment's respite
"Nothing", Swift Commander Tomas Thorn had eyes for the bastards now.
"Fulani?"
"Some before the guns blew them away"
"Now?"
"None who are stupid enough to move"

Behind them a hundred guns, arrayed in batteries continued to pour death down into the valley below. Armoured tractors stood ready to limber up and pull them out at a moment's notice, whilst overhead a half dozen Scavengers swooped and dived, keeping as best a watch as they could.

"Well and truly pounded, sir" Colonel Graham Sebastian McLaren saluted.

"Yes", Alberto rose to his feet, "but what is?"

"Always a good question" Graham nodded, "If there were any Natives down there, they're dead"

"If not" Thorn had also risen to his feet, "then we blew up a riverbank"

"Lots of those around here" Graham pointed out.

"Lots of Natives too" Thorn could not ignore those after what they had done to his fortress.

"Always lots of Natives", the general huffed, "Its the ones with the Damned lights that we have to worry about"

"Yes sir"

"Sirs!", a young runner came up, panting, her long hair plastered to the side of her face.

"Report", as the most immediate in the chain of command, Graham spoke to her.

"Radio from sector 2 reported beings of light"

"Beings!" Alberto growled, "Who gave them *that* appellation?"

"The officer, sir"

"Of course", the general looked at her, noting for the first time her youth; a cadet, even, "Of course", he smiled more readily, "Where?"

"West 2-7-0 Sector 2"

"Colonel, the guns"

"We will re-orientate...Ten minutes"

"I will instruct the flyers", Thorn rushed off to find the Imperial Airforce's radio car.

"Your name...?" the general asked the runner.

"M...Marissa Timms, sir"

Overhead, two solitary Wildcats had replaced the antiquated bi-planes. If an attack came, they would be as good...if as good would ever be good enough again.

~

They zoomed in at night, targeting their prey with precision, way ahead of any Native force, and far in advance of any machinery specifically designed to detect them. Guards at their stations were struck down silently before they had the chance to even notice their attack. Servants going about their business were cut down, sliced in half before they knew what hit them. Slaves were ignored, left to stare in wonder as the lights passed, and made their way to their target

Leonora awoke, knowing that something was wrong. Drills on her father's estate had inculcated an acute awareness when something out of the ordinary occurred. She lay in her bed, and cast her senses around the room - nobody, but the area by the door was brighter than it should be. She assessed her options, more training of her father's, and decided that lying still would be the best. Don't invite attack if the enemy might just pass on by, not if you were weak and defenceless.

For a full five minutes nothing happened, and Leonora Bunny began to think that she had miscalculated, but her father's warning remained in her head - don't assume, always beware being stared out, don't give up sooner than the enemy. As she lay in the deep and luxurious bed that the Viceroy had provided, she found that she had time for thought. This was a million miles away from her home South of London, a million in effect, some many hundred in actuality, though she had forgotten just how many.

It moved. She squealed. It came for her. . .

~

The sex had been fantastic, the Battle Captain had taken it up the ass and demanded more, and Lieutenant Samuel Simeon Parker had strained to satisfy her all night. They had ended up dripping and filthy, and washing it off in a long cold shower. Now, at four hours beyond Midnight he was moving slowly, carefully back to his lodgings from the Captain's in the Viceregal Palace.

But something was wrong.

He first realised it when he came upon the dismembered body of a guard, his legs in one place, torso and arms in another, and head rolled away into a corner. Unsure whether it was some sort of trap, Sam had blanked it from his mind, and moved quickly on towards the barracks.

136

His cousin, Orlando Elias Parker would only be on duty another half hour, and if he did not get back within that time...well, he was fucked, well and truly fucked.

Passing a communicating corridor, he gave in. Down the darkened extense, he could see the body of two servants, sliced apart lying in their own mess, and beyond them a guard impaled upon a torch, what was left of her. He threw up against the wall, and drew his pistol. Visions of his mother and father, proud upon his graduation, flashed into his mind and he hardened his resolve. Whatever was happening here was wrong; he would investigate.

He stepped over the dismembered bodies and shuddered. A force way beyond his ken was doing this, but there could only be one - the lights. They were here in Timbuktu, inside the Viceregal Palace! What hope was there?! He moved on, seeking an enemy to engage.

He found it outside one of the guest apartments, somewhere he had never been before, and somewhere he was not cleared to be that early morning, but regular guards were gone...or dead...or, he dreaded to think, and he could walk in.

The light was in the entrance way to a room, seeming to be engaged in some act. He raised his pistol then lowered it. It had never done any of the others any good. In desperation he thought "light" and reached for the lone phosphorous grenade upon his belt, issued only in the last few weeks, and an experimental technology. He heard a whimper from within, and acted.

His aim was off and it impacted against the wall, bursting into a blinding light that he had to dive to the floor to shield himself from. The light above faded then staggered, then came a high-pitched scream. He did not wait to think, but threw himself forward, rising off the floor in a single move and dashing into Hell.

The light was whizzing around the room, disintegrating into fiery embers that which it touched, but clearly unable to tell which way was what. A girl lay prostate and terrified in bed. He dragged her from it, and slapping her face calmed her enough to get co-operation and pull themselves out of the room. The wounded light shot about then increased in intensity.

As he pulled the girl after him, the light went from yellow to white, then the world exploded behind them.

Chapter Ten

Red faces abounded all around, some from embarrassment, and some from anger. The volume level had risen dangerously high, and a half dozen guards now took up positions on the edge of the room, watching with some concern as the visiting Count berated his host.

"Only the valour of one officer prevented that *thing* from possessing my daughter!"
"To be fair..." Gunther began again.
"One man!" the Count drowned him out, "Where were your guards?!"
"Dead!" Gunther finally snapped, "That thing sliced through servants and guards killing them instantly until it got to your daughter."
"You are a disgrace and an imbecile!"

The Viceroy slapped him, and as Count Roger Alejandro Schenk went for his sword, two guards moved swiftly from the walls and grabbed hold of his arms.
"Release me you sons of currs!" he bellowed.

Archbishop Jensen upended his carafe of iced water over the man, happy to have a means of displaying his displeasure about the events of the previous evening. To be forced to visit a High Temple of the Unicorn was just so disgusting for words, and having to have the Order's local High Acolyte on the governing council was a mighty slap in the face.

"You fucking little shit!" the Count roared.
"How rude", Jensen smiled sardonically and helped himself to another carafe from off the table beside the wall, "Perhaps we could return to the purpose of this discussion?"
"My daughter, you bastards!"
"Quite", Samuel Guy looked up from where he had been sat at the table, reading the report, "If we have finished with the histrionics, perhaps we can take note of an important fact?"
"Light fights light" Luisa Maria Valdez pointed out.
"But that is not what we are missing" Samuel said.

The Count nodded to him, and the Viceroy in turn nodded to the guards who released him and retreated to the wall, keeping a watchful eye on the distance between the Count's hand and his sword.

"What is it?" he asked.

"That it was not going to kill your daughter" the octogenarian said quietly.

"What?!" Roger's ire was rising once again.

"It had ample time to do that according to your daughter's report, and despite her delicate age, the detail in her report confirms for me that she is correct."

"She is", Roger knew that for a fact; he had trained her well.

"Then the light had another motive."

"It does not always kill", Wolfgang had also remained seated at the table during the furor, "The lights seem to work in co-operation with the Fulani, and these", he indicated a set of reports everyone had ignored, "state that over a dozen slaves saw it pass through the palace. *No* servant or guard has survived to make that report."

"It ignored the slaves?" the Archbishop shrugged, "So? Everyone ignores slaves"

"How did it distinguish between servants, whom it killed automatically, and slaves, of whom it killed none?"

"It has intelligence", the Viceroy now finally retook his seat, and gestured for everyone else to do so, "We are already coming to the conclusion that it is some kind of lifeform, whether daemonic or faerie..."

"Despite common myths, those would be the same" the Archbishop snapped.

"If it made the distinction, then it chose to ignore the slaves" Wolfgang pointed out, "They could not have been overlooked on appearance alone as most of them do not look much different from servants, most of the time."

"I think I see", Count Roger sat finally, "It chooses to spare the slaves?"

"They are no worth", the Archbishop shrugged, "Why waste energy killing them?"

"Perhaps" Luisa said, thinking in military terms, "It depends how their energy is focused."

"I think, perhaps, *we* have something there..."

The voice came from a thin reed of a man, dressed in ornate but antiquated clothes, sat a little apart from the others, as if observing - which was the only status that the Archbishop, for one, would acknowledge him in.

"The Order?" asked Luisa

The man rose. High Acolyte of the local branches of the Order of the Unicorn, Quentin Eros Frobisher was here at the direct 'request' of the Count, a 'request' backed up by a telegraph from the Imperial Court requiring all Realms of the Empire to accord favoured status to the Order of the Unicorn.

"In the last few weeks, the Order has been carrying out extensive research at our facilities within Albion", when stated like this the word only could refer to the continent across the sea, the Heartland of the Empire, "We have studied reports, such as they are, from here, as well as more detailed reports from incidents across the Atlantic."

"What are those?", Gunther was surprised that he had not been informed, before.

"Over a dozen airships have been attacked by lights, three have been destroyed, the others made some kind of landing, but sustained heavy damage."

"They are attacking the airships not the people on them?" asked Luisa.

"It amounts to the same thing when the airship is destroyed" Count Roger pointed out.

"What is significant about our studies, is that there appears to be no energy decrease between the start of an attack and the last action in it. We even have cinematographic footage that correlates this."

"By which you mean that when it kills people it does not dissipate its energy?" Archbishop Jensen asked, interested despite himself, and overcoming for a brief moment his loathing of the man.

"Yes", the High Acolyte smiled at him, "Whatever discharges there are, the energy remains at a constant level"

"So it could have killed the slaves without wasting resources?" Luisa had worked that out for herself.

"Indeed" Quentin nodded.

~

For a moment all remained at peace, the strange contraptions on the hillside almost as if a giant had abandoned his playthings in the garden and gone in for tea. Then the diffusers began to work, and a noxious cloud floated on the wind, down towards the woods.

The diffusers continued to release the gas, a gentle hissing perhaps like a dozen grasshoppers going all at once, then the silence was broken by an agonised cry, a war-song taken up again and again within the trees as the gas soon found its victims.

Up-Master Vingatani was lying in a fox-hole level with the foremost diffuser, a careful watch on the wind, a more careful one upon the tree-line in front. He pulled the field telephone cable clear of a snag, and spoke into the headphones secured upon his head,
"Delivery underway, so far no sign of primary target"
"Understood" growled a crackly voice in his ear.

Beyond, the Fulani continued to die a hideous death as the nerve gases found them, and did their evil magic, but neither the Up-Master, nor those back beyond the ridge in the radio-truck, cared about the Natives - however many were killed, it was a good thing, but they were not the target of interest.

"Got one!" the shout was only in his ears, a scout somewhere beyond the contraptions ejaculating into the air.
Still, he winced and waited for the co-ordinator to speak.
"Where?" demanded the crackly voice from the radio car.
"Up ahead!"
"Be more precise"
"Er, special grid position 3-6-9"
"Got it"
"Options?" said another voice.
"Take it out", he heard himself say.
"Agreed"
"Understood"

"Ready the Device" ordered the crackly voice.

142

Up-Master Vingatani wormed his way out of his foxhole and squirmed backwards, keeping low even though the immediate likelihood of a Fulani attack was gone the same way as their screaming, dying men. He slid the communication wire under his arm, and crawled uphill towards the brow of the hill.

A fallen tree lay across a small depression, neither of which was what it seemed. Inside the depression, the Device lurked, the tree both cover and a prop for the various arms which were secured now to the backs of its limbs.

He rolled into the depression, and came to his feet
"Selector!" he said.
"Up-Master Vingatani", Selector Baines looked up from where she was both plugged into the communications system, and supervising the charging up of the energy core of the Device
"Ready as ordered"
"Good", she handed the communications relay over to another tattooed warrior, and together with the Up-Master approached the velvet-upholstered chair upon which Professor Kyle was reposing, sipping a brandy and watching events with interest.

The professor smiled at their approach,
"Is the world ready to witness my genius?" he asked, pleasantly
"We are", Baines had long reckoned that playing along with the man by altering words to mean both what they needed to, and what he wanted them to, was the best way of dealing with the Professor
"I am ready for my Godhood" he announced with a pleasant smile
"Excellent", Baines motioned towards the control panel, "Only you can do this, Professor"

That part was not flattery, but truth. The controls were hideously complex, and only a mind as chaotically organised as the Professor's had a chance of working through them.
"Target at optimum position!" the warrior who now manned the communications relay called across.
"Then it is time", the Professor rose and stepped up to the control plate, "Device fully charged", he read off the meters, "Calibration acceptable, target bearing please."

The warrior called it out.

"*Now* shall the world witness my genius!" he yelled.

And pulled hard on the lever.

~

A fountain tinkled, and birds sang. Overhead the sun beat down whilst a gentle breeze took the edge off it. The garden courtyard was secluded, cut off from the rest of the palace by thick walls, and heavy curtains over the doors. A cat walked by, brown fur mottled with black, ears pricked up. green eyes wary.

Joanna Jessica Jones - 'Triple' or 'Trip' to her friends - was not unhappy about guard duty in such a place. She knew that some of her fellows would have considered it unbecoming of a professional soldier to be sitting around on a marble bench, watching a child play. But this was a child who had survived an encounter with the lights, and she was a Schenk to boot, scion of a famous dynasty.

Joanna was not used to children. An only child, she had volunteered for the cadets upon entering her teens, and spent her formative years in various camps and schools across Albion. Her first action had been in the Caribbean, a runner for General Short himself, from which she had progressed to regular frontline service in China, and then a promotion to guard status here in Timbuktu. Aged only twenty-two, she had already seen several corners of the world, and knew that none was necessarily any better than another.

"I am confused" Leonora Bunny had finally stopped her investigation of the pebbles, and came to sit next to her bodyguard.

"Yes?", Joanna did not think 'my lady' appropriate for one of such tender years, but neither did she think some childish term of endearment would suit. Treat children as regular people and they would usually respond well, she thought.

"The light did not kill me" the eight year old said.

"Thanks be to God", a strong faith in the Imperial Church was one thing that Joanna *had* got.

"It did not want to kill me...I think" she said.

144

There was silence awhile, as Joanna had no answer to that. Then the girl sighed and shook her head,

"I did not like it" she proclaimed.

"The lights are evil", Joanna had heard the priest say that the previous Sunday.

"It did not want to hurt me, but I did not like it", she ran the two statements together, "Did it want to do something else to me?"

"Like what?" Joanna asked, then wished she had not.

The girl was shaking her head,

"I have read my father's books on war... A light cannot rape or pillage"

"Er..." Joanna tried to remember to treat the girl like any other person, regardless of age, "Perhaps it could in a different way"

"My maidenhood would not have been at risk" Leonora Bunny declared solemnly.

"No..probably not" Joanna admitted.

"Was it going to kidnap me?" the girl asked.

"There are no reports of any ransom demands", Joanna said, before realising what she had let out. She hoped that the girl would not realise the implication, but had forgotten that a powerful young intellect sat next to her upon the bench.

"The lights have taken captives before?" she asked.

"Er", Joanna was absolutely not permitted to release this information, "Please ask His Imperial Highness", she spluttered.

"Yes then..." Leonora Bunny continued on, "Who?"

"I...er...that is..."

"It must be someone important" the girl concluded.

"It is not confirmed" Joanna tried to rescue the situation.

"I see"

The cat walked back, giving them a narrow berth, but with its eyes and ears trained upon them.

"Do the lights kill animals?" Leonora Bunny asked

"I...I don't know"-

"Do animals see the lights?"

"I don't know that either..."

"What about slaves?"

"They saw the light" Joanna knew that much.

"But..." the girl tugged a strand of hair into her mouth, "It didn't kill them."

"Hmmm" Joanna was getting confused, and worried by the conversation.

The uncompanionable silence was broken by the entry into the garden of a robed Acolyte, his head shaven and his eyes bright,

"Mistress Leonora?" he said.

"Me?" the girl stood up.

"I am Acolyte Theodore Hart."

"...of the Order of the Unicorn?"

"That is so", he smiled, "Your father wishes me to give you instruction."

"In what?", Joanna was concerned, rising to her feet, "I am the duty guard"

Theodore looked at her, and nodded

"You may come too...His Lordship wishes for me to begin instruction in the Heritage of the Chivalric Orders"

"Very well", Joanna looked to the girl, "Do you understand?"

Leonora Bunny nodded,

"My father wishes it, it is important"

Joanna wondered what it was like to have such faith in a parent.

~

The green and the grey were everywhere, it seemed to Lieutenant Samuel Simeon Parker. After being awarded the Ribbon of the Golden Cavalry, he had been granted a few days leave, his misdemeanour in being in the palace without permission being completely overlooked on the basis of its fortunate consequences.

Now, he walked in the sunshine, and frowned at the numbers of Europan uniforms present in the city. He had never known more than a few before – the Europan Consulate had been small, its staff few, for their were few interests to represent, such was the historical antipathy between the empires. Now, of course, with Europa at war with the Caliphate and with rumours flying around that the Egyptians were allied to the lights, common cause had quickly become established.

The old consulate had been closed down, and the Europans had moved into a brand new building, originally earmarked for a hotel but now given over to a far more urgent purpose. As suited a large building, trains running across the Northern desert had brought in Europans to man the place, and now they seemed to be everywhere.

Sam knew that that was because his eyes were attuned to see them – enemies they had always been, and now in the unlikely role of friends, he could still see them. Obviously they were more numerous here, in the centre of Timbuktu, where the hotel had been constructed for commercial reasons. Out in the suburbs there would be fewer, even none. But the palace was in the centre, and the squares and shops, cafes and taverns, were his natural haunt – as well as that of the foreign consulates.

Europa was not alone in having a consulate in Timbuktu, and in fact those of other nations had traditionally been larger, more heavily staffed than them. Now eclipsed, there were constant brawls brewing up in the evening, as High Brasilians, or Halychians came to blows with Europans trying to muscle in on their favourite drinking places, or brothels, or chatting up girls who had long swooned to the money and looks of the Brasilians, if not quite the latter for the Halychians.

The Zanzibari, and the Abyssinians went along with things more easily, the one occupying different haunts for the mostpart, the other used to playing second fiddle to whoever was more numerous.

Samuel Simeon Parker went into one of his favourite stores. Along with the ribbon, the award had come with a thousand crowns, and with the news from the South unremittingly bad, he was determined to spend it whilst he still could. He stopped and stared around at the empty walls, denuded of carpets, and the empty shelves.
"Ah, Lieutenant", a swarthy individual emerged from behind a curtained area, "Congratulations on your honour"
"Thank you", Sam gestured around the barren store, "Are you selling up?"
He knew that things were getting bad in West Africa, but surely not

that bad!

The merchant laughed,
"Your new friends had a consulate to outfit, and to my credit, they preferred my goods for it"
"I see", and Sam did see, for this place had always been one of the best in the city, selling high-quality goods imported from all over the Empire, and out.
"My order books are full as well", the merchant grinned, albeit in apology, "It would seem that several high-born Europans wish not to live in the consulate and are buying, or perhaps renting, mansion houses in the city"
"Oh...", Sam had not foreseen that, but of course it made sense, "Very well, I will try Barnie's"
The merchant laughed,
"He might still have *some* stock...he was always on the edge of respectable"
"Good luck", Sam shook his head and left the store.

He understood the merchant's warning – Barnie's had also sold out of most of their stock, and what was left would be the second-class stuff that the owner tried to secrete amongst the good, in the hope that nobody would notice. It might fool people in Timbuktu, but it clearly had failed to fool the Europans.

Giving up on the stores, he headed instead to his favourite restaurant, noting with annoyance as he approached, the queues snaking around the corner. No doubt the Europans had chosen to dine here too...

~

The room smelt of pipe tobacco, spilt brandy, and old man, but it was home. Leatherbound books took up two whole walls, an open fire with a thin, old cat laid out in front of it another, whilst the fourth had set within it a series of waist-high windows looking out on a formal garden, exuberant with fountains and small trees, but devoid of bright colours.

Samuel Guy sat in his favourite armchair, feet up on a foot-stool, a satin gown wrapped around him, despite the warmth of the fire. In an hour, his servant would bring him the business accounts for the previous day and he would spend until lunchtime going over them. But for now, he sat back with a glass of steaming coffee, mixed as usual with the first brandy of the day, and perused the newspapers which he had flown in from all parts of the Empire.

Of course, the further away they came from, the more out-of-date they were, those from Kamchatka most so as they had been flown in via China, India and Zanzibar. But he had long ago partitioned time in his mind, and his sense of "current" was as if he had a time-machine, and each zone was so many days out of kilter from where he was. Much of the more global news was no longer relevant, but he read the provincial newspapers for their local news, or their local take on international news. It was always simplest to rely on meetings at the palace, and his own contacts within the telegraph offices, for the most immediate information but often the detail was missing, something perhaps deliberately withheld, whether at this end, or at the point of origin, and when it all came down to it, he preferred the evidence of his own eyes.

"Hmm...", his eyes strayed to a sidebar in *The Kamchatka Chronicle*, "Bulgarian Patriarch backs Uprising". It was dated two weeks ago, but there had been no news out of Europa that their troublesome province was in rebellion. No doubt the news was being censored, and without any direct reporters there, Albion's own newspapers were lacking in information. Kamchatka, no doubt, had received its news via an Eastern cable, probably even via the Caliphate. He wondered how things were really going in Europa's ill-starred war, especially if they had had to keep this news quiet from their newfound ally.

In fact, there was very little news on the war in any of the major newspapers. Only *The Tunis Herald* had anything substantial, and that was a report of a naval clash off the Cyrenaican coast, no further details, dated two days ago. Maybe he would invite the newly-appointed Europan Commercial Attaché to dinner, and pump him...

Chapter Eleven

"I am approaching the co-ordinates now", Guy Simonis Meredith was keeping a wary eye out for lights, but so far there was only open land, with ahead the area where it merged into the luxurious forest, stretching away to the South.

"Is there any sign of them?" the voice in his head asked, with an effort to mask the concern that was being felt.

"I...no", Guy swept the Scavenger lower, the bi-plane responding to his hands like a trained animal, "There's a hole"

"A hole?" the voice said, "Captain, we are not receiving you clearly"

"There is a hole" he said louder, more enunciated, "Actually it is more like a bowl, like somebody scooped out a part of the ground."

"Captain?" the voice was all concern now, "Can you hear me?"

"I said its like a bowl, or a scoop!" Guy shouted back

"Captain, are you there? We cannot hear you!"

Then the aeroplane went dead.

"Bulgarians!" Guy muttered a curse that had been fashionable thirty years ago when he had been a young man.

At that time, the newly-conquered people were not sitting happily beneath the Europan yoke, and it seemed that not a day went past when there was not something in the newspapers about rebel activity. Of course, those days were long past now, but men and women who had served alongside Europans in Georgia had picked up the habit, and old curses die hard.

The aeroplane came back under his control, still dead but with its precipitate descent aborted, and the veteran Grand Captain was able to bring it to a slow glide in on the grassland. The landing was not pretty, the wheels hit a bump and the aeroplane flipped over onto its back, but he had been in worse, and with the engine cold nothing untoward happened. Struggling out of his harness, and dropping to the ground, he crawled on his hands and knees and was sick in a corner as the adrenalin rush dissipated.

Clambering slowly to his feet, he looked around. There were several things in his favour, he knew. There had been no enemy in sight, the

Controller knew almost exactly where he was, and it was not raining. On the other hand, there was a great hole in the ground where there ought to have been a Special Unit. That it had not been heard from for over thirty-six hours had resulted in his being dispatched to investigate. It clearly was not there, but why was there a hole instead?

As his rescue was only likely to come from above, he decided that he might as well go and have a look at the strange bowl-like hole. Any aerial craft would see him against the stark emptiness, and his crashed Scavenger would indicate he was in the vicinity anyway. Poor thing; he looked at the veteran aeroplane and shook his head; strange the way sentiment could lead the mind.

He headed off towards the hole.

~

Leonora Bunny was impressed. Even her father did not have one of these! And since she was sure that he had everything that money could buy, then that meant that money could not buy these. Also, since he was a high-ranking nobleman, of a famous family, it also meant that rank could not buy one also. Her father also had influence, that much was obvious from this trip alone, but he did not have one of these, so influence and connections could not buy one. In all probability, therefore, these could not be bought at all, in the ordinary way of things - like armoured battlewagons, or Wildcats. No matter how much money, how great a rank, or how much influence someone had, they could not buy those for their own use.

The televisual apparatus must be something like that. From somewhere far away, relayed, as the Acolyte had attempted to explain, across re-transmitting stations, she was receiving live, if rather broken, pictures from a High Temple in Iberia. The man speaking was an Imperial Historian, again the Acolyte had explained this to her, a famous man who could not possibly leave his university but whose time was at the command of the Order.

She learnt that there were twelve Chivalric Orders, of varying lineages, but none younger than two hundred years, when the Order of the

Buffalo had been accepted by the then-Emperor. Of these, by far the most important was that of the Unicorn, which traditionally had Imperial Patronage, and by far the most despised was that of the Serpent, which had become perverted and debased over the years. She had a bit of an idea what the first of those two words meant, but no idea about the second. The Imperial Historian made it quite clear, however, that the Order of the Serpent had no fabulous Temples, no standing at the Imperial Court, and no honour. She wondered just what it was that was so bad about it, but whilst she could hear almost every word that the other spoke from Iberia, there was no way for her to speak back to him. This was instruction only, and she sat and dutifully made notes as she was instructed

Outside the room, Joanna was bored. The Acolyte had been pleasant enough and brought her fruit juice and scones, but she was forbidden to enter the room, and could only stand outside, and make sure that nothing that was not permitted entered. On her belt she had a single phosphorous grenade, clipped there since she had received her assignment. There were not many of them in West Africa, though a ship was enroute from Albion with a hold full. Since her colleague had seemingly driven away one of the lights with such a device, anyone who was in contact with the girl had been instructed to wear one.

To Joanna, it was a dangerous piece of technology she would rather have had nothing to do with, but she could not deny Samuel Simeon's use of such a thing had either killed or wounded the light, or otherwise made it flee. It was a light, who could tell what had happened to it? One of her friends was dating Sam's cousin, and through her, Joanna knew all about his night-time escapades, and how he had come to be in the palace when he should not have. Rumour had it that his Captain had received her orders, reassigning her to the Upper Volta, but rumours were always rife and only time would tell.

But Sam was a hero, had received the Ribbon of the Golden Cavalry from the hands of the Viceroy himself, and was no doubt even now living life to the full, his few days leave and his thousand crowns bound to ensure that in a city like Timbuktu.

Acolyte Theodore Hart reappeared, the sun shining off his bald pate, his eyes equally luminescent, and Joanna wondered if he had been smoking, or imbibing of some substance, something that was said to open the mind to great things, though she shuddered herself at the thought of losing control.

"It is nearly over", he held a pocket watch in his hand, regarding the second hand sweeping around, "The Imperial Historian has a lecture to deliver to the Hidden University in a few minutes. There will be a brief lag whilst the re-transmission stations pass on the last segments, but on the hour exactly he will cease to broadcast."

"I see" said Joanna, to whom everything the man had just said was gibberish.

"We count down now...ten, nine.." he smiled, but she did not join in, so he shrugged, "I will fetch the girl for you."

"Thank you"

Five minutes later, Leonora Bunny stood before her once more, a heavy notebook under her arm, a pensive look upon her face, though that was not much different from her usual sombre expression. In fact, Joanna thought, she had never seen her smile, but then again she could well be traumatised by what had almost happened to her.

"Are you ready?" she asked gently.

"It was most instructive" the girl said, not to her guard but to the Acolyte who smiled warmly at her

"I am sure that the Order will schedule another session for you, though it is not likely to be with Professor Knox. He is a very busy man, and much sought-after on the televisor."

"I understand", she sounded happy enough with that, "He was good, but sometimes talked too fast"

Theodore Hart laughed,

"Yes, many of his students feel the same, but few are bold enough to say so!"

"Oh", the girl looked at her feet, "I will remember that"

Joanna touched her arm, and led her from the courtyard, through a series of ante-rooms to a postern gate in the Temple. Emerging onto a side street, they were met by two more guards who were standing by a steaming black limousine.

"Back to the palace", Joanna told them, holding the door open for the girl.

~

"Elven Battle Boots!" Awfy was not one for profanities, and had adopted one of his aunt's old sayings early on in his career. It was not an altogether strange exclamation, though more often favoured by those of a certain generation, or of a more rural lifestyle. However, there were occasions that it seemed to fit, and this was certainly one.

"Prepare to deploy", Grand Captain Elijah Ramirez had no time to consider his passenger as he ordered his bridge crew to bring the airship *Xerxes* down low over the grassland. He had been unhappy at first when the Viceroy had commandeered his vessel, but when he had been invited to a private briefing and shown the photographs of the devastation of the fortresses, and learnt that Imperial Prince Alexander was missing, presumed captured (though nobody quite said how they presumed this), he had allowed himself to be convinced. The company was being paid well, and he would still receive his wages, as would his crew. Only now, did the potential dangers of the added duties become apparent.

"Secure us one hundred yards short of the edge", Sub-Commander Katerina Delilah Spinks commanded.

"Deploy!"

The ropes lashed down, but of course in this wilderness there was nobody to take them up. Instead, each was weighted with lead, and teams of crewmen swarmed down on lines to grab a hold of them and take up the strain. It was common practice on smaller vessels, especially those serving out-of-the-way places, but for a behemoth of this size, it was unusual. But then, so was it being here.

Awfy continued to stare out of the viewing port, ignoring the men and women who were struggling to tie the airship down, his eyes only for the giant bowl ahead; an area that looked as if some god had reached down with his spoon and scooped up a helping of earth and trees...and rock...for the original contours of the land could not have been like that. He spotted a figure moving in the distance, and smiled to himself; it was never good to lose a hero, and he had had a feeling that Guy Meredith would still be alive out here. The Imperial Airforce had refused to send any of its dwindling number of aeroplanes, and Awfy wondered what the Grand Captain out there would have to say about that. Instead, it had fallen to the Shadow Service to convince the Viceroy to send this giant airship out, just to pick up one man, but the Viceroy was not an idiot, even if he was sometimes a pompous ass. He had agreed mainly because he needed to know what had happened to the Special Unit, than because he cared about the life of one single pilot, but saving the latter's life, if it could be done, would have knock-on consequences of its own, and whilst not included in the main calculation, were there as supporting evidence.

The *Xerxes* bumped slowly to the ground, and Elijah Ramirez rose from his throne-like seat, rubbing the small of his back,
"I do not fancy trying *that* too often" he said.
"What time-span do we have?"
Elijah smiled thinly,
"As short as possible if you please, we are not much use on the ground"
"I understand"

Awfy left the bridge, picking up guards and a cinematographic crew on the way. They exited quickly and headed towards the hole, where Guy Simonis Meredith was now making his way towards them.
"Captain" Awfy called as they approached, "Are you well?"
"Yes, yes", Guy was shaking his head, although at something else, "This is insane."
"Insane?" Awfy reached him, and looked at the veteran pilot with some concern.
"Look at it!" Guy gestured behind him, "It looks smaller from the air, but I have just completed walking its perimeter..."
"It *is* vast" agreed Awfy.
"What happened here?"

Awfy could only shake his head, and instruct the film crew to begin shooting. The guards fanned out, but beneath their feet there was only rock, smooth and clean as if newly cut. They walked around in some confusion, then grouped back together by the cameras.
"There are two possibilities", Awfy had been thinking as he had watched them, "Either the Device did this, or the lights did"
"It is funny how we speak of 'the lights' to mean some malevolent . . .

force" Guy pondered on his choice of word, "Creature? Being? Force? Which is it?"

"The best minds in the Empire are hard at work on that."

"That is little comfort", Guy was not being disrespectful, "Do they have a captive light?"

"I do not believe so."

"Then their conclusions are not likely to be any better than our own."

"That may be so", Awfy allowed.

"Sir!" one of the guards had gone into the trees to urinate, and now came running back up the slope, arms wheeling wildly, "Sir! In the woods, sir!"

"What?!" Awfy stepped forward.

The guard looked momentarily confused, his eyes leaping from his own lieutenant, to the Grand Captain then to the Shadow Service man. His lieutenant gave an almost imperceptible nod, and the guard addressed Awfy,

"Uh, sir...There are bodies in the wood, hideous bodies....Fulani"

"The Fulani aren't *that* hideous" Guy said; in truth, he thought some of them rather pretty, the menfolk included.

"*These are*!" insisted the guard, "Oh my God..."

"Lieutenant with me", Awfy headed off the way the man had just come, the lieutenant and half a dozen guards close behind, Guy bringing up the rear at a more sedate pace of his own.

The woods were shadowed, damp ... and stank.

"What the Heck..." the lieutenant pulled a handkerchief from a pocket and wrapped it over the lower part of his face.

"Over here sir", the woman's voice was flat, devoid of emotion.

They gathered around her, looking down at what they had found.

"What did *that*?!" the lieutenant was horror-struck.

Awfy knew the answer, visions of multicoloured tanks coming into his mind.

"The Special Unit" he said flatly, "They had...weapons that would do this."

"God's toenail", the lieutenant grimaced, "I am not sure I care what has happened to *them* anymore."

"Care not about them, but about what happened" Awfy advised him,

156

"An act can happen to others also"

"Yes", the lieutenant nodded, then turned to the woman, "Fetch paraffin from the ship and douse the woods. We will fire it as we leave."

"Yes sir"

The party emerged back into the clear, fresh open air of the hole, the lieutenant stopping and staring around him,

"Was this wooded?" he asked.

"A grassy hillside, I think" Awfy replied, "It ran down to meet with the trees"

"What did this?" he asked.

The Shadow Service man could only shake his head...

"Sir, long-range radio transmission from Greencape Station"

Captain Hector Aloysius Leclerc took it, and read it with a frown,

"Order additional lookouts" he instructed.

"What is it, sir?" the first officer was not going to be dismissed without knowing. He had taken the sealed envelope from the radio officer and delivered it as instructed, but he did not like being in the dark.

"Greencape have informed us, using the top-security Atlantis code, that two ships have been sunk by the beings of light within their waters"

"Merchant ships?" he asked.

"If it matters, one was a transport from the Azores, another a submarine completing a proving voyage from out of Brest."

"Have any other vessels seen the lights and survived?"

Leclerc stared at him,

"Interrogate a piece of paper, would I?"

The first officer blanched.

"Now go and post those lookouts"

"Yes sir"

But it was too late. As the *Perseus* cut through the waves, a pair of lights homed in from the South.

"Lights!" yelled a lookout, a lad on his first seagoing voyage

"Helm hard to North" Leclerc had no idea what to do.

The lights were not a threat he knew how to counter. He could order the ship about, fire its guns off, but how could you escape light?

"Lights following and closing on us" the duty officer relayed reports from above

"All weapons bear and fire"

"Free fire" the duty officer commanded.

The cannon and machine guns opened up, but the lights came on.

"Signal full power, push the engines beyond maximum" Leclerc was just going through the motions.

"Engine room responds aye" the duty officer was all calm on the surface.

"Lights closing astern"

"Damn" Leclerc slapped a hand against his thigh, "Instruct the radio room - issue the emergency signal"

"Nobody can get to us in time!" the first officer was angry.

"Our duty is to make a report!" the Captain told him.

"Duty be damned!"

Then the lights struck, cutting through the hull of the ship, slicing it apart...

~

"Logic?" Imperial Duke Gunther Luis Leander snapped, rubbing his head

"Of course", his guest was plump, and bald, and resplendent in yellow robes, "Cyclops runs on logic alone"

"Explain it more carefully", Samuel Guy was tired, but his mind was as alert as ever. He knew that the Lord Guardian was jumping too fast ahead of himself, on something that needed to be taken slowly.

Pedro Leonidas Jenkinson took a moment to collect his thoughts,

"Cyclops functions on a logical basis - something is either on or it is off, it is either so, or it is not so."

"With you so far" Luisa Maria Valdez was fascinated by the strange man sitting opposite.

158

"When there are numerous feeds there are multiple logical calculations to make"

"Aha", Gunther took a sip of a fruit cocktail, "Go on"

"These calculations impact upon others, until there is a whole matrix, each one impacting others"

"Hmm" Gunther frowned

"Life is an analogy", the Lord Guardian said, "You make a decision today, but what are its antecedents, and what events led to those?"

"So, you are simply talking about something in reverse?" Samuel Guy eyed the man carefully

"If you could chart the start of the process leading to a decision, that would be so"

"Continue", the Viceroy instructed.

"Cyclops reduces down the multiple outputs until it has computed a conclusion"

"No..." Gunther shook his head, "Again please"

The Lord Guardian sighed,

"That is the logic, your Highness", a bit of smooth talking usually worked wonders, "It is like a series of mathematical equations, worked through until you come to an answer"

"I will take your word on it", Gunther was wary of looking a fool, "And these answers are true?"

Pedro Leonidas peeled an orange with a sharpened fingernail and considered for a moment,

"If the inputs are all true, then the output is true"

"You mean that if people do not lie to Cyclops, it does not lie to you?" Luisa asked.

"If I told you that nine balls were red and one blue, what would be the chance of getting a green one?"

"None, zero" Gunther could follow that.

"But if I was colour-blind and three of the balls I thought were red were actually green, then your conclusion would be wrong"

"Cyclops relies on correct information being fed into it", Samuel Guy said wearily, "I think we understand that."

"It relies upon it, and its answers rely upon it", the Lord Guardian knew that he had to press the latter point, "If something is incorrect, even by omission or confusion, then the ultimate computation could be wrong."

"Very well" Gunther sat back in his chair, "I assume you believe that Cyclops has been given correct data."
"Why do you assume that?" Luisa asked.
"Because if not he would not be here" the Viceroy smiled at his military liaison officer.
"That is correct", the Lord Guardian confirmed, "Cyclops has given a provisional answer to what it was asked."
"Provisional?" Samuel Guy caught onto that word.
"If more data becomes available, Cyclops will recompute, and it is possible that later data will substantially change the equation so as to affect the outcome."
"That sounds like an excuse" Wolfgang had remained silent until now, having had no problem following any of it, but he could not resist a swipe at a rival to the shadow service.
"If Cyclops were human, perhaps it would be", Pedro Leonidas admitted, "But it is not. There is no excuse, only truth."

"Very well" Gunther had finally got his mind around it all, "What are Cyclops' conclusions?"
"The lights are alive, or are directed by some being that is alive. The intelligence behind them is real-time. Their ability to travel is linear, but on a scale not yet evaluated. That they are acting according to an intelligent plan, even if it is beyond our understanding. That it is possible that light may combat light."

There was silence for a moment, then the Viceroy coughed,
"Can you explain the first one; I do not understand the qualification?"
"Of course, your Highness", Pedro Leonidas was relieved to have finally got this far, "If you send a dog off after sheep and command its movements with whistles, the sentience is not with the dog, but with you. Admittedly, in this example the dog is alive, but the guiding intelligence is yourself, stationed some way away."
"So it is possible that the lights are alive, and are controlled by another being that is alive?" Luisa had cut through the analogy.
"Oh..." Pedro Leonidas sat back hard upon his chair, "That is an option, and is within Cyclops' parameters."
"Its what?" asked the Viceroy

"The output feed on that question", the Lord Guardian smiled at him, "I was merely summarising, but Cyclops' output allows for that situation within it"

"Oh...good"

"Let us hope it is" admonished Samuel Guy.

~

Chapter Twelve

Dusk was drawing its untidy veil across the land, a dangerous time, especially when the enemy were known to be on the move. Darkness was falling in patches across the land in front, the valleys and the wooden outcrops dipping out of sight as they faded from view. Except in one spot where as the darkness all around deepened, so did the light there seem to intensify, shimmering and moving as if it came from the windows of a train, though no train would carve such a circular route within one place. Besides, there were no tracks down there; this was frontier country, truly now since the advanced fortresses had all been destroyed, and whatever was moving down there was not of Albion's doing.

Honour Ensign Ralph Cornelius Vane swallowed, and dropped down from the conning tower into the crowded interior of the armoured battle-wagon. People were moving about, the duty shift changing as one crew went for a lie-down and some food, the other rose from the bunks and made their way to their stations. One person who was not moving was the Elite Marshal, sat at the centre of a web of machinery, his eyes glued to a scope that rose up from the side of the leviathan.
"Sir", Ralph waited patiently.

Humphrey Odysseus Brown was in his early sixties and a veteran warrior. He had seen all of the conflicts of the modern era in his time, and had indeed authored two volumes of memoirs about them, books that were used on the one hand in the Elite Training Colleges, and on the other had become best-sellers amongst the public. But whilst he had fought Kazan and Egypt, Caribbean rebels and revolutionaries, Chinese warlords, and Indian princes, and before now, a decade ago, even the Fulani when attached to New Lisbon, he had never come up against an enemy as dangerous, and as perplexing, as the lights.
"You could see them too?" he asked the young man.

Ralph nodded,
"Yes, sir...I would estimate twelve to twenty of them"
"That is a mighty concentration", the Elite Marshal did not exaggerate
- even a single light was a serious problem.

"I think they are waiting for full darkness sir."

"What do you base that on?" Humphrey Odysseus was truly interested. That a man did not have rank did not mean that he lacked in brains, and often in his career he had been saved from a potentially disastrous course of action by opening his ears and listening to the dissenting view of a junior officer.

"They are restless, sir, moving about like cavalry before a charge."

Sitting in an armoured battle-wagon, cavalry could sometimes seem an outmoded concept, but it was still the prevalent form of warfare in many parts of China and the Deccan, and as an Honour Ensign, the young man would be conversant with it from his ceremonial training. And if the Fulani warbands were infantry, then perhaps the globes of light did indeed play the role of cavalry to them, albeit more on the scale of ancient kataphractoi than the fast-moving sabres of today.

"They no doubt know that we are here", the Elite Marshal was pessimistic that the dug-outs and netting had kept such an enemy as the lights from noticing that his armoured brigade held the heights, "They have never shown themselves leery of a fight"

"I think so, sir"

"Yes", Humphrey Odysseus sighed; how did one prepare to fight an enemy that one could not defeat? In all the recent history of Albion that had not been a calculation that anybody had had to make. Even the loss of the French interior to Europa had not been against an enemy who was invincible - it had been an even fight, and Albion had lost. But people preferred not to dwell on that these days.

He motioned for the duty captain to approach. As a battle-wagon with a double rotation of crews, it also had two Battle Captains sharing responsibility for it, an incongruous situation except that as the flag-vehicle of the Elite Marshal he was always there to preside.

"Yes sir?", Amelia May Hamilton ducked beneath the gunlayer's sights, and made her way across to what had become known, outside of the Marshal's hearing, as his 'Nest'

"Instruct all vehicles to be ready to move out immediately. Keep a shell in the chamber, and another ready."

"Yes sir"

The former would give away their position, except that the Elite

Marshal was sure that the enemy knew it already. Armoured battle-wagons in revetments usually kept their engines charged down so as not to advertise their presence. The latter command was potentially risky in case of a hit upon the gun barrel, or a fire in the interior, but against the lights it probably made no difference.

"Movement sir!", the observer was upfront in his own little compartment, lying flat and sighting along the line of advance. Stationary, he had as good a view of the distance as did any of them, but in a battle that was not his role, and his reports would change to immediate instructions on steerage and manoevring.
"The lights?" Humphrey Odysseys gripped the iron rail beside him
"Starting to spread out sir, coming this way"
"Open fire as soon as the range is closed"
He knew it would do no good, but what else was there to do?

~

"This cannot be!" Imperial Duke Gunther Luis Leander read the report that Luisa had just handed to him, "They *knew*?" he asked.
"You will have to ask our friendly Lord Guardian that, sir" she replied.
"But even I did not know the name of the ship", he protested, "I was to be informed when it had arrived"
"I do not think this is an ordinary leak in intelligence", Luisa Maria Valdez had grown in confidence during her superior's extended absence on the front, "If the lights knew, then they have different ways of learning things"
"You *are* beginning to sound like the Lord Guardian" the Viceroy warned her.
"I apologise, your highness" she smiled.

He sighed and balled the report up, throwing it against a painting of the current Emperor's father which hung upon the wall,
"So the one weapon we suspect works against the lights has gone to the bottom of the Atlantic along with the *Perseus*?"
"Yes sir", she shrugged, "It makes perfect strategic sense from the lights' point of view"
"We are now convinced they *have* a point of view?" he ran a hand through his hair.

"They, or whoever is controlling them"

"Very well", he sat down heavily upon a chair, careless as to which one it was. With only himself and his military liaison in the room, who would care if he left the grander chairs empty?

"It is the third vessel sunk in the Near Waters", she reminded him of what he may have forgotten.

"Yes..." he searched his memory, "Why were the others sunk?"

"A show of strength perhaps, or perhaps the lights were testing their capabilities"

"Not because of any intrinsic value in the vessels themselves?"

"One was a transport from the Azores; I cannot remember what it was carrying. The other was a submarine out of Brest on a proving voyage - I do not even know if it was armed."

"Targets that would not create too big a stir?" he wondered.

"Ideal for a test" she nodded.

It was getting late, but there was no council meeting for the evening, and the Viceroy did not feel that he could face his papers after the news he had just received. He rubbed at his eyes; these days he was beginning to look very haggard.

"Do you think these lights know what they are doing?" he asked.

"In what way?" Luisa had taken the Viceroy's sitting down as in invitation for her to do also.

"They have sided with Natives, rebels and maybe even slaves, against the greatest force for civilisation that this world has ever known" he protested.

"It is easier to control the primitive" she said, then frowned, "Or perhaps, they mean to have us all reduced to their level?"

"May God save us from *that* fate!" Gunther growled, inwardly shaking at the images it conjured up.

~

"Back! Back! Back!" the officer in the conning tower screamed into the communicator as the light came out of nowhere and shot at them broadside on.

The driver was clearly well awake, and the armoured battle-wagon shot backwards, bumping over something, and slewing down an incline, but it served its purpose. The light shot forward across the bow, then found another target.

Once again the main gun fired, shuddering the gigantic vehicle, and sending a shell flying out in a stream of smoke and flame. Where it landed, the officer atop could not tell. All the survivors of the Elite armoured brigade were firing, probably at nothing or in hope alone, and explosions were dotting the skyline, or thundering up nearer as a shell ploughed into some structure unseen in the darkness.

Somewhere to the right a huge explosion rent the air, and he turned in time to see the barrel of a gun flying through the air in a cloud of less identifiable debris, the death mark of another of the proud battle-wagons.

Below, Battle Captain Nehemiah Davis was hunched over the radio, trying to make sense of the situation outside that had rapidly descended into a chaotic melee as the enemy had attacked. Nobody had brought any of the lights down, and whilst machine-gun fire cut swathes through the Fulani that had swarmed after them, their death did not appear to affect - or bother - the lights in any way. They were systematically hunting down and destroying the armoured battle-wagons.

"Are we defenceless?" the gunlayer had grown tired of blasting away at far-off trees, and came to lean next to his captain.

"Like a Native with a wooden stick going up against a machine gun" he said.

"Worse than that", Elisabeth Leclerc was filthy with the oil of the engine, "At least a stick *can* kill a man"

"Do we have a*nything* that can kill these bastards?!" the Battle Captain asked plaintively.

After a moment's pause, the gunlayer spoke up,

"We have a few star shells; they're experimental, designed to act like flares"

"Maybe we can burn the bastards", Nehemiah stood up, "Get them loaded up"

"Sir"

"And driver, keep us alive long enough to fire the damned things!" he called.

166

"Yes sir!", the driver quite fancied staying alive himself, anyway.

Outside, another battle-wagon, this time one of the smaller - relatively-speaking - trapezoids, careered down the incline towards them, its tracks blown apart, smoke gushing from a fire aft. Even as it did so, men and women could be seen jumping from its shell, landing to try to roll free. Most did; a few unlucky bastards fell into the path the stricken vehicle was taking, and their agonised screams added another layer of Hell to the air.

"Two lights closing!" the officer on the conning tower, clenched his buttocks and vowed not to disgrace himself.
"Target!" the voice of the Battle Captain came over loud and clear.
"Target aye!" the gunlayer seemed happy about something.
"Fire!"

The main gun bucked, and the battle-wagon staggered briefly backwards, then the star shell exploded on the ridge ahead. Shielding his eyes against the unexpected light, the officer could hear a high-pitched keening noise, but see nothing with the after-image blasted upon his retina.
"Fire!"
The main gun bucked again, and a second star shell exploded ahead. This time, the officer knew to duck, and waited whilst the bright light washed over him.

Blinking tears from his eyes, he rose and stared at where the approaching lights had been. There was nothing there...

~

Like everybody else out on the streets, Lieutenant Samuel Simeon Parker froze and looked around in amazement.
"Air raid...?" he stuttered.
There could be no doubt that the sirens were sounding, a wailing plaintive rising and falling designed to strike fear into the heart of man. Only the deaf could have missed them, and even they would be wondering at the suddenly confused mass of humanity standing on the city streets.

A Zanzibari, resplendent in his robes of many hues, walked across to him,

"You are an officer", he said, a fact that would have been hard to deny given the uniform, "What do we do?"

Sam blinked and returned to the moment,

"Perhaps it is a drill, but even so the safest option would be to comply with procedure"

"And what is that?"

"Um...", Sam realised that the man was right; the issue of what to do when an air raid hit Timbuktu had not been part of his training either. He struggled to remember what he did know,

"There is a...vault on Magog Street, I think it has a sign outside saying it is a designated emergency shelter"

"Magog Street?" the Zanzibari nodded, "That is five minutes away"

Sam shrugged and the man hurried off, a fair few others in his wake, people who had watched the exchange and believed that the guard lieutenant had given instruction, not somewhat garbled advice.

The sirens continued to sound, and now Sam saw to his alarm that the airships tethered at the airfield had clearly all been instructed to leave. It was emergency procedure, to get them airborne and out of the way as soon as possible, but his spine chilled as he realised it could mean only one thing.

Others were now looking at them, a pair of Europan consulate guards who clearly had seen action, crossing swiftly his way

"You", they stabbed a finger in his direction, "tell us what is happening"

Sam took a swallow,

"The evidence of my senses says we must be under attack"

"Yes", the older of the two gestured at the rapidly-departing airships, "but who and how?"

"That I do not know"

"Pah!", he turned away in disgust, and with his colleague headed quickly back towards the consulate.

Sam reckoned that they had the right idea, and turned towards the palace, shocked to see tracer rounds already streaming into the sky, their sound buried beneath the rising hubbub all around him.

"What the Hell is going on?!" he snapped, turning to run back to his duty station.

- - -

Francis Elias Bannerman was running around like a madman. Over the last two days, brand-new Wildcat aeroplanes had arrived first by train to Timbuktu, and then by truck to the airfield, and now a crazy mishmash of crews, some veteran, some current, and many newly-training were running to their craft, the markings upon not a fair few were still damp with paint.

"Get them up!" Station Commander Laurent Clermont Judd looked way older than his late twenties after the events of the last few days, and this was now putting a crown upon things, he thought.

"Roll-out! Roll-out! Roll-out!", Samantha Denison was twenty, beautiful and pregnant. Neither her age nor her condition were factors taken into consideration in the middle of a war, and she was now standing in the middle of the field, waving her arms at first one Wildcat, then another.

In the cockpit of his new steed, Grand Captain Guy Simonis Meredith stroked the smoothness of the instruments, and took a deep breath. He could see his young lover out there, rushing around making sure that the Wildcats were really all ready to take to the air, pausing every now and then to check on something, or to fix something that a fresh new pilot had overlooked. Twenty Wildcats, but how many would survive the day?

Francis looked up and met his eye across the grass, and they exchanged a wave, heavy with feelings, then it was Guy's turn to move, Samantha motioning him forward with wide open movements of her arms. He moved, bumping the aeroplane across the grass, and attaining the makeshift runway, just as the craft before him leapt into the sky.

A wide smile upon his face, Guy throttled up, and sent the Wildcat hurtling down the runway. As it soared aloft, he thought that at least this time he would know what to shoot at.

~

"The reason is obvious", Lord Guardian Pedro Leonidas Jenkinson was by far the calmest man in the room.
"We *know* it is obvious!" General Alberto Smith had returned only an hour ago from the front, "We are short on aeroplanes, with our losses in the South, and now our armoured brigade has been shattered at the front."
"Not all is bad there", Prince Gunther Luis Leander had already received a detailed report on the battle.
"The problem", Wolfgang eyed the man in yellow as if *he* was the problem, "is not Egypt, but Cyclops"

"How so?!" the Lord Guardian was on his feet, stomach protruding from his gowns as he pushed himself to full height.
"Is it obvious after the event, why was not it obvious to Cyclops before?" the senior Shadow Service man demanded.
"A fair point", the Viceroy looked up at the only one standing in the room, "We can sit back and say 'Oh yes, that is why they attack' but it would have been useful to know beforehand."
"To know?" the Lord Guardian shook his head, "You are asking for an Oracle."

"Is that not what Cyclops is?" Wolfgang eyed him sternly, "Why rely on it if it only tells us what we know or can work out."
"Cyclops could have listed probabilities", Pedro Leonidas was sweating not with strain but with anger, "but what would you have done with them?"
"This attack", the Viceroy stared at him, "If I understand probability, it is 1-in-1"
"It is now", the Lord Guardian sighed, "Beforehand, of course not - there were many other possibilities, the most likely one being that things would remain as they were"
"Most likely according to who?" the Viceroy demanded.
"You" Pedro told him.

There was silence, then the Viceroy waved him to a seat,

"Very well" Gunther said, "That is as it may be. What is the Caliphate going to do next?"

That was the major question on everyone's lips - the Egyptian air raid had come out of the blue, quite literally, a whole six squadrons passing over the borderlands from the East. A mixture of gun batteries, and what aeroplanes there were to scramble, had made them pay a heavy price for this, but the railyards had been smashed, several streets of salubrious housing flattened, and panic created in the commercial heart of the city. With the retaliatory capacity almost zero in the area, it was a move that the Caliphate could take safe in the knowledge that it could land a blow, and as things stood get away with it.

But Gunther suspected that there was more to it, than that.
"We have been fighting their proxies for decades, here, in Abyssinia, and in Georgia, and they have never seen the need to declare war on us."
"They have never dared" General Smith added fiercely, "The war would be long and bloody, but we would destroy them"
"We could hardly conquer them" Samuel Guy protested.
"Their defeat would have destroyed their power" the general told him, modifying his tone as he reminded himself whom he was speaking to.
"And now they do not fear defeat?" asked the octogenarian.

"Fear or belief?", Luisa Maria Valdez asked, looking up from her perusal of the damage reports upon the city; in many ways they had been lucky, but it was clearly not intended to be a decisive strike rather a statement of intent...but what intent?
"They believe it is not possible to lose?" General Smith looked at his aide, "Is that what you mean?"
"I would think it would be a prerequisite to attack, sir"
"I see what you mean"

Gunther looked from one to the other,
"Why would they believe that?" he asked.

Chapter Thirteen

If Albion City was, in common parlance, the "City of a Hundred Spires", then London was the City of a Single Spire, that of Saint George's Cathedral, reaching up high into the sky like a beacon for an incoming airship. In fact, city ordinances required that no building be constructed within 300 feet of the cathedral's height. London was not to be drowned in the modern; it was to remain a monument to the old. That was how it retained its pride in the world it found itself in.

Dionysus Rothgar Excelsior walked out of the reception building of Barnes Airfield alone, carrying a case in his hand, and a bag over his back. Whilst travelling from Albion aboard one of the fully-militarised airships, he had been secure, and whilst passing through the terminal he knew that Elite Guards, with direct orders from the Emperor, were keeping an eye on him.

Now, stepping forth onto the paved way, and walking up towards the elevated railway, he was on his own. To be honest it was a relief; ever since the rather anti-climactic rescue from the Yukon, when five military airships had flown in and met no lights at all, he had been surrounded by people. Only when secluded with the Grand Master of the Order of the Unicorn had he known a moment's respite, and there too had he seen what must be done. He carried letters from the Grand Master to the Arch Master of London's Arch Temple, and to the High Acolytes of Britannia's other High Temples. He would see them in time; first he had to get into London itself.

The station was clean, all chrome and glass, newly reconstructed as part of the Imperial Airship Service's centennial the year previous. Although it was crowded, the crowds were good-natured, waiting in lines rather than pushing to the front, and Dionysus had no problem slipping right in amongst them. He could have ordered up a limousine from London, or even an armoured wagon if he had been so minded, but the Grand Master had been clear - lose yourself, he had said, and so Dionysus was losing himself.

Once seated aboard one of the four cars of the train, he removed his black leather overcoat, and his gloves and stowed them inside his bag, instead replacing them with a woolen jacket, and a cap. He pulled off his boots, black leather also, and replaced them with a beaten-up pair of dusty brown ones he had bought in a second-hand shop back in Albion City. Finally, he emptied out the contents of his case into a smaller bag which he removed from the larger one, then placed the case, now empty, on the floor beside him. That would be something to conveniently forget in the rush to leave.

A few people watched him, but none showed much interest. To them it was just the actions of a man who had been on show, reverting to his normal persona upon returning home. Such were common within Britannia, within London especially, people who had to seem to be other when they journeyed to other Realms of the Empire, but when they came back to the Homeland, they were glad to shake off the pretense, and put on once again that which made them British. Dionysus was just doing it in reverse, but nobody was paying enough attention to understand that.

The train clattered above parkland, country palaces in the distance, soon giving way to mansion houses, and then to salubrious suburbs as they approached London itself. Snaking in from the South-West, they passed through an increasingly industrial heartland, before crossing the Thames and arriving at Charing Cross, one of the three main railway stations serving London.

Dionysus made sure that he was up and into the first rush for the doors, all the more easier to conveniently forget his case. Shouldering one bag, and with the other gripped tightly in his hand, he rode the flow, out through the concourse and into the courtyard beyond. Steam taxi cabs competed for traffic with horse-drawn carriages, the latter for the romantics and the tourists, and sometimes for those who did not mind paying more if it meant they did not have to queue.

However, he chose the third option and began to walk, passing swiftly across a wide thoroughfare and into St Martin's Square. There he dodged hawkers and whores, and headed up a broad tree-lined avenue, North towards the Arch Temple of the Unicorn which lay at the juncture of Oxford Street and Aldgate Way. It was a bit of a slog in the sunshine, but Dionysus enjoyed looking through the trees to the establishments set a dozen or so yards beyond. There were inns and coffee houses, bookshops and emporia, the latter with goods from China or India, Patagonia or Australia, from all across the Empire in fact.

He smiled at posters advertising the plays and shows to be seen in the many theatres and show-houses upon Aldgate Way, and took especial notice of the smaller flyers posted to trees, lamp-posts and even to the side of the ornate ironwork of the green-painted benches. Dominion Viceroy - as the British called him - Hercules Troubadour Rannoch would be giving a speech live at the Palais Aquitaine two days hence, and all True Britons were encouraged to be there. Dionysus laughed inside at their conceit; Rannoch was by rank but a High Provincial Governor, Britannia ranking on the same level as Shantung, or indeed of Kamchatka, an autonomous High Province that existed yet within another Realm. But the British were proud of their lost heritage, and pretended yet to a status that did not exist. As for 'all true Britons' one could only guess what that nonsense would be all about.

It was true of course that there *was* something unique about Britannia's position. If he had wanted to see the Realm Viceroy, he would have had to fly to Bordeaux, where the Viceregal government had relocated in the last century after the Europan conquest of Paris. But Bordeaux was a city that at best equalled London, and in some ways was outdone by it, and the remnant French provinces were as a crust left once someone has carved out the heart. But Bordeaux administered from Iceland to Iberia, even though the Viceroy in modern times had not dared to command his deputy in London, only to suggest. So far there had been no great clash of wills, but that was mainly because of the non-entities sent to Bordeaux, administrators who were under the thumb of the Marshals responsible for maintaining the French frontier, men who had no time for the greater scope of European politics.

Dionysus shook his head, and emerged into Central Square. To the West the broad leafy road of Oxford Street stretched, whilst to the South-East, Aldgate Way ran back towards the river. Straight ahead of him, on the Northern edge of the square, was the Arch Temple of the Unicorn, set in luscious grounds, and with a series of domes replacing the spires that in other cities would have thrust high into the sky.

There were only a dozen Arch Temples within the Empire, each with between five and twenty High Temples under their control; beneath those, of course, were the lesser temples, often several within a major city, much sparser out in the provinces. London's Arch Temple boasted of being one of the oldest such institutions, though its actual buildings were less than one hundred and fifty years old.

Dionysus paused only to drop the letter he carried into the ornate brass postal box by the open gates, then he turned and made his way along Strange Avenue, heading due East along a roadway elevated some thirty foot from the ground below as it demarcated one of the mainly hidden contours of the city. The hotel where a reservation had been made in his name was at the far end, its portico rising from the roadway, three floors falling below this, down to the streets at the base. Traffic was light, but he knew that city ordinances prevented deliveries and through traffic during the day - the Grand Master of the Unicorn had been most insistent that he learn such things by heart.

There were no steps to climb, and he walked between a pair of impassive silver-coated doormen, up to the carved oak reception desk. Their job was not to keep people out - if anybody needing throwing out, there were bondsmen inside to do that. British nobility could be hard to spot by eye - some had great rank, but straightened circumstances, others just dressed in a fashion that the enlightened of Albion City would have thought of as below their status.

"Joshua Janus Capell", he spoke his identity to the receptionist, a blond woman of indeterminate middle age whose hair colour no doubt came out of a bottle. His name had been chosen for him, the Capells being a once-great noble family long since fallen on hard times, but a name that would still have some distinction attached to it.
"Room Ten", the woman palmed a key seemingly out of midair; it was big and heavy and of the finest steel, "For your comfort we suggest you hand the key in each time you leave"
He took it and tested its weight, nodding
"I think I will do that"
"Its straight ahead at the far end, you have a room overlooking

Captain's Gardens"

He nodded and moved off through a set of double-doors, shooing away two slaves who approached in the hope of carrying his bags. It was not a long corridor, and the room at the far end was indeed well-described, the door facing towards him as he approached. He opened it, stepped through and locked it behind him, sliding home the top and bottom bolts for good measure. A quick stride to the window showed that did indeed have a fabulous view. From three storeys up, he could see the entire length of Captain's Gardens, a large privately-built park that had long-since been purchased by the city authorities.

Drawing the curtains he took off his clothes and lay down on the bed. Five minutes later, he was asleep...

~

If there had been a throne in London, then Sarah Alexandria Dunelm would have been the power behind it. As it was, there was only a carved oak council chair, and she did not relish trying out the phrase 'The Power behind the oaken chair'. It was bad enough that her nickname from school had been Sad!

"Do you think this is a good report?" she tightened her vice-like grip on the man's genitals and he proceeded to squirm, squeal and swear, and other things beginning with 's' too, as evidenced by the sheen upon his face and the foul smell rising up from below.

"Filth!", she released him and turned away, pivoting to come back with a kick to his head that sent him sprawling.
Two slaves, lash marks fresh upon their naked backs, stepped forward.
"Take him away - and get rid of him properly"
They did not need to hear 'or else' for they had experienced it that day already. As the prone agent was dragged away, leaving an unpleasant odour, and a brown trail on the floor behind him, she sighed and walked across to the cabinet against the far wall.

The room was spartan; the cabinet, a chair, and a table set with unfortunate devices, being the only furniture within it. The walls were grey, the floor concrete, and light came solely from four old gaslights set centrally in each of the walls. There were two doors - both now at the opposite end from where she stood. One was the door the agent had been dragged out of, leading to the lower levels, and eventually to a drop-hole into the Thames below. The other was the door he had entered from, at the base of an ornate staircase that led up, through a mid-level doorway, to one of the many corridors in the palace above.

Sarah opened a cupboard set within the cabinet and withdrew a bottle of finest Azteca Spirit, dead worm floating happily at the bottom - she assumed it was a happy spirit, drowned in the alcohol of cacti. Pouring a strong measure into a mug, she downed the lot, then replenished it, sipping at this one.

Oh, what weak fools were men! The agent should have been ruthless, killed when he was in danger of being caught, but instead he had slunk away, hoping to return to his target, but never getting there, and then coming here, all downcast to report a failure. What did she want to know about failure! He had tried to spice it up by entering observations, a few of which would prove useful, but the majority of which were already known to her - how else had she decided on the target but from information she already had? He was a waste of space, hopefully by now an ex waste-of-space, on his way to becoming fish food.

She had already decided that she would have to do this herself. Hercules Troubadour Rannoch would not like it, but Rannoch often decided not to know about things he would not like, especially where she was concerned. It was easier for him that way, and freed up his mind to concentrate upon government, and upholding the laws of the 'dominion', laws that she was constantly and unfailingly breaking in his name.

"Bah!" she swallowed the last of the Azteca Spirit, and threw the glass against one of the walls. One of the slaves would clean that up - or they would fail to, and she would enjoy applying the lash again.
She headed over to the stairway, mounted halfway, then used a series of keys upon her belt to unlock the several locks on the heavy iron door halfway up. Passing through she swung it shut behind her, and

locked them all again. Unless one exited via the drop-hole into the river, one had to come this way. Her basement was a sealed unit.

In the corridor she paused to lean against the wall, focusing her mind, as well as channelling the alcohol to where it would be most useful, an old whore's trick that an old whore had indeed told her. Lifting up her dress, she urinated upon the carpet, then with her mind in equilibrium, she headed down a side-turning towards where she knew the Viceroy would be.

He was, of course, sitting in a small hall, at the end of a twelve-person table, with a fire burning in the grate since this room, deep within the palace complex here at Whitehall, had no windows, only a couple of skylights, usually filthy and incapable of letting in light. Instead a couple of gas-lamps on the wall did the job, showing Rannoch sat with the usual jug of ale before him, two of his drinking companions beside him, laughing at his jokes, or more probably so inebriated they were laughing anyway, regardless of whether they were funny or not.

Sarah gave them no more attention; had they been anyone of note, they would not be behaving like this, it was obvious. She moved to stand directly alongside the Viceroy, and placed her hand in his lap,
"Would you like me to take care of your cock?" she asked.
He rose, and then frowned
"As long as you mean this", he indicated his tent, "And not the animal you did it with last time"
"That was a joke, and you laughed hard" she reminded him of her little game.
"Oh, I did, good", his mind was clearly befuddled as usual when he was not working.
He unbuttoned himself,
"Please take care of it"
She did.

~

"Thank you", Dionysus handed in his key as he exited the hotel, the woman behind the desk this morning not a false blond, but someone of at least half-Indian extraction judging by her colouring. London was

178

like that, though, he remembered; the descendants of the many concubines taken by employees of the India Companies still occupied a high social rank, whereas in Albion they would have to start again from the bottom.

He strolled forth onto the bridge-like road, noting with annoyance that the warm weather of the previous day had given over to wind and drizzle. London was like that, he also remembered from his briefing with the Grand Master. he paid scant attention to the shops, inns and emporia that plyed their wares upon the raised roadway, and headed with a purpose back towards Central Square. The rain was coming down harder now, and people were raising strange little fabric platforms above their heads, bumping into each other, and threatening to decapitate him, it seemed.

He walked in the roadway, the dearth of day-time traffic making it far safer than it would have been back home in Albion City, and entered Central Square to find a giant armoured battle-wagon parked in the centre. For a moment he thought it was aimed at the Arch Temple itself, but after a minute's damp observation he realised that this was some kind of mobile recruiting station, the flanks of the vehicle plastered with posters, now sagging in the rain, and the soldiers at the front handing out pamphlets to an increasingly dwindling crowd.
"Interesting" Dionysus said to himself, and walked behind the leviathan, and through the gates into the Arch Temple

The foregrounds were open to anyone, and the Order did not attempt to impose any barriers to whom could enter. Should untoward behaviour occur, a couple of Acolytes would escort the guilty out, or in the case of recalcitrants employ their lightning staffs to encourage departure.
Dionysus smiled at a young woman breast-feeding a baby in the shelter of an oak tree, and at an old man sitting smoking an ancient pipe out in the open upon a bench, presumably not caring about the rain, though that probably depended on what was inside the pipe.

He passed through a small second gate and up some steps to a recessed doorway where he pulled hard on a brass bell-pull. Inside, a bell sounded

"That works", he nodded to himself, impressed at the detail of his briefing.

It was exactly two minutes later - again, as per his briefing - that the door was opened, and a wizened ancient looked out at him

"May I help you sir? Do you require instruction?"

They were separate questions, the first offering a direct reply to a direct need, the second enquiring whether the larger services of the Temple were being looked for.

"Yet the Lord testified against Israel, and against Judah, by all the prophets and by all the seers, saying, Turn ye from your evil ways and keep my commandments and my statutes, according to all the law which I commanded your fathers and which I sent to you by my servants the prophets"

The wizened one blinked

"The Arch Master will see you now, sir"

Dionysus followed him in, and the door seemed to close behind them of its own accord - again, in line with how he had been instructed.

The interior was fresh and cool, lit from every direction by a clever positioning of windows and skylights, and giving the impression of being even more vast than it was. They ascended a flight of marble steps, and walked along a rooftop passage, roofed but open to the elements, before passing through another door, and along an internal corridor to a doorway guarded by two men. These were clearly very serious in their endeavours, dressed in black leather, with knives and staffs upon their belts, and sub-machine guns cradled in their arms.

"High Acolyte Philippus Andreas Bosch to see the Arch Master" he said to the men, who must have known who he was by now.

"You may enter", the guard stressed the first syllable, "He may not"

"I am..." Dionysus began but was warned off by a gun barrel to his throat

"I will converse with the Arch Master", Philippus assured him, and passed on in, leaving Dionysus staring at the impassive faces of the guards. *This* had not been in the briefing from the Grand Master.

~

Sarah could knock back shots of Azteca Spirit like there was no

180

tomorrow. Used to drinking it in vastly greater quantities, and still retaining her faculties, she despised those who could only take it in small measures, but loved them for how easy it was to get them where she wanted them.

"This damned rain", the soldier was in his late twenties and pronounced the middle word damn-ned, indicating an education in one of the Northern boarding schools.

"You enjoy handing out pamphlets to the weak and cowardly?" she squeezed him intimately below the table.

"As God is my witness, no", he shook his head, and blinked in an attempt to clear the fog, "But some of them are just misguided, having taken false instruction. We can..." his mind swam, "Er...we can re...un-misguide them", he smiled triumphantly, and she poured another measure into their glasses.

"What time do you have to be back at the base?", she knew precisely where the armoured battle-wagon had come from, having seen the order sitting on Rannoch's desk two days ago

"Dusk", he shrugged, and belched, "Oops, yeah we have some hours"

"Unless it stops raining"

He peered out vaguely at the torrential downpour bouncing off the ground,

"Not anytime soon"

"But what if it does and you are not there?"

He paused with the glass halfway to his mouth and struggled to get his mind around that one,

"I bet I would not be the only one" he said.

She laughed,

"They do rooms by the hour here" she told him.

The Falcon Inn was a respectable establishment on the South-Western corner of Central Square, its downstairs an inn, its first floor an exclusive restaurant, and its second floor accommodation for rent as the customer required. The barmaid looked at Sarah and smiled conspiratorially, recognising a fellow predator, if not precisely who she was.

"Two hours - fifty crowns"

"He is paying", she placed the soldier's purse upon the bartop and the barmaid withdrew six twenty-crown coins

"Paid" she grinned.

"Up", the man said, leaning on her, "I need to get it up"

"Yes you do", Sarah was determined not to be disappointed in that area, despite the far more important things she had to do with the man.

- - -

"Blond, blue-eyed, mid-twenties, can't count", Sarah hissed at the idiot barman who had replaced the woman she was looking for

"Oh, you mean Leona - she *can* count, she just prefers not to"

"That would be her", Sarah put steel into her voice, "Fetch her now"

"Not without payment", the barman knew what would lie in store, and demanded recompense for it.

"Twenty now", Sarah flipped him a coin, "Twenty if you are back with her in five minutes"

"Right!", he ran off.

It was four minutes when he returned with her, the half-naked Leona still struggling to fasten her blouse around her, to the whistled delight of the drinkers nearby

"There", Sarah flipped the barman the promised coin, "This didn't happen"

"Er...right...no" he went off to serve a long-suffering customer whose glass had remained empty for far too long.

"What do you want?" Leona had finally managed to tidy herself up and was looking at her in some annoyance. No doubt already paid, it would be her professional pride which had been hurt.

"Read this", Sarah passed her a thin sheet of brass, embossed and stamped, with enamelled information on the other side.

Leona read it, turned it over, read it again, and set it down heavily before her

"Fuck" she said.

"You will do as I say?"

"I quite like my breasts", the barmaid pointed out.

"Good - remove the body in Room 20, and make sure nobody knows it was ever there"

"Oh Hell...why?", she shook her head, "I mean why did you?"

182

"Matters of state, that is all you need to know"

"But if he doesn't report back, and his body is never found, he'll be listed as a deserter" Leona hissed.

"Is that my problem?"

"This isn't the first time he's done promotional duty outside, I've spoken to him - he has a wife and six children!"

"How sad for them"

"If he's listed as a deserter, they'll be sold into slavery!" she snapped.

"If you refuse to do as I say, I will have you arrested for treason, and *your* family will be sold into slavery", Sarah promised.

"Shit", she ran a hand through her hair, "I'll do it"

Sarah smiled, and watched her go, then headed out into the pouring rain. Only one man was standing by the armoured battle-wagon trying to shelter beneath its gigantic gun, but rain seldom did one the honour of coming straight down, and he was getting just as wet as if he had rolled in the puddles now developing all around.

She gave him a wide berth, passing round to the rear of the vehicle, and located the compartment that her recent lover had told her about before he died.

~

"Lord Homer Johannes Schenk", the Arch Master introduced the man who stood to his side, slightly in shadow within the dimly-lit room, "His brother was Governor of New Lisbon"

"Ah, my lord", Dionysus used the courteous form, not as an inferior or as an equal, but in respect for his loss, "You have my sympathies"

"Thank you", Homer looked back towards the Arch Master who smiled and gestured towards a triangle of sofas set in the middle of the room where the light did meet, that from the sole window blending with that from the sole skylight to produce a cube of luminescence seemingly alien to the rest of the room.

Dionysus had been made to wait over an hour, and had ended up sitting on the floor outside, his back up against the wall, running over in his head the instructions and teachings of the Grand Master back in Albion City. Nothing that had been said had prepared for his, but had he not been instructed, he would not have been surprised at being kept waiting, just perhaps at the length of time of the delay. He had composed his mind back into a happy state by the time that the High Acolyte had opened the door from within and beckoned him forth, the guards this time being perfectly happy for him to pass between them.

"It is time that we dwelt on higher things" the Arch Master said.
Aged seventy, he looked younger, a healthy diet and regular exercise staving off the rigours of time. Born to an impoverished Irish family, Seamus Agamemnon Cowan had seen the Order as the only way out of the depredations of his upbringing and had dedicated his life to it. Having served in temples as far away as Kamchatka and Australia, he had also done Pioneer Work in Borneo, in Ceylon, and in Tibet, which is where he had come upon the knowledge that was at the heart of this meeting.

"Lord Homer is here at the express wish of the Great Chamberlain", the Arch Master added, in case Dionysus was wondering at his clearance, which indeed he had been
"Good, please go on"
There was no doubt that the Arch Master would know what subject matter was at the heart of this meeting, and the seventy year-old needed no additional cue to break right into it,
"It is true", he said, "Whilst in Tibet I saw one with my own eyes, frozen in ice, but a light none-the-less"
"It was known to the locals?" asked Dionysus.
"To the monks", the Arch Master nodded, "They worshipped it as some sort of representation of the Divine"
"Did they ever attempt to release it?", Dionysus pressed.

There was a moment of silence, then Homer gave the answer,
"I was there two years ago", he said quietly, "attached to the Imperial Military Mission out of Yunnan. Our remit was to ensure that Tibet remained on the right side of the Great Alignment within China, and to that end we came with armoured wagons, Scavengers and ... Special Units", he coughed.
"You saw it?" Dionysus knew all about the expedition and its success, and wanted the man to cut to the chase.
"I was amongst a party chosen to accompany Elite Marshal Phoebus

184

McLaren on a tour of the monasteries in the centre of the country; it was Lhasa's way of showing us friendship, but they did not mean for us to go where we did."
"How do you mean?" asked Dionysus.

"We were at a monastery down in one of the valleys, bored out of our minds by that time with the ringing of bells, and the chanting of chants, when one of our young bucks came back."
"Young bucks?" Dionysus pressed.
"He had been seeing one of the monks in a way I am sure the lamas would not have been happy with, and told us that there was *another* monastery in the heights beyond, not on our maps, and not mentioned to us by our hosts"
"Amazing how a cock in the ass loosens the tongue", Dionysus snorted.
"No outsider had ever been there since the party of which the Arch Master was a member", Homer went on, "The Dalai Lama had declared it to be off-limits after that, and its existence had been expunged from the records. If it truly was a representation of the Divine, they did not want outsiders seizing upon it, and taking it from out of their hands"
"Sensible, considering" Dionysus said.

Too many native peoples had tried to buy off the global powers by showing them their treasures and hoping they would be impressed; instead they had invited in rapacious hordes and gone down in flames, whilst the global powers had fought over the spoils in bloody war. Tibet had retained its independence by playing the game of the Great Alignment, but its position could be undone by a global power deciding that it was worth the blood, the money and the effort to conquer her. Lhasa had come to the decision that the best way to keep the wolves at bay was to hide any evidence that they had anything that the global powers wanted.

"The Elite Marshal had to go back to Lhasa, and left the expedition in the hands of Battle Captain Joseph Creary, and myself, with five troopers to accompany us. I do not believe he placed much faith in the tale, but he required it checked out."
"Your report?" Dionysus looked at the Arch Master, "It was not known

to the Elite Marshal?"

"Hardly", the old man coughed, "It was a report made within the Order, and which rested on the desk of the Grand Master. What he chose to do with it is not my concern."

"But now..." began Dionysus.

"Now you are here, and it is clear that the Grand Master has released the report to the Imperial Court. It was always his decision."

"I understand", Dionysus bowed his head, "Go on"

Lord Homer Schenk nodded,

"We killed the monks of course - they were insistent that we should only look, but that was not our remit"

"How many monks?"

"Up there, about twenty"

"In your time, sir?" Dionysus asked the Arch Master.

"Perhaps thirty, but it was a hard place"

"I see. What happened then?", he addressed Schenk.

"Captain Creary was determined to release the thing and take it back to Yunnan. It would have made his name, and earned him upwards of a hundred thousand crowns in prize money"

"Since I never read about any of this in the newspapers, or in the confidential reports, I assume that something went wrong?"

"Very", Homer ran a hand across his brow, "We detonated the charges and the light broke free...I was the cameraman, in a hide so as to get the best footage...I did *that!*", he said, shuddering.

"It attacked?"

"In the course of a minute everyone else was dead, and it did not go...I was in that hide for forty-eight hours, then I could take no more and I ran..."

"It was gone?"

"My mind was gone", Homer was unapologetic about that, "I have no recollection of how I got back to Lhasa, but I remember walking in through the gate and seeking out the Elite Marshal who was about to depart the next day."

"You made a full report?" Dionysus asked.

Homer met his eyes,

"No" he said, "I said that the monks had attacked us, and in the battle I

186

was the only survivor...and that when I went out looking for the light, there had been nothing there"

"And?" Dionysus knew that there was more.

"It was a lot to live with... When we got back to Yunnan, I put in a request for furlough and was granted it. Back here in London I sought my cousin out and he told me to report it to the Order"

"Who and why?" Dionysus was not judging, just in need of information.

"Because my cousin stands high with the Order as the senior dynast within the Schenk lineage"

"Who?" pressed Dionysus, feeling that if he were more familiar with Britannia, he would probably already have known this

"Count Roger Alejandro Schenk" Homer said quietly, "And if you are going to ask where he is, he headed out for Timbuktu a week ago"

"Why?"

"You are asking *me*?"

For a moment, Dionysus did not understand, wondering whether it was information he himself was supposed to have, then he realised that the fellow's tone was implicatory of another.

"Why?" he asked the Arch Master.

"Some things are outside of your remit", the seventy year old rose and headed over to a darkened corner, from where he removed a slim file from a shelf, "*This* is your remit"

Dionysus rose and took it, walking back into the light to properly see, "Photographs from both expeditions?" he asked.

"Those from the second are stills extracted from the reel of film that Lord Homer brought back with him"

"And the earlier shots - you took these?"

"Myself, or one of the monks under my instruction" the Arch Master confirmed.

"Two years ago...", Dionysus leant against the back of one of the sofas, "We knew about the lights two years ago..."

"No", the Arch Master was back beside him, "We knew about *a* light that had subsequently disappeared"

"But still", Dionysus began, and then the world blew up.

~

Sarah had chosen her hiding place well, and when the armoured battle-wagon exploded from a ruptured fuel line, she had been sheltered from the force of the blast. As it had dissipated, she had run into the aftermath of the storm, and attained her objective even before everybody else had managed to pick themselves up from off the ground.

Running between the gates, now hanging crazily from the gateposts, she passed where a young woman lay impaled by a branch, a mewling infant dusty and bruised upon the floor beside her. Smiling, Sarah ran on, leaping over a couple of old men who lay in grotesque pose, a pipe rammed down the throat of one, an upturned bench having smashed the skull of the other.

She passed through the second gate, ignored the heavy door which had buckled but not swung open and circled round the temple, passing a couple of shattered windows before she found one that she liked the look of. Heaving herself over the sill, she found herself in a laundry, naked female slaves just stirring as they recovered from the shock. Killing half a dozen with her dagger as she passed, she exited into a service corridor and ran down its length towards the service elevator at the far end.

People were beginning to move, and she could hear voices milling around from all directions. Crouching inside the small square space, she depressed the button, and shot her hand back in before it was sliced off by the sharp upwards movement. A half minute later the elevator shuddered to a halt, and the door slid open. Sarah rolled out, cut the throat of a young man who was crouching on the floor, staring at her in amazement, and ran on deeper into the complex

~

"What..." Homer struggled to his feet, "What...?" he muttered.
Dionysus was still on his hands and knees and crawled towards the outer door, but it was locked.
"Urghhhh..." said the Arch Master, thrown against the wall, and

188

bleeding heavily from the mouth.

"Ahhh..." Homer gripped the sofa and looked around, through the dust, into the gloom. The lamps had gone out, and even the skylights seemed somehow fogged, unable to pass as much light through as they had done previously.

"Help!" Dionysus, banged on the doors with his fists, but there was no response.

"Oo..." Homer looked over to him, "The....the...secret door" he said

"What?" Dionysus had raised himself up to rest upon his knees, "The what?"

"Uh..." the Arch Master made his last sound upon this world.

Two minutes later, Dionysus and Homer were tearing at the panelling behind a curtain, the one fogged in mind but determined in purpose, the other wondering where the controlling lever had got to.

"Its a secret door" Dionysus panted, "Probably the controls are secret too"

He had his breath back by now, and was focused solely on getting out of this room

"But I saw them" Homer protested, "When the Arch Master let....out"

"Let what out?"

"Um...I am not allowed to say"

"Oh", snapped Dionysus, "I see"

And he did see - the delay had been because the Arch Master, with the Schenk dynast in company, had been seeing somebody before him, somebody who did not want to be there when he himself was admitted to the chamber.

The door swang open. A Hellcat rushed in, stabbing Homer a dozen times in the breast, whilst Dionysus lunged past and careened off the wall, before finding his footing and tearing off down the secret passageway. A moment later he heard footsteps behind him - whoever she was, she was after him. He ran on faster...

Chapter Fourteen

"Where are we?"

It had been a long journey, first from the Yukon aboard one of the five military airships which had rescued them, to Navaho City, and then on to the coast at Port William. From there she had transferred to one of the airships of the Great Southern Company upon which they had flown far to the East, avoiding both the Incas and High Brasil, to attain Patagonia from a direct Easterly direction.

Overflying the coastal plain, they had come to here, high in the mountains, where a team of diminutive slaves was now drawing in the lines, and bringing the airship to a safe landing upon the glacier.

"Fort Fluffy" Grand Captain Gerald Blakeney said, adding "They mis-spelt a native word...I forget what it was"

"Fluffy", Ramona Elise Carding nodded, "Good..."

"Our orders are to land you and your cousin here."

"Yes", Ramona bit down on her lip, having hoped that somewhere along the way she would have managed to shake off the Eyes of the Great Chamberlain, but it appeared that the bitch was along for the ride, in its entirety.

"I will ensure she is deployed upon the ice in proper fashion"

"Deploy her upside down for all I care!" snapped Ramona, departing from the bridge.

Tabitha Clarissa Theresa had other ideas about that, and walked sedately out of the airship, a pair of stalwart troopers carrying her bags until she was firmly upon the icefield.

"Hmmm.." she said, "Fluffy?"

"An unfortunate mis-spelling, highness", the taller of the troopers had done her good service on the journey.

"It is just as well", she looked around them, "A proper description of this place, and nobody at all would come"

"That is truly a good point, highness", the shorter fellow had not had the pleasures his companion had, but wished not to seem to upset by it.

"Our breath is almost freezing here," she told him, "I think perhaps the other would"

"Come on" the taller trooper slapped his comrade on the back, "Good

190

luck, Highness!"

From one God-forsaken hole to the next! Tabitha Clarissa Theresa was not happy. It was all very well being the Eyes of the Great Chamberlain, but he appeared to want to look into places that no sane person would ever go. From the Yukon she was now transported to the heights of the Patagonian Mountains. Nobody came here - nobody apart from Fort Fluffy's denizens, and half of those were probably mad.

"Swift Commander Terrance De L'isle"
he introduced himself to them, a pair of junior officers to his rear
"Swift Commander?" Ramona looked around at the bleakness all about, "Surely we do not have an Imperial Airforce base up here..."
"Not a base" he agreed, "I have a single Webmaster, complete with skis if you recall the design"
"I recall the design", Tabitha snapped, "It is why it has the name, after all"
"Yes, highness"
Like a duck.

They moved in his wake, across the ice-field, the two juniors ignoring them, not even offering a hand on the more difficult sections. Ramona watched them with interest. Tabitha vowed to kill them as soon as it was politic to do so.

"In here", Terrance indicated a small doorway set into the rockface, "That is unless you fancy a climb up that?"
He indicated the cliff above them, upon which a path could be seen carved into the side for some of its length.
"Is that a path?" Ramona asked out of interest.
One of the junior officers chose to answer her.
"It was", he said, "Fifty years ago - now it is the remains of a path. We send young bucks up there to learn that they do not own this landscape"
"We will go via this doorway, thank you" Tabitha snapped.
"Of course", Terrance held it open for them.

~

"Port William?", Arthur Spinks knew that he was a long way behind the chase, but he was all that they had.

"These prove it", the man was in his forties, fat and with a drinking problem, hence his willingness to deal, and to sell the boarding cards to the Order.

"Pay him" the Dragomaster said.

Leopold Hubertus Scheer handed over a purse of coins.

"Good. Good", only now was James Calhoun beginning to believe he had made the right choice.

He took the coins and left. Scheer looked to the Dragomaster who shook his head,

"We are not strong enough, and, besides, his urges *are* strong enough that he will not give away the goose of gold"

"These are genuine?" Scheer handed over the documents.

Spinks needed only to give them a cursory glance before he nodded, "Very"

"So..." Scheer was only an Acolyte, albeit one of long-standing within Navaho City, "Do we know more?"

"More and yet less" Spinks said.

"How is that so?"

The Dragomaster considered his answer. Navaho City was a relatively open place, dominated by none of the services, nor any of the Orders, but its very openness meant that vehicles, vessels and people passed in and out at a regularity that was hard to put a finger on. They had struck lucky with Calhoun, reckoning that if an airship had brought someone in, another airship would be taking them out, but he was only a small step along a greater process, he knew only from B to C, but it was obvious that their prey would no longer be at Port William, it was only a stone upon which they had already stepped.

"Take him out in a week or so", Spinks resumed the role of his rank, "What we really need is the manifest of all airship services out of Port William in the last week"

"Is that available anywhere but there?" the Acolyte asked.

"It has to be filed", Spinks knew that for sure, "But would be in a secure code"

"What about Cyclops?" Scheer was uncertain whether to voice the thought, but had run out of alternatives.

"Cyclops.." Spinks rubbed at the unshaven stubble upon his chin, "Perhaps I should pay a visit to the local station"
"It is the relay for Port William", Scheer pointed out.
"Then I certainly will" Spinks affirmed.

- - -

"This is highly unusual", Roberta Henrietta Gilbert only sounded defiant; inside she was rejoicing as it seemed that pay-day had finally come, "But perhaps we could give you a limited tour"
"Thank you", Spinks stepped through the doorway before she could move aside, and held the door open for Scheer to join him
"We are a poor establishment" Roberta smiled, her shiny teeth blending in well with the sheen of her bald pate.
"Then, thank you Lord Guardian for admitting us"
"This way" Roberta led them to a private room.

Twenty minutes later they were substantially lighter in their money belts, and she wore a brighter smile upon her face,
"Here is where the Rods input the feed" she gestured down below to where a handful of the strange eunuchs sat in commune with their stations.
"So the feeds come in from places around here?" Speer asked, playing the role that his superior had decided for him.
"Of course", she pointed to a black-skinned individual, "He is passing on the feed from Apache City."
"What about Port William?", Spinks hoped that now would seem a natural place to position the question.
"Oh, that is largely automated" Roberta shrugged, "But some feeds come in straight to Gold"
"Gold?" the Dragomaster asked.
"Come this way"

Gold proved to mean a dingy office smelling of sweaty female feet and sour milk. But it had a console, and a ticker-tape spooler, and Roberta sat down on the single stool as if she owned the place - which she did.

"If it is marked Urgent, the system spits it out here.", she gestured around her, "It requires a Lord Guardian to make the decision"

"What decision?" Spinks asked looked around him with a wrinkled nose.

"Why, whether to pass it along its original line alone, or to duplicate the input into other lines"

"What do you mean?" Scheer stood on the edge of the room, breathing in the pleasant dampness of the corridor outside.

"Something might come in on a single line, requiring relay to a single line. Cyclops cannot evaluate whether it has significance that should be fed in to other Rods in Albion City. It requires humans to make that decision"

"And you do?" Spinks asked, zoning his nose out.

"Port William, right?" Roberta brought up a series of flashing inputs, "Now, if I choose to isolate one of these, its feed would be displayed here alone"

"Can you choose one?" Spinks asked.

She was about to protest that none of the feeds had anywhere near that kind of importance, but then realised that in her position she could always get away with running a test run, and flicked a switch. Two minutes later the ticker-tape spewed out.

"Grand Pacific Railways report an increase in Chinese agitation on their Northern coastal line", Spinks read it with some surprise.

"If this was of wider import I would duplicate the pass-through" she said, then grinned, "If we were at war with China..."

"If such a thing were possible" Scheer breathed.

"...then I could send duplicates of this to the Rods dealing with grand strategy, the Imperial Fleet, and so on"

"And if you did not?"

"Then their input would be false, corrected only when the original feed hit the system and propagated"

"In what timescale?" Scheer pressed.

"An hour perhaps - enough to want to get it right beforehand!"

Spinks was impressed, but not happy.

"Is there a record of this?" he asked.

"The tape is stored in the vault" Roberta allowed, "We cannot of course store the impulses"

194

"Perhaps one day we can", Henry James Jones walked into the room and looked from his fellow Lord Guardian to the two interlopers, "You are not from the Order of the Unicorn", he said.

Roberta had frozen in horror, her private enterprise undone by the arrival of her colleague, but Spinks narrowed his eyes and nodded, "Dragon" he said, and waited.

"Good enough", Jones sat in the chair that Roberta had rapidly evacuated, "What are you interested in?"

"An airship passed through here enroute to Port William", Spinks said, "We need to know where it went from there"

"One moment", he picked up the telephone, "Canticle" he said to the operator, then a moment later, "Jules, its me, Hen"

The conversation could only be heard one way but Spinks heard the man ask for and apparently receive the information he needed.

"The *Auroch*" Jones said.

"That is a military vessel", Spinks agreed, "Where has it gone?"

"Five hundred crowns" the Lord Guardian said.

"Very well"

"And a contract"

"I see"

Anyone with a contract was not exterminable; he or she had to be used in future, that was how the system worked, even if venal bastards would play it for their own gain.

"It is a good deal" Jones insisted.

Scheer looked at Roberta, prone against the wall, regarding the proceedings in shock.

"What about her?"

"Oh yes", Jones drew a dagger and cut her throat, "Happy?" he asked.

"Fuck", Scheer lunged into the corridor.

"Happy" agreed Spinks looking the Lord Guardian up and down, "Five hundred crowns"

"Good", Jones sat back upon the stool, "The *Auroch* went to Patagonia"

"*Where* in Patagonia?" demanded the Dragomaster.

"Fort Fluffy", Jones replied..

~

The train rattled across the Southern provinces, crossing over giant spans of bridges as it moved through the floodlands, and entered the South-West. Small settlements fell by the wayside, and the train stopped less and less, the most recent of which was at the small city of Saint Richard's. Nobody had got off the Azteca Express, and only a couple of people had got on, merchants heading for the Southern border, and a naval officer, fresh off his patrol ship and heading home to see his family in Yucatan.

Harold Swan Buckmeister lay back upon the bench-seat and eyed the container that the gorgeous woman he had spent two very lazy days chatting up, had left behind. It was a steel cylinder, about a foot high, and from this angle he could see that its bottom flanges were crenulated, and that there appeared to be small holes in the raised base. Why would an air-tight cylinder need holes in it?

He sipped at his spiced rum, and stared into space. She was a wow, unmarried, unattached, and travelling alone to the Isthmus. He was going there for business reasons, but his wife and four kids back in Saint John's were far far away, and he could play the bachelor to her mystery quite easily.

Ah, here she came now, weaving her way through the swaying throng of the bar car, carrying a small tray upon which were balanced another spiced rum for him, some indeterminate fruit cocktail for her, and a plate of small fried fish that the train had no doubt picked up at Saint Richard's.

"Here you are", she somehow managed to flash her breasts without moving, again.
He took the glass and sipped from it,
"Divine, how about you?"
She peered at him,
"I am divine" she decided.
"I meant your drink..." he had had two days of this kind of banter.
"Peaches may be divine, but not apples"
"Why not apples?"

"It is commonly thought that they were the fruit offered by the serpent in the Garden of Eden."

"Hmmm" he sipped his rum, and regarded her, sex plastered upon crazy religion as per usual, "Who made the Garden of Eden?"
"God of course", she laughed, "Or Satan, if you believe the other version"
"If God made it then everything in it was divine"
"Even the fruit of the Tree of Knowledge?"
"It was there"
"So the Serpent only fed the divine to the divine?"
"I think so", Harold had to admit to himself that he was rather confused on this matter, "Is that significant?"
"If it is so, what did the Serpent do wrong?"
"He disobeyed God" Harold was pretty certain on this.
"Had God commanded the Serpent not to feed Man, or only Man not to feed on a certain fruit?"
"I see your point", and indeed he did, protruding through her blouse, erect and very, very interesting.

"But I think you are a Heathen" she said, seating herself, and taking up the steel cylinder again.
"A Heathen?!" he was somewhere between outraged and astounded.
"You go along with the Imperial Church because it is easier than not doing", she sipped at her drink, "You agree or disagree according to what scripture seems like to you... You seem to care little if it is in opposition to what many people think"
"Many people can think wrong" he pointed out.
"How many?" she asked.
"As many as are wrongly convinced"
"Millions?" she snuggled down beside him.
"There are millions of Mohammedans" he pointed out.
"You are seeing the truth" she agreed and brushed her hair against his feet.

~

She did not say "Helena Larennia Alexandra" as the woman behind the desk at the Telegraph Office did not look the friendly sort. A walking corpse was not very believable at this time in the morning. But she needed to say something; the operator at her father's estate would take the message, whatever it was, but he would only pass it on if he thought it worthy of the attention of an Imperial Duke.

The woman was tapping a fountain pen upon the pad,
"If you do not know what to say, please go away and work it out. We have tables set aside for that purpose", and she gestured beyond to a small hallway where half a dozen meager tables sat, two of which had people perched by them on stools, keenly trying to work out messages that would be cheap enough to post at one crown a word, but clear enough to the recipient to know exactly what was meant.

"Remember the Golden Lake", she said slowly, "and the way the sunshine on my birthday danced upon the waters –stop- Remember how we laughed that this was the perfect painting made by nature and yet in its transience was but a figment –stop- Remember how I tried to paint it back at the castle and spent a week on the colours only to burn it in the great fire in my adolescent frustration –stop- If you remember this, you will remember me –stop-"

"Woh, lady", the woman counted up the words, excluding the stops as it was over twenty words long, "You sure you got 76 crowns to spend on this?"
Helena drew out her purse, and counted out three 25 crown coins, and one small crown piece. It was a large proportion of the money she had earned at the launderette, but she could not let her father go on thinking she was dead.
"Very well. If you wait, I will bring a receipt"
"Thank you"

It was not a receipt for the money, but the acknowledgment from the recipient that the message had got to its target. Sometimes they could take hours, but this was only a couple of hundred miles to the North, and any telegraph to the estate of an Imperial Duke would automatically be routed via the priority lines.

Helena had seen it in the paper the previous night, whilst busy ironing other men's shirts, and folding other men's sheets – it seemed only to be men who used the launderette, usually coming in in the evening, and often going upstairs to the cheap prostitutes who had flats up there whilst they waited. "The Albion Crier", the newspaper had been, left by one of them on the bench at the side, and she had perused it whilst waiting for one of the big steel machines to finish its business. The report of her own death, confirmed by her father's estate, had come as a bit of a shock – more so, the date and place of her funeral, in the Announcements section. She almost thought about going, but that would be giving in, when her quest was just beginning to bear fruit.

Purely selfishly, it would have made more sense to let everyone think her dead – nobody looks for a dead person, but she could not do that to her father. Besides, she was not absolutely sure that this was not some trick by those she was hunting, and if it was, they for certain would know that she was not dead, so there would be only false safety down the route.

"Here you go", the woman came across to the bench she was sitting on, and handed her the telegraph receipt, "I hope he remembers you", she said.
"Yes", Helena smiled, "I hope he does, too"

With that she turned and left the Telegraph Office, and walked down the street, picking her way through puddles that had begun to work their way into the road surface after several days of incessant rain. Usually at this time in the morning she was still asleep, her body having adjusted to the rhythms of her new work pattern. She wondered what her father would say if he knew she was working til 3 a.m. in a launderette – but at the moment, that would be the least of his worries, all things considered.

The job was seven days a week, but she did not mind; the money was good, considering she had no experience, no references, and had given a name that was made up out of her head. Mr De Salle was a good boss, he let her get on with things, but at the same time made it clear to the men that she was there to iron their shirts, and wash their clothes, and that if they wanted the other they should go upstairs where the girls were, of course, also his tenants. She would start at seven and work with only a half hour to eat her supper, but as she was being paid for the time worked, it was better that way, and, besides, waiting for the machines gave her the occasional break every time she cleared a backlog.

After work, she would usually go to bed until Midday, then go out in the afternoon upon her quest. Today, she had made do with three hours sleep, so as to get to the Telegraph Office by seven; she would feel it later, in the small hours, but for now she was energized, and determined to use the extra time she had to good effect.

As usual she walked to the elevated railway station above The Matador Inn, and caught the train in to Lower Slaughter. She had tracked things this far, and had achieved something that, as far as she was aware, none of the many who wished the Serpent destroyed had done. She had identified an Acolyte and believed she even had a lead on where the elusive Grand Temple was. It was become a quest for her, a mission to avenge the dead professor, and she was determined to reveal all, and in so doing destroy the Perversion for good.

~

What it was, they did not know, but the light had guided them from the moment it had freed them, and it seemed to be keeping them safe.

Lucille Drusilla Marguerite still did not quite trust it – how do you trust a ball of light? It has no face, no visible emotions, no voice. But it was helping them still, and she respected that. Respect, but not trust, perhaps that was so.

The group was small, every now and then shrinking as one or more ex-captives went their own way, every now and then growing as one or more returned. The Elite Guard was combing the countryside looking for them, not she suspected because they really cared about a couple of dozen escaped prisoners, but because of the principle of the thing, especially the longer they managed to elude capture.

Some had been taken, she knew that, either ones who had broken and ran off on their own from the start, or some who had left the group and tried to break out of the hills on their own. The light was keeping them safe, but it was not taking them anywhere, at least nowhere fast. The forest was their friend, the hills their ally, but it became too much for some, people used to the city, who wanted to return. The result of trying was too often death as the Elite Guard was not in a mood to make prisoners of the runaways.

The young cousins were still with her, and had opened up a lot in the time they had been traveling the forest. The boy was called Elias – he refused to give any more name than that. His cousin was called Sarah Anne, but again, on Elias's say-so she had withheld her family name. Lucille Drusilla did not know if it was significant or childish fancy, but had filed it away in her memory as something to take note of at the appropriate moment.

"It is moving", the speaker was a tall, rangy man of indeterminate colour, his ethnic background perhaps part Berber, part black, and the effect a curious blend that made him stand out, and yet blend in.
She looked up from where she had been crouching peeling potatoes, and nodded. The light was indeed moving off, very slowly into the woods, giving them time to pack up their few belongings and catch up with it before it would move away faster, causing them to walk swiftly, occasionally even to run. Once she had seen a patrol pass mere yards behind them after they had run to catch the light, and ever since then she had had faith that it knew what it was doing.

"Maybe it will move towards a town this time", the speaker was an elderly black man, one who had not yet struck out on his own, but who was beginning to exhibit the familiar signs of one who was reaching the edge of what his city-upbringing could take
"Do not be in so much a hurry", Lucille Drusilla told him, "What is time? We will return when we return. There is no rush to do so outside of your mind"
He nodded, uncertainly
"Perhaps you are right" he said.

But she knew that come the dawn he would no longer be with them. Whether he would die, or come back to them later, she did not know…

~

"I see the light..." Tabitha Clarissa Theresa stared at it with something akin to wonder.

Unlike the lights that had attacked the airships back in the Yukon, or the lights on the film footage, exploding through and out of that island, this one was trapped, frozen in time, a glacier encasing it for all eternity...or until someone was stupid enough to release it.

"Nobody has been stupid enough to release it", Swift Commander Terrance De L'isle said, caressing her rump with his groin.

"Thank God for that" she said.

"For this?" he asked, rubbing harder up against her.

In the time since her arrival, she had quickly exhausted the few troopers willing to take a chance with someone known to be the Eyes of the Great Chamberlain, and had ended up in the bed of the only Imperial Airforce officer based at Fort Fluffy. He was good, but he was not *that* good.

"Stand here", she yanked him round to her side, "*That* could kill us in an instant if it was released" she said, pointing at the light.

"It must have been here thousands of years" Terrance pointed out.

"Of what relevance is that?" she was mock-angry, but it sounded bad.

"It has not been released in all that time" he said, but did wonder whether her proximity was dimming the lights of his brain. He would never have behaved this way with the other Dynast, that bastard who had come with his Treasure aboard the airship.

"What I am saying", she squeezed hard and made him yelp, "is that *we* must not be so stupid as to release this..."

"Why would we?"

"Because we usually are..." she said, and turned away from it, "I think a guard should be posted here."

He frowned at her,

"It is a principle of the base that any may come and gaze on the light" he said.

"They can still come, but there will be a guard here"

"How can you trust a guard?" he wondered.

"Women" she was certain on this point, "Men can so easily be seduced. Post women from the garrison, and arm them with live weapons."

"Inside the base?" it was another local rule that had somehow grown up, and now she was threatening.

"Unarmed weapons are not that much of a detriment to the determined - or the delusional"

"You fear that?" he was shocked, and freed her hand from his member, "You believe that somebody here may be delusional?"

"The Serpent has its hand in many places" she said.

~

"Coatzacoalcos", Harold Swan Buckmeister mangled the word in his attempt to say it.

She smiled at him, and rubbed him where he wanted rubbing,

"Not a coat and a coal", she said, and bent her head to end conversation for a moment until she got her fill, "Co-at-za-co-al-cos"

"You sound so sexy with a full mouth" he said, wondering why his wife was never this attentive to his needs. Somehow they had had four children to date, but Esther May did not know half the tricks that this beautiful creature did.

She swallowed and released him,

"Tehuantepec" she said, and laughed.

"That is...." he searched what remained of his memory, "That is the province!"

"I did not suck *all* your knowledge out of you" she smiled.

"Not quite" he said, lying back and looking round the small compartment.

After entering the Azteca provinces of Albion, they had decided to take up the rent on a berth together, paying enough that the steward had thrown out some poor aesthetic to make room for them. The fellow had been furious, berating them publicly in the bar, but a day later had been found dead of an apparent heart attack, and dumped from the train as it crossed a swamp - much less paperwork that way.

"Ahhh..." he looked up at her, drinking in the sight of her, "You are soooooo mysterious!"

"I am?" she giggled and brushed her breasts against his face.

"You are many things, Sylvia"

"I am many things", she said, and sat back.

The name was a game, as they said, and he was playing it.

"What's in Panama for you?" he asked.

"An opportunity" she said.

"For what?" he was curious.

"Too many questions", she got up and straddled him, "You have work to do"

"I'm doing it!" he proclaimed.

Chapter Fifteen

Bordeaux, Vice-regal Capital
Realm of Europe
Empire of Albion

"Ah, Consul"
"Your Eminence"
"Come in please"; Aspen Thylacine Groat was more of a clerk than a noble, more of a pawn of the military than a commander of armies, and more a tool of the Great Chamberlain than a true representative of the glory of the Empire, but he did his best.

Johannes Georg von Witzendorff, on the other hand, was most things that his host was not. Appointed Consul of Europa at the age of only forty, he had now held that post for ten years, and risen in the rankings of his home empire accordingly. A Serene Highness by the honours and property that had accumulated to him, he did not use that form here in Bordeaux, where Albion's ways would find the phrase sitting too oddly with their own ideas on such things.

"There is much to discuss", von Witzendorff was always to the point, but unfailingly polite, even when being discourteous. One former minister of a former Viceroy had tried to get him reprimanded over a letter he had written, but the forms used had been respectful, even if the message had not been. That was his interpretation of Europan diplomacy all over.

"I understand that there has been a second battle in the Eastern Mediterranean", Admiral Louis Hieronymus Gravelines was the Viceroy's number two, First Minister within the immediate province, and Senior Aide within the Realm as a whole.
"Details are still sketchy", Von Witzendorff spoke only the truth, but given the less than happy outcome of the first battle, off the coast of Cyrenaica, he had little wish to talk about such things
"Of course", Gravelines bowed his head.

"Cognac", the Consul answered the unasked question as the Viceroy himself prepared the drinks for them, "Ah, thank you. Now to business..."

"Please" Aspen T Groat had quickly learned that that was more or less the only thing that von Witzendorff lived for.

"We are now full allies in war", the Consul sipped delicately at the amber liquid, "but we have yet to purposefully unite any of our resources in the joint endeavour"

"I am authorised to require the fleet at Valencia to join up with the Tunis squadron and sail to your aid as soon as you request it."

"Hm", the Consul's utterance was somewhere between a laugh and a snort, "That is not quite what my government had in mind."

"That does not surprise me", Admiral Gravelines had expected as much, but form required the Viceroy to make the offer.

"I have been requested to ask for the full design specifications of your Wildcat and Hellcat aircraft, and to enquire into your...ah, rumoured...use of light weapons"

"Light weapons?" Aspen T Groat frowned, "We have several squadrons of heavy armoured battle-wagons deploying to Tunis, but I am uncertain about light weapons..."

"You misunderstand me", the Europan looked carefully at his host, and decided that it was genuine, "Yes, you do", he said, "I meant to refer to weapons that consist of light..."

"Light?", the Viceroy pointed towards the electric fitting upon the wall, "That kind of light?"

"The same", von Witzendorff nodded, "Although rumours have it a thousand times more powerful"

"I know of no such weapons."

"Hm", the same noise again, "I do not doubt you, Your Eminence, but if you could pass my enquiry to the Imperial Court, my government would be most grateful"

"As you wish"

"And the aeroplanes?"

"I cannot answer for the Imperial Airforce precisely, but I foresee no problem with the Wildcats. We hope to begin deploying additional squadrons to Tunis this week, and it is certain that some will be landing in your Tripolitanian territory at some point"

"And the Hellfire?"

Aspen T Groat rubbed at a pimple upon his cheek,
"I am familiar with them as an idea", he said slowly, "but I believe the Admiral would be better placed to answer, as they have largely been deployed within the Imperial Navy"
"Admiral?"

Gravelines winced. He had direct orders from the Grand Admiral in Albion City himself to avoid this subject, but now it had been dumped in his lap. Quickly he ran over the rationale and the specifics as far as he understood them to be, and smiled
"I believe that the Imperial Court would require reciprocation on this matter" he said.
"Oh?" von Witzendorff sounded genuinely intrigued.
"One of your *Blitz* aeroplanes would be acceptable"
The Consul coughed, whilst the Viceroy merely looked blank.

Von Witzendorff recovered his poise quickly, and mimicked confusion,
"I can ask my government if there is such a thing in existence" he said
"When they have confirmed it, perhaps discussions about the Hellfire can resume" the Admiral said.
Aspen T Groat looked at him, uncomfortably, but did not like to challenge anything that a military man said. Instead, he smiled weakly at the Europan,
"I am sure it will all work out" he said.
"Oh..." von Witzendorff was caught out by the banality, "Er, yes" he managed, "I am quite sure, also, that it will..."

~

Bristol
High Province of Britannia
Realm of Europe
Empire of Albion

The sun was setting, the light dropping low before it met the horizon and merged with the darkness beyond. In the twilight, the temple looked deserted, no lights shone at its windows, no shadows moved within its grounds. But it was far from deserted, it was simply in mourning, and forbidden to show a light until true dark was upon them.

High on the Clifton heights, the temple overlooked the river far below, whilst its other aspect faced down towards the bustling second city of the High Province. Immediately below, was Clifton Village, long a mixture of up-market townhouses and popular taverns. The former might be home to a count, or to a duke, with his family driven away each morning in a limousine, and his children attending one of the many Imperial Schools in the immediate vicinity. The taverns were home to a better class of whore, popular bands, and the occasional poetry recital, bustling with an influx every night from the city below. Clifton was somewhere to come to, for these people, not somewhere to be, and it retained its exotic nature even if the entertainment was often not much different from that on offer in the better parts of the city centre.

"One more", Dionysus Rothgar Excelsior placed his empty glass upon the polished bar-top and watched whilst the same over-thin barmaid took it and refilled it with expensive Iberian liqueur. In many places it would have been an extravagance which would have marked him out, but in The Spotted Owl, as in all of Clifton's taverns, it was a popular drink with those pretending towards elegance. That he truly had it was no concern of the woman's, and she thought him as false as the farmer's son ordering it once a week on the wages earned by delivering groceries to the town houses up this way.

"Ahhh.." he breathed, and looked around.
With the imminence of nightfall, the day travellers and tradesmen who

populated the place were now giving over to adventurers up from the city below. He spotted a couple in felt hats, gay lovers without a doubt, and students at the University he did not need to even make a wager upon that. More complex were the old man, with his white beard, and the young girl, with her naked thighs and short brown hair. She was not a whore here, and something about her manner made him think she was not a freelance, even if a place like this had tolerated those not upon its books. She was all for this man, and he was all for her. Needing something to occupy his mind for a small while longer, he continued to watch them.

It was then that he saw it, and in seeing it could hardly believe the evidence of his own eyes. She delved deep into a bag of russet velvet and pulled something out, putting it into a voluminous pocket of his gown, but the angle had been perfect, and he had seen what it was. He looked away, sighting a mirror so he would be able to see if they had marked him, to see if they came anywhere near him, for if they did he did not wish to be anywhere near them.
"God", he whispered, but it was true.
He had known they were here somewhere, but to find them like this, he shook his head. What bearing would it have on his meeting later?

- - - - - - -

"No", the shaven-headed Acolyte continued to bar the gateway
"Do you know who I am?" Dionysus Rothgar Excelsior demanded
"It is not for me to care", the Acolyte was in his late twenties and built like a battleship
"I have authority from the Grand Master to see the High Acolyte" he said.
The other shook his head,
"We got the letter that you left", he indicated the brass post-box, "It is no longer acceptable"

Dionysus considered leaving and going elsewhere. Surely they would not all be such pains, but what if they were? What if his slinking away from one in defeat made the others more defiant, more certain in their refusals? He could hardly return to Albion City and inform them that he was not welcome in any of the temples!

"The Order of the Serpent" he said.
The Acolyte paused, and turned back, eyebrows arched.
"What about them?"
"Do you know who their local agents are?"
The man laughed,
"There are no local agents; the city no doubt has a few poor deluded souls, but..."
"You are unaware of the proximity of the threat."

Dionysus waited, and the Acolyte shifted, then nodded,
"Wait on the bench - I will relay your words to the High Acolyte"
Dionysus sat upon the marble, cold in the darkness, and able to see the path of shattered quartz only by the light of the Moon reflecting off it. It was some ten minutes before the fellow returned, with an older, slimmer man in his company.

"If this is some ploy, your name will be forever dirt" the newcomer said, and Dionysus did not need any introduction to know that this was the High Acolyte
"In The Spotted Owl" he said simply, "An old man with a white beard, and a young girl with short brown hair"
"What of them?"
"She passed to him a snake, a viper I think, from her bag to his pocket..."
"Perhaps..." the High Acolyte looked up at the Moon, "Yes, perhaps"
He nodded at his underling,
"Let him in - but only let him out when you have confirmation from my person that he is to leave"

Dionysus followed the man up the path, and realised only then that they thought him complicit in the killings at the Arch Temple.

Palace of Whitehall
London
High Province of Britannia

"Bulgarians!" Erasmus Pioneer Farley bounced off the wall, steadied himself against a painting that swayed at his grasp, and walked with a swaying purpose back towards the small hall.

"Ach!" Hercules Troubadour Rannoch, self-proclaimed Viceroy of this self-proclaimed Dominion, looked up and belched, "Molly can't have taken you that long!" he protested

"I got lost", Erasmus walked into the bench and fell heavily upon the floor, "Fuck..." he muttered, clutching at his bruised shin.

"Lost", Francis Shade Carrington was the third member of the unholy trinity who met every day for their heavy drinking session, "You couldn't get it up!" he laughed, "Even Molly couldn't make you stand!"

"I get you", Erasmus pushed himself to his hands and knees, "I will get you" he panted.

"You couldn't even get up Molly's arse!" Francis guffawed and downed a pint of ale in one swallow, swinging the jug in the air, "Poor little Molly" he sang, "I should go see to her..."

From the door, Sarah Alexandria Dunelm watched the three men, and smiled to herself. This was perfect, drunkenness on an epic scale as usual, and such petty debauchery that she cringed inside to think that these pathetic specimens thought themselves great by wallowing in it.

A bell rang. Francis continued to laugh, and Erasmus continued to curse, but Rannoch stood up, sighting Sarah in the doorway as he did so,

"Bell?" he belched

"I hear it", she was for once unsure of what was happening.

How was there a bell in here? Why was it ringing? It was completely outside of her experience and, more worrying, of her knowledge.

A man ran down the corridor towards them, and Sarah only just resisted the urge to draw her sword and skewer him as he skidded to a halt,

"Battle Captain Derek Faran!", he saluted

She looked at him and made a mental note; yes, she had seen him before, in the outer guardhouse, but it was one of Rannoch's rules that no Elite Guard officer be allowed within the heart of the palace. Who the Hell had let the bastard by?!

"I like not your kind!" Rannoch was standing now, pointing at the unwelcome guest.
"I present His Illustrious Highness, William Augustus Chance, Grand Duke and Great Chamberlain of the Empire of Albion!"

"Holy Fuck!", Rannoch dropped to one knee.
Sarah backed into the room, and made her way to his side, also falling to her knees in quick obeisance.
Erasmus was still scrabbling for a purchase that would pull him up, kneeling as he tried a chair, though it kept moving away with his exertions.
Francis had eyes only for him, laughing and jeering as he continued to sit at the table.

The Great Chamberlain entered... He paused and waited until his eyes accustomed to the darkness, and then nodded at the kneeling Viceroy and his woman, and frowned at the kneeling, but confused Erasmus. Then he took in Francis, still seated
"Kill him" he commanded
The Battle Commander drew a pistol and in almost the same motion loosed off a shot, propelling what remained of Francis Shade Carrington against the wall.
"Ugh", Rannoch looked at the ruin of his friend, then felt Sarah's fist in his kidneys, "Welcome to London" he gasped, and the Great Chamberlain smiled.

"Stand up", he said.
Rannoch and Sarah stood. Erasmus scrabbled at a chair but it fell over, and he collapsed upon his face
"Kill him", the Great Chamberlain said, and another pistol shot rang out.
Into the ensuing silence came the sound of running feet, and a dozen Elite Guardsmen fanned out into the hall. An officer approached the Great Chamberlain and saluted,
"Grand Captain Roman Vardis, I received your command, sire"
"Good", the Great Chamberlain looked from him to the Viceroy, "You will accompany me to the Audience Chamber."

Time froze as Rannoch stared at Sarah, completely lost somewhere between the drunken haze and the shock of the arrival of an almost mythical figure. She laid a hand on his arm, and slowly drew a bronze slither from a hidden pocket, proffering it to Battle Captain Faran.

"Captain-General of the Security Directorate of the High Province" she said, and waited

It was a dangerous game, but it worked - slowly, but it worked.

The Battle Captain passed the bronze to the Great Chamberlain who perused it carefully, drawing out a template from an inside pocket of his own and measuring the exact spacing of certain characters. At length he nodded,

"You may accompany the High Governor"

"Thank you, sire"

- - -

The Audience Chamber was little-used in recent decades, dusty and dark, cobwebs hanging everywhere, but this did not seem to phase the Great Chamberlain, who probably already knew about them. He waited whilst a couple of lieutenants cleaned the oaken chair, the twin to the one in the council chamber, and then seated himself down.

"Let all herein proclaim their name and true rank" he said, an ancient form, but one which had two excellent uses in practice; on the one hand, it forced undercover officers to reveal themselves on pain of death, on the other it meant that any who retained their anonymity were automatically traitors upon their discovery.

"Hercules Troubadour Rannoch...uh", he looked at the floor, "High Governor of the High Province of Britannia"

"Sarah Alexandria Dunelm, Captain-General of the Security Directorate of the High Province of Britannia"

"Grand Captain Roman Vardis, Elite Guard, Overseer of security, Palace of Whitehall"

"Battle Captain Derek Faran, Elite Guard, Duty Officer, Palace of Whitehall"

"I accept these as true and full declarations made upon pain of death" the Great Chamberlain said, and with the example of the 'Viceroy's two late drinking pals to go on, nobody could doubt him,

"Let all know that I am here by express wish of His Imperial Majesty, the Emperor of Albion"

Nobody said anything, for what was there to say?

"All executive and military officers within the capital will present themselves within one hour" he said

"But..." Rannoch dragged his gaze from off the floor, "Who is to keep order...?"

"One thousand Elite Guard are even now landing in a dozen airships at Saviours Field, North of here."

"A th...thousand...." Rannoch stuttered

The Great Chamberlain pierced him with his gaze

"High Governor, you have allowed the Arch Master of the Order of the Unicorn to be assassinated in your capital, and made no moves whatsoever towards apprehending the culprit."

"I...uh?" Rannoch looked towards Sarah.

She nodded a mite of encouragement at him, then looked to the oaken chair,

"We have dismissed our erroneous initial assumptions" she told him.

The Great Chamberlain nodded,

"Coincidence and the recent nature of visits does not a culprit make."

She knew that better than anyone, and could only nod her head in agreement.

They seemed to come from nowhere, and yet be everywhere. Leona stood at the doorway of The Falcon Inn and could only stare in amazement as the hundreds of Elite Guard, resplendent in their white and gold marched past, the lights of the establishments, and of the posts, shining from off their uniforms.

It did not end. Two score guards took up residence in Central Square itself, setting up roadblocks and stopping any vehicle that tried to pass which, as night drew on, was a lot as deliveries could only be made in the hours of darkness under city ordinances.

Customers grew thin, scared by events, or too intrigued to pay for an hour of her time, and the outside seats became packed, despite the cold, with people crowding round to just watch the new arrivals and try to get a handle on what was happening.

"I am Invicta Commander Jessica Ilaria Monroe"
All life seemed to stop around her as the woman pushed her way to the front and waved an ivory card at the young man behind the bar, "You will fetch for me Leona Halliday and David Jenkins at once."
"Um" the man knew a rising panic.
"No harm will come to you if you comply" the woman said.
"Le....Leona is by there", he motioned to where she was stood, in the centre of a group, watching the Elite Guard within the square, mingling with a half dozen regulars who were chatting amongst themselves.
"And David?" she asked
"He....uh", the young man wracked his brain, "I think he took an old man upstairs."
"You have two minutes to find him"

Smiling as the barman ran off, Jessica picked up a drink abandoned by someone who had been beside her, but was now running out of an external doorway. Her rank was . . . unusual. It existed outside of the services, it was to be found upon persons of any rank or none; it was not Elite Guard, nor army, not Imperial Airforce nor Navy, but it was to be found within all of them, albeit at an exceptionally rare rate. Within common parlance it fell within the catch-all term of Eyes of the Great Chamberlain, but whilst an Eye was a single agent answerable only to him, and with all power, there existed yet a parallel service where ranks remained, and where subordinates could be co-opted. Jessica belonged to this, and nobody wanted anything to do with her.

"You are Leona?" she said as the woman approached.
Leona looked her up and down, and shrugged
"Somebody told you that I was, so yes" she was determined not to seem too easy a catch
"That is acceptable"
The young barman returned with another of his kind in tow
"You are David Jenkins?"
"I might be..."
An Elite Guard stepped out from behind the crowd and swept his legs from under him

"Fuck..." David said, "Yes..."
"Things go better if you answer" Jessica told him.

Several dozen people were now standing in a loose semi-circle around them, bounded on the other side by the bar itself or, no doubt, they would have been all around them. Jessica had no wish to disperse them yet; the power of the Great Chamberlain depended at least as much upon fear, rumour and supposition, as it did upon the law, and she was far from having created enough of that yet.
"I am sure you remember the night that the Arch Master of the Order of the Unicorn was killed" Jessica said
"A fucking battle-wagon exploded!" Leona fingered the scar upon her forehead, "And that bitch dragged me from a client's bed."
"I am not a bitch!" David turned on her.
"The bitch who told you to" Leona snapped, "She killed..."

Jessica approached the woman,
"She killed?" she asked
"Oh fuck", Leona sagged, "If I tell you I'm fucking dead, she made that clear"
"You will explain" the Invicta Commander said, certainty in her voice.
"She had a .... a sort of card.... bronze"
"What did it say?"
"That she was the fucking head of the Security Directorate!" Leona was almost screaming, convinced that she was dooming herself to an agonising death, but knowing that she had no alternative, "She'd fucking killed him in the room upstairs."
"You will accompany me to Whitehall."
"Oh...shit" Leona sagged.
"No harm will come to you"
But the barmaid only looked at her...

~

"Sir.." the official hovered on the edge of the Vice-regal bedroom.
It was well-known that Aspen T Groat went to bed early, and was usually happily tucked away by nine o'clock. This night that was to his detriment.

216

He blinked himself to full wakefulness, and stared at the doorway where a vaguely familiar figure hovered
"Are we under attack?" he asked.
"Not as such", Cedric Thaddeus Mobion coughed.
"In some way?" Aspen reached out and found a light-pull, turning on the carven lamp beside his bed.
"I...um" Cedric was not sure how to break the news.

Aspen swung his legs over the side of the bed, and buried his toes in the luxurious carpet,
"Tell me" he commanded.
Cedric nodded,
"Communication from Albion City....the Empire is taking direct control of Britannia..."
"What?" Aspen struggled to his feet, "What does that mean?"
Cedric looked at his midriff, bare where the pyjamas had spread open,
"The Great Chamberlain and a thousand Elite Guards have landed at London, sir. They are taking the whole of the High Province under . . . direct control."
"What?" Aspen had now grasped the fact, but the reasons escaped him, "Why?"
"No reason is given"

There was silence for a moment, whilst he contemplated the ruin of his professional career, but it gradually dawned on him that he did not have much of that as it was. Rannoch had run Britannia as his personal fief, as had High Governors before him, and Bordeaux had had little real say there. So, in real terms an Imperial re-assumption there did not affect his power - but what about the perception of his power? That was more important, being already low. If it seemed that the Imperial Court was knocking him aside, he might as well hire a boat and shoot himself out to sea.

"Order the senior representative of the Elite Guard to the Audience Chamber" he said.
"Sir?" Cedric was beyond confused.
"Instruct Admiral Gravelines, Marshal Dos Santos and Marshal Lefebvre to be there...on pain of death"
"Sir!" Cedric squealed.

"Invite the Arch Master of the Order of the Unicorn and the High Masters of the Dragon, Bear and Wolf to attend"

"Now?" Cedric panted.

"And send the criers out; all nobles of ducal rank or higher are to be allowed within the precincts...", he paused, "We will speak at Midnight precisely."

"Sir!" Cedric protested.

Aspen speared him with his gaze,

"Do I need to ask someone else to do this?"

The implication was obvious and Cedric shook his head,

"I will begin at once" he said.

As he left, Aspen sagged back onto the eiderdown, wishing as he did in moments of weakness for his cousin's body to lie beside him, but it had not been allowed, the family council had said she must marry a duke or higher, and so she had, and he had been left with memories, memories which taunted him at moments such as this,

"Oh Becky..." he said.

- - -

"By Grace of God, Imperial Viceroy of the Realm of Europe for His Imperial Majesty, the Emperor William VI", the herald had been carefully instructed what to say and how to say it, "His Eminence, Aspen Thylacine Groat"

No applause followed, but it never had, but as he stepped onto the platform that had been hastily erected in the centre of the Audience Room, he could sense an unease amongst those that had been 'invited'. He nodded, and smiled inwards to himself,

"The chimes of Midnight have spoken", and indeed they had a moment earlier, "and I am pleased to see that so many of you could find the time to be here."

His tone was ironic, and so it was taken, except that many of those there did not believe in his power to command, and had come simply because the words had sounded ominous, or because news of events in London had reached them and they did not wish to put themselves and their families at risk.

"I spoke with the Lord High Chancellor an hour ago", Aspen did not say that it had taken two hours to arrange this, nor that the fellow had been condescending in the worst degree, "and I can assure you all that whilst Britannia has been re-adepted, the rest of the Realm remains firmly under my control"

He paused and looked into the eyes of some of those before him. First Minister Admiral Gravelines looked interested, and occasionally confused, but both Marshals looked furious, mutinous even. Of the dukes who had come, at least half their number looked thoroughly befuddled, but he could tell those who had had prior knowledge, and those for whom his words had resonance; the latter were the ones to trust going forward.

"For decades, Britannia has been a High Province apart from the rest of the Realm, governed as if it were a viceroyalty in its own right, and ruled by men who thought that ancient history placed them above the laws of the Empire."

"Exactly!", the Duke of Anjou was a notorious drunkard and had probably been deep in his cups when the criers had found him

"Tonight, the Great Chamberlain himself has taken back oversight of Britannia. With a thousand Elite Guards, he has imposed the will of the Imperial Court, and made its Governor know where the will of the Empire lies."

The latter had taken some urgent calls to London to ascertain the continuing status of Rannoch, but those on the other end had eventually confirmed he remained in place.

"Absolute loyalty to the Imperial Court is needed", he had sat in the dark and worked this out for himself, "In the face of the threats before us, this night I have permission to demand the Test of Loyalty from everybody here."

This was radical, but at the same time building a house of bricks baked in the sun. The Lord High Chancellor had agreed that it was a good idea. The organs of government at an Imperial level were notoriously hard to get anything out of at short notice, so his one conversation with the Chancellor in Albion City had covered as much ground as he could possibly twist to mean different things in the short time available.

"The Realm Justiciar has agreed", he had the man all but tied up back downstairs, "All will take the Test of Loyalty for immediate report to the Imperial Court."

Given that form of words, nobody could refuse...

Chapter Sixteen

Why was she walking in the dark? Richildis stumbled against a log, and reached out for a hold, surveying the ground in front of her in the gloom. Where was she? Had time passed so swiftly since the destruction of New Lisbon, that she could truly have wandered this far inland? She had no memory of it, so she sighed and walked on.

Where she was, she had no idea. The contours of the country were completely unfamiliar to her, and the forests had all gone, replaced by a few groves of trees, such as that through which she now clambered, and ahead mainly open land...upon which there was some movement.

She blinked and wished that there was more light from the stars, or from the sliver of a Moon. What was out there, moving? Was it friendly? She knew nothing of the plains, and these seemed more desolate, more empty than she even remembered from her reading.

Taking a deep breath she considered her options; remain in the copse, and hope nothing was in there with her, or move into the safety of the open, and hope nothing was out there to get her. She blinked again and knelt as a group of men walked quickly by, hunched over and carrying guns... Fulani! She felt her legs moisten as she could no longer control herself. Were they hunting for her, was she the prey and they the hunter?

And then something moved on the edge of her vision...a light, but... And then she remembered... Before she could scream, the crash of a hundred guns boomed out.

- - -

"Shellshot, plus two hundred yards and falling!" Lieutenant Gareth Samson Evans did not like his role, but somebody needed to do it.
"Pull back", the woman at his side insisted.
"Count it out" he snapped.
"Fuck this!", Rebekah Ilona Webb spat a stream of tobacco juice over the cupola of the armoured wagon, and sighted at her pocket watch,

"Thirty", she said.

"Hold course" Gareth's voice sounded strained even to himself.

"If you say so..." the driver's voice from below was strained.

"Twenty" Rebekah said.

"Hold"

"I'm holding!"

"Ten"

"Mark"

"Seven, six, five, four, three, two

"And turn!" Gareth yelled.

All along the line, the armoured wagons swept round in a semi-circle and raced back the way they had come, the rapidly receding barrage chasing them as they returned to their own lines. In the light of exploding shells, Fulani warbands could be seen being blown to bits, but all around them the lights still came on, somewhere approaching twenty of them in pursuit.

"Cease fire!" Colonel Graham Sebastian McLaren yelled and all along the line, the guns shuddered to a halt.

"Twenty", Swift Commander Tomas Thorn had been seconded to the Artillery for that night, "No effect"

"Twenty lights coming our way", MacLaren spoke into a radio link of command rank

"Understood", the voice was tense but unmistakably that of General Alberto Smith.

"Lock down" the Colonel ordered his own emplacement, setting men and women scampering to secure the shutters that had been built over their entrenchment in the previous few days.

It would be a manoevre enacted up and down the line; nobody wanted to stand casually in the way of an advancing light and die when they did not have to.

- - -

Richildis shook herself as the guns fell silent. The lights had gone, but she still remembered... Shaking she raised herself onto one knee, and wept. Day after day they did this! They released her without memory, then they came back for her. What the Hell were they? Truly daemons!

But this time the guns had disrupted them, but now they had fallen silent... She shivered; were the guns destroyed, the gunners dead? Would the lights be coming back for her?

She staggered to her feet
"No...." she hissed.
Not this time. They would not take her again.

Then the sky exploded, and fire rained down upon the world.

- - -

"Bank and roll!", Guy Simonis Meredith had no idea if the other Wildcats in his squadron were following his command, but if they had any sense they would be. He was a veteran and he was still alive; these were characteristics those who remained with him could only aspire to.

He rolled his Wildcat as a light shot past underneath it, and smiled. Finger on the trigger, he righted his aeroplane, and sighted
"Take that you bastard" he hissed.
And fired

Phosphorous shot exploded out of the cannon, blowing up all around the light. When it cleared, it was no longer there.
"Scratch one fiery daemon" he said to himself

- - -

"Target and fire!", Elite Marshal Humphrey Odysseus Brown was focused in the moment, over-riding his Battle Captain as he controlled events at hand.
The armoured battle wagon bucked as the shells flew out.
"Lights closing from three directions!" Honour Ensign Ralph Cornelius Vane had volunteered to remain up top, believing that if he survived the battle he would have a sight to describe. Now, he sounded as if he were regretting the decision.
"Number Four, assistance please" Humphrey Odysseus spoke into the command link

"On you", Battle Captain Nehemiah Davis sounded confident.

A moment later, his armoured battle wagon burst out of a recess in the ground and opened fire. When the smoke cleared, another of the lights was no longer there.

"Keep it up!" General Alberto Smith's voice echoed through the radio link, "We have the bastards on the run!"
"Target and fire!" the Marshal shouted into the chaos of the interior.
"Target aye!" the gunner confirmed.
"Fire", the vehicle's own Battle Captain, Amelia May Hamilton managed to get her command in before the Marshal's, adding, "If you don't mind, sir"
"Feel free, Captain", he smiled at her enthusiasm.

"Still one light on us!" Ralph's voice was definitely strained.
"No target!" yelled the gunner.
"Where is it?" the Marshal demanded.
"Directly above us!" Ralph was now cowering in the cupola, hoping that it would somehow go away, "Agghhh...!" he screamed.

There was an instant of silence then a blinding white flash.
"Ensign?!" the Marshal did his duty, calling for him.
"Um" said Ralph.
"Ensign?", he was amazed he was still alive, "What happened?"
"A Wildcat got it...sir"
"Thank you", Humphrey Odysseus sagged back in his chair, "Thank you" he said again.

"All units press the attack", General Smith was having nothing short of outright victory that night.

"Locate a target and engage", the Marshal commanded.
"Advance", Amelia May was back in her element; a running enemy was a known quantity.
"Target bearing five hundred yards and crossing lateral"
"Target"
"Target aye"
"Fire!"

- - -

Lying prone on the floor, Richildis watched in awe as the armoured battle wagons swept past, firing sunbursts at the remaining lights, supported by aeroplanes that dropped from out of nowhere to explode their own constellations against them. Somehow it was working.

The lights were in retreat...

~

Dawn brought the sound of ringing bells, and all Timbuktu poured onto the streets. Criers roamed the boulevards and avenues announcing the victory, and if their strident voices were not enough, trucks with placards were parked at strategic locations, the signs proclaiming the glorious day to one and all.

Count Roger Alejandro Schenk moved through the city with an escort of a half dozen Elite Guards, people moving quickly out of his way as they recognised both his importance and his purposefulness, even if they had no idea who he was. Approaching the postern door at the side of the High Temple of the Unicorn, he knocked and after only a moment was admitted, the guards spreading out to cover all the ways in and out of the complex.

Quentin Eros Frobisher met him in an inner courtyard, by a crystal fountain, and motioned him to a seat
"Events move quickly", the High Acolyte of the Order of the Unicorn said.
"None quicker", Count Roger agreed, and perched himself upon the marble bench.
"Things are so far in our favour"
"My cousin's death was not expected" the Count frowned, then shook his head, "But it is of no consequence in the greater scheme of things."
"I am glad that you understand that."

"What can we expect?" Count Roger could not remain sitting for long, and was back up on his feet.

"They will strike soon"

"Where?"

"Location can not be determined", the High Acolyte shrugged, "Cyclops has calculated the probabilities based on the inputs that we suggested to the Lord Guardians."

"And if they were wrong, or lacking, then Cyclops is wrong."

"But if they are right..."

"Then it gives us a start..", the Count paused by the fountain, "A chance is better than a guess."

"Exactly"

"Where?" the Count turned back towards him.

"Cyclops gives equal probabilities on Kalgoorie, Patagonia and Shoshona."

"What is our coverage?"

"Shoshona is not within it; it is a mountain city with a small population."

"Do we have the mines and the ice fortress covered?", Count Roger was keen to show that whilst his knowledge might be remiss on one front, it was full on the others.

"Completely"

The Count snorted,

"If our coverage were complete, then there could be no chance."

"I misspoke", the High Acolyte inclined his head, "We will know at once if they are able to move in these places."

"But not in Shoshona?"

"Unfortunately..."

"My airship can be recalled", the count was thinking out loud, "I have no doubt that the Viceroy would give immediate clearance."

"Out of here?", the High Acolyte smiled, "I have no doubt of that"

"Then I should go there"

"As you will"

"As God wills..."

"Indeed."

~

"This way my lady", Alban Wentworth had no idea of the woman's status, but the fact that she was out here alone, and that she seemed to have survived several encounters with the lights, demanded a certain respect of him. He was not entirely sure quite what her half-raving tales meant, but he knew where he had to take her.

"Where are we going?", Richildis looked up and around her.
She had lain low during the night, even after the cannons had stopped firing. The armoured wagons had come back, shooting up any Fulani who still roamed the area, or who lay wounded and unable to fly. Her ability to hide had made her wonder how many of the Natives were still out there, so even as dawn had come she had not moved. It had taken this strong trooper, recognising that she was not one of them, to haul her up and get her moving back towards the lines.

"I'm taking you to my commander", Alban smiled his wide, generous smile, "He will be very interested in what you have to tell"
"Oh", she supposed it made sense, and allowed herself to be led on.

As they approached the ruins of the defence line, now being shunted aside by heavy earth-scoops attached to some of the older battle-wagons, an Elite Guard stepped forward, his weapon raised,
"Identification" he demanded
Alban handed his over
"And her?" the guard pointed his weapon at Richildis who began once more to shake
"Have some sense, man!" Alban angrily stepped in front of the gun, "I'm taking her to command"
The guard frowned,
"I am not sure where the Elite Marshal is..."
"General Smith is in overall command", Alban reminded him.
Reluctantly, the man let them through.

"You are taking me to see a general?" Richildis hung onto his arm
"I did not actually say that" Alban smiled, "I said he is in command. I am taking you to see my commander"
"Oh", she did not ask any more questions

- - -

Awfy had not been amused to be allocated a tent upon his arrival there that morning. As the general's aide said, however, he was not even the most senior Shadow Service operative remaining in Timbuktu, so would be treated as a liaison unless General Smith said otherwise. Considering all the other things that the general had to do that morning, it was no surprise that he had not even considered Awfy's situation, so in a tent he had remained. It did have the advantage of being away from the other command posts, and of being some way back from where all the heavy earth-work was going on. Combined, this meant that his agents in the services were finding it surprisingly easy to come and go, without giving away anything of their loyalties.

"Sir", Alban Wentworth parted the tent flaps and stepped inside.
To his surprise, Awfy was alone, no guard and no aide in sight.
"Trooper", Awfy's mind raced down the personnel files, "Wentworth" he added, then caught sight of the woman almost hiding herself behind him, "And?"
"She has not spoken her name", Alban told him apologetically, "I found her out there", he pointed.
"Beyond the front?"
"Yes sir"

Awfy led the clearly terrified, rather filthy and definitely very smelly woman to a seat, and turned to the Trooper,
"Speak to Lieutenant Tessa Vardis in the Catering Corps; get her to bring some hot water, bowls, towels and a change of clothes, "She is about her size"
"Yes sir"

"A drink?" Awfy indicated a trestle table laden with water, brandy and a small portable stove upon which some coffee was brewing.
"Water" she said
Behind her back, he tipped a measure of brandy into it and handed it to her. If she noticed, she didn't say, but perhaps she was too far gone for that. He let her drink for a moment.

"How come you were out there beyond the front?" he asked, gently but with blazing curiosity

228

"The lights keep taking me, then releasing me"
He froze and stared at her,
"They keep doing this?" he asked
"Each time they release me I don't remember...until they are just about to take me again"
"You remember now, though"
"They were just about to take me when your guns drove them off"
"I see"

He turned as Alban returned with the lieutenant in tow. She took one look at Richildis and nodded,
"If you two gentlemen will wait outside, I will have the lady fit to receive visitors in a few minutes"
Awfy and Alban walked around to the back of the tent, out of anyone's direct line of sight. Ahead of them lay an open expanse upon which convoy after convoy of supply trucks could be seen heading their way, and pulling off into the coralled areas that the Logistics Corps had established for them.
"We are going on", Alban sounded dubious
"They have the scent of blood in their nostrils"
"I do not think the lights bled"
"But they certainly seemed to die" Awfy pointed out.

"You may enter now" Tessa came round to find them
The woman certainly looked and smelled better, clad in a light-fitting dress of the lieutenant's, her hair combed, the pungent odour now scrubbed clean.
"Her name is Richildis", Tessa told them, "She comes from...New Lisbon"
"I see..." Awfy wondered just how much improved her mind was, and whether she was speaking truth or delusion, "Thank you, lieutenant, that will be all"
"I will come by tonight, sir, to see if there is anything more I can do"
"Very well", he watched her go.

"Now", Awfy lowered himself onto a stool and beckoned for Alban to seat himself likewise, "I would like you to tell me slowly, and from the beginning. Don't worry about anything you forget or are not sure about, just keep going, and when we get to the end...we will see what we have there"

"Yes...alright", she nodded

And she began

*~

The airship rose, like a black cloud passing before the sun, and then it was gone, heading West towards the Atlantic.

"I am not sad to see him go!" Luisa Maria Valdez said, with some feeling.

"It is certainly a welcome departure", the Viceroy breathed a sigh of relief.

"Let us hope it is a journey full of much turbulence", Archbishop Jensen had already discarded half a dozen curses as unChristian, and this was as bad as he thought he could get away with.

"But the poor girl..." Luisa protested.

"Oh...very well", the Archbishop sighed, "I hope the count gets the shits"

She laughed.

Imperial Duke Gunther Luis Leander turned round and moved towards where two steam limousines were gently hissing in the shade. Their drivers and guards stood around, one smoking a cigar, another perusing a copy of The Timbuktu Gazette, no doubt looking up the prices of slave girls at that evening's market.

"This morning's other business cannot wait" he said.

"You could make it wait", the Archbishop pointed out as he headed for the other limousine

"It is in none of our interests if we do"

"Perhaps", Jensen was still riding the high of getting rid of the count, and he grinned.

A few minutes later, the two limousines sped away from the airway, one back to the Archbishop's Palace, the other, carrying the Viceroy and his military liaison, back to the Viceregal palace, and for a meeting that had been requested before dawn.

230

Hence, it was no surprise to find the Europan Consul fuming, pacing the ante-room, and generally making the servants' lives a misery as he demanded to know when the Viceroy would be free to see him...and again...and again.

"Ah, Your Eminence", Gunther Luis Leander had read the credentials of the man when he had first arrived, and had decided that despite the honours he might hold within the Empire of Europa, he would be addressed as any other Consul would be, when within the walls of his palace at least.

"My government will not look kindly on this delay", Giacomo Ludovico Orsini was a scion of one of the oldest noble families in the province of Italia. Before that country had been swallowed up by Europa, his great-grandfather had gathered large estates in Epirus and Albania, and it was upon these that the current owner based his wealth. Possessed of several titles within the multi-layered heirarchy of Europan titles, the one that Giacomo preferred for himself was Duke, although to be sure this was only an Aristocracy of Italia title, and he held the title of Count within the Imperial Aristocracy.

"Matters of state", Gunther Luis Leander cast his cloak at a servant who nimbly dived to catch it, performed a roll in mid-air without touching the ground, and turned away to hang it up, "Unavoidable, I am afraid"

"Hmph", Giacomo had made his protest, now he had business to get down to, "If we may begin"

"Of course", the Viceroy opened the door to his office, "Please take a seat. My military liaison officer will also be attending."

Giacomo took one look at the Galician, decided she would look better in a different, more naked, profession, and dismissed her from his mind.

"Lights attacked our armoured battle-wagons outside of Benghazi last night", the Europan said as he took his seat, "We took over ninety percent losses..."

"My condolences", Gunther knew what was coming next, but was not about to pre-empt it.

"I believe my congratulations are in order with regard to a similar engagement that your forces fought last night to the South of the city."

"I did not think you would miss the bells", the Viceroy laughed
"Information would have been welcome."
"You are welcome to ask for it." the Viceroy was waiting for something of some value to be spoken here, "The criers and the trucks I sent out gave a good overview of the battle."

"I concede that", Giacomo picked at some fluff on his collar, "My government needs to understand how the battle was won."
"Phosphorous, chiefly", Gunther shrugged, "I am not au fait with the exact composition of the shells"
"And the tactics?"
"Are unlikely to work a second time" Luisa Maria put in, adding, "In many ways it was the classic tactic that William the Bastard used at Hastings..."
"The Bastard of Hastings?" Giacomo proved ignorant of medieval English history.

"Skirmishers ran, the defensive wall seemed to collapse, then a strong counter-punch was delivered to the enemy as they threw themselves forward."
"A full military briefing will be delivered to the Consulate", the Viceroy added, "As soon as I receive one from General Smith"
"Very well", Giacomo balled his fists, "My government needs to ask for assistance in the immediate case..."
"Please ask", Gunther was always intrigued when people acted like this, shy of asking and telling him they had to ask something. In many things it had been this way since childhood where as son of an Imperial Duke if the captain of the football team had decided not to select him, he felt that he had to ask if it was alright to tell him first. Not that Gunther had particularly enjoyed kicking a ball between two posts anyway; it had always seemed rather pointless to him compared to shooting and hunting.

"Can you spare munitions and commanders familiar with them? My government has informed me that we need to counter-attack with these weapons at once, or Tripoli itself will fall."
"Hmm..." Gunther was intrigued.
As far as he knew the Viceroy of North Africa had already been co-operating with the Europan commanders in Tripolitania; in fact had

not armoured battle-wagons and Wildcat squadrons already been deployed through Tunis?

"I thought..." he began.

The Consul waved a hand,

"Only you have engaged the enemy with these weapons. I know not whether any are en route to your forces in the North, but only you have used them, and had success with them."

Gunther smiled; it was funny how things turned out. General Alberto Smith had already reported that morning that he was having problems with the Marshal of the Elite Armoured forces over who was in control of the advance.

"I will order Marshal of the Elite, Humphrey Odysseus Brown, to head to Tripoli at once with his command crew, and will ensure that a cargo of phosphorous is sent up with him."

"Thank you!" Giacomo was astonished, but bit back on it, "My government will be truly grateful."

The Viceroy rose,

"If it helps to defeat the lights, then it is the interest of all Christendom"

"Quite", Giacomo bowed and departed

Gunther grinned at Luisa,

"Inform General Smith of my decision and ask him to break the news to Marshal Brown...I do not feel quite up to it"

"Yes sire"

*~

The *Londinium* sailed into the night, her black flanks merging with the darkness, only the golden lion and unicorn embossed upon them shining back with reflected starlight.

"We are passing over Greencape now", Grand Captain Christopher Nicomedeus Holand was polite in his tone, but rarely used deferential words to his passengers. He was the ultimate authority upon the airship, and he did not want any to get ideas literally above the station.

"Thank you", Count Roger Alejandro Schenk was standing by a viewing port, though to say true, all he could see out of it were stars above, and a couple of small lights below; this close to the coast they could be towns or ships, he did not know.

"We are cleared on Greencape Station", Samuella Josephine Reit was a statuesque blonde, somewhere in her middle thirties, and with piercing blue eyes that the count had already learnt not to look into.
"Thank you, lieutenant", the Grand Captain nodded and looked up, "Course for Albion City, and then route for Shoshona"
"Yes sir", the muscular red-headed woman at the wheel replied.

- - -

Leonora Bunny lay on her bunk, kicking her legs in the air, and reading the book that Joanna had given her as a parting gift that morning. She would miss the female soldier, but the book was so good that it drove all such thoughts from her mind. She knew she would have to resume her studies as soon as they arrived in Albion, but for the moment there was no tutor aboard the airship, not even an Acolyte of the Order of the Unicorn, and it was back to being a holiday, like it was when they had first set out from London.

The book was a historical comedy, set in the court of Emperor William IV and all about the young women who came to the balls for the first time. Its author, Hariette Delaney, had captured a spirit of the time and imbued it with a light humour, appealing to intelligent girls of her age. She laughed aloud at a description of a girl from Tehuantepec being surprised that they wore dresses for the formal dances, something not in her largely Azteca custom!

The airship bucked, sending her bouncing back onto the bed.
"Turbulence?" she asked, knowing all about such things from books, but her one journey so far, that from London to Timbuktu having been mercifully free of such things.
It happened again, this time almost tipping her onto the floor
"I don't like this!" she said, to stop herself from crying

- - -

234

"Port engines unresponsive", James Aardvark Camberley looked at the readouts in alarm and confusion, "I cannot understand it sir!"

"I can.." Count Roger turned away from the window, "Blazing debris is falling into the ocean"

"Message from the topmost lookout…" Samuella listened to the faint transmission, and swallowed, "Lights sir, two of them attacking the rear."

"About 180!" Christopher Nicomedeus Holand yelled, "Jettison ballast and immediate rise!"

"About 180 aye!"

"Jettison ballast!"

The airship bucked, twisted and tried to turn around, but without one whole set of engines it lurched drunkenly about. The ballast fell, but the intended lift was counter-attacked by the uneven weight at the rear and the *Londinium* was threatening very nearly to sit upon her tail.

"Sir!" screamed Samuella.

"Belay that!" Holand could tell when something was going badly wrong, "Issue the emergency distress call and blow the bags, we are going to have to ditch"

"Fuck", Count Roger turned and ran from the bridge

He tore down the passageway, elbowing aside crewmen who were staggering around in confusion, balling over a woman who was standing still at a junction, weeping.

As he ran the airship bucked and heaved, every now and then dropping beneath his feet so that he slammed into the walls, or crashed swearing to the floor. Then it levelled out, beginning to descend more evenly, no doubt on the final leg of its death dive.

He rounded a corner, panting, his daughter's compartment up ahead. He could see her now, standing in the doorway, bloodied nose dripping down her dress, eyes full of terror, but trying with her strong personality to get a hold on herself and work out what to do.

"Bunny!" he staggered towards her, calling her pet name, cutting through her fear back towards her earliest memories, back towards where she would know that safety lay, "Come to me!"

And the light came through between them, slicing through his body, sending arms and legs flying, his head bouncing to lie at the child's feet. Leonora Bunny screamed, and then the light touched her, and both of them vanished.

- - -

The *Londinium* crashed into the sea, as good an emergency landing as the Grand Captain could have hoped for. As the flotilla of ships out of Greencape closed upon the wreck, it became clear that neither the Count nor his daughter was to be found numbered amongst the survivors in the water.

Chapter Seventeen

Shoshona, Albion

Lightning arched across the sky but no rain came down, the dogs howled and the horses frighted in their paddocks. Inside the city's only tavern, ironically not named either The Frighted Horse or The Howling Dog, but the rather more prosaic *Princess Arms*, the High Constable sat at a table, gambling his monthly pay against his nemesis in a game of bridge.

"Four no trumps", Deucalion Bennington Hart was a merchant of good standing in Shoshona, from a family that had first come to the region two hundred years ago when it was a place for trappers and hunters. Now, it was at the heart of a different community and the single rail-line that ran in from Assiboinia was its life-blood, though the roads and trails around still linked the community closer than any more distant form of communication.

"Five hearts", Reynauld Riel had been High Constable for five years, and had felt his life slowly slipping away with every one of them.
"Five no Trumps", Deucalion smiled.
Reynauld looked at his cards, then across at his partner, another Constable, silent sturdy John Halstead who sat in on these games so as to earn the percentage of any winnings if any, all losses incurred being borne by his boss. Halstead shrugged, imperceptibly. Deucalion sighed,
"Pass"

Deucalion's own partner this night was wild Jo Hetherington, a farmer from down the valley, with her flame-red hair and a fore-arm strength that had broken many a man's arm in an arm wrestle. She laid her cards out before her, and Reynauld whistled to see them,
"Right..." he said
Deucalion laughed,
"You could pay me now" he said
"I'll make you earn it" the High Constable snarled.

- - -

The rain finally began to lash down, quieting the dogs, drenching the horses and sending those few people still out and about at this hour scurrying for shelter. Only one person remained without, drinking in the wetness, dreaming in the air.
"Soon" she said, "It will be soon"

~

Fort Fluffy, Patagonia

The light shone eerily in the ice, blazing out from its frozen prison. As was usual now, a female guard stood on duty, a sub-machine gun with live ammunition slung across her breast.
"I only wish to pray to the light", the speaker was half Native, half the daughter of a colonel, once posted here, but departed ten years ago, leaving her to grow up part of the fortress, part outside of it.

Serena Bramley sighed; despite the much-publicised attacks by the lights in West Africa, some still held out that *this* one was different, was holy or special in a mystical way. Orders were to let anyone through to the light, but to shoot on sight anybody who attempted to blast it free. Somehow, Serena did not think that the poor girl was one of those.

She knelt before the light and stared dutifully into it for so long that Serena forgot she was there. It was only when she heard a strange sound, that she turned, too late to avoid the blow, but quick enough to deflect it. The knife arced down onto her arm, slicing into the tendons, causing her to let go of the gun.

"Whaaaa!" Serena yelled, turning and twisting as the girl grabbed at her throat
She released herself enough to make a fist with her good hand, and slammed it into the girl's midriff, flooring her, kicking her in the head for good measure

"Did you call?" a guard came trotting down, not too fast in case it had just been a trick of his ears

"Ahhh... " Serena was bandaging her arm with a strip torn off the prone body's dress, "That attacked me..."

"Her?" the guard was sceptical

"Who else?" Serena looked around, "There are no faeries here"

He looked at the light, still encased in its icy prison

"Except that" he said

"Possibly", she tightened the bandage upon her arm.

Panama, Albion

"Panama - All out! Panama - All out!"

The white-suited station porters, many of them black, and not a few of the rest of Native birth, strode up and down the sides of the Azteca Express, banging on the doors and windows with ebony canes, until all of the former were open, and the blinds on the latter pulled up. Then they drew back and let the slaves in, men and women stripped to the waist who would do the heavy work whilst the porters served in the role of overseers.

"*Nobody* touches this!" Sulvia slapped back the hands of a grasping slave woman, and hefted the steel cylinder out of the train herself, "You boy", she addressed a lad dressed only in breaches, "Carry the rest of my luggage"

"Yes mistress", he smiled white shiny teeth and she felt a tingling inside of her, ""To where?"

"If there is not a carriage waiting for me, then the director of the hire company will be flayed alive."

"Yes mistress"

A few minutes later they stood in a walled courtyard whilst a melee of drivers milled around, fighting for space as they hefted their placards.

"Sylvia de'Ath" one said, in bold black lettering and she nudged the slave boy that way.

"That is me", she said to the yellow-and-black uniformed driver, "You have a sealed carriage suitable for up-country as I wired?"

"Yes lady", he indicated such a vehicle behind him, with four strong-looking horses pawing the ground, "Just as you wired"
"Good", she let herself be helped up and inside placing the cylinder on the seat beside her, and indicated that the slave boy pass the rest of her luggage inside.

He did so, and grinned
"What is the punishment for running away with me?" she asked
He laughed
"Nothing if I don't come back"
That was very practical, she thought.
"Then get up and we'll see if all your muscles are as strong as those on your shoulders."
"Yes Mistress!" he shot on up.
"Drive on!", he banged on the connecting wall, and the driver raised the whip, bringing it down gently and manoevring the carriage out from the busy courtyard.

~

Fort Fluffy, Patagonia

"You are cleared for landing", Lieutenant Colin Hamer bit down on he stem of his pipe, "I don't think people will be happy to see you - we have....a situation"
"Understood, Fluffy, we'll land the passengers and be away"
"Very well, *Flying Fox*"

Colin sat back in his chair and blew smoke rings towards the ceiling,
"Where is The Eyes...?"
"Probably still in the bed of our fancy flyer" Marietta Espezia Guiscard was lazing back in her chair, one shapely leg crossed over another, "Should I get her?"
"Hell, no" Colin laughed, "There will be finer sport if she finds out in her own good time."
"What about The Bastard?"
Neither of the two Dynasts had become popular in this mountain fastness since their arrival, and Marietta was never one to give undue deference.

"Where is *she*?" Colin asked.

"Behind you"

The Lieutenant whirled around, pipe skidding across the floor, and gaped up into the face of Ramona Elise Carding moved slowly, and silently, into the Flight Control Office.

"The *Flying Fox*?" she asked

It was infuriating, but the Shadow Service had nobody of any worth here, and all of her information was being obtained by sneaking around on her own.

"Landing now..." Colin managed to force out.

"Clearance?"

"Direct from Port William" he replied.

That told her nothing. Ramona shoved him aside, and sat down on his chair. Things were not as they seemed at Fort Fluffy, and the Governor was still investigating the incident before the light. Opinion tended to acquit the girl on the basis of a deranged mind, but to Ramona that would be too simple an explanation.

"Passenger manifest?" she asked.

Colin was scrabbling around on the floor, so it was Marietta who answered,

"Two only", she had been listening in, "No identification"

"Yet" Ramona turned and nodded, "I will go and greet them"

"But Security will already have despatched someone"

"Then there shall be one more"

With that Ramona strode out, leaving Colin to clamber back into his chair, and attempt to locate a shred of his tattered dignity.

- - -

"I don't like this place!" Leopold Hubertus Scheer had been growing glummer in recent hours as the *Flying Fox* had neared the landing point in the mountains. A native of Navaho City, he was happy in the sun...

"It *is* warmer inside" Dragomaster Arthur Spinks told him.

"It couldn't be colder" Scheer growled.

"Security Commander Hawk Monroe", a slim man greeted them midway across the ice.

"And I am Ramona Elise Carding", she smiled at the discomfort both of the man she stood beside, and the two she stood facing.

"Er" said Scheer, looking towards his master.

"Very well", Spinks knew that their prepared bluff was not about to hold up in the face of such a senior member of the Shadow Service, "We would speak with you alone"

"That is not permitted" the Security Commander jumped in.

"It is permitted if I permit it" Ramona snapped.

"Do you permit it?" Spinks asked.

"I permit it"

"I must protest" Hawk said feebly

The Dragomaster just grinned at him.

Inside, Ramona led the two new arrivals to a room carved into the ice, with the Security Commander insisting on standing outside.

"Dragon?" she guessed .

"Ah...that would be yes" Spinks said, "Is it a problem?"

"For my part, no. You do need to be aware that there is an Eyes here..."

"Eyes?" Scheer muttered, perplexed.

"...of the Great Chamberlain?" Spinks was suddenly rather less sure of himself.

"It might be better for you to be someone else" Ramona said.

"Do you have anyone in mind?" the Dragomaster asked.

"Oh...", she smiled, "I think I do..."

~

242

Albion City (Imperial Capital)

"You understand your orders?"

Hector Badger was a recent recruit to this area's Constabulary, having put in for a transfer from his rural parish when his mother had died. He knew he still had much to learn about plying the trade in the big city – the biggest of cities – but this was mighty strange in anyone's book. But he was not stupid, and the orders were certainly clear enough, "Yes sir" he said.

"Good", Charles Ronaldo Harkness was not normally on active service like this. As High Constable of the district, he usually directed operations from afar, though he liked to keep his hand in on investigations. This was not an investigation – it was action, but he was here, and given his arrangement with Doctor Kahn, he really had no choice but to be here.

Helena Larennia Alexandra was ahead of them, crouching behind a wall, looking ahead at a set of steps leading up to a non-descript doorway. Inside, the Constables knew, was a single young male, someone who was not at all known to their surveillance.

Known only to the High Constable, the active surveillance had been upon the female dynast, someone declared as dead, and buried. He had labelled her by her assumed name, as a laundry attendant, and created an operation to watch her. They had watched and they had seen. Seeing what they had seen, he had decided to let her run, but to keep a close eye upon her.

Now, she was crouched, waiting and watching the featureless building of old grey stone. Above, a train rattled by anonymously upon the elevated railway, but nobody here had eyes for that.

"Is she going in?", lieutenant Eleutheria Stevenson had joined the constabulary at sixteen, and was steadily rising in rank, having attained her first commission now at the age of nineteen.

"It does not look like it", the High Constable frowned, "I think she is waiting"

"What for?" asked the woman.

"Who..." said Hector Badger, pointing as the door was being opened from within.

"All hold position" Charles Ronaldo Harkness realised that he had miscalculated.

The youth who came out was clean-cut and well-enough dressed, if not in any sort of finery. He carried a bag over his shoulder and locked the door behind him with a large key that he then bestowed upon his person. Without appearing to look around, he trotted down the steps and moved off quickly. Behind him, Helena rose from her hiding place and slipped after him.

"Targets one and two" the High Constable quickly relayed instructions; if they remained together, no problem, but if they split up he would have to assign teams to each. But as it seemed that the woman was surreptitiously following the youth, he hoped that they were all going to the same place...where-ever that was...

Dodging from hiding place to hiding place they moved in a silent chain up the deserted street towards the cross-roads ahead. There the youth paused and seemed to drink in the air, for all that it was full of the fumes of coal in its many aspects. Passing across, and dodging only an ancient bicycle ridden by an equally ancient man, the youth approached the beaten-up prospect of an old chapel.

"I don't believe it!" the High Constable exclaimed.
"It would seem so", the young lieutenant watched as the youth palmed a second key from somewhere on his person and unlocked the door, passing quickly within.
"What?" Hector Badger was now thoroughly confused.

Helena Larennia Alexandra paused only briefly before running up to the door and slowly trying the handle. It did not budge, and she hunkered quickly down behind a ruined wall.
"Well, sir?" Eleutheria was not one to rush matters, but she had an eye for strategy.
"Target one is not the target", Charles Ronaldo made his decision, "Target Two is the target- surround the chapel and wait my command."
"And . . . Target One?"
"Ignore her - do *not* shoot her!"

"Yes sir"

- - -

James had grown in stature during his mistress' absence, and this day was tasked to deliver the sermon to three young acolytes, fresh in from the country fields. The network brought them, as it sought them, and he knew not where they were domiciled, only that they would be here, at the Grand Temple, at this allotted time.

He approached the tattered cloth of the old altar and placed his bag upon it. The youngsters were kneeling, one boy and two girls, perhaps old enough to have entered the cadets if their families had wished it, but instead here, before him, because a greater force commanded, He looked them over, and decided that he would have one of the girls later, a prerogative of rank, and one that he was beginning to enjoy in his new-found elevation.

"I bring the future" he said to them, and they gaped and gasped as he withdrew the steel cylinder from out of his bag and carefully unscrewed the top.
Biting down on his fear, he coaxed the inhabitant out of its den, and held it aloft by its midriff
"The Rising is upon us!" he intoned.
"The Rising!" they gasped, and he decided which one he would have, her heaving young bosom depositing a load within his trousers, even at this distance.
"A new way is coming!" he cried.
"Coming!" they repeated.
"Coming...." he gasped.

And the walls blew in.

- - -

"Holy fuck!", Eleutheria skidded to a halt, knife replacing gun in a swift action as the young man beside the altar swung a snake in her direction. Her slash missed, but she was able to dive and roll clear before he curved round again with his unnatural weapon.

Of the acolytes, the boy surrendered on the spot as two Constables emerged from a shattered window to cover him with their weapons. The girls tried to run, one cut down by pistol fire before she had gone a dozen yards, the other cleaved in two by a short sword as she attempted to flee out of a side exit.

Only the youth remained, swinging his snake and chanting something that did not sound like any language the constables had ever heard. Given that Hector Badger was fluent in the languages of the Iroquois, and that the High Constable himself had seen service in Assiboinia as a young man, it seemed certain that this was no dialect of a Native people. Even the Azteca did not speak like this. It could be truly foreign, but how so?

"Put the snake down!" High Constable Charles Ronaldo Harkness approached the fellow.
"The Rising is upon us!" James intoned.
"I dare to say it is", Charles Ronaldo had little doubt about these things, "but yours is over for now"
"A new way is coming!" he shouted at them.
"Oh fuck this...", he drew his pistol and shot the bastard between the eyes.

As he fell, the snake slithered from his grasp and disappeared beneath the altar.
"Sir!" Eleutheria gasped urgently.
He looked slowly at the body, then at the dilapidated altar.
"No", he said, "Soak this house of evil in paraffin and fire it."
"And the bodies?" she looked at the three now lying about them.
"Let them burn"
"Yes sir"

He turned and strode outside. The woman was standing outside of the chapel grounds now, hands on hips, confusion upon her face,
"Come here!" he shouted across to her, "Your Highness"
Constables about him froze and stared but with their officers inside the chapel none dared to ask the question. He waved them on,
"We arranged your death so that you could serve us" he said.

246

She moved hesitantly back towards the railings,
"You have been following me?"
"Your drive was stronger than ours" he said, "They killed your professor, and you found them."

"Are they all dead?" she asked.
"All but one, a mere lad"
"And the Grand Mistress?"
"She was not here"
"I know..." she sagged upon the railings, holding on with her fists, "That is why it was so easy - the priest was but a youth..."
"But highly placed"
"The Serpent moves quickly and often" she had read a lot in a few weeks.
"The Lore of the Serpent is true, but it cannot escape from the facts", he had been reading a lot too, "The Grand Mistress may be on the move, but *this* is the current Grand Temple."

"Ready to fire, sir" Eleutheria looked with curiosity at the woman now standing but scant yards away, apparently in friendly conversation with her boss.
"Destroy it completely" he commanded.
"If only it were so easy", Helena Larennia Alexandra said, "...The Order of the Serpent"
"They will know your wrath" he said.
She smiled,
"I can go home?"
"Is that possible?" he was confused, knowing how loose they had played with her life, her assumed death, and her burial.
"My father is no idiot"
"As you say"
"I can go home"

He paused, then nodded at his men ran from the building and the first whisps of smoke began to rise from its sides,
"The Grand Temple of the Serpent", he smiled, "Yes, you can go home"
"Thank you..." she said.
He nodded, as she walked away, back towards the elevated railway

and a ticket back to a life she had almost forgotten in her quest to escape its bounds.

Shoshona, Albion

"I am truly sorry" she plunged her knife into his neck and a few moments later Deucalion Benington Hart lay dead at her feet, pumping his life blood into the dirty puddles of the sidestreet.

She stood as if waiting for a reply, and when one did not come turned and mounted the dead merchant's horse. Given that she sometimes stayed the night in the stables, unknown to anyone, the animal was not unused to her presence, and let her, after a few skittish moments, command it to move off.

Jocasta Hetherington watched from behind a merchant's cart, heart in her mouth, pistol in her hand, and head somewhere in the clouds. Had she really seen the mad little bitch kill Deucalion? They had all grown up with the crazy child amongst them. True she was more or less a woman now, but to kill him? What could he have done to her? She shook her head - of course, in theory, a powerful figure in the local community could have taken advantage of a poor orphaned girl, but everyone would have known, there was no likelihood that he had abducted her, or snook into her hovel for some evil purpose. The girl was just that - a mildly dirty, rather ragged creature who lived amongst them. But now? Jo did not know whether she was more outraged or curious - what on Earth was going on?

She followed at a discreet distance, the girl seemingly to have to no urge to make her steed go at better than a trot, and although it was wearing, Jo was up to the challenge. She had been working on the farms since she was three, a bit of exhausting exercise was nothing new, though it was hardly welcome either.

Before long they were well outside of Shoshona and heading into the country, the hills rising towards the mountains all around. The sun had just about given up for the day, and the shadows of night were beginning to fall, but on these deserted roads it was no difficulty for Jo to follow the murderous little bitch to where-ever she was going.

That destination proved to be the Caves of Wakini, a rather uninspiring entrance set between a rockfall and a stagnant pool in the lower hills. In past times bears had perhaps lived here, but the trappers had long since seen those off a century or more ago. Perhaps a raccoon or even a coyote ventured this far, but against a well-armed human neither was a threat. The girl clearly felt none, for she tied the horse to a stake she drove into the ground, and with only a small paraffin lamp for company she headed into the caves.

Jo heaved to a halt, watched by the horse, who knew her well as one of Deucalion's friends and business partners.
"Zebra" she shushed the animal to quietude, and drawing her knife, followed in the other's foot-steps.

It was soon truly dark within the cave, and only the jittery light of the girl up ahead gave any clue as to where she was, and where she was going. Jo followed as quietly as she could, just managing to keep the girl in sight, gaining a lucky break when she stopped to consider a split in the tunnel for some moments, allowing her pursuer to catch up close enough to see which one she took.

Some indeterminate time later, they passed over a rocky outcrop and between two gushing pools, apparently linked beneath the rocky bridge by some kind of cataract. The girl entered a side cave and was still, Jo having to duck down behind an outcrop to wait and see what she was doing. The paraffin lamp was still strong, obviously newly-filled, indicating to the watching woman that this was no mere whim, no flight after the event, but instead a purposeful venture that everything else was subordinate to.

A moment later she emerged, something wrapped around her arm. Jo stared through the darkness at it - what was it? Some kind of rope? And then it moved.

"A feast in the dark, sister" the girl said
Jo shivered but did not move

"The Serpent will feed - it is hungry!"

Again, she tried to remain still, but as she did the girl moved forward, and only then did Jocasta realise that she was not holding the paraffin lamp. Yet a steady glow was pervading the cave, but where did it come from?! Jo began to know real fear.

The girl laughed,
"It is written - this night, the Rising is upon us!"
And she strode straight towards where the woman was hiding...

Chapter Eighteen

Kalgoorie*, Australia, Empire of Albion

The sun beat down upon the dips and dells, burning the red-brown soil, slicing into a hundred houses, a dozen parked-up trucks and beating down fiercely upon the backs of a thousand slaves, under the watchful eyes of their overseers.

"The day is ripe", Bernicia Vivienne Coburn was a tall and buxom woman of thirty. Standing in the small shed, she seemed to fill it, despite the space all along the sides.
Geraint Flyn was a small man, a clerk, a nobody from Hamilton on the coast who had worked his way up to Administrative Officer here at Kalgoorie. He was not easily intimidated, not least because few dared, and even fewer held the ground once he had spoken his affiliation,
"I serve the Unicorn" he told her, and waited.

Bernicia was a typical woman in Geraint's limited experience, argumentative and not easily won over by logic. Thus he was not surprised when she just laughed at this announcement, and placed her over-large hands upon the desk,
"The Rising is upon us" she smiled, in a completely un-smiley fashion.
Geraint ran a hand through his thinning hair,
"There is a doctor in the camp, if that is what you need"

"You mistake me", Bernicia had come round behind the desk, outraging Geraint's sense of propriety but overwhelming his ability to contest it, dominated as he now was by the woman leaning down over him.
"Um" he said, "What do you want?"
She laughed and backed off, leaning against a window frame and staring out at a couple of dozen slaves being executed in the weekly round-up, "This must end"
"What?" he looked around the barren shack, "What must?"
"This", she indicated the window and the scene outside that was beyond his vision, "The future is upon us"

"Rising? Future?", he was beginning to get a distinctly bad feeling about this, "I will telephone for the camp Commandant."

"No!", she slammed a surprisingly heavy fist down upon the telephone, shattering it, and looked him squarely in the eye, "I seek the release of my sister."

"Ugh?" his power of speech was rapidly deserting him, "Sister?"

"Svetlana Maria Kuropkin"

"I...I thought you said your name was...Coburn" he whispered

"You recognise her name, of course"

"Halychian witch!" he spat, then realised what she was implying, "but....but..."

"You can release her or die..."

"Um", he looked down at the desk and contemplated life in a world where he was known to have abetted the escape of a slave to the Serpent. There was no hope there at all, "Die" he said

She slit his throat.

(*) On the lines of contractions of other native tongues, here we see a multi-syllable native word being stripped of an element and reduced from Kal-gor-lee to Kal-gor/ree

~

Panama Province, Empire of Albion

The boy was dead, but that was life . . . life, and death joined, as the Serpent had it, and in this case the serpent had well and truly had it. Most of them froze with terror when the snake was inserted, but this one had squirmed and frighted the creature. To die of a snake bite in the rectum was not a pleasant death, but it was not slow either. Sulvia had retrieved the snake and placed it back within the steel cylinder, then called on the sole Acolyte manning this high jungle fastness.

"Grand Mistress?", Ferdinand Bristol Napier had been born to a good family, and had served as a cadet during one of the many interminable wars in the Caribbean. There he had met a High Acolyte of the Serpent, and changed the course of his life, slipping away from the army of Albion and ending up here, in Panama, not technically a deserter as the crimes of cadets remain on the books only for a couple of years. Now in his thirtieth year, he had no fear of Constables or investigators investigating that ancient crime. He had many more recent ones to concern them.

"The slave failed the test" she said.
Ferdinand looked at the grotesque grimace on the face of the dead slave boy, and knew what had happened. Like all recruits to the Serpent he had gone through it himself, to be literally possessed by the serpent, and like most he had frozen still until the ordeal had ended. But there were always those who writhed or spasmed, and a death like this was not so uncommon to be rare amongst their number.
"I will dispose of the body", he bowed, and with the muscular strength in his shoulders, hefted the slender lad up onto them.
"You serve well" she told him.
"Mistress" he said, and was gone.

The door swung shut, and Sulvia relaxed upon the sofa. Before his untimely death, the slave had served her well, and her appetites were truly nourished for the moment. There were more important things to think about, but the Serpent taught that to focus on them one had to break through baser things by indulging in them, and getting them out of the way. That after all was the lesson of the Garden of Eden...

She picked up the telephone and manually dialed a series of numbers. The first few routed the call via a secure private exchange South of the border, well away from snooping ears of who knew which agency of the Imperial government. Compared to Albion, Corrientes was a pathetic little principality, one of half a dozen on the Northern rim of the Southern continent which were pulled between the competing influences of Albion and High Brasil. Its biggest advantage was its poverty, making anything for sale, and the Orders worked hard to increase their position there, the first stop, as it were, after leaving Imperial territory.

"Channel Two", the voice was heavy and gravelly but spoke clearly.
"So he drove out the man, and he placed at the East of the Garden of Eden Cherubims"
"Understood", there were a few clicks and hisses, and then a new connection.
"This is the demesne of Raymond Alfonso Lopez", the voice again was clear, and its choice of language indicated that whoever had picked up the call knew from whence it had originated.
"I need a fast ship", Sulvia said.
"From where to where?"
"I will return to Panama City, but I need to get to Tumaco in the first instance."
"I will send my own yacht to pick you up."
"What is its IPN?"

An Individual Patrol Number was how vessels in these waters were identified to the navies of the competing powers of Albion, Corrientes and the Incas in Peru. Valid across all three jurisdictions, an IPN could get you out of much trouble - or into it, if the authorities had black-listed you, but only fools fell into that trap.
"312-219-007" the voice said, "Do you copy?"
"Copied", she acknowledged, "Is four days enough?"
"I will instruct my captain to depart at once", he paused, "When you see the ship, ask for Pietr...there is no Pietr but he will understand"
"Understood"
"May I terminate now?", the voice was in this, as everything, deferential.

254

"Terminate"

The line went dead, and Sulvia herself hung up.

It would take her no more than a day and a half to return to Panama, and she was not keen to spend too long roaming around the city. An agent of the Serpent was always marked, whether the enemy knew that they were or not. It was always a matter of time, a question of how long it was safe. She would remain here until it was necessary to leave. Ferdinand would be no fun, but there were slave boys and girls on the local estate she could borrow, or hire, or even buy if the mood took her. She would not lack for things to amuse her...

~

Panama City, Empire of Albion

"Well?!" Caitlin Elizabeth Howard was a petite young woman, but she more than made up for this by the identification that she carried.

"Ungh", High Constable Luis Maria Valdano was never happy to see people like her, and their credentials served only to freeze his blood, even in such a place of heat as was Panama.

"I have been instructed to investigate why this death was not rated top priority" she told him, using all of her five foot height to its full.

"But..." he bit it off, knowing that nobody argued with such a one and gained by it, "I apologise for the oversight", he muttered.

Caitlin nodded, as if such things were common-place in her experience, which they were. As an Invicta Commander, she acted as an agent for the Great Chamberlain, and through him the Imperial Court, over-riding all local authority, whether military, civilian or religious, and she had at her beckoning anyone she asked for, once they had accepted her as genuine, usually a task that would take a military commander no more than five or ten minutes. People angered an Invicta Commander only at their own dire peril, and because of this few even embarked upon that course of action. Everybody knew where it might lead, and it took a brave soul even to demand proof of the assertion that such a rank was indeed held - although the penalty for impersonation was to be dismembered alive, and fed to the fire in stages.

"Full name?" she looked at the autopsy sheet and shook her head; how could people be so sloppy!

"He was Harold Swan Buckmeister of Saint Johns"

"Definitely?" she asked

"We have, ah, carried out extensive investigations"

"Now you have", she said, and tossed the autopsy at him, "Then you did not"

"Ah...he was a passenger who appeared to have died from natural causes"

"Snake venom...", she spat, "It is perhaps natural to the snake"

"Many apologies"

"Desist!" she raised her hand, tired of the incessant apologising, "Be useful henceforth and I will see to it that the first part of the report is summarised in brief."

"Yes", he said, nodding vigorously, "We have interviewed those of his fellow passengers whom we were able to trace."

"How many?"

"Er...three", Luis Maria looked sheepish, but Panama was a place to come to in order to go somewhere else, and not many of those arriving from the North hung around more than a day or two before moving on.

"And the crew?"

"Um..." he took a deep breath, "Whilst it is true that the train that formed the Azteca Express on its Southward journey is still here, a new train was waiting to depart, and did so within forty-eight hours with perhaps three-quarters of the same crew aboard.."

"Ah", she had not foreseen that, "Where would it be now?"

"Perhaps exiting the Azteca provinces?", he was not sure, but this seemed a fair guess, "We could perhaps instruct the Constables at Saint Richard's to intercept it in a day or so."

"I will liaise, do not do anything"

"Yes, of course", he nodded.

"These...three passengers you found, what are their statements?"

Luis Maria drew them out of a faded pink folder that had perhaps once been red,

"One is a drunkard and spent all of his time in the bar car; he saw the

256

deceased in the presence of a beautiful woman many times, but cannot remember anything about her, other than that"

"She has that knack" Caitlin said.

"Er...." the High Constable peered at her, "Who does?"

"Go on - the other two?"

"Um...yes", he gathered his shattered wits, "Another observed that at meal times, the deceased was sometimes to be seen in the company of a....he terms her a loose bedraggled whore..."

"Anything more?"

"Some strange statement that she sometimes put food to take away into a metal case she carried with her..."

"Of course"

There was a pause, then Luis Maria coughed.

"Ah, right, um, the third person was a woman"

"Some people are" Caitlin reminded him.

"Oh yes... She said that she had seen the deceased and a woman together on several occasions, but when the train came in, the woman exited alone and left the concourse attended only by a slave boy."

"Because the deceased was dead" Caitlin pointed out.

"Because she had killed him?" Luis Maria was no further forward despite all of this.

"Without a doubt"

"Why....er, why are you so certain?", he wasn't sure that he should be asking this of her, but did not think he could do his job unless he knew.

"Because she is the Grand Mistress of the Order of the Serpent..."

Fort Fluffy, Patagonia

"General Engineering", Tabitha Clarissa Theresa read their credentials with a raised eyebrow, "There is a problem here?" she asked.

Arthur Spinks drew himself up to his, admittedly not very impressive, full height,

"You have a light here... Central directives are to make sure that all such non-combatant lights remain in this state."

"A fair point", the dynast looked across to where Swift Commander

Terrance De L'isle was watching the proceedings with a distinctly unhappy look upon his face, "What do you intend to do?" she asked.

"This is a collar", Spinks indicated the contraption that Leopold Hubertus Scheer hefted up into the air, "We intend to place this around the light."
"It *is* in ice, you do know that?", Terrance was no longer able to restrain himself.
"This device does not require penetration of the ice", Spinks was certain that he was not about to accidentally release the damned thing, "We will place it in between its position and its potential egress."
"And what good will that do?" the Imperial Airforce officer fingered the thing with suspicion.

Spinks coughed; in similar circumstances he would have thrown them out on their ears, but he had to continue to bluff the man, apart from the fort's Governor the most influential fellow upon the base,
"If the light attempts to move from its imprisonment towards freedom, this device will intercept it"
"Hmmm..." Terrance was interested, despite his general scepticism, "Can you use these things akin to mines in combat zones?"
"Um", Spinks did a rapid calculation of gambits in his mind, "That is the hope, certainly"
"Brilliant!" the Swift Commander came forward, all smiles, "May I accompany you when you install it? I really am most fascinated."
"Of course", Spinks said, hiding his dejection.

Ten minutes later, the contraption dumped back into a storage cupboard, Spinks and Scheer stood before Ramona Elise Carding in a deserted room that had once been some kind of alcohol store, at least to judge by the couple of bottles almost embedded in the ice which was busy reclaiming this part of its lost territory.
"Excellent", the senior Shadow Service officer beamed, "You even convinced me that you were idiots from General!"
"It is somewhat demeaning" Spinks pointed out.
"But very useful" she reminded him.
"And we still have to put the piece of crap into position"

Ramona laughed

"But it is priceless! Nobody will know it does not work unless the light gets free and kills us all, at which point nobody will care!"
"That is a point" Spinks agreed, "I feel like I am playing Imposters with a family of particularly naughty children!"
"It is a good game" Ramona said, "But we must play it well"
"Yes"
"And you?" she looked at Scheer.

The Acolyte blanched,
"I do the best I can, Highness"
She regarded him for a moment, then nodded
"Yes, I believe you do" she agreed.

~

Albion City, Imperial Capital

"The Grand Master of the Order of the Bear!", the herald was young, not much older than a cadet, but sonorous of voice, hence his selection to serve within the Imperial Palace.

Horace Aloysius Despenser stood and waited whilst the short, shambling man entered the grand audience chamber. The newcomer bowed and grinned,
"I heard that you were in charge!", he laughed, "The cat is away, will the mouse play?"

"What can a bear do to a mouse?" Horace asked, motioning the man to a seat.
"Eat its feet whilst it hibernates?" the newcomer laughed, "But let us not fence, I am here to call in the debt, old friend"
"Bulgarians..." muttered Horace, Lord High Chancellor of the Empire of Albion.

"The newspapers are so full of the hunt for the Serpent Queen, and the alleged feud between the Dragon and the Unicorn, but nine of us are left without"
"Of course" Horace nodded, "Tea?"

"Beer"

"Er, right", he signaled to a slave hovering on the edge of vision and a moment later two frothing glasses of beer were brought forth upon a tray, "Proper Albion beer", he said.

"Is there such a thing?" the Grand Master sipped from his, "This is not bad"

"Is that not what I said?"

The man looked at him and shook his head,

"No" he said.

Jeremiah Nathaniel Gold had not been born to the Bear, as most of its remaining adherents had been, but instead had served his time in the Caribbean, fighting the insurgents and returned home disillusioned in time to hear the final speech of the great Bear orator of the last generation, Douglas Kershaw, asking to what men were addicted, why they fought, and whether the false idols most cleaved to made any sense at all. Instead of the Imperial Church, Kershaw had advocated allegiance to the Order of the Bear, and Gold had chosen so, rising in the next thirty years from a disaffected young veteran to the Grand Master of a global order, albeit one mentioned only in the second breath of commanders who remembered their politics.

"The debt…" Jeremiah said slowly and softly.

"I will hear your proposal", the Lord High Chancellor had not got to where he was today by being easily blackmailed, or pressurized.

Jeremiah looked around the vast hall and nodded,

"I do not see the Emperor here", he said.

Horace made no comment, but waited.

"Nor did I last year when I attended a ceremony awarding medals to those of exceptional merit in Georgia"

"What of it?", Horace affected disinterest.

"Then I saw the Great Chamberlain", he looked up at the dais, "though perhaps 'saw' is to overstate it"

"Now you see me", Horace both completed the other man's statement and pre-empted it.

"Very true", Jeremiah drained his glass and placed back upon the tray, "The debt?"

"What do you want?", Horace sat down heavily and motioned his

260

guest to do the same, "We are not about to change the machinery of government to cater for the interests of a small Order"

"One is always happier when the other speaks his true feelings", Jeremiah was not insulted, "How about a trade before the repayment? If you find value in the trade, then the repayment of the debt will follow…"

"Very well", the Lord High Chancellor sighed.

"The Grand Mistress of the Serpent is trying to get into Corrientes", Jeremiah said

"A supposition?" Horace snorted.

"The Bear has people in Tupaco, this is fact"

"Hmmm….she will have to sail there, I assume?"

"From Panama"

"Where we have the Elite Guard mobilized" Horace pointed out.

"And that has been successful so far?" Jeremiah snorted.

"The first time it is will be the last time it needs to be"

"Sophistry!" the Grand Master of the Bear made a sound somewhere between a laugh and a snort, "A gambler could say the same for a lottery…"

"I think the odds rather favour us more" Horace smugged.

"I think you have not asked Cyclops to calculate them" Jeremiah returned.

There was silence for a moment, then the visitor tried a different tack,

"You should ask yourself why a General Engineering team commandeered an airship for Fort Fluffy", he said.

"Fort what?", Horace was bemused.

"Its in Patagonia", Jeremiah said patiently, "Fort Fluffy has been the official designation of this fort for over a hundred years."

"If you say so"

"And my question?"

"Is irrelevant", the Lord High Chancellor rose and shook his head, "You come here and speak in riddles; what am I supposed to make of this?"

"Your ignorance is instructive", Jeremiah agreed.

"I think the debt has lapsed", Horace smiled widely, "The Bear clearly is of no consequence"

"You will not say that!" Jeremiah was in his face.

"You are irrelevant!" Horace laughed, "There is only the Unicorn – and the Serpent, but we will soon destroy that"

"Now your ignorance is alarming"

"There is no debt here", Horace shook his head, "I was a fool to think there was"

"What does the Emperor think?" Jeremiah snapped.

"You are no longer welcome here without an invitation – none of the lesser Orders are"

"This is a day that will live in infamy", the Grand Master had the other up close and was breathing angrily into his face, "People will write whole histories about this!"

"You have two minutes to depart or I will set you up as a training exercise"

"You bastard…", but Jeremiah left

A minute later, Horace crossed to a plinth and the statue of a buxom woman, manipulating one of her breasts,

"Target in external corridor three, estimated position one hundred yards. Terminate and dispose of"

"Yes sir" came the voice, dispassionate as stone.

Chapter 19

It was dark, more than dark - there was no light at all, but even that was not the weirdest. Leonora Bunny knew that she was lying down, somehow, somewhere, and that something was watching her - somehow, in the dark. She wanted to cry about her father, but nothing seemed to work. She knew that she ought to be scared, but fear did not come. She thought about her home back in Britannia, but though she could visualise it, she could not mourn it. It was all very strange - and that ought to have been frightening, but somehow it was not.

Some time later a light seemed to come on, and she was in a room with white walls, a white ceiling, and a white floor, lying upon a white couch. She stirred and rose slowly into a sitting position, blinking at the light, looking around her in confusion. Memories streamed across her consciousness, thoughts chasing each other unto exhaustion, and she sat there, eyes focused internally, body seeming as if frozen in time.

"We hope you are rested?"
The voice came from nowhere, and she blinked, looking around, but nothing had changed.
"Who are you?" she asked, but still fear would not come, though she knew that it ought.
"We are the grains of the sand and the droplets of the rain" the voice said.
She thought about it a while, who knew how long, and decided that it was something profound, but that only people with certain aforeknowledge would have understood. She did not think her ignorance related to her childish years; many adults would not have understood either, she was sure.

"Why cannot I see you?" she asked.
"There is no thing to see", was the reply.
"There must be something", she thought about her lessons, "There can be no light without fire, even if that fire burns on a scale that man can never see"
"You are learned" the voice said, "but you cannot see us"

"I could see the lights", she protested, though without emotion she felt it more as a point made in a mild discussion, although knowing that it was not
"We are manifest"
"Is that not the same as being?" she asked.
"That we would not know"

There was another silence - minutes, or hours, perhaps even days. There was time, but there was no measurement. She blinked,
"Why did you kill my father?"
"The term is a biological curiosity" the voice said.
"Not to me" she said, but the anger, fear and guilt would not come out; they were there, guiding her thoughts, but they would not transcend.
"You need to come with us" the voice said.
"I am with you", she was sure of that.
"We are moving"
"Where?"
"Humans have such a limited understanding of spatial temporal matters."

There was nothing for a while afterwards, and then there was a light in the room, a glowing globe that seemed to come straight out of the fabric of being, not entering, just being.
"You know not to ask" the voice said
"You can hear my questions before I ask them?" she said
"Some", the light circled around her, "This brings to you familiarity?"
"It is familiar" she answered, if that was what they meant.
"Merge and be one and we will be elsewhere"

She did nothing, but also did not stop the light as it closed and merged with her. A moment later everything flashed out of existence, and she was on a hillside in the rain. She started to cry...

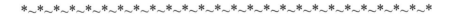

Somewhere in Albion

"Uhhhh", Sebastian Patrick O'Brien stretched and looked around him
Same old shack, same old walls, same old calendar dated five years

before and showing models who were probably now married with children. It made him sick, well mad, or perhaps just annoyed. But it seemed to be no way to be spending his life, but that was the essence of guard duty, and those he was guarding did not want to be drawing too much attention to themselves by renovating the guard post.

"Huh?" he stood up as a commotion became clear outside. Pausing to listen, he could hear a half dozen voices, give or take, and they did not sound happy. "What?"
He grabbed his gun from the rack, fastened on his helmet against the incessant rain, and pulling his cloak tight around him, stepped forth into the night.
"Who goes there?!" he demanded, looking around.

"Insect in the halls of infamy!", the speaker was a tall, rangy man, dark in countenance but with eyes that blazed blue in the beams of Sebastian's torch and hair that seemed to speak of sand itself.
"Are you addressing me?" Sebastian hefted his gun to bring it to bear on where the man was coming slowly down an incline.
"You and your kind" the man said.
"You make assumptions about people you do not know", Sebastian was reluctant to shoot him out of hand, and was half-hoping that banter might win the day, all the while remembering that there were several more of them out here.

"He speaks true", a girl emerged from behind a rock, "We do not know this man!"
"Perhaps", a boy had materialised, as it seemed, by her side.
"Children?!", Sebastian looked from the man to the kids, and frowned, "Are you on the run?"
"And if we were?" the man did not seem happy at the children's actions, but for the moment he was playing their game.
"As long as you are neither Unicorn nor Serpent, we can offer you sanctuary here."

The man seemed to freeze, and a moment later Sebastian's blood did the same. A dozen more of them emerged from out of the darkness, and trooped down to stand behind their leader, or spokesman. But what really made him clench his buttocks tight, and think of anything but a sudden desperate need to pee was the globe of light that seemed to glide down the hillside towards them.

"You...you..." he blurted, and slapped himself round the face, an old remedy a long-dead sergeant had once taught him for those times when senses were all one had to go on, but were being overwhelmed, "That is a light"

"It is", the girl came down the slope towards him, "It is our guide"

"Oh..." Sebastian continued to eye the thing warily, but knew enough from newspaper reports not to be so stupid as to open fire on it, "Does it communicate?"

"Not quite", the speaker this time was a beautiful woman, dusky of skin, and...

"Oh my God!", Sebastian dropped to one knee, "You are Lucille Drusilla Marguerite!"

The light seemed to freeze in motion, and the woman came up to him, "That is my name" she affirmed, "but I do not know you..."

"This", he waved a hand behind him, "This is a Dragon installation.... Your....your uncle commanded it to be"

"They will treat us as kin?" she pressed him.

"Without a doubt", he rose to his feet, "The niece of the late High Dragomaster.... We will be honoured"

"Then let it be"

Sebastian looked at the light,

"If I let that in..." he began.

"It will enter whether you let it in or not" she pointed out.

"How can I condone it?" he demanded.

"It has led us through the country from the slave train" she said, simply

He nodded, and swallowed,

"I need to inform them not to attack it"

"Not all guards are as sensible as you", the man said, coming up to them now, speaking neither a question nor an insult, just a fact.

Sebastian looked into his startling blue eyes,

"They are not" he agreed.

"I will help to frame the call" he said.

There was an awkward silence before Sebastian was able to find a riposte to that

"With respect" he stammered, "this is Dragon business....sir"
"Shall the axe boast itself against him that heweth therewith?"
"I....I see", Sebastian lowered his gun, "How...?"
"Why do you think the slave train was formed?"
Sebastian eyed him, and sighed.
"I see", he said again, "Come; let us make that call"
They disappeared inside the shack.

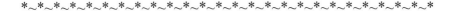

Surrey, High Province of Britannia

Sometimes it seemed that all that it did was rain. As she walked the hills and forests to the South of London, Sarah Alexandria Dunelm swore within her heart to kill the rain, to chop the rain's head off, to somehow dismember the individual droplets...but it was just a way of venting her frustration.

The Great Chamberlain had reduced Rannoch to a mere cypher, a ticker of boxes and a scrawler of signatures, and for her, they had taken over many of her security duties. But she retained her position, and on the basis that any operation not deemed the Chamberlain's business, was still hers, she had kept back several reports, and was now out hunting, dressed in simple leathers and with over a dozen lethal weapons about her person.

The quarry, in the hunter's sense, was not a single person but an organisation, but she had experience of those as well, and she had perseverance amongst her secret weapons. She paused beneath an ancient tree, and using its canopy as cover unwrapped the map - she was somewhere near Windsor, out in the woods towards Ascot, an estate formally owned by the crown but long-since alienated to the Despenser family, whose current status at the Imperial Court was no small part of the reason that she was here.

Sighting landmarks from the map, she folded it away and moved off, up a wooden slope, and then over a ditch, beyond which she at last gained her first sight of the target - a large, sprawling nineteenth century manor house. Of course, the Lord High Chancellor did not live here, being always across the Atlantic in Albion City, but he owned it, and various members of his family used it, either as a holiday home, or as a base for their visits to Europe. She had been unable to find out who exactly was in residence now, deciding not to put out any feelers on the matter in case the Great Chamberlain's agents picked up on her asking, but she was sure that somebody would be there - there was always somebody there, even if just a dissolute cousin taking advantage of the fact that no more senior member of the Despenser family was using it at the time, so moving in until he was turfed out some weeks later.

She also knew that it was not fortified, and that security depended on Despenser family retainers rather than on Elite Guards, and that the former were often rather lazy and distracted, finding the joys of the house more to their liking than traipsing around in the woods upon patrol, especially in weather such as this. Nevertheless, she was skilled at what she did, and reckoned she could have got past them anyway.

She crawled forward until the hedges and fences bounding the property came into view, and made a series of calculations as to the best route, and alternatives to take in an emergency. Then she flitted quickly from the tree-line to the nearest hedge and began her penetration.

- - -

Behind her, Jessica was having an even worse time of it in the rain. Tracking a prey such as this, one had to invert what you knew - cover was great, but if the hunter was checking the cover behind her as she moved, it was unsafe. Consequently, Jessica had often been reduced to slithering on her belly across fields or woodland, using her shielded binoculars to keep the Captain-General of the Security Directorate in view.

Invicta Commander Jessica Ilaria Monroe had been tracking her for some weeks now, not personally of course, but using agents sworn to the Great Chamberlain, but until now there had been nothing of particular note to report. The agents reported that she was hated, but feared, and that her own type of terror usually got things done, though with little acknowledgment of Imperial laws and edicts. The more pressing cases before the Security Directorate, the Great Chamberlain had kept for himself, but Sarah Alexandria Dunelm had sworn her loyalty in the Audience Chamber, and could not be removed without good cause. Jessica was pretty sure that she would have one now.

She rose and ran through the woods, beneath the sight-line of her prey ahead, cresting the rise and merging once again with the sodden earth as she scanned the land ahead. The great house lay invitingly before her, and there was the Captain-General, just passing beneath a hedge, some kind of rabbit run or perhaps a terrier hole allowing her to squeeze through.

Jessica was in two minds how to proceed from here. As an Invicta Commander, she had the Great Chamberlain's prior approval for whatever action she took, whoever she had arrested or executed, or had to kill in the line of her work, but which path was actually the best one for the Empire was not immediately clear at this juncture. Also, whilst she was sure that she could tail the Captain-General successfully, she was not absolutely sure that she could sneak up on her and cut her throat, though it was certainly an option.

Nobody would complain - not even that dog Rannoch who was so much under her thumb. Without her, he would lack the backbone to speak up to the Great Chamberlain, and become even more the rubber stamp that the Great Chamberlain was already turning him into. None of the Security Directorate's agents or employees would miss her, and in fact many were already working more for the Great Chamberlain than they were for her. By invading the estate of the Lord High Chancellor, Sarah Alexandria Dunelm had put herself beyond the bounds of the law, and Jessica could kill her at once, if that was to be the outcome.

Ahead, her prey was using the shadows cast by the house itself as cover as she ran at a stoop across a patch of open ground. If she continued on this course she would enter via the servants wing, and be lost to observation. Jessica rose, and made to follow directly in the footsteps of the woman before her.

~

Somewhere in Albion

The group standing before the barracks-like buildings of the base looked decidedly ill at ease as the light approached, leading a motley group of men, women and children down the dimly-lit path. Sebastian Patrick O'Brien walked to one side, gun pointed at the ground, but keeping his own eyes upon the light; after all, he only had their word for it that the thing would not harm them.

"I am the Dragomaster", a tall, thin man somewhere in an undefined middle age stepped forward, his sharp black eyes going from the light to the man who stood at the head of the newcomers, then to the woman at his side, "Yes" he said, "You are Lucille Drusilla Marguerite"

"I am" she said
"And you?" the Dragomaster looked at the man beside her
"I will hear your name first", the newcomer said sharply.
"As you will; I am Gervaise Salvatore Calvo"
"Claude Jameson Marquez"

Either the name meant nothing to the Dragomaster, or he was not going to show what it did mean. He nodded sharply, and then indicated the people behind him, beginning to introduce the officers and acolytes, all the while keeping the light firmly within his field of vision.

Behind the leading adults, but ahead of most of the newcomers, the two children walked closely side by side, eyes scanning the base all around them, looking every now and then to the guard who still walked a little apart, as if he didn't quite trust them.
"He doesn't like us" Sarah-Anne said.
Her cousin watched him a moment, then laughed
"He doesn't dislike us; he just doesn't like the light"
"But it has helped us" the girl protested.
"I think it helps only us" Elias said.
"Why?"
But to that he had no answer…

270

~

Surrey, High Province of Britannia

Samson Osvaldo Despenser frowned as he looked through the binoculars,
"Marie!" he called his sister over, "I can see a girl on that hill…crying"
"A girl?", Marie was slender, slight and slow.
She came across to his side, and peered through the window out into the rain,
"I can't see" she said.
"Use these", Samson prodded the binoculars at her, "Over there",; more gently he guided her elbow so that she was pointing them in the right direction.
"I can see a girl" she said, "Yes she is crying in the rain…"
"But what is she doing out there?" Samson retrieved the binoculars and adjusted the focus, "You know", he said, "She looks vaguely familiar but I'm sure she doesn't live round here"
"Oh…" his sister said.

Making up his mind, the second cousin to the Lord High Chancellor moved across the room and pulled the bell. Not twenty seconds later one of the butlers was opening the door,
"You rang, sir?" he asked.
"Pickett, yes?"
"Yes sir"
"Pickett, there's a young girl sitting on the North Hill, crying"
"Crying, sir?"
"I can see her through these", he checked that she was still there, and nodded, "Send someone out to see if she is alright, and whether she wants to come into the warmth."
"Here, sir?" the butler sounded rather shocked.
"She looks vaguely familiar – I can't think why"
"Very well sir"
"And make sure you send a woman out with whoever goes; we don't want to scare her any more than she already is"
"Yes sir"

The butler exited and a moment later his stentorian voice could be heard echoing down the hallway. Samson was at the window, again "Why is she just sitting there?" he asked.

Marie gave no reply, not having any answer.

- - -

Sarah paused, bloodied knife in her hand and looked around her. She had the strangest feeling; was there a cat perhaps out there, watching her? She had always been able to sense when one was doing that, hidden but with eyes upon her. She carried out a quick, but detailed, survey of the lawn to her rear, the upturned pots to her side, and the darkened kitchen right in front of her, but apart from the bloodied body of the kitchen boy before her, she could see no life. But there was definitely something…

She moved into the kitchen, not a main one, just a small room that the servants used for cooking their own meals, and at this time of the day it ought to have been abandoned. Unluckily for the lad who now lay with his throat cut, it had not been, though she was unsure what he had been doing. Logically there might have been a girl in there hiding, but she had come upon only him, taken by surprise, and dispatched him. Nobody else was inside. She shrugged; perhaps he was taking this last little secret to the grave with him, he could hardly deny him that.

She moved quickly into the interior, passing through dimly-lit corridors, moving swiftly past doors behind which the usual hubbub of life, or love, could be heard. She would kill if necessary, and anyone who saw her would be necessary, but killing for its own sake was only a distraction, though sometimes it had an effect later that one wanted to create. Not this time, however.

She moved swiftly on.

- - -

Jules Pickett had carried out a quick calculation, and after ascertaining a couple of basic facts had had one of the house slaves bring him a telephone. He had placed a call through to the stables and instructed a couple of the grooms, one of whom had to be female, to mount up and ride out straight away to the North Hill. Between receiving his instructions, and two horses galloping out of the stables there had been less than five minutes.

"There", Roger Gilbert was a muscular lad of seventeen, and had been brushing down the house's prized stallion when the telephone call had come through. To have a chance to actually ride the animal, and at the gallop had been priceless, and though he was doing so bareback, he was loving every moment of it.

"I see her", Charlotte was his cousin, twenty years of age and one of the few females in the stables who were not numbered amongst his lovers, not for any reasons of family propriety but simply because she preferred her own kind, and never gave in to temptation to swing both ways.

They slowed to a trot and approached the girl who was clearly drenched to the skin. The child could not be more than ten, probably younger, and was sitting weeping, but now looked up at their arrival, her glance more one of confusion than fear.

"Please can we take you inside?" asked Charlotte; it was not exactly the way that the butler had told her to phrase it, but she felt pity for the poor child and did not want her out here any more than was necessary.

The girl blinked and looked from one to the other of them,

"Where am I?" she asked.

"At the Despenser estate outside of Ascot" Roger said, "Where did you come from?"

But she only shook her head.

"Can you ride?" Charlotte had jumped down from her mount, and was holding the reins, motioning to the saddle that had fortunately still been on the animal when the butler had called.

"Of course I can" the girl said, but made no move.

"Prove it!" Roger had either a brainwave or a serious mental malfunction, but only time would tell.

The girl stood slowly up, rivulets of water running down her dress, and Charlotte could see some older stains near the neck of the garment, ones that looked suspiciously like dried blood, now as sodden as the dress itself. If someone had done what she feared they had to her, Charlotte vowed to kill them.

But the girl approached the horse without fear, and took a hold, a moment later vaulting up into the saddle,
"I ride alone" she said, proudly.
Charlotte looked across to Roger who shrugged
"You are always welcome to hug my body" he said.
His cousin sniffed, and got up behind him.
"Show us that you can ride him" Roger said, feeling a mite more secure now that the girl had proved that she at least knew how to mount up.
The child looked at him,
"Is this a competition?" she asked all serious.
"It can be, if you want"

She nodded and looked down the hill,
"That is the stables down there?"
"That is where we are going"
"It is a race?"
Roger did not know what to say; one thing he was certain was that the current Despenser resident would have him lashed if he caused the death of a child on their property,
"It is wet" he said.
"You do not think I can ride as well as an adult" the girl said.
"I think it is possible, but I do not even know who you are"

There was silence for a moment, then the girl nodded
"I am Leonora Bunny Schenk"
Roger did not find her middle name amusing, being almost a hundred years too young for that; once it would have seemed a strange choice, but ever since Princess Berenice in the 1950s had been called Bunny by the newspapers, people had been including the name as a full and correct name in their children's names.
"Schenk?" Charlotte knew rather more about politics than her cousin did, "Are you related to Count Roger?"
"I was" the girl said, sadly
"Was?" Charlotte gasped.
"The light killed him"

And with that, Leonora Bunny was off down the hill, riding at a mad-cap pace towards the stables.

"Shit!" her action had caught Roger out, and he quickly kicked the stallion into action, tearing down the hillside after her, amazed at how fast and steady the girl could go in such awful conditions…

- - -

"Hell!" Jessica swore and dived back behind the hedge as a child on a horse came tearing past her. She had been so focused on closing the distance to the house that she had failed to note the rest of her surroundings. How bloody stupid could she be?! But her prey had entered through a beat-up door, and from what she could see in the doorway, she had already killed. The Invicta Commander had been trying to cut her off by reaching one of the lounge patios where the door stood open, when the girl and horse had almost ridden straight into her.

She raised herself slowly, then ducked down again as a second horse thundered by. Were these people mad? Everywhere was wet, and as she raised her head she could see that the second horse was not even saddled.

"Despenser without a doubt" she said, speaking the familiar superiority that followers of the Great Chamberlain felt towards the family of his deputy, the Lord High Chancellor.

Making sure that the horses were now gone, she rose and moved off, quickly closing towards the open door and hoping that her prey was not busy slaughtering the inhabitants of the great house.

- - -

"I say…" Samson put down the binoculars with a puzzled gaze and walked to the bell, giving it a mighty heave.

This time a woman answered, hot towels and soap in her hand

"I am ready to warm the child up, sir" she said

Samson looked at her, then barged past and stared around the upper hallway beyond, before singling out a burly man who was stood at one end, reading a book to a small boy.

"You, what is your function?"

"Er...family retainer sir... George Hampton at your service"

"Are you armed?"

"Er, yes sir", he passed the book to the child, and drew out a long-barreled pistol.

"Good" Samson was happy enough, "There is a woman sneaking up towards the patio lounge just below. If you could fetch her...?"

"Yes sir", he made to move off then frowned, "What if she does not want to be fetched, sir?"

"I hardly think that she is coming here to pay her respects" Samson said, "I would prefer her alive though; corpses are not good at answering questions"

"Yes sir", the man handed the boy over to a young woman and trotted off down the staircase.

Samson leant thoughtfully upon the doorpost, then noticed the woman with the towels hovering by,

"Go and see to the girl; I will meet with her when she is decent."

"Yes sir"

"Sammy?", Marie had moved to her brother's side, a puzzled frown on her pretty vacant face, "Why is there a woman sneaking around in the gardens?"

"Exactly", Samson patted her forehead affectionately, "That is exactly the question I want to ask her"

"Oh good", Marie basked in her brother's praise.

- - -

The man did not scream, but his head bounced and rolled, to come to rest at Sarah's feet. She paused in her moving down the corridor and looked down upon the suddenly sightless eyes with interest,

"So..." she said, nodding, "That is how it will be"

She rounded the corner, to find the rest of the man scattered around a small ante-room, and a globe of light hovering in the centre of the room.

"Hello" she said, and nodded, "You make quite an entrance"

The light was unmoved by this.

Sarah sheafed her knife, and kicked the severed hand of the man out of her path, squatting down before the light and looking up at it,

"Are you here with me?" she asked it.

The globe of light whizzed around a small circular perimeter of its own devising before returning to its original static position in mid air.
"Excellent" Sarah snorted, "That could mean yes, no, or something else"
The light did it again, and she grinned
"If that is signaling agreement about my comment, then your first answer was also an affirmative"
The light did it once more.
"Of course", she said, "You might just be fed up with the sound of my voice"
It did not move
"Interesting…"

- - -

"Lie down on the floor!"
Jessica froze and stared at the man. He had been standing directly behind the curtain as she had entered, frozen still and out of her perception. She nodded and did as she was commanded.
"Hands out" he said, and she obeyed.
"Make one move and I shoot you" he warned as he patted her down and removed an assortment of weapons, raising his eyebrows as he did, and sending them spinning back out onto the patio.
"Get up slowly and take off your trousers and underwear"

Jessica did as commanded, throwing the soaking wet garments at the man's feet. Let him look upon her genitals if he wished; it was of no concern to her.
"Now move", he seemed quite uninterested.
"Where?" she spoke for the first time.
"Through that door and up the stairs to the left"
"There is a killer in the house" she said, though she did as she was bidden.
"I ask no questions of the family" he said.

Jessica puzzled on this as they exited the lounge and began to mount a staircase, a couple of younger men with guns bearing on them at the top, though their eyes kept straying down below her waist.

"I am here to protect the family" she said.

He said nothing

"The killer is a woman…"

"You are wrong" he laughed, "The Lady Marie would not harm a fly"

"Down there" she said, but he prodded her in the back and she quietened down

They passed the two men with guns who still stared low, ogling the sight down there, then approached a pair of large doors, ajar with the sound of voices from within.

"Wait" he said, and knocked.

"Bring her in" a male voice said.

He prodded her and she passed through into a sitting room, met by the raised eyebrows of a noble dynast and the nervous laughter of a young woman…no doubt this Marie who would not hurt a fly. She bowed

"Invicta Commander Jessica Ilaria Monroe" she said

Samson stared at her, then nodded

"Samson Osvaldo Despenser and this is my sister Marie Alethea"

"Delighted", Jessica bowed at the young woman who giggled the harder

An elderly man entered behind her, and waited

"Pickett?" Samson asked.

"Sir, the girl is in the stables…"

"That is good work. Has the woman gone to her?"

"Yes sir", Pickett waited.

"Thank you"

He still did not move

"Is there something more?" Samson asked with a sigh, realizing that there had to be some reason why she had been sitting on a hill in the rain, and if there was, it was probably something very bad that as senior dynast here he was going to have to do something about.

"She claims that her name is….Leonora Bunny Schenk" the butler said

"Schenk?!" Jessica ejaculated.

"That is why she was familiar" Marie said, tugging on her brother's arm, "Remember the ball last year at the count's estate…"

278

"Very much" Samson nodded, "I may even have danced with her as a courtesy"

"Sir?" asked Pickett, anxious to be away from the naked buttocks of the woman he was standing behind.

"Good work" Samson said, and looked at the woman, "Arm the retainers and get them to check the house. There is something very strange going on here"

"Yes sir", the butler sounded resigned.

"You are an Invicta Commander?" Samson looked back at the woman, "Can you prove it?"

Jessica slowly reached into an inside pocket of her jacket, wary of the man with the gun behind her, and drew out an ivory card that she proferred to him. Samson regarded it for a moment from a distance, then crossed over and took it, checking it quickly and nodding,

"The Great Chamberlain may not be a friend to the family" he said with ready wit, "But he is no enemy.", then looking over the woman's shoulder added, "Holster your weapon and fetch her trousers"

"They are completely sodden, sir" the man pointed out

"Here", Marie had removed the shawl from around her shoulders, "You can wrap this around you"

Jessica smiled and took it. It made an impromptu skirt, but it would do for modesty's sake.

"You need to let me hunt down the woman who is killing your servants even now" she said

Samson looked at her, then at his sister, and whatever his doubts about her words, the fact that his sweet, rather dim sister was in some potentially serious danger decided him

"Yes" he said, "I need to know, though"

"Are you sure that you want to?" Jessica asked

He considered it for a moment, then nodded

"Tell me"

The Invicta Commander did,

"She is Sarah Alexandria Dunelm, Captain-General of the Security Directorate...and suspected High Acolyte of the Order of the Serpent"

"Oh..." he looked down at his feet, "I have met her with the Viceroy"

"High Governor" Jessica corrected him from the previously-common usage, "Are you saddened at the prospect of killing her?"

Samson laughed and looked up

"That would be exactly what I was not feeling!"

"Then do not fear, the Imperial Court wishes her disposed of, and the Great Chamberlain is the ultimate authority in Britannia, even over the Security Directorate"

"I see", he said, and he did, "then Rannoch has nothing left"

"Except his name and titles" she agreed, "Do you mourn?"

"Hardly"

"Then let me kill this woman"

He nodded, the asked

"Is she here for me or for the child?"

Jessica froze

"Fuck…" she said; she had been so focused upon the fact that this was a Despenser residence, that even though she had been startled by the information about the girl she had failed to factor her in.

"I thought so", he said, "Do your job. I will protect the girl"

"Yes", and she ran from the room

Samson crossed to the telephone and lifted it up,

"Priority Line" he said

The response went from deadness to a buzzing noise and then a human voice in brief seconds

"Priority Line" a starched woman responded, "Misuse of this service…."

"Shut up" he snapped, "Get me Swift Commander Torquil Larson at Camberley; this is an emergency!"

"Transferring"

"Larson…" said a languid voice some ten long seconds later

"Samson" he said, "I've got an emergency situation on the estate"

"Heck", Torquil was suddenly all business, "Why don't you call the Guard?"

"They can't get here in time!" Samson restrained himself only just from shouting, "There is a High Acolyte of the Serpent here, and Leonora Bunny Schenk, and no I don't know why or how, but the count will kill me if anything happens to her"

"Third Squadron is at battle readiness; I'll get them up now, and order

them mid-air"
"Timing?"
"Five minutes to arrival"
"I need the men not the aeroplanes, make that clear"
"It will be"

The line went dead, and Samson sagged against the armchair.
"What is going to happen?" his sister was at his side
"I don't know" he said, shaking his head
"Contraction" she pointed out
He laughed and tousled her hair,
"They say that one forgets under heavy stress"
"That's better", she leant close in against him.

From somewhere down below there came the sound of a gunshot.

Chapter 20

Cuzco, Inca Empire of Peru

"The serpent has possessed you"

"Yes", said the girl whose rear end still felt sore from the invasion

"You will swear"

"Yes" she said.

"Here is the text", Sulvia handed her the ancient words, and the girl spoke them clearly, if occasionally blankly as she came across phrases which had long ago lost their meaning in common parlance.

"Break this and you die" Sulvia took the text back.

"Yes" the girl said.

"Good, now kill him"

The girl crossed the cellar to where a youth was strung up, hands high above his head upon a beam, legs chained by ankle restraints into the earthen floor. She looked up, her face blank and waved the long-bladed knife that she had been given. The youth moved away as best he was able, but it was not far. A foul smell filled her nose, and in disgust she killed him, plunging the knife high into his chest, again and again and again until his blood soaked her, and she stood naked, and red before the Grand Mistress.

"That was well done", Sulvia took the knife and licked the blade, "You need relaxation" she said to the girl.

"Yes" she said

"I will enjoy licking the blood from off your body"

"Yes"

- - -

The next morning, the girl was safely returned to her family, and Sulvia exited the cheap dilapidated house in the rundown part of the city, an easy rent in ready money, disposable as it was no loss to lose the deposit when prices were as low as these. Swinging the steel cylinder, she stepped up onto a beat-up tramcar, and drank in the lustful glances of the local men. She was still rosy from the night's excesses, new acolytes to the Serpent giving themselves with absolute abandon to their initiator and there was little that she had wanted to do that had not been done. The girl was exhausted, sore and bruised, but she was now inducted completely, and the Order had a strong new Acolyte deep in the heart of the Inca state.

The tram rattled through the city streets at last entering a more salubrious area, bounded by high-walled palaces and containing within it the factories and warehouses of the foreign powers. Here every other face was non-Native, a mix of all the global powers, from Albion to Zanzibar, from Kazan to Europa. There were even Chinese, representing the various sub-national powers of the so-called empire, some few Japanese, and an Indian or two from one of the stronger princely states. The Inca Empire was everybody's playground, and though the court survived by playing them off, Peru's power relative even to Corrientes to the North was certainly on the wane.

At a stop before the Halychian Embassy, Sulvia got off and moved across to where a small queue of people was standing in line, patiently waiting to present their documents and request entry into the Eastern European empire. She stood behind an old Inca woman, and a man with her who was clearly only half-Native, being lighter of skin, and more angular of feature. He smiled at her, ignoring the disapproving tutting of the older woman,
"You are going to Halych?" he said, using the Quechuan spoken colloquially by all members of the empire, and easy enough for visitors to pick up.
"I hope to in some weeks" Sulvia replied, not exactly a lie, although she did not know where the Serpent would lead her in that time frame; maybe to Europe, maybe to Africa. All she knew was that Albion was too hot for her, and after what she had to do in Patagonia, she was going to need to be on another continent altogether soon afterwards. The embassy did not care what you did between presenting your application and claiming your entry papers. She could take an airship to Edo and back, for all they cared. This was one of several escape routes she would set up, but who knew whether she would use it?

"Next!", the Inca Guard were gaudy in their imitation of the most colourful of global uniforms, the regiment doing guard duty today seemingly to base their colour-scheme on that of the more exotic Zanzibari, dazzling and startling in equal measure. If they thought it demeaning to be keeping order amongst the crowds seeking to leave the Inca Empire at each of the global powers' embassies they did not let on. in fact seeming to be proud to be doing their duty by doing so.

The crowd shuffled forward a few yards, behind her Sulvia registering the arrival of several more people into the queue. It was still early and by Midday the queue would probably stretch down the street and round the corner. Such were a common sight in Cuzco, and the score or so of people ahead of her represented only a small wait in the scheme of things, a couple of hours at the most. She smiled back at the half-bred man,
"Your father was from Halych?" she asked.
"Wodj" he said, "but he returned there before I was born"
"It will be your first time there?" she asked.
"If they let me in" he said.

~

Surrey, High Province of Britannia

The gardens were littered with blackened and burnt-out Hellcats, the hybrid rocket-and-propeller aeroplanes still smoking in many places, their husks burnt down to the metal, devastated by what had befallen them all.

He looked from them up to the ruined house, and swallowed. A day ago it had been a beautiful, if somewhat functional, piece of architecture, the symbol of a major family's wealth and worth, but now it was collapsed in upon itself, the windows blown out, the roof caved in, the doors burnt up, and the interior a blackened and annihilated ruin.

"The horses are all dead, my lord", the Elite Guardsman who reported no longer looked white and gold, instead his uniform was smeared black and grey, his face dirty, his hands caked with filth.
"Were the stables fired?" Great Chamberlain William Augustus Chance looked up

284

"No, my lord, they remain intact...but the bodies within do not"
"Is there a child?" he asked.
"Not in the stables, my lord"
"Very well"

"Sir?" Grand Captain Roman Vardis was as filthy as his men, "We can find nobody alive at all"
"None of the pilots?" he indicated the wrecks all around them.
"A few bodies sir on the threshold, cut to pieces....not by man"
"By a light", the Great Chamberlain nodded, "and the rest burnt in the inferno..."
"Why did it burn like this, sir?"
"Because the light willed it", the Great Chamberlain sighed, "I spoke to the Lord High Chancellor this morning"
"Of course", it was after all his house.
"It could not have burnt like this on its own"
"The cousin had nothing in it that may have?"
"Nothing", he shook his head, "The Lord High Chancellor was receiving regular reports from various agents he had amongst the staff"
"Were there any that would be of use to us....here?"
"One"

The Great Chamberlain resumed his walk towards the patio ahead, moving from between the parked and burnt-out Hellcats, followed at a distance by the majority of his retinue, the while Elite Guards continuing to pick over every detail in every direction.
"Leonora Bunny Schenk..." the Great Chamberlain said.
Roman Vardis wracked his memory,
"She drowned off Greencape with her father...after the light destroyed the *Londinium*"
"She was here"
"She can't have been!", he coughed, "I mean..."
"Her death and that of her father has not been reported in the news" the Great Chamberlain knew that because he controlled the news, "The agent reported her arrival as nothing more than a curiosity since she had arrived alone"
"Alone?", the Grand Captain frowned, "I thought she was eight, nine, something like that"
"She is...was....is"

"We do not know if she is dead?"

"There is a lot we do not know" the Great Chamberlain said.

Albion City, Imperial Capital, Empire of Albion

"There are many problems" Lord High Chancellor Horace Aloysius Despenser was defensive, despite himself, "It is impossible to be completely on top of all of them."

Dionysus Rothgar Excelsior just looked at him. They were seated upon a couple of oak-and-leather chairs before a fiery brazier, situated in the dead centre of one of the lesser halls in the vast palace complex. All around, in the darkness and the shadows, Elite Guardsmen stood and waited - for a change of shift, or for something untoward to happen, it was all the same to them.

"The, ah, Grand Master of the Order of the Bear is dead" Horace Aloysius attempted to make it sound like mere conversation, but failed.

"You killed him" Dionysus had no doubt as to that..

"I..." began the Lord High Chancellor.

"It is of little matter now", the Imperial Prince told him, "What is of more concern are these reports."

He indicated two especially, though his eyes took in a few more.

"These ones?" the Lord High Chamberlain flipped one over, "Shoshona City?", he shrugged, "A wild and lawless mountain fastness I have no doubt"

"Mountain might be correct", Dionysus had read the file, "A murder, a theft, and a disappearance"

"Which seems to be obvious!" Horace Aloysius protested, "The woman killed her lover, stole his horse, and rode off"

"Why?"

"Do we care?"

"And where is the crazy young woman?"

"Maybe murdered also - perhaps she saw one of the crimes"

"It is an interpretation", the Imperial Prince allowed, "But I have spoken to the Lord Guardians"

286

"Oh...?"

"They report that the Unicorn requested analysis of anonymous data, one output of which was Shoshona"

"What does that mean?" the Lord High Chancellor was far from being the most technical man in the Empire.

"Sadly it would seem that those who know are either not saying, or are dead"

"Perhaps we can force the Lord Guardians to talk!" Horace Aloysius had little love for their ways.

"Not without destroying Cyclops!" Dionysus was having none of it, "Send a party to Shoshona"

"But why?" the man protested.

"Because I command it"

Truth be told, he did not have the power to command, but he had the influence to make the Lord High Chancellor's life very difficult if he refused to even consider it, and a command was a good excuse if there should be nothing there after all.

"Very well" Horace Aloysius said.

"I commiserate on the destruction of your house" Dionysus said.

"Thank you", he blanched, "It makes no sense..."

"Sense is made if your house is seen as incidental"

"How can it be incidental? It was mine!"

"Perhaps you are incidental?"

The Lord High Chancellor stared daggers into his eyes, so Dionysus thought better of pursuing that track.

"More like", he added, "it was chosen because it had the power to pull in the players and adversaries"

"I see what you mean"

"The report of the presence of the Schenk girl is......disturbing"

Horace Aloysius could only agree whole-heartedly; he had dismissed it when the agent had reported it, but now with what had happened afterwards he knew that he could not dismiss anything

"If she were truly there, how and why...?"

"Sitting on a hill, crying in the rain", Dionysus made clear that his own sources were the equal to the Lord High Chancellor's.

"My agent said she acted like she was whom she said, a born horse-rider, brave and noble"

"He has been reading too many historical romances" the Imperial Prince snorted, "but accounts say that Leonora Bunny was - or is - an experienced and skilful rider, despite her tender years"

"It was really her?"

"That I cannot say - it is possible that the lights can now duplicate human form"

"Then we are doomed!" the man stood up quickly, all but knocking over the brazier as he did so, "It cannot be!"

"I hope it is not" Dionysus agreed, "but we have to consider all possibilities"

"But if people are not real..."

"You cannot even know who I am!" Dionysus grinned at him

The Lord High Chancellor opened his mouth and backed away

"No" he said, "No....!"

Dionysus laughed

"I hardly think so" he said, lowering his arms to his sides.

Horace Aloysius could only stare at him the more.

~

Surrey, High Province of Britannia

Battle Captain Derek Faran was not happy with his duty. The Great Chamberlain and Grand Captain Vardis had gone, and now he was left with but a dozen Guards to keep a watch over the burnt-out shell of the Despenser estate, and keep the handful of Acolytes of Cyclops safe. These latter, their shaven heads making them seem more than usually spooky, were picking their way through the rubble and the still smouldering timbers, making notes and gathering data. What good any of it might do, Faran had not a clue, but it was by order of the Great Chamberlain and one did not dare to question.

The work did not stop for nightfall. The Acolytes had taken up one of the stable blocks, hastily cleaned of its equine and human detritus, and now they worked in shifts, one lot sleeping in there whilst the other worked with heavy electric torches in the ruins. If anyone was of a mind to shoot them, then they had perfect targets, but it was not snipers that the Elite Guard were worried out, rather it was the lights, or as the newspapers were beginning to term them, 'The Lights'. He thought the capitalisation a fancy, but people were like that, and the newspapers most especially of all, despite constant vigilance by the Imperial Censor.

"Nothing to report, sir", the Guard was one of the more beautiful women under his command, but she was tired and bedraggled and looked like only a week in bed - alone - would restore her to her usual glory.
"Good", it might be boring and routine, but not being under attack was certainly not a bad thing.
"Lieutenant Parker requests that he extend his range onto the North Hill" she said.
The Battle Captain thought about it for a moment, then nodded,
"To the crest only - from there he can see if we need him down here; beyond it we lose out"
"Yes sir", she moved off and he watched the tired sway of her rear.

"Captain", the Acolyte was young, female and bald, and she was filthy from the soot and ashes, her robe now black whatever colour it may have been before. But she was holding something in her hand.
"What is that?" he frowned at it.
"It is ivory", she wiped it down with a cloth, "An identification plaque"
He took it and read it,
"This was found with a body?"
"A female impaled upon a long-bladed knife, trapped under some beams we have only just moved"
"Can she be identified?" he tossed the ivory into the air and caught it, "I mean, can we match the body to this?"
"Perhaps only by dental records" she said.
He sighed, knowing very well what that meant. There was definitely a probability here, but the Great Chamberlain had asked for certainty; of course, the longer that the Invicta Commander did not report in, the more likely that she was dead.
"Were there any other bodies found near her?"

The Acolyte swallowed and nodded,
"Body pieces", she coughed, "- a young boy"

"Boy?" he asked, "You are certain?"

"About four or five years of age", she said, and nodded her bald head, "Yes - we are certain"

"Too small anyway", he shook his head, "Pieces....you mean that the light did this to him?"

"It would appear to be so..."

"I think I should report that at once"

"Yes Captain", she turned and walked back towards the ruin, whilst he crossed hurried to the tent which had been erected in the shadow of one of the burnt-out Hellcats.

Shouldering aside the entry flap he nodded to the guard, and approached the radio operator, handing him the ivory plaque.

"Ah", the man took it and nodded, "You need to report this?"

"And something else" Faran said, waiting.

It became clear that he was not going to say anything more, and also that by his silence he was requesting that they leave the tent. He could not order them to do so, but after a moment they took account of his position and departed. Quickly he retuned the radio to a frequency not on the listed guide,

"Bristol" he said, urgently.

"One moment", the woman's voice was thin, rising with the static, then falling away, "I have Bristol"

"Battle Captain Derek Faran at the Despenser estate" he said.

There was a moment's silence and then

"This is the office of the High Acolyte, please proceed"

"The light sliced up a child, a young boy" he could feel the horror of his words, but kept his voice steady

"This is confirmed?" the man was shocked, not by the crime so much as by what it signified.

"It is to be doubted that anyone else had the time to do it."

"This is a pattern shift", the man was thinking aloud.

"It shows that they are not rational!" Faran spat.

"No...they will be rational, but to some plan that is shifting before our sight."

"Every madman thinks that he is sane" the Battle Captain pointed out.

"But like a dog that turns on its master, the lights are not human, they think in a different manner to us."

290

"Why do we need to understand them?" Faran protested, "We know how to kill them"

"But do they die or just go back to where they came from, to come again?"

"I thought they died..." he was less sure now; how could they tell?

"That is why we need to understand them"

The connection went dead, and static reigned. The Battle Captain reset the dial to the proper frequency and then placed a call to the Palace of Whitehall, informing the radio operator that they had recovered the identification plaque of Invicta Commander Jessica Monroe, and that the body next to it was, on first examination probably hers, but that they would need her dental records to confirm. London assured him that they would be flown out at first light.

Faran exited the tent and nodded to the two men who frowned at him, but went back inside. He tossed the ivory plaque into the air and looked up at the starless sky. The heavy clouds were obscuring the light, and he looked to find significance in this. But he was too tired, and after a moment of fleeting thought he pocketed the plaque and trudged back to his post. Come morning a new set of Guards would come up from the Camberley base, but this was his domain until then.

"Report?" he asked the first guardsman as he passed.

"Nothing to report, sir"

"Good, carry on"

"Yes sir"

He hoped that it would be like that for the rest of the night .

Chapter 21
Albion City, Imperial Capital, Empire of Albion

He staggered back, staring in horror at the crossbow bolt protruding from his chest, lost his footing and plunged down the spiral stairway.

On a rooftop, across the way, a man crouched in the lea of a chimney and smiled grimly to himself. Those older stone towers still had open arrow slits, a folly on the part of the designers who had aimed at recreating old Europe here in the New World, and had had little thought for security this deep within the Imperial Palace.

He wound another bolt onto his crossbow, content to bide his time. His mission was clear - vengeance, and it would be his.

- - -

"We sent them by train to Assiboinia", Elite Marshal Valeria Luisa Craven was making her report of readiness, "They stand ready to assault the city, should you so wish it."
"Their approach is so far undetected?" the Lord High Chancellor asked.
Such a consideration was why going by airship had been ruled out. After the events in the Yukon, not to mention the death of Count Roger Schenk, it was giving too much warning to the enemy to move in that manner.
"Yes sir", Valeria was deferring to his civilian rank here, "Do you wish to order the attack?"

Horace Aloysius Despenser wished for no such thing, but he was bound by his agreement with the Imperial Prince, and one did not gainsay such a one lightly, especially not when all the pieces had been placed upon the board.

"The attack has to bag us our suspects", the Lord High Chancellor stressed, "Anything less is harassment of a settlement that should be enjoying our protection."
"We understand the law, sir"
"And do you understand the Serpent?"

"I have read all the briefings, sir"

"You have never faced them?"

"Until recent, military action was not permitted."

"Oh yes", he had forgotten how swiftly things had changed, "Just remember – an agent of the Serpent can pretend to anything, they do not care – not for honour, not for name, not for decency"

"Yes sir", she sounded bored.

"Then on your understanding be it, order the attack."

"Yes sir"

- - -

Elite Marshal Balthazar Erasmus Hunt stopped and watched as the party of guards cleared away the body at the foot of the staircase.

"What happened?" he asked.

A trooper paused, looked at him, then moved on. Balthazar sighed; the Imperial Palace was so full of higher ranks that the lower ranks could choose to ignore those they did not know. If one was not in their immediate chain of command, then one might as well be commanding Native levies in Shantung. So used were they to ignoring senior commanders that even an individual who had a legitimate call on them could fall by the wayside.

For his part, Balthazar knew that his current appointment allowed him only to call for audience with the Great Chamberlain twice a month, and to continue to represent the affairs of the islands of the Eastwind Chain, such as they were. Even the Lord High Chancellor had failed to acknowledge that the first meant something in the Great Chamberlain's absence, whilst in the face of attacks by the lights, war with the Caliphate and dramatic events in Britannia, the Eastwind islands were low on anyone's list of things they wished to speak about.

Dejected, he stood and watched as a couple of young female guards carried out the dead body taking him through the outer door towards a waiting cart. Like much within the Imperial Palace, there was a false reality about this – it could easily have been done by a steam car, but tradition demanded a cart with attendant horse, and within the walls that was what the dead got..

Balthazar moved on, wondering what had really happened to the fellow – had he slipped and fallen, or had someone pushed him? He would hardly discount the latter, what with things that had been happening lately…

- - -

"Dead?!" Horace Aloysius Despenser stared at the messenger in shock, "Are you sure?"

"Yes sir", privately James Horner thought the man a moron; how would he have not have been sure? How would he have dared approach him, if he had not been sure?

"But he was alive this morning!" the Lord High Chancellor protested

"Hmmm" James was somewhat confused as to how to answer this gibberish, "He must have been killed after you last saw him alive", he ventured.

"No!", Horace Aloysius sat down hard, "Why him?"

"We do not know sir."

"But….why him?"

James looked at him and frowned,

"We…do…not…know" he said again, more slowly.

Grand Captain Alain George Rowlett had not been anyone special in the scheme of things; he had held no great rank, no great responsibilities and no great knowledge. He had come and gone as many of his rank did. But he had been the Lord High Chancellor's Personal Adjutant, and his death felt like a body blow to him.

"I thought…." Horace Aloysius was slowly collecting himself, "I thought that all crossbow bolts sold had to have a unique identifier stamped on them?"

"Yes sir"

"Then we have him!"

"No sir"

"What?"

"There is a stamp sir…it says "Vengeance is mine""

"What?"

"It means that whoever fired the bolt, made it himself"

"No!" Horace Aloysius surged to his feet, "Make sure that it does not mean that!"

"Um…"
"You will make sure of that or die!"
"As you wish, sir"

James hurriedly extracted himself from the audience, and strode quickly back to the Guardroom, his mind foaming and frothing. Was the man speaking sense? Could he possibly be? What if he was simply mad or grief-stricken? Maybe they were lovers? Who knew…

- - -

He shifted his position slightly and looked down as the striking woman came out a side door and headed towards where a sleek black limousine had steam up, its driver and guards standing to attention as she approached. He took in their white and gold uniforms and smiled. This would certainly send a message to the Lord High Chancellor.

He fired…

~

Fort Fluffy, Patagonia

"Another airship is enroute..." Lieutenant Colin Hamer shrugged and looked across the room at his colleague.
Marietta Espezia Guiscard laughed,
"Well we have had the Unicorn and the Dragon; who next, the Serpent?!"
"The...the Dragon?" he stammered.
"Oh please...." she laughed, "General Engineering?! Those men?!"
"You think...?" he looked at her hard.
"How much engineering have they done?"
"The Collar" he spoke in capitals.
"As if that makes any sense" she laughed.

"Fluffy, this is *Huascar*, respond please?"
"*Huascar* stand by" Colin looked across at Marietta, "What do you think?"
Marietta sat up in her chair, bracing her feet upon the ground,

"You seriously think it's the Serpent come to visit?!" she was scornful.

"Of course not!" he snapped.

She rose and took the microphone,

"*Huascar* this is Fluffy, please land on the scheduled icefield."

"Understood, Fluffy; will comply"

Colin looked up at her and shook his head,

"So what have you invited into here?" he asked.

"Some Incas...?" she suggested playfully.

"You don't know that!"

"No", she sat down, "Because agents of the Serpent are the most logical..."

"Hmph", he looked down at his instruments and vowed to give her a good seeing to one day.

Chapter 22
Shoshona, Albion

"Welcome to Shoshona, your highness. I am Constable John Halstead."

"Constable", Imperial Prince Dionysus Rothgar Excelsior walked away from the giant tethered form of the airship *Pandora*, and with the Constable as an escort passed through the ranks of slaves, maintenance men and overseers who had come out to greet the aerial vehicle.

"Elite Marshal Kennedy has secured the city but is leading an attack on a cave complex in the hills beyond."

"Yes", Dionysus had had an update about the impending operation whilst enroute aboard the *Pandora,* "Do you have any further information?"

"No sir"

They passed on through a white stuccoed building, and through to a tavern which had been commandeered by elements of the Elite Guard.

"Your highness, I am Battle Captain Cyrus Sabbath Cavendish. The Marshal has instructed me to bring you up to date."

"Very well", Dionysus lowered himself into a chair and waved at one of the barmaids who still seemed to be working inside, albeit to a different clientele.

"We have rounded up six suspects, sir" Cyrus hopped from one foot to another, indecision about whether or not to seat himself growing until he decided to remain standing, "These are their names and positions." Dionysus took the list and ran his eyes over it.

"Nobody significant?" he asked, "The only noteworthy one seems to be this Branson, railtrack engineer?"

"He claims innocence", Cyrus made it sound like a crime in itself, "but we do not think he was anything more than a basic acolyte."

"There has to be a High Acolyte here" the Imperial Prince was on his feet, "Cyclops indicates this."

"Yes sir", Cyrus took the list back, "The Marshal believes she has gone to ground in the Caves of Wakini."

"She?" Dionysus speared the man with his eyes, "You know who she is?"

"Certain indications, but there are definite reports that she has been seen near the caves in recent weeks."

"And you have been instructed to take me there?"

"Sir?" Cyrus was momentarily lost by the jump in conversation.

"If you have not previously been so instructed, Battle Captain, you are now definitely instructed."

Cyrus swallowed, and nodded,

"I can have a battle wagon here in ten minutes"

"Very well", he made his way over to the door, "The city is secure?"

"Yes sir"

"I will take a brief perambulation."

"As you will, sir"

Albion City, Imperial Capital, Empire of Albion

A sudden rush of Elite Guards sprinting past made Balthazar stop and stare. A moment later there came a deal of shouting from the courtyard without, and another half dozen guards descended from a tower doorway set near where he was seated, trying to get some work done. He rose and strode over to the window, looking out towards where the dozen or more white and gold uniforms were gathering by some steps. Someone appeared to be making frantic efforts within the centre of the group and as they parted briefly, he was able to make out a definite pool of red, under a body that looked vaguely familiar.

Then another couple of Elite Guards ran in from beyond the archway, and the view was blocked once more.

As more Elite Guards poured into the courtyard and began to turn their weapons upon the doorways and windows facing into it, he decided that for once his rank might actually prove useful in this situation, and picking up his helm from the sideboard, fastened it about his head and strode quickly from the room.

"Sir!" one of the troopers saluted him, "We would request that all personnel remain where they are at this time."

"Who is the senior officer here present?"

"Commander Faye Rashelle Galloway, sir"

"Negative", Balthazar looked him sharply in the eye, "I am."

"But, sir..." the guard was momentarily at a loss, "You are outside my chain of command"

"This is an emergency situation" Balthazar began to move across to where the majority of Elite Guard were still grouped around the body, "Elite Marshal Valeria Luisa Craven?"

"Yes...yes sir", the same guard was at his heels, clearly at a loss, "Crossbow bolt sir"

"As with Grand Captain Rowlett."

"Yes sir, the same"

"Vengeance is Mine?", Balthazar had his sources after the event, even if he had been excluded from the detail of the previous assassination whilst it had been going on.

It was one of the Elite Guard from around the body who answered, straightening up with bloodied hands she wiped upon her trousers, "Yes, the same", she frowned at him, "I am Commander Galloway."

"Elite Marshal Balthazar Erasmus Hunt"

"You are taking command?" she sounded neutral.

"Given the nature of the emergency."

She nodded slowly,

"Accepted, sir. I am afraid that Elite Marshal Craven was killed instantly. There is nothing we can do."

"I assumed so, given a professional assassin."

The group of guards had now parted to allow them unobscured access to the body. Balthazar stood before her, looking down at the animated features, now stilled, the raven hair now bloodied by the fall that had come after the bolt had impacted, after it had already killed her.

"Sir", the guard was young, uncertain of himself, but addressed the Marshal, rather than the Commander by his side, "Given the angle of her fall, I am fairly certain the assassin fired from a rooftop..." he paused, then added, "Probably up there, sir"

"Very well", Balthazar looked where the young man was pointing, "Take two others and find access to that point. Report back as soon as you can on anything you find"

"Yes sir!", the fellow tapped two of the closest guards and together they ran for one of the tower stairways.

"Elkwood Hart is but two weeks into his posting here" Commander Galloway's words were said in a flat tone, but it was obvious why she had said them.

"He is the one who made the report." Balthazar said, "He showed initiative and he is alert."

"As you wish", the Commander stressed the middle word.

"Indeed," he returned his attention to the body of the other Elite Marshal; he had difficulty in even thinking in the form of 'his fellow marshal' after the way many had treated him in the months since he had been assigned to the Imperial Palace.

"Sir", a junior officer approached from the steps that Balthazar himself had come down, "A message has been sent to the Lord Chancellor."

"Of course", Balthazar answered before the Commander could, "He is the command authority."

"Yes sir", the officer looked from the Commander to him, then decided that whatever was going on, he would work with it, "Battle Commander Grey has also been informed."

"Good", Balthazar knew the latter by name only, as would anybody within the Imperial Palace. The Duty Commander for the Red Guard was a natural contact in an emergency.

"We are not going to refer the case?" Commander Galloway made clear what her answer to the question was.

"Of course not, but courtesy is courtesy" Balthazar told her, "Someone is taking out top level officials and we need to stop them."

"We need to know why!" the Commander hissed, "How can we stop what we do not understand."

"I know why", Balthazar said slowly, "I know why - but it makes it no easier to stop."

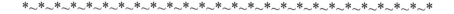

Caves of Wakini
Shoshona, Albion

"Down!"

The trooper threw himself to the floor and rolled as two jets of flame seared above his head.

"On! On!"

A half dozen troopers rushed on in, storming through the dying flames and the smoking rocks, guns pointing every which way, up and down, round and round, seeking a target that was not there.

"Locate!" yelled the commander following them into the cavern.

"No target", the trooper was female, suited up and otherwise undefined in her uniform.

"Move!"

A moment later Imperial Prince Dionysus Rothgar Excelsior strode into the cave, looked around then approached the point guard,

"The High Acolyte?"

She shook her head,

"I don't think so, sir. So far they are all youths, boys off the farms. We think we are after a girl, an outcast that lived within them."

"That sounds like the Serpent"

"But we've not seen any sight of her"

"She was here?"

"Those we questioned said so before we went in."

"I doubt they are all Serpent." Dionysus laughed.

"That is statistically improbable sir."

"Fire! Fire! Fire!", the commotion came from down the passageway.

A moment later there came a scream, agonised and brief.

"Male!" yelled a hidden voice, "On! On!"

Dionysus followed, his own weapon drawn, running past a blackened, smoking, twisted ruin of a young man before entering a narrow passage, snaking down, the roof closing in, the walls almost kissing in places. Ahead of him a dozen troopers ran, fired, yelled and dashed. In part it was bravado, in part it was the hope of intimidation. Noise, noise, noise to both chase out the fear from themselves and the hope from their foes.

"Your Highness?" a junior officer of indeterminate sex prevented his advance beyond a pinnacle, "We have someone pinned down"

"Her?"

"I don't think so, sir"

He nodded and allowed himself to be led to an outcrop,

Albion City, Imperial Capital, Empire of Albion

The first of the pairs slipped into the room, moving silently, dark against the walls, striding along like shadows made manifest. Only when the second pair passed in front of one of several stand-alone lamps illuminating the hall, did people look up, and stare.

Horace Aloysius Despenser was immediately on his feet, fury upon his visage,

"Out!" he shouted, "You are not allowed in here!"

None of the four black-uniformed figures responded. Instead they completed their path, and now took up positions, weapons drawn, visors down, inscrutable and silent.

Others were on their feet now, the morning's business forgotten as the Lord Chancellor's outburst had had no apparent result, and he was clearly working himself up to a more blazing anger.

"I demand you leave now!" he yelled, moving to within a few feet of them, "Now!"

Balthazar Erasmus Hunt entered the room from what for the last few days had been his field office, a nice suite adjacent to the hall from where he had been running the so-called investigation into the murder of his colleague, Elite Marshal Valeria Luisa Craven. That the Lord Chancellor should explode in a fiery outburst was not too unusual, but the words that Balthazar could hear him shouting had confused, and alarmed him.

Now he stood in consternation, staring out at the two pairs of Black Guards, agreeing with everything the Lord Chancellor was saying - yelling - but feeling that somehow they were, both of them, missing the point.

302

"The Black Guard are not allowed general access to the palace!" the Lord Chancellor was shouting again, "Your role is solely..."
"To protect the Emperor"

The voice was wizened, if a voice could be wizened. It was one part wheeze, one part scratch, but it was powerful and resonant and it cut through the room like a battleship on the Thames. Silence was absolute as people leapt from their seats and crashed to the ground. Balthazar himself swept his legs out from under himself and crashed down onto his knees. The Lord Chancellor was slower, shock freezing his movements until the fierce icy gaze of the septagenarian laid itself upon him.

"My.......My lord!" he gasped!
It was a truism that nobody had seen the Emperor for almost two years, but like most truisms it was false. Very ill and generally too weak for official duties, he had remained within his private apartments, but there had been private audiences, private meetings and family occasions. The Emperor had retained his grip on the apparatus of state, choosing whom he saw, who was invited to meetings, and who had the favour of meeting him in his sickroom. Whilst the Great Chamberlain had been in place the Lord Chancellor had not been in favour, and since then...he had not been in favour either.

With another phalanx of Black Guard either side of him, Emperor William VI hobbled across to the oaken chair that the Lord Chancellor had been sitting in, his ebony stick tap-tapping in front of him.
"You are relieved" he said into the air, "I am retaking direct control."
"But..." Horace Aloysius Despenser looked up, "sire, are you, I mean...?"
"Capable", the Emperor eased himself into the seat, "I am capable."
"Yes...yes, of course, I did not..."
"Thank you", the Emperor waved a hand at him and he finally lapsed into silence.

"Rise!" one of the Black Guard, indistinguishable from any of the others bellowed, and as the inhabitants of the room staggered to their feet. He turned towards Balthazar, "Elite Marshal, you are to make your report."

Balthazar swallowed and rose, crossing to stand before the Emperor,
"Your Imperial Majesty"
"The Eastwind Islands?" William VI proved he was not uninformed, "I see you have outgrown liaison."
"Yes sir"
"Explain"

Balthazar nodded,
"The assassination of Elite Marshal Valeria Luisa Craven left a hole in the immediate chain of command, sir. The situation was obviously an emergency and I stepped in to do my duty."
"Hmmm", the Emperor leant forward upon the knob of his stick, slowly rotating it about the point embedded in the floor, "Your report?"
Balthazar looked at the Lord Chancellor, then away again,
"In general, sir, the identity of the assassin was obvious"

There was a shocked intake of breath, then the emperor slowly wheezed out,
"Yes", he said, "It would be to a good man."
"Explain your answer", the commander of the Black Guard was now standing beside his Emperor.
Balthazar nodded,
"The Order of the Bear strikes back."
"Back?" barked the Emperor.
"The...ah..."
"Speak?!" the guard commander demanded.
"The Lord Chancellor had their Grand Master killed within these walls."

"I..." Horace Aloysius Despenser swallowed, "His Imperial Highness, Prince Dionysus Rothgar Excelsior has been kept fully informed."
There was silence all round, then the Emperor nodded
"Very well" the Emperor's gaze drifted between the two men, "There will be a Grand Convocation."
"Convocation?!" the Lord Chancellor was aghast, "But the Bear...?!"
"They will already have a replacement in place.", Balthazar said, "Either emergency protocols or they will have had an emergency meeting to appoint one."

"But..." Despenser blanched, "I ordered his predecessor killed!"

"There is a..." Balthazar searched for the word, "bigger problem"
"What?!" Despenser swept round towards him.
"The Serpent"
"What?!"

"The Elite Marshal is right", the Emperor rasped, "The Serpent have not been declared Anathema. They must be invited to Convocation."
"But they won't come" Despenser was confused.
"They will come", the Emperor coughed, "They always come"
"They are always here" Balthazar did not so much correct as enhance the Emperor's words.
"But we are fighting a war against them." the Lord Chancellor was confused.
"The Unicorn smites the Dragon." the guard commander said, shocking them all into gape-mouthed confusion once again.

"Oh yes", the Emperor slowly rose to his feet, "My sons, the Great Chamberlain and my Viceroys may think that what they do not tell me, I do not know.", he paused, "That is very foolish."
"Yes, Your Majesty", Balthazar found himself grinning, "It is *very* foolish!"

Chapter 23
Fort Fluffy, Patagonia

"I don't believe it", Lieutenant Colin Hamer was out of his chair, the piece of paper flapping in his hand, "Grand Convocation!" he tried to exclaim but squeezed out in a strangled whisper.

Marietta raised her eyebrows and took the paper upon which he had decoded the transmission,

"By Express Order of the Emperor"

"Everything is by Order of the Emperor" her colleague pointed out.

"Express Order, that means His Imperial Majesty has ordered it in person."

"All ranking officials of the twelve Grand Orders are instructed and required to present themselves to Convocation on pain of....death", Colin stumbled over the last word.

"I think we have a few guests we need to inform", Marietta was on her feet.

"...of the twelve Grand Orders..." Colin's eyes had returned to this part of the message, "Twelve"

"Every child knows there are twelve Grand Orders" Marietta frowned.

"There are only twelve", Colin swallowed, "when you include The Serpent!

"Well" Marietta was all but silent for a moment, "That will be different" she opined.

~

Ramona Elise Carding walked into the viewing chamber, pleased to note that since the incident with the girl security on the ice wall had been doubled.

"Commander", she nodded almost pleasantly at Hawk Monroe who stood on one side of the light, a female guard opposite, "All is quiet?"

"More so than usual", he shrugged, "That demented girl's attack on Serena has made people more wary."

"Wary?", all her Shadow Service training sparked upon hearing that.

"Lest we think they too are Serpent."

"And yet," she looked back at the light, "Some of those who stay away *will* be Serpent."

"Double bluff?"

"Triple too", she said thoughtfully, "Some of those who come will be Serpent."

"Too many bluffs and we won't be able to tell them apart.", the Commander warned her.

"Who comes the most?"

"A couple of young lovers – girls from the stores. And the Bear, of course."

"Ah yes, of course. Our newest guest."

Identifying herself as Samantha Messalina Gold, the sole passenger on the *Huascar* had explained that her brother was the recently deceased Grand Master of the Order of the Bear. Fresh from Tupaco, a Bear stronghold from among the principalities bordering the empire, she had claimed to have come to Patagonia to put as much distance between herself and the Imperial Capital as was possible.

For her part, Ramona suspected that she had hidden motives. After all, if the Unicorn and the Dragon did, why not then the Bear?

~

Colin handed the message to Arturo Spinks, aware that in so doing he was making the man aware that his cover had been blown.

Spinks took one look at the paper and blanched,

"Convocation" he gasped, holding on to the doorpost for support,

"There has not been one in my lifetime."

"By express Order of the Emperor" Colin found himself saying.

"I..." Spinks staggered to the bed and sat down, hard, "All twelve Grand Orders..."

"The Serpent" Colin whispered.

"All twelve orders..." Spinks shook himself and rose to his feet,

"Leave me", he said.

Colin left, the echo of the door slamming behind him like a full stop upon the moment.

~

Silently, she closed the door to the shack and picked her way back over the ice field to where Swift Commander Terrance De L'Isle was standing, hands on hips, a sardonic smile upon his lips. As he began to gesture towards the Webmaster, a score of yards away, he saw the look upon her face, and his smile died.

"Something?" he asked as she came within range.

Tabitha Clarissa Theresa nodded, her mind still racing with the implications of what she had been told,

"When is the next airship due?" she asked.

He was taken aback at the unexpected question and struggled to focus his mind,

"Regular shipping? Five days. But you well know we could get another arrival with but a few hours' notice."

"I am interested in departures", she came closer to him now, letting his hands envelope her body.

"What comes in must go out. People could have left on the *Huascar,* had they wished."

"True", she slipped out of his embrace, "But we can hardly trust to that kind of chance."

"I am missing a key chapter in this discussion.", he admitted.

She realised that for the first time, and looked back towards the shack. Once an Air Force command post, it was now scarcely used, more of a relic than an operational building. To her, as an Eyes of the Great Chamberlain it would have been open anyway, but as the lover of the senior Air Force commander on the base it had been his pleasure to show her. But what she had learned was still rocking her world, even now after these several minutes.

"Grand Convocation" she said quietly.

"I…I'm not sure I understand"

"The Emperor has ordered all ranking officer of all Grand Orders to the Imperial capital – on pain of death."

"He has?"

She mistook him and smiled at his surprise,

"By express order of the Emperor. That means it was given in person – which it would have to be. No official however Great or Grand could so order."

"You are leaving?" he spoke the unspoken words between them.
"I am a ranking officer in the Grand Order of the Unicorn."
"I did wonder"
"I must go at once. Time is limited."
Terrance gestured towards his aeroplane,
"We are not far out of Fort Fluffy, the Webmaster's tanks are almost full."
"What is its range?"
"It could get you to the Land of Fire."
"To Firestone?"
"They always have an airship ready for immediate dispatch."
"Very well", she hugged him, but it was now awkward between them, "To Firestone."
"To Firestone", he said, resignation and the excitement of adventure blended in his voice.

~

Colin stopped in confusion, having opened the door in anticipation of a welcome that had not come.

For a moment his senses took in the naked woman upon the bed, head down, rear end raised as the other woman - the Bear - rammed something up her behind. For a moment a witty comment rose to his lips. Then it died when he saw what the other woman was inserting.

"I..." he gasped.
"Ah", the woman turned but her hand still skilfully continued to insert the barely quivering serpent into the greasy tunnel of the other.
"Um..." Colin tried, his mind trying to decide whether to run or somehow stand his ground.

"Your time was coming" the woman told him.
"S...Serpent!" he spluttered, "You are not Bear, you are Serpent!"

"So named", and she smiled revealing an unseen miniature gun from beneath her free hand.

Colin could only stare in amazement as she shot him down.

~

"That was a shot." Spinks froze in his stride.

"What was?" Leopold Hubertus Scheer also froze and strove to listen.

"One shot, small gun. Makes it sound further away than it was."

"I heard nothing", the other protested.

"Training", Spinks for once on this day smiled, "Dragon training you will receive one day."

"I look forward to it."

Serena Bradley came running round the corner, gun drawn, one arm still bandaged up,

"Where?" she demanded looking at Spinks, able to tell in one moment that he had heard it too.

"Somewhere in that direction", he indicated towards the left, "It was but momentary."

"Come", she instinctively took command, "You are armed?"

It was not allowed for them to be, but after the attack upon her she had been aware of more and more personnel surreptitiously carrying weapons. She saw no reason why these two would be any different.

"Yes", Spinks said, "We should go."

They went.

~

Rashelle Vickers never saw it coming. One moment she was standing beside Commander Hawk Monroe, guarding the light. The next she was collapsed upon the floor, choking out her last gasps as the weighted cord fastened round her neck.

Hawk Monroe ducked into a firing position, searching for targets, moving just fast enough to evade a bolas that moments later whipped over his head to clatter uselessly against the wall of ice.

A head popped up and he shot it down before realising a moment afterwards that it belonged to one of the pretty girls from Stores.

Another movement, someone scrabbling for cover, then a shot, high and wide, pinging the ice about the light's imprisonment. If it was deliberate it had no chance of denting that, it if it was wild...he fired again, missed.

Running feet, coming from two directions. Hawk stayed low and close, firing again in the general vicinity of the last shooter, wary about the newcomers.

"Friend!" yelled Ramona Elise Carding, skidding round a corner and kneeling beside him, "What have we got?"
"Yon lesbians" he spat, not at their sexuality but at the greater truth that he had seen but not noticed, "We marked them as frequent visitors to the light."
"So we did", Ramona ducked as another wild shot spat chunks of ice from the wall over her shoulder, "Two shooters?"
"I think I downed one. The other isn't as accurate."
"Incomers!" Ramona's ears had picked up the second set of running feet.

A pause then a shot, and the second woman from stores sprawled dead from her hiding place, blood running in a puddle from her heart.
"Identify!" Hawk rose carefully from his position.
"Bear", she emerged, another woman some steps behind.
"So named", Hawk said in the ritual phrase, "Are there any more Serpents out there?"

As an answer she raised her gun and fired. Ramona collapsed next to him, blood running from her head,
"Rocket" she commanded, keeping him covered with her gun.
The woman behind her limped up, a rudimentary explosive device fashioned around what had once been a signals rocket. Still keeping him covered they swapped weapons, the other woman limping to a position clear of the other, weapon fixed firmly on Hawk's head.

"The rising is upon us!", she raised the rocket and unhitched its firing mechanism.

"No! Don't fire that!! It'll free the..."

"Light" said Sulvia.

And fired.

Also by Grey Wolf

All artwork used in Never The Dawn
by Derek Roberts

Printed in Great Britain
by Amazon

16584457R00181